# A TIME TO HEAR

# A Time to Hear

S. J. Knight

C.M.P.A.

404 Shaftmoor Lane
Hall Green
Birmingham B28 8SZ

2006

First published 2006

©2006 The Christadelphian Magazine & Publishing Association Ltd

ISBN 0 85189 164 0

*ACKNOWLEDGEMENTS*
Illustrations and Calligraphy – Paul Wasson
Cover Photography – Nigel Moore

*Printed and bound in Great Britain by
William Clowes Ltd, Beccles, Suffolk*

## AUTHOR'S NOTE

This is a work of fiction, not exposition.
There was no Banayim – no Dan, no Ammiel.
But there were people like them – faces in the crowd –
people like us.

S. J. K.

## Chapter One

DAN was nine years old and far too old to suck his thumb, but somehow it just crept in by itself as he drowsily listened to the adult voices murmuring above him. His face was pressed on the sleeping mat, but one eye could still see past the blurred shape of his nose and its encircling fist. He could see the stiff hairs of the mat standing like grass stalks, a crumb of bread among them like a pale cratered boulder, and a wide awake ant exploring it busily, making as much fuss as Aunt Etta at a funeral. Beyond the ant the beaten earth floor sprouted a small dark thicket of legs – nine smooth stool legs and six hairy people legs with lumpy toes like old tree roots. The faces high above them were thrown into silhouette against the wall.

Dan stared sleepily at the shadows moving against the puddle of yellow light on the rough plaster. The mud walls still held some of the day's heat, but the evenings were growing chilly now, and soon the threads of stories old and new, false and true, would be unfolded with the blankets, shaken out, and rewoven into the family memories. Last year when friends came to talk away long wet nights, Dan was allowed to stay up and listen – tucked up on the nearest lap until he had to go to bed. Aunt Etta's was the best – she was so soft and squashy and comfortable that she took longer than anyone else to complain of Dan's sharp young bones, so he got to stay up longer.

But it would be different this year. The sad fact was, he was growing too big to curl up on laps as if he were an orphan lamb. As Dan thought about this, he decided that perhaps a sleeping mat in a dark corner was even better. If he kept very quiet, people forgot about him and what he should and shouldn't hear – or perhaps they thought he was sound asleep. That's when the most interesting things were talked about, and Dan patched together the invisible pieces of his life.

Dan snuggled deeper into his blanket, and watched his family's shapes on the wall. The beaky nose with a curling moustache and beard below and fuzzy hair above, was his father, Ammiel. Dan thought his father looked very much like his own sheep. He was big, and woolly, and warm, and of course, he smelled of sheep too. Dan shifted his gaze, feeling the lashes of his covered eye brush against the mat. The egg shape with the big ears – a head which looked like a water jar, thought Dan – that was Uncle Bukki. Uncle Bukki – a water jar – yes, a water jar with a crack in it. The big tent shape between the two men was Aunt Etta, and occasionally a nose poked out of the tent, first to the right, then to the left, as her shadow turned from one man to the other.

Dan had nearly fallen asleep when a sudden rumble of laughter from Ammiel flicked open his eyes. He pulled out his wet thumb and listened.

"Ah, leave me alone, Etta!"

"Quiet! You'll wake the boy!" hushed Aunt Etta.

Dan instantly shut his eyes.

"A man should marry again and two years is long enough – too long. There's Asa and Helen's Anna needing a husband – a hard worker she is and a good dowry goes with her. And you with a boy to raise, and needing brothers and sisters …"

Dan held his breath again as his father answered warningly, laughingly.

"Her mother's a Greek, Etta!"

"Pah! Greek by birth, Jew by faith. *A Syrian ready to perish was my father …*'. And what's that to do with Anna herself, raised a good Jewish girl all these years …?"

"Yes – all these very many years …"

The jar and the wool were jolting with laughter again, the tent tossed a little and sprouted flapping hands.

"Cluck, cluck, cluck! Like a lot of hens, you men! Peck and scratch! To dismiss a woman for what none can change – her age and breeding! Peck and scratch! And I suppose you are both such good catches yourselves?"

The tent crumpled down between the water jug and the woolly head, which finally stopped rumbling.

"It's a proper wife you need, Ammiel. And Anna has many good years in her yet. Not like me. I'll not be here for ever."

"Come now, Etta! You're strong as a horse."

"No."

"What do you mean, Etta?"

Dan held his breath. *Not be here forever!* Why not? Was Aunt Etta going to leave them? What would they do then?

3

"Ammiel – what a stupid brother you are – you never see me except when I am bending over your son, or your food, or your washing, or your everlasting lambs!"

Aunt Etta's voice trembled. Alarmed, Dan quietly raised himself, unnoticed, on one elbow and looked directly at the three around the oil lamp. Uncle Bukki was scratching his beard unhappily. He didn't like weeping women. Dan's father was patting Aunt Etta's hand clumsily.

"What is it, Etta?" he asked with concern. "Do I treat you as a servant instead of my sister?"

Aunt Etta shook her head and covered her eyes. "You have not seen."

"What? Seen what?"

"I can no longer straighten myself. I am always bending. And it is getting worse."

"Worse!" Even Uncle Bukki looked sober.

Still unnoticed, Dan lay down quietly again, his eyes wide and his ears straining.

"For more than a year I have told myself it is just stiffness, or cold, or overwork. But every month I am a little more stooped, do what I will."

Ammiel chewed his beard and grunted. "Like mother, may she rest in peace."

"Yes, like mother. And her mother before her. She ended her days with her head almost on her knees …". Aunt Etta's voice died away.

Uncle Bukki's jaw dropped. "Horrible! It's in the family? Will I get it?"

4

Ammiel scowled at him. "You fool, Bukki. You're my brother-in-law, not a blood relation."

Aunt Etta sniffed angrily. "It is only the women in our family who suffer this affliction. Nothing can be done. Mother tried many cures which only caused her pain. I blame Eve, of course. The mother of all living and the mother of all living women's woes. But – the will of the Lord be done. Though why this should be His will …" She broke off and Dan knew she was glancing to his corner. He moved not a muscle, and she lowered her voice.

"You see why you must find a wife, and a mother for the boy. In a few years, his Aunt Etta will be of no use to anyone."

The concerned voices sank to a drone, and Dan shrank deeper into his blanket, shivering a little, remembering the old woman in the Magdala market, who was huddled right over, and who always looked haunted and angry. She scared him. Was this how Aunt Etta would be? She was so big and fat, and was always out of breath when she had to pick up things from the floor. If she was to be bent so sharply in half – surely she would be squashed – would she run out of air and choke? Dan quickly took a very deep breath , and reactively stretched his back as straight and far as it would go. The tide of sleep ebbed swiftly, leaving him uncomfortably high on a prickly bank of wakefulness.

"Enough now," murmured Ammiel. "The boy is stirring. We will talk in the morning. This is not for his ears."

The wavering golden light on the wall was snuffed into a smudge of oily smoke and the three black shadows gulped by the greater darkness. Aunt Etta crept in beside Dan's thin body, turned over and sniffed quietly a few times. In the far corner Uncle Bukki banged his elbow on the wall and muttered something sharp under his breath. Dan heard his father's knees crack and a deep sigh, and knew that Ammiel was praying. He always took a deep breath and sighed before he began, as if he was first breathing in incense and then expelling all unworthy thoughts. Dan wondered if God actually read the words as Ammiel was framing them in his head, like reading a book – or if He just heard them as if they were spoken aloud, as clearly as they were heard in the synagogue.

He imagined the words floating up like wisps of smoky incense to far-distant heaven. Would they be swallowed in the clouds? Dissolve if rained on? Dan saw interesting pictures of an unspoken prayer making its way up past the stars, past the moon, hovering about with hundreds of others to be attended to. What if one prayer got mixed up with another? What happened if God was not pleased with it? Or if bits of it were good and bits of it were not? Did a displeasing prayer just come tumbling back to earth with a thud ... land as a curse on someone ... or just sizzle up in a clap of thunder? Perhaps that's what lightning was – there must be a lot of bad prayers around in the winter ... his father always said cold weather made people selfish. Was his father praying right now about Aunt Etta's affliction? Surely that would be a good prayer and fly to heaven true and straight.

Dan thought of his own prayers for his mother. It was such a long time ago. He had only been a little boy then. What had happened to those prayers on the way to heaven? Had his child's voice been too weak or feeble for them to get all the way there? Were his words too simple and lame, not strong and powerful enough to reach? Or had there been so many tears and fears in his head that God couldn't read the words at all? Even big strong Ammiel had been afraid and tearful then, and his prayers hadn't worked either. Many times when he had stumbled over his reading at school, Dan had felt the crack of the rabbi's stick on his knuckles, and so he knew it was impossible to read through tears. And fear filled your head with a kind of fog where you couldn't see or think at all. Perhaps happy people had a better chance of having their prayers heard. But Ammiel had told Dan he must "call to God in times of trouble." Perhaps there were different ways of calling? There were so many things he did not know … which nobody told you about … which he was shy of asking in case he was supposed to know already …

His drifting thoughts were interrupted by another deep breath which indicated that Ammiel's prayer was finished. This time it was always a sharp intake of resolution, followed by a sigh of resignation as he rolled from his knees into his blankets. Soon all was quiet. After a few false starts, Ammiel's gentle snore began its nightly rhythm. Only Dan lay awake, his bony spine soaking up warmth from Aunt Etta's well padded back, staring into the darkness and wondering about all he had heard, and all he did not understand.

## Chapter Two

DAN woke suddenly as his warm blanket was flipped open and his black curls were scratched lightly. Obediently he slid out of bed, pushing the blanket back towards Aunt Etta's bulk. Outside, Ammiel and Dan splashed their faces with cold water from a pot by the door, and scrambled over the rocky hillside in the chilly twilight of dawn. Squatted by a tiny, burnt-down fire on a flat rock, old Caleb was waiting for them at the opening of a rough circle of thorn bushes. Inside was what looked like a valley of small boulders. Some of them were stirring.

"A good night." He nodded towards the sleepy flock.

"That's what I like to hear," Ammiel replied, squatting down and warming his hands. "How's the Queen of Sheba?"

He leaned over to stroke the nose of a particularly fat sheep who lifted her head and grunted scornfully. She shuffled forward on her knees and flopped down closer to Ammiel, her head almost in his lap.

Caleb grinned. "Still bossy, but slowing down these days, like the rest of us. There's a another season or two left in her, though. Maybe this year we'll have more twins out of her, maybe triplets."

"Triplets!" Dan was excited. "That would be special, wouldn't it!"

Ammiel motioned towards his leather bag. "Mmm, maybe, if nothing went wrong. Hurry up, son – before the growls in our stomachs wake the very rocks." He raked the coals aside with the end of his staff while Dan dived into the bag, pulled out a cloth bundle and unwrapped it.

Caleb's eyes crinkled in appreciation as the boy's quick fingers pulled apart a lump of dough, slapped the pieces into shape and dropped the flat cakes on the hot stone. It had been Dan's idea to bring dough and cook it so they would have hot cakes for breakfast instead of cold bread.

"A useful boy," Caleb grunted, carefully untying the opening of a skin bottle.

Ammiel glanced at his son, who was engrossed in patting the dough flat without burning his fingers. He answered in a low voice.

"Mm – but too much alone. Etta thinks he needs brothers and sisters."

Caleb chuckled and gave Ammiel an unsubtle nudge.

"Oho, indeed?"

"Etta thinks I should ask for Asa-and-Helen's Anna."

"Oh, *Etta* thinks again! – what do *you* think?" but Ammiel only shrugged. Caleb's sharp eyes, the colour of old bracken, glanced sideways.

"What about Dan?"

"Ssh – he doesn't know."

Dan looked up and blushed.

"My ears are sharper than you think, father," he answered clearly, "and I heard you talking last night."

10

"How much did you hear?" asked his father quickly.

"Only a bit ..." Dan flipped the cakes expertly with a flat stick.

"But what does *Ammiel* think, hey?" Caleb persisted, in a louder voice, with another big nudge.

Ammiel rubbed his chin thoughtfully, wondering whether Dan had also heard them talking about Etta's back. He wouldn't try to find out now – not in front of Old Caleb. He had been a good friend for many years and was almost like family – but not quite. He was also a talker. Reacting from his long quiet hours with the sheep, Caleb chattered constantly when he had an audience, whereas Ammiel was content to think his own thoughts quietly no matter where he was.

"Blessing first, talk later." Ammiel took a deep breath.

Dan and Caleb automatically dropped their eyes and repeated with him their morning prayer.

*"Blessed art thou, Adonai our God, King of the world, who causes to come forth bread from the earth ..."*

Ammiel had made this commonly used blessing especially their own by adding to it words which were both familiar and mysterious to his son ...

*"... Thou our Shepherd, lead us beside still waters, and show us thy Messiah. Amen."*

As he chanted the words, Dan felt the usual sensations – the strangely comfortable confusion in imagining God as a shepherd like his father, and the old itch of being muddled about the Messiah. He watched as his father and the old shepherd devoured their breakfast. He chewed his own more slowly. Why did Caleb always eat so quickly? Nobody was going to snatch it away from him! He reminded Dan of a hungry dog with a bone, jealously

11

guarding it from others. And why did his father always lick his fingers in the same order? He licked them quickly, beginning with his little finger and finishing with a quick suck of the tip of his thumb. It always made Dan want to laugh to see his father apparently sucking his thumb, even for a second. He wondered if Ammiel had ever had the same trouble as he did, when he was a boy. That tiresome thumb would just sneak in when he was asleep. Perhaps Aunt Etta would tell him if she was in a good mood. She was a lot older than his father, and sometimes teased him with older-sister jokes.

Dan started on the next round of cooking, and as he knelt by the little fire he thought he must look like a pagan fire-worshipper, praying over the coals. He liked hearing about the strange things the pagans did – they seemed so interesting, if silly. He wondered if Judaism seemed just as silly to the pagans, and if the pagans had a big thing like the Messiah to look forward to. *Why do we always pray for the Messiah?* Dan wasn't sure he really knew who Messiah was. Where was he coming from? *And how would he get here?* What would he do when he came? Everybody talked about Messiah and looked very holy, but *I wish someone would explain it properly instead of supposing I know all about it already!* Dan rolled up his next hot cake and put the whole thing in his mouth at once. What would he do if his father married Asa-and-Helen's Anna as Aunt Etta advised? The one with the Greek mother, but raised as a good Jewish girl. Dan had never seen her and had no idea what she was like. *What sort of a step-mother would she be?* He stopped chewing while he tried to imagine it.

Ammiel caught Dan's thoughtful eye.

"Well? If you don't like the food, blame the cook!"

Dan gulped his mouthful and blurted out, "Are you really going to marry Anna, father?"

Caleb guffawed. "Look out!"

Dan looked at him crossly. More mysterious grown-up jokes. He was tired of never knowing enough.

"Why is it funny?"

Ammiel quickly shook his head at Caleb, and motioned his son close, wrapping his thick cloak around him. "It's still cold yet – here, tuck in beside the Queen of Sheba. Caleb's laughing at me, not you."

"But why?" Dan snatched another cake and held it in his teeth while he wedged himself between the warm hairy sheep and his warm hairy father. He inhaled the familiar odour of sheep mixed with comforting smell of hot bread, and began to feel better.

Ammiel replied slowly, choosing his words with care.

"Well, looking for a wife is usually a lonely young man's passion. He imagines a cosy, rosy married life with a pretty woman and can't wait to begin. But I'm not lonely, nor young, so perhaps that's why I don't feel much passion about it either. You see, I had a pleasant enough life before I had a wife, and now I'm living very peacefully without one."

Old Caleb nodded emphatically. He had no qualms about speaking bluntly, even if Ammiel did. He leant forward and tapped the coals crisply with a stick. Tiny sparks sprinkled the air.

"Dan, your mother was a good woman, may she rest in peace. Good looker, good worker. But she had a sharp tongue, my boy, a very sharp tongue."

Dan remembered the bright eyes, the shining dark waterfall of hair, the busy hands, the hasty kisses and quicker slaps, the restless feet, the scoldings and the high pitched voice. Ammiel smiled down at him and dug a handful of dried grapes out of the bag. He dropped them slowly one by one into Dan's lap as he spoke.

*"A continual dropping in a very rainy day and a contentious woman are alike,"* he said. "King Solomon says so, and when it came to women, he knew what he was talking about and no mistake. Your mother snatched my heart so fast she made me breathless, son, but she was hard to please, I can't deny it. It suddenly went very quiet when she died. When my tears dried, I got to like the silence. Your Aunt Etta knows my ways, and Bukki ..." His voice died away. Somehow there was never anything to say about Uncle Bukki. He finished, lamely, " Well, it's peaceful with the sheep and I'm used to it. And it's peaceful without a noisy woman in the house, and maybe I've got too lazy to change."

"Oh," said Dan, pulling Sheba's long floppy ears absently. He thought about everything he had heard since last night. He knew the lazy one in their house was not his father. He knew Aunt Etta would become crippled by her back. He also knew Uncle Bukki would do nothing to lighten the load and that this worried everyone except Uncle Bukki, who never worried about anyone but himself. The Queen of Sheba nibbled lazily at his fingers, begging, and he gave her a raisin. He thought for a while longer.

"Is Anna a lazy woman, father? Or is she noisy like mother was?

He slid out from under his father's cloak and slapped the next round of cakes on the stone. He was turning them before he realised Ammiel hadn't answered.

"Father?"

Ammiel was staring at the coals, which were darkening even as the lofty sky began to flush with sudden colour.

"Ah – no," he said, sounding a little surprised. He paused. "No – I remember – Anna was always busy. And so quiet you hardly know she's around ..."

"Hm!" Caleb grunted. "No beauty, though."

Ammiel slowly pulled apart a piece of cheese, gazing at the fire still, and dropping the fragments in his lap without any idea of what he was doing. Sheba sniffed at them hopefully.

"You're right," he said absently. "No beauty – not used to admiration and attention and making a fuss. Certainly not a Queen-of-Sheba – no beauty at all – but quiet ... gentle."

Suddenly he threw his curly-haired arms in the air and gave a shout of laughter, scattering cheese and crumbs, and startling fat Queen of Sheba, who bleated a protest. Bits of cheese landed among the frying cakes and melted on the stone.

" '*Out of the mouths of babes and sucklings has thou ordained strength!*' King David was a wise man in truth! Etta is right, but it took my son to show me sense. Dan, you're a wise man too! A small Daniel!"

Dan's mouth twitched. It was a well-worn joke but it belonged just to him and his father. And he never tired of being called a small wise Daniel. It made him feel a man-to-man warmth.

Old Caleb sucked his crooked teeth happily and nodded as he greedily picked up bits of cheese and poked them into his mouth with grimy fingers.

"Three wise men – Solomon, David – and Dan!"

15

"Yes, a Daniel – a revealer of secrets!" chortled Ammiel – suddenly jubilant – cramming his mouth full of hot bread and speaking with unaccustomed rapidity between gulps. "Today he revealed to me my own heart! I must have been asleep all these long months! Today in his innocence he revealed that what I really crave for my old age is comfort and peace, ministered to by a gentle wife. Who knows – she may even love me at the last! Dan, this is man's business, but you've earned a part in it. Will you come with me to Anna's parents?"

"Yes," said Dan, swelling with pride, amazed and glad to see the unusual sparkle and exuberance in his normally placid father. He hugged the Queen of Sheba to squeeze all these unexpected emotions back into a more manageable package. If this Anna was quiet and gentle, it would be a change without dread. He wondered if she would like Uncle Bukki and Aunt Etta. And if they would like her. He wondered if she would want to marry a bushy, brawny, wool-smelling shepherd, and if she would want to be a stepmother to anyone. He hoped she would be kind as well as quiet.

The cheese toasting on the stone sizzled with a tempting smell. Dan scraped it off with a stick and tasted it. The others saw the expression on his face and tasted it too.

Caleb smacked his lips. "Delicious! A new treat! Better have this at the wedding feast."

Lazy Queen of Sheba was coaxed to her feet with a scrap of this luxury, and she waddled off to pull at the short grass between the stones. Ammiel was making short work of the remaining food. The sun bounced above the horizon and spread the hillside with tentative colour. It warmed Old Caleb's white hair to pale yellow, sparked gold lights from Ammiel's red-brown curls and showed a new glint in his eyes as he threw back his head to drink from the water skin. He wiped his mouth with the back of his hand and slung Dan the bottle.

"It's nearly time to move the sheep."

He waded through the flock which was now awake and beginning to graze. Last year's lambs were still attempting to sneak up and bunt milk from weary mothers who sent them sprawling. "Time to grow up! You're not a baby any more!" they seemed to say and Dan laughed to see how cheekily the youngsters tried their luck. Satchel in hand, he followed the men around the flock, ready with the flask of vinegar, tub of wool-fat, and precious pot of healing ointment. Ammiel and Caleb worked swiftly but thoroughly – patiently inspecting ears, hooves, tails and bellies and murmuring reassurances to each sheep in turn. A stray thorn stuck in the membrane of a cloven hoof, an infected eye, a sore teat, a lovely fat brushy tail jerking unhappily in the agitation of early fly-strike – all quickly noticed, and deftly treated. As always, Dan marvelled that such scatty, silly animals were so meek and willing to submit even when treatment was painful. In their shepherds' hands they became calm, and almost sensible.

Inspection over, Dan strapped up the satchel, packed the remaining food away in the leather scrip, smothered the fire with earth, and retied the water skin. Caleb rolled up his blankets and tucked them under his arm, but Ammiel shook his head as Dan shouldered the food and water.

"Leave it. Go back with Caleb after all, Dan," said Ammiel briskly, pushing away the loose thorn barrier with his staff. "I'm taking the flock to join with Samuel's goats on the west slopes. We've agreed to keep them together for a few days. There's water and plenty of pasture for them all, and the goats will love the shrubs. One of Samuel's boys will take a message to Asa for me. I will ask him to expect a visit from me within two days."

Caleb winked at Dan. "Asa won't be guessing about that visit, you know. Your father and Anna played together as children ... but ..."

Ammiel snapped his fingers warningly at Caleb and gave his son a gentle shove.

"Go back to Aunt Etta and tell her what we talked about. It will make her happy and spare me her questions for another day at least! Caleb, bring him with you tomorrow morning. And no more gossiping! I'm sure he'll have a host of instructions from Etta to give me."

He waved them off with a grin, and lifted his rich voice in a buzzing melody. *"Come on, my darlings! Come to Abba! Come on, my darlings! Come to Abba!"* He dropped his voice to a normal tone and remonstrated, "Sheba, no pushing! Holah, Golan, Geba, Almon, Hephzibar ..." Then the odd little tune began again, *"Come on, my darlings! Come to Abba! ..."*

Caleb and Dan strode away, hearing Ammiel's special call fade into the answering bleats of seventy three sheep ambling out of the fold.

"Caleb?"

"Mm?"

"Do you think Asa-and-Helen's Anna will want to marry my father?"

Caleb screwed his seamed face into even more wrinkles to think about it. "She will if her parents want her to. She's a dutiful woman."

"Yes, but do you think she will want to?"

Caleb looked down at Dan's small feet dancing over the stones and thought rather sentimentally about the rocky scramble of life ahead for the boy. He patted Dan's thin shoulder.

"Your father's a handsome man, even if he's not young. And he has his own flock to make a living with. Rich enough to hire me, after all! And he didn't beat his first wife. Why not?"

Dan dismissed the tantalising question of men beating their wives for the moment. He was more worried about something else. "She might not ... *want* ... me. Or Aunt Etta. Or Uncle Bukki ..."

"Oh, you're too small to bother her. And your Aunt Etta's too sensible to get in her way."

"Uncle Bukki?"

Caleb considered. "Well, now, your Uncle Bukki, you know, he should really be making a home of his own anyway. Maybe we should persuade Uncle Bukki to find a wife too." Dan thought of Uncle Bukki, with his lazy ways and his whining voice, and the funny shadow of a water jug made by his head.

"Who would want to marry Uncle Bukki!" he giggled suddenly.

Old Caleb cackled. "Who indeed! But with God, nothing is impossible!" He waved his leathery hand and branched off towards his daughter's house.


Dan scurried down the last hill towards their house, and still thinking over all the things he had heard since yesterday. So much was crammed in his head there hardly seemed to be room for it all. The shock of the overheard conversation by lamplight. Talking it over like a man with his father and old Caleb. His father deciding

19

that Anna would be a good catch after all. And thanking Dan for it! Aunt Etta would be very pleased. "Who would care for the family?" That had been Aunt Etta's worry, and now if Anna and her parents agreed to the marriage, this problem would be solved. But nothing could cure Aunt Etta's diseased back, which would curl over like an autumn leaf.

There she was now, bending to wash her face outside the house. She lifted her head. "What are you doing back here, boy? Is all well with your father?"

"Aunt Etta! Father says to tell you! He is going to speak to Anna's parents!"

"Oh, is he?" Aunt Etta watched Dan carefully. "About what, if I may ask?"

Dan snatched the towel from her shoulder and waved it cheekily above his head. "I know all about it," he boasted gaily. "He's going to marry her if she'll have him, and then …"

"And then what?" said a sullen voice from the doorway. Uncle Bukki was shuffling out, rubbing sleep from his near-set eyes and scratching himself.

"And then we'll all be happy …" faltered Dan, suddenly uncertain, dropping his arm. The cloth trailed in the muddy puddle beside the water jar.

"Yes, Dan," said Aunt Etta firmly, rescuing her towel and wringing out the wet corner as if she was wringing someone's neck. "Then we'll all be happy together! I'm very glad." She rubbed the back of her neck briskly and mopped her wet face.

Uncle Bukki crossed his stumpy arms and squinted at her.

"Oh, yes, we'll all be happy together!" he agreed sarcastically in his gargly morning voice. "We'll all be very happy when she starts breeding and there's no room for us any more. We'll all be very happy when she decides her husband's old brother-in-law doesn't belong in her home. We'll all be very happy when she doesn't want a fat old bent-up sister-in-law taking up space and making extra work ..."

Dan's mouth dropped open. Aunt Etta's eyes narrowed to slits and with a swift flicking movement she snapped her wet towel right in Uncle Bukki's face with a crack like a whip.

"You stop that at once!" she hissed. "How dare you speak this way in front of Dan! Ammiel has been more than good to you! If he turned you out tonight you'd have had more charity from him than you deserve! Would you begrudge him joy after all his sorrow?" She caught sight of Dan's horrified face and fumbled her purse from the depths of her bodice. "Here Dan!" – thrusting a coin into his hand – "run to the shore and get me some fish – the boats will be in by now – go!"

She turned for another sharp word to Bukki and Dan fled obediently from their angry voices. He thought he had just sorted it all out – and now he was as bewildered as ever. Why was it all so complicated? Only last night he had heard the first rumblings of change. And now the rumblings were becoming an earthquake. Perhaps it wouldn't be as simple as old Caleb had thought. What if Uncle Bukki was right?

The shepherd's house was inland a little way, removed from the gregarious cluster of the tiny fishing village by the sea. Dan emerged from the intervening rocky scrub and swiftly threaded his way among the small houses which were already bustling with early morning activity. His thoughts joggled about as he tried to outrun them. He jumped over a scavenging dog, pushed past a huddle

21

of toddlers who were squabbling over a lizard, banged his elbow on an inconveniently placed hand-cart, and dodged his way through the narrow crooked laneways towards the fresh welcome of the beach. Not paying attention to his feet, he ran through something smelly and felt it squish between his toes. It was warm, which only meant one thing … suddenly the sea was more inviting than ever … he ran faster … Dan swung thankfully around the corner of the last house and there was a loud smack as he collided with someone coming the other way. It was too much! Dan dropped his coin and howled in good earnest, clutching at his eye, which was already swelling like a mushroom.

# Chapter Three

A stifled groaning made him open his other eye. A bigger boy was drooping against the wall holding a large fish under one arm and gingerly feeling his jaw with the other hand. They each opened their eyes at the same time. The older boy spoke first.

"Ow! Ow, ow." Then he began to laugh in spite of his pain. "Your eye! It's a pigeon's egg!"

Dan swallowed his tears at once and glared at him. His head throbbed. The lump above his eye certainly felt like an egg, and he was sure it was turning black. He began feeling in the dust for his coin. The boy squatted next to him.

"What's lost?"

"My fish money."

The boy put down his own fish.

"I'll help." He rubbed his jaw again. "Ow – thought you'd broken it."

He hunted beside Dan, who by now could only see out of one eye. "Here it is!"

He looked at Dan's lump, which was growing all the time.

"Hen's egg! Better put cold water on it."

Dan squinted at him and nodded.

The boy pulled him to his feet and they made their way to the beach where the icy water bit their feet. The bigger boy eyed Dan's face critically.

"Maybe even a goose egg, now!" he exaggerated cheerfully.

Dan was bending down to splash his eye when someone called out.

"Johanan? Where are you?"

The boy looked up towards the houses. "Here!"

A woman trotted towards them across the sand, the long, heavy blue tassels of her light mantle kicking giddily with every step.

"Was it you I heard groaning?" She was very big and tall, with straight black eyebrows and a quirk to her wide mouth – and there was something unusual about her eyes. She saw Dan and gasped.

"You haven't been fighting this little boy?"

Johanan shook his head indignantly.

"Ran into him round a corner. His eye, my chin." He slapped his hands demonstratively. "Smack!"

The woman put her arm round Dan. "Poor lamb! Does it hurt?"

"No," Dan lied. His face felt very lopsided.

"My jaw hurts!" the other boy offered, but she ignored him, examining the confused Dan, and smoothing his curls. She dipped the end of her veil in the water and gently held the cold cloth to his sore lump, increasing his headache. Now he could see what was strange about her eyes. One was brown and one was hazel.

Embarrassed, Dan said faintly to the giantess, "I must go – I have to get some fish."

"Johanan – take his money and run back to the boats to buy his fish. The poor little thing can hardly see. No, better yet, give him yours so he can go home at once. I'm sure he is in pain, and his mother will want to fuss over him. Why, it's a wonder he's not knocked senseless!"

Poor Dan by now was feeling rather wobbly. All this

24

tenderness was a bit much, and he was feeling more like a baby every minute. Johanan rolled his eyes and handed over his slippery fish with a wink. Rather helplessly, Dan dropped it on the sand, wondering why the world kept sliding sideways. The woman picked him up in her strong arms.

"Come on, *dodi,* you've had a nasty bump. I'll take you home to mother. My cousin will bring your fish. Where do you live?"

Dan closed his eyes and felt himself swaying with each step she took.

"I ... feel ... sick ..." he muttered, and promptly brought up his breakfast all over her.

Johanan jumped clear and laughed. The giantess shook her head at him, turned around, marched back to the water and swiftly cleaned them both up. Swaddling Dan's damp body in her equally damp woollen veil she carried him as lightly as a lost lamb to a house close by. Her laconic cousin rescued his fish, and hugging it to him, sand and all, ran after them. Dan was too dizzy to notice that he was entering the same house where he had received his bump. He was dimly aware of sinking onto a soft sheepskin, being draped in something warm and dry, and having something bitter held to his lips. A little hammer in his head tapped him firmly down into a black well full of coloured sparks and from there he floated backwards into grateful darkness.

Meanwhile Aunt Etta had given Uncle Bukki such a good roasting that he had stalked out of the little mud house and gone off to cool his temper elsewhere, leaving Etta to all the household tasks. Well, of course it was women's work, but – *Catch Bukki even lifting a finger to tend the herb garden!* Etta thought resignedly. She sighed to herself, wishing that Dan had not witnessed such a nasty outburst. Little Dan had been very grown up about Ammiel deciding to remarry, and great big Bukki had been so childish! It was all the wrong way round.

She took the cover off the large water pot and ladled a little into a pan. Deftly Etta washed the cups and bowls with her fingers, dried them carefully and put them on the neatly made shelves which long ago had been her wedding gift to Dan's mother. She ran an appreciative hand over the glowing wood which fitted perfectly into its own little niche in the whitewashed mud wall – *such a lovely smooth finish.* He'd only been an apprentice, but that young carpenter had seemed to understand that a woman needs to take pleasure in the little things of her own world. She wondered how he'd got on in life. Well, his wife would be a lucky woman. Etta threw the water onto the little patch of mint beside the house and sternly plucked out a creeping weed hiding under the hairy leaves.

Next she took up the beds and draped the blankets over a bush to air, thinking about the fish Dan would bring home. She would fry it, or make soup – or perhaps wrap it in herbs and mud and bake it very slowly. It would depend on the size of the fish, and what *that* depended on was the mood of the fisherman selling it, and what kind of a night he'd had. Etta lifted the sleeping mats, and shook them in the rapidly warming sunshine. She began to sweep the floor with a small broom. *Time this broom was mended ... Must get Dan to collect some good stiff straw for it ... though Marta says water reeds are as good ... and Ada swears by fine twigs, herself. Each to her own. Where is the boy? He should be back by now.* Perhaps there was a crowd down at the boats, and he had been lost among the drapery of the eager women. He would have to wait a long time while they all haggled, and be attended to last of all. Probably they would try to cheat him too. She smiled to herself. Dan was small, but he was not stupid. She had taught him how to bargain in the market place. He was quick with figures for his age, and knew how to stand his ground even with that cunning little old fig merchant, Zaccheus. *Hiy–Yi, but that man has the money! And no wonder, with his cheating ways! They say in his younger days he swindled someone with cakes of cow dung padding out three bushels of dried figs, and it wasn't discovered until the poor man made a wedding gift of them to his bride's family and nearly had a knife at his throat for the insult*!

Etta couldn't help chuckling over the old story as she patiently swept the dirt floor. Likely the gossip was only half true, and anyway, old Zack was amiable enough. He worked hard, and did the rounds of all the markets from here to Jericho and back. *Can't bear to trust his money to servants, and works himself to a shadow, silly man! No fat on his little bones, that's for sure.* Etta shook her head indulgently, recalling both his blandishments and his tantrums during some of their bargaining battles. Zack was a character, all right. You paid for his extravagant compliments with extra figs if you weren't careful, that's all. *Dan is so late with that fish! Perhaps the catch was poor and the boats late.*

Etta trimmed the wick in the lamp and refilled it with pale yellow olive oil. It was second pressing of course, and sputtered just a little, but it was bright enough for their needs. She thought of the lovely clear light which burned in the synagogue lamps and which to her was a hypnotic symbol of keeping the Faith. *That reminds me – it's more than time that young man went back to synagogue school!* Ammiel had kept the boy very close by him since his mother died. Well, it was proper for a boy to learn his trade at his father's knee, and a boy passed early from the care of women ... but a little paternal selfishness was there, Etta thought compassionately. True, Ammiel should make a shepherd of him, but the Law and the Traditions must be learned – and schooling was to be prized, as the backbone of the Faith.

Besides, the boy was far too young yet to be with old company all the time, and a stepmother would mean adjustments all round. He'd need the steadiness of regular school and boyish company. *I'll talk to my brother and tell him enough is enough.*

Dan should go back to morning-school very soon and continue learning his letters and more advanced figuring, and the holy writings. *Where is he?* Dan was a solitary boy, and never dawdled to play when on an errand. Come to think of it, he had no particular friends – thought Etta. This wasn't right either, and another reason to return to school. A boy should have friends. And a boy should learn to play before he learned to work (Etta's thoughts continued rather contrarily) or he would be a very joyless man. *But he had better learn to work as well!* Etta corrected herself wryly, or he would be a very ... a very ... he would be ... well, he would be very much like Bukki ... She sighed and propped her broom upside down to save the worn straws. She pulled a face, coiled part of her veil on her head, settled the water jar on the resulting pad, and walked slowly to the well. *Maybe Dan will be home when I get back.*

Of course, Rachel was there, with the latest scandal. "Dabab" was her nickname. Rachel the Gossip. She was always first to the well, drawing her water and then lingering till a worthwhile crowd collected before scattering her freshest titbit for them to devour. It was hard to get a word in sideways with her crafty tongue in full flow. *Dabab–ing away already*! Etta could tell by the way the women were leaning towards her sly little face. *That one draws unhappy secrets out of people as expertly as she draws water. Well, practice makes perfect,* she thought sardonically.

"No, I said *Marah,* dear. *Not* our potter's wife, Marta, – how could you possibly confuse them? I'm sure I speak clearly enough, but of course, your mother went deaf early too, didn't she, poor soul. Marah All-Alone, I'm talking about. Well, she's rarely a visitor here these days, despite her old friends … though we all know how hard she works, poor thing! But what's a woman to do without a family? A good place with the biggest dyer in Magdala and she actually left!"

The fat, toothless woman beside her worked her wrinkled mouth disapprovingly as she impatiently shouldered Rachel aside. "You know those stinking vats gave her the vomits, *Dabab,*" she lisped curtly.

Rachel blinked at hearing the nickname spoken to her face. "Sickness is a visitation from God," she said primly. "Sickness is earned, and to say less is sin. And look where she went next – I ask you! Taking service with those ungodly Romans at the hot springs of Tiberius, and never a day off for the Sabbath! I believe her father was a devout man, may he rest in peace, if he can, while turning in his grave no doubt. *Tiberius!* And on the Sabbath! Of course, that's old news now … But, the most tragic thing! Marah was seen in broad daylight two days ago … just wandering about, with *wild eyes* and her hair uncovered – such a sight! – And she was wringing her hands, *babbling to trees*! and whispering nonsense to anyone who'd listen … and not a word of sense could anyone get from her … Now *what* do you think …"

Aunt Etta forgot Dan momentarily in her annoyance and interrupted loudly.

"I think she was giving an excellent imitation of the Dabab!" she called out waspishly. Hot springs, at Tiberius or no, sounded like Paradise for her own aching back. If it came to that, what did anyone know of lonely Marah's ailments? Perhaps she had private aches and pains of her own.

Rachel looked taken aback.

"If anyone but you said that, Etta, I would be very offended," she said in a hurt voice. "But we all know how hard your life has been these last few years, and no doubt you are not quite yourself today. So I forgive you," she added sweetly.

Etta snorted, but Rachel continued patronisingly, in a voice soft enough to intrigue, loud enough to force attention.

"Of course, all this is too dreadful – poor Marah! But what can one do to honour the law of the fatherless? She has repelled all *my* offers of friendship ... and it *must* be admitted that she brings bad luck ... with that broken betrothal when her poor father died leaving nothing but debts ... rather mysteriously, you must admit ... because we all expected there was a good dowry tucked away – and so did her intended –" here the Dabab dropped her voice, adding in a chilling whisper, "*and what with her mother taking the leprosy all those years ago ...*"

A suppressed shudder rippled around the well and the women involuntarily averted their heads as if a leper had edged into their view. Rachel drew breath.

"Well, it certainly seems ..." she paused for effect – "that the strain has been too much for her – and with spending all that time working for pagans over a graveyard on all those Sabbaths – what could you expect?" She settled her pot on one shoulder and took in all the expectant expressions around her with a single swooping glance.

" It is clear that Marah All-Alone *has a devil ... maybe even two!*"

Nodding emphatically, Rachel turned away at once, and left the well busy with chattering voices and hastily called questions, all of which she grandly ignored.

She was an expert in timing, Etta thought sourly, and knew exactly when to make her exits to the greatest effect. She dropped in just enough yeasty information to get imaginations started, and then withdrew to let them ferment. Her thrill was simply in poking it in and watching it gradually puff up. Nobody could ever accuse *her* of actually cooking the sweet bread of slander, no matter how much she enjoyed tasting the crumbs. Any attempt to discover the source of her rumours met with a very pious response.

"Oh, no, my dear, I'm not saying it's *true,* it's just what I've heard. Oh, I can't tell you who told me! You wouldn't want me to betray a confidence, would you?"

The eventual truth – or half-truth – of many of her whispers seemed to justify the Dabab. But it was an unspoken fact that Rachel's deceptively sympathetic probings aggravated many a sore which would have healed faster left the ministrations of time, wisdom, and the hand of the Eternal. Etta had had enough! She elbowed her way unceremoniously to the mouth of the well, snatched at the bucket rope and raised her voice to change the subject.

"Never mind the Dabab – and never mind poor Marah's imaginary devils – has anyone seen my little Dan today?"

Etta's friend Marta arrived at the well just in time to hear the question. Despite the quirky lock of silver which striped the front of her brown hair, the pomegranate shape of her robe showed she was a still a young wife with happy expectations. "He's not up the hillside with his father today, Etta?"

The grey streak blew free from her veil and tossed in the morning breeze. She tucked it back with a lean brown hand. It wasn't like Etta to worry for nothing. The others shook their heads. True, their little community was close to Tiberius, and there were stories about child-eating soldiers with which they scared their children into obedience – but really … Dan wasn't a baby after all.

"Ammiel didn't need him for long this morning – and I sent him out early for fish as I often do." Etta hauled on the rope, and tipped the bucket into her jar. "He should have been home this last hour." She dropped the leather bucket with a splash and

31

began hauling up the next load. She would not relate the whole story in front of the others.

Several had seen Dan running past this morning, but none had seen him return. The women finished collecting their water and drifted off in talkative pairs and triplets. Now they had two pieces of news. Not that Dan's tardiness was exactly news, but it was a good starting point for the morning's conversation. While talking about Dan, they could bring in the whole subject of his mother's sad death, Ammiel's reluctance to quickly remarry for the child's sake and whether it was wise for him to keep on that hopeless Bukki – after all, his sister was now dead – *and in death may she rest in peace, for she found none in life*! they whispered – and while on the subject – was Ammiel a fool or an angel to treat him so well?

The busy tongues had plenty to savour even before they returned to the discussion over whether Etta was really fit to mother a lively little boy at her age – and how slow and bent she was getting, and now of course she was panicking when the child was out of sight … and so it was that those with either too little or too much excitement in their own lives were gratified in the contemplation of someone else's problems. Marah All-Alone's mysterious affliction was almost forgotten for the moment, but of course, that was a far meatier topic, to be chewed over at length. It would keep very nicely for later.

Etta leant on the worn edge of the well and waited for Marta, who was polite by nature and as a result, was often the last one drawing water even when she arrived at the same time as the others. Now they were alone, Etta told her why she had sent Dan off in a hurry. Marta nodded consolingly. They all knew Bukki.

"Perhaps he wanted to stay away till Bukki calmed down," Marta suggested, pulling up the rope with the firm swift movements of long practice. "Or maybe he decided to stay and clean the fish himself."

Etta considered. Possible, but unlikely, unless he borrowed a knife from a fisherman, who'd be unlikely to lend it. She could think of nothing else. She lifted her jar to its position on her head with an effort, spilling a little. Marta steadied it with a laugh.

"You'll have to straighten up a bit or you'll lose some more!"

Etta tried to smile as Marta swung her own jar easily to her head and settled it.

"Ah – I'm just getting lazy in my old age!" She nodded at the large bump in Marta's gown. "Easier for you, oh thou little *shaduf*!"

Marta pictured the Egyptian irrigation shaduf – waterbucket at one end, counterweight at the other – and burst out laughing so suddenly she nearly unbalanced her jar. She laughed until she had to lean on the well for support – but finally her giggles subsided. It was clear that Etta's thoughts were busy with absent Dan, even though she added a chuckle to Marta's peals of laughter. Of course, Bukki would be sulking somewhere, Ammiel would be out all night. Etta was looking worn out these days – and there was no-one she could send to look for the lad.

"Oh, I'll die of your jokes one day!" Marta gasped cheerfully, straightening up with an effort. "Come on, Etta. We'll take our water home and look for him ourselves."

They walked together – hips rolling, knees and ankles softened – bodies steady from the waist up. A sinuous, gliding walk learned from childhood. A graceful walk with no jarring movements, the water barely moving in the heavy pots on their heads. Marta slowed her pace to that of the older woman, pretending that she was tired. Etta wasn't fooled. So far along, and no sign of a waddle in her young friend yet. No, Marta wasn't tired! Etta lifted her fig-black eyes and smiled properly for the first time that morning.

"You're a good friend, Marta."

"Well, you never know," said Marta gaily, ignoring her thanks, "perhaps by the time we've taken my water home, and then yours, he will have turned up." She giggled again. "*Shaduf*, indeed!"

Gentle swirls of laughter and dust followed their softly padding bare feet.

Half an hour later the two women neared the shepherd's house, calling Dan's name hopefully. There was a movement in the scrub and they turned expectantly. No Dan! – but a gangly lad – freshly scratched legs sprouting from a short tunic sprinkled with sand and scales – lurching out of the bushes, panting.

"This the Shepherd's place?"

# Chapter Four

ETTA tried to dissuade Marta from accompanying her to the house by the shore, but her friend insisted. Johanan eyed both of them dubiously. Neither of them looked fit to carry Dan back home, but it wasn't his business to decide that – just to fetch anyone who was at the house.

"He's probably all right," he said chirpily. "Just a faint. We hit hard, you know – cracked my jaw too!"

He noticed Marta's nervous glance at the white fleshy lips which were pouting through the neckline of his bulging tunic, and dived a hand into his bosom.

"Oh, sorry! Forgot this."

He pulled out the stiff fish and handed it over triumphantly.

"Dan bought this?" gasped Etta. "It's huge!"

Johanan shook his head. "Mine. Well, was. Now it's yours."

Etta shook her head in turn. It was beyond her. She dug out her medicine satchel of herbs and ointments while Marta took the fish, dropped it in a deep dish and covered it with cold water. Both women moved quickly, but Johanan danced about impatiently till they were all hurrying down the track to the village together.

Seeing that no useful information about Dan could be got out of the messenger, Etta tried unsuccessfully to find out about his family. She didn't remember having seen him before and knew no local Johanans.

"Who is your father, lad?"

"Dead."

"Oh – your mother's name, then?"

"Mari."

Etta rolled her eyes at Marta. From Galilee to Jerusalem, Miriams, Maris and Marahs appeared like manna on the ground, as if naming a girl-child for bitterness was a either a warning or a charm against it. Marta rolled her eyes too, with a giggle, thankful as always that she had narrowly escaped 'Bitterness' by a mere syllable, at her mother's insistence that her little girl should be a 'Lady'.

Etta puffed along behind the boy, who strode at a tremendous rate. As if to mock her, swallows darted through the air, flipping about nonchalantly, skimming the ground with insolent ease. If Dan was here no doubt he'd be asking a dozen questions about how they did it and wouldn't she love to be a swallow too? Pesky things, filling the air with their shrill cries all day long – but yes, right now she'd love to be a swallow! If only that boy would slow down. She called him back with another question, still trying to extract information.

"Is your mother in the village?"

"No."

"Whose house are you staying at?"

"Not staying. Just visiting."

Marta and Etta exchanged frustrated glances.

*"H'mph!"* said Marta's eyebrows.

*"Manners!"* said the twitch of Etta's nose.

"Whose house are you *visiting?*" persisted Marta.

The boy considered.

"My uncle's, I think."

*He thinks! Doesn't he know? And who may his uncle be?*

"Or maybe it's my cousin's –or perhaps my mother's."

Marta shrugged to Etta in comic despair. There was not much to be got out of this boy. One thing they both realised, though. To be so unconcerned and ignorant about whom in the clan owned a spare house! Certainly this family must have money behind them.

Etta hoped they weren't Sadducees. They always had plenty of money, and knew how to spend it. Of course, they didn't believe in Resurrection, that was why! After all, if you only have a life now, you have to have Paradise now, as well – or miss out. Not for them a humble life, with a hope of later inheriting Abraham's promise. Later was too far away, and they couldn't believe in it. They wanted it all, and they wanted it now. They usually got it too, Etta reflected wryly. *Living in Rome's pocket!* They were not nice people. She would rather not be obliged to a pompous Sadducee. But perhaps that was unfair. If a Sadducee had opened his house to an unknown urchin with a sore head, then he – or his wife or his family – could hardly be pompous, or "not nice" … but then, sometimes folk did good things for bad reasons. Etta shook her head a little. A cynic, she was becoming! Better to believe the best of people – if you could. She tried to picture a gentle, benevolent Sadducee taking the sea air and watching the children play on the beach – just as a thorny bramble scraped her ankle and snatched her hem.

Etta tugged her robe from the clutches of the insistent bush and pulled her thoughts back to reality. A Sadducee – with a little house down here? *Not very likely!* Tiberius, now, Herod's showpiece, would be a very different matter. It was very modern, Roman of course, and full of luxury and beauty – *if you like that sort of thing* … but Etta broke off, and mentally slapped herself for dishonesty. Of course she liked luxury and beauty as much as anyone, even if she had no share in it – and Herod's touch was in the Temple buildings too, so there was no use pretending it wasn't attractive. Oh, and there was no doubt her stiff back would appreciate those hot springs! She fairly craved the hot springs, to be truthful.

But you just couldn't get around the fact no self-respecting Jew would live in Tiberius – why, it was built over an old graveyard! Not that this bothered the Sadducees much … not so as you'd notice, Etta added sarcastically. Sadducees weren't concerned about respect for the dead, the uncleanness of graves or other such "superstitious traditions". *And money sings sweeter than tradition!* After all, they'd get precious little power or position – and the wealth that flowed on from them – without an important Roman or two on their side. And if bodies weren't raised, who cared about a graveyard? Well, they'd get a shock on Resurrection Day, she thought with grim satisfaction. Hi-yi! The long dead looming up through their marble floors and frightening them all into fits! She strode on more cheerfully.

Meanwhile, Marta, whose thoughts as well as her feet were keeping pace with Etta's, was wondering if Johanan's mysterious rich uncle could be a Pharisee. A Sadducee surely wouldn't be interested in maintaining a house in such a humble place, but a devout Pharisee might take it into his head – perhaps to force the ignorant classes to take more care in observing in the sacred rituals, which they often ignored. It was all very well for the rich, but time itself was a luxury to the poor, with every moment spent in earning bread or taxes. Perhaps he was a scribe, or had plans for building a synagogue! That would be a blessing indeed. All the synagogues at Magdala were small and crowded, and a long walk to school for the smallest boys. And everyone knew the Rabbi was bad-tempered! Yes, a local teacher would be a big help. It was all very fine for the sages to declare that a village of even ten pious men could support a synagogue, but they didn't mention how it was to be paid for! So of course, there had never been one built.

A fine crop of boys had been born five years ago, and even a class under a tree would be better than a crowded floor in Magdala. Marta hoped the baby she was carrying would be a boy. She would hate to end up like Zipporah in Cana – always another girl! Poor Zipporah and Barak had eleven girls before the all important son arrived, and how they would get them all married off was yet to be imagined.

Happily oblivious of their speculations about his family, the boy trotted ahead, occasionally wheeling back around them like a sheepdog to hurry them up. The women were both breathless by the time they reached his house. Marta sat down on a bench, holding her side, and waved Etta on, panting, "You go – I must catch my breath."

Etta clutched her satchel, stifling a sudden nervous qualm as the boy led her to the upper room.

The light was thickly filtered through woven blinds which stirred on the warm air, and flowed in a speckled river over the child on the floor. Etta hardly noticed the tall woman folded beside him in the shadows, fanning him with a palm leaf. She bent over her nephew, carefully touching his damp curls with her fingertips and feeling his cheek with the back of her hand.

"He is better," the woman whispered reassuringly. "He woke from the sleep of shock an hour ago – it was only brief. See, his skin is warm and dry, and he breathes easily. You won't need your medicines – this is the normal sleep of a weary child. But I thought he should see his mother when he woke …"

"The Lord bless your kindness!" Etta responded quietly.

Johanan was fiddling with the low blind, and just then it slipped from its peg. As the sun flashed in, the woman on the floor lifted her straight eyebrows questioningly and gave a charmingly crooked smile.

"Well, well! It's Etta!" she murmured. "Then this must be little Dan, your brother's boy!"

The sun lit Etta's face, but mingled relief and recognition brightened her eyes.

"My dear! What a surprise – what a pleasure!"

"Johanan, put the blind back at once!" The woman rose, stooping like Etta in the low room, and held a finger to her lips.

"We won't wake him," she suggested softly. "Healthy sleep will refresh him. Johanan will stay with him, won't you?"

The boy nodded gratefully. He hadn't run so far or so fast for a long time. And his jaw still hurt when he touched it. Lucky he hadn't broken a tooth! Much they cared. It wasn't as dramatic as lumps or black eyes – women liked to see something for their sympathy. Maybe he would get a good bruise, though. He stretched himself on the floor with a happy sigh and pulled a cushion under his head, but the light was in his eyes. He jumped up, dropped the blind still further, and settled back comfortably, lazily watching the motes dancing on a thin stray sunbeam which trickled through the woven straw, until, lulled by Dan's quiet breathing, he too fell asleep.

The two women joined Marta downstairs and a sudden bubbling of pleasurable chattering frothed in the room, ebbing and flowing on the warm tide of mutual acquaintance.

"And here's young Marta, too! You were a mere betrothed child when I last saw you – and look how you've grown!"

Marta giggled at the double meaning and proudly satisfied all the usual feminine questions about her condition before asking some of her own.

"Oh, do tell us – that exasperating Johanan was no help to our curiosity. Whose house is this – and what in the world are you doing here instead of in Cana?"

"It's my Uncle Joseph's, bought for old Esther, his nurse. She was raised here, you know, before taking up service with the family."

"Of course, we remember old Esther, we wailed at her funeral ourselves – but had no idea of the connection!"

"Oh, I think she kept much to herself. The house was the result of a very old promise!"

"Really?"

"Yes! The story goes that when Uncle was tiny, and in trouble, he used to beg, *"Pleathe don't thmack me, Ethter and when I'm a big man I'll buy you a houthe by the thea!"*

The friends laughed at her squeaking mimicry of a little boy's lisp. They laughed with feminine tenderness for childhood bribery, and in the pleasure of their unexpected meeting – but they were also laughing because Dan was safe.

"And he kept his word!" said Etta, marvelling.

"Yes he did, but thankfully, not his *lithp*! That's my darling Uncle Joseph for you! So, when dear old Esther died happily by her own seashore Uncle wasn't sure what to do with the place. He was too busy to leave his beloved Island." She handed around a plate of fresh figs.

"And?"

"And, he wrote to ask father's advice ..."

"Don't tell me – your father asked you," Etta prompted, accepting a fig and sinking her teeth into it with pleasure. Such rare respect from a father to a daughter in matters of business was a thing to be prized, indeed. But then, he had always treated her like a son, right down to her education. Perhaps being so strong and tall had something to do with it, Etta thought with a wistful pang at her own diminishing height.

Unaware of her friend's envy, the tall one nodded. "He was too busy, and mother hasn't been very strong this year – so here I am, looking it over, fixing a few things, and dreaming up ways to make it useful. *And* minding my scamp of a cousin. Aunt Mari asked if I'd take him on the pretext of errand running and general help."

"Pretext?"

"Of course – otherwise why not take a servant? But Johanan's been restless lately. It's hard to raise a boy without his father. Aunt Mari's been anxious about the company he favours, and thought getting him out of Jerusalem for a while would do him good. As a matter of fact, when I saw that poor lamb's face – I thought he'd been fighting."

"It's just his age," said Marta in a rather superior fashion, pulling open a black fig and turning it inside out. The coral coloured flesh sprawled over her fingertips like a live thing.

"First all Legs and Loudness. Then all Hair and Horseplay."

She devoured her shredded fig and licked her fingers daintily after each mouthful, looking insufferably complacent.

The mismatched eyes regarded her with amusement.

"Yes, Marta dear, that's very good, and of course you'd know," she said very politely.

Etta nudged her gently with a fat elbow. "It must be that lock of white hair giving you all that instant experience."

Marta blushed a little. "I do have five younger brothers!" she said defensively, swallowing the fig in a hurry and laughing at herself. "And please don't say, 'Just you wait!' I've been hearing a lot of that lately."

The tall woman patted her arm. "May your child be perfect in body and soul. And pay no attention to the teasing of jealous old virgins."

She said it easily, knowing there was no bitterness in their honest envy, and Marta smiled, knowing it too. She rose and thanked her hostess.

"I really have to leave you if I am to finish my work before my husband is growling for his dinner. There is always so much to do – and I still must get to the Magdala market!"

"Oh, but I will certainly come with you, my dear – I have food to buy too and you can show me the best merchants – or rather, the worst, so I can avoid them. Etta?"

Etta shook her head.

"You go – I have a magnificent fish to cook for tonight which some good angel provided." She hesitated. "Are you quite sure Dan is all right?"

"Yes." A pause. Quietly, "My brother taught me a good deal about such things …"

Etta and Marta stared.

"Your *brother*?"

"It's a long story – and you know, all families have their secrets," was the hasty reply. "Perhaps we will share ours some time … but not today. Now, Marta, let's be off. Etta, let Johanan accompany you back to your home when Dan wakes, and you must send him on whatever errands you please. It will do him good. And please do come back and see me soon! Johanan accompanies me on a visit home tomorrow, but we will be back here by the new moon."

Brushing aside their thanks, she put a long, gracefully draped arm around Marta's back and practically swept her through the door. Marta flung an expressive look back over her shoulder at Etta, and they both mouthed, *"She has a brother?!"* before the door closed between them.

Aunt Etta was truly astonished. *Lips tight on that one!* she warned herself. And say nothing of Ammiel's plans either. What the Dabab wouldn't do with that little morsel, no matter how innocently it came to her! She smiled grimly. And think how she'd like to be the first to hear of those plans! Well, tonight the well could hear all about Dan's little accident instead. While Rachel gossiped about something harmless, at least she would be letting other poor folk alone …

"He's awake!" Johanan stuck his head over the steps.

# Chapter Five

"DAN, my little man," said his aunt that night bending over the fishy dishes, and rubbing them hard, "you gave us a fright today and no mistake!"

Dan was feeling fine, and wished Aunt Etta wouldn't call him her little man. It made him feel anything but. Luckily she didn't do it often. There was a fuzzy bit in the middle of the day, but that was all. His headache was completely gone, and he had a puffy black eye – and a nice lump – which made him feel quite important. And he had made a new friend. He liked Johanan and determined to see more of him if he could.

Aunt Etta had baked Johanan's big fish with herbs. It was sticky and delicious – and had even cheered up Uncle Bukki, who had come home, swaggering slightly, just in time for the evening meal, and was now in a very good mood. Uncle Bukki always seemed to – well, he seemed to *swell*, a bit – when Dan's father wasn't home. Then he sort of shrank again when Ammiel returned. Dan wondered why or how, and couldn't find an answer, but it was very interesting to watch anyway.

Dan was washing a handful of flat fish scales in a small bowl. Tomorrow he would spread them on a sheet of thin bark and leave them to dry. He had an old chipped pot half full of them already.

These would be the biggest in his collection, and Dan wondered how they'd look when they were dry. If they lost too much of their life, he wouldn't keep them, he decided. Dan saved all the lovely big flat iridescent scales for his treasure box. One alone didn't look very special, but a heap of them glinting in a box held some charm, and Dan had ideas for them.

There would be fish soup tomorrow, with lots of bones to be wary of first and suck afterwards, and a nice big slab of cold fish to wrap in flat bread and take to the hillside for his father, and Caleb too. That would be a real treat, especially for old Caleb. He lived with his married daughter when he wasn't out in the fields, and she wasn't known as "Keren Extra Pressings" for nothing. Even Dan knew what that meant. The first pressing brought the best oil – deep golden green – like the depths of the sea – or so he had been told by one of the fishermen. He had never been out on a boat, though he thought it would be a wonderful adventure. You could press the olives a second time and get a paler oil with less flavour. Or you could squash them up again for a third pressing, and still get oil, but it was cloudy and full of bits – much cheaper, and not very good. The bits held water which made the oil spit in a hot pan. Aunt Etta liked it to oil leather and wood, even if you had to rub off the flaky bits afterwards, but she didn't like it for cooking. Extra Pressings probably did, though. Dan wondered if she was really poor, or just really mean. One day he'd know. One day he'd know a *lot*.

Night poured over the hills. The lamp was lit and trimmed. Dan took the washing–up water outside for Aunt Etta and tipped it over the dark herb patch, slowly, so their shallow roots weren't disturbed. He especially liked the mint with its cool, fresh taste. He felt among the leaves, plucked one carefully and put it on his tongue, feeling its hairy texture and gently biting its edges to release the flavour. Sucking his leaf, he tilted his head and looked at the stars out of his good eye. *What are those stars anyway?* Yes, God created them, but what were they really? *They must be something to do with ... oh! what?* Well, they were something to do with God, anyway, because they were in Heaven and so was He.

Sometimes Dan imagined they were the eyes of all the angels, watching what happened on earth. He wasn't sure if he liked that idea or not. It could be comforting or rather alarming, depending on what you'd been doing. He chewed his leaf properly and swallowed the fibrous pulp, feeling a cool sensation follow it down the warmth of his throat and a minty aura float up through the back of his nose. Did angels ever ...? No, never mind ... actually he had a lot of questions about angels, but just now it really was stars he wanted to know about.

Stars seemed to be *alive* – white cinders sprinkled in the sky, like the glowing sparks which danced recklessly in the darkness when you tapped the dying coals of a fire. Dan knew nobody could count them. The Holy Scriptures said nobody could tell how many there were, and anyway, you couldn't put a mark on them to stop yourself counting the same one twice. Ammiel had told him about the Patriarch Abraham, the Father of the nation, whom God had promised *"as the stars of the heavens ... so shall thy seed be"* and sometimes they'd see how many stars they could count. Some were so faint you weren't sure if they were really there or not. When they gave up on counting, Ammiel would patiently point out the starry patterns which could show a man his direction at night, while his son struggled to pick them out of the mass overhead. Now Dan searched the sky for familiar constellations, but they were hard enough to find with two eyes, let alone one, and he was getting a crick in the neck.

He thought of the fat fig Johanan had given him to eat on the way home. He'd been hungry after losing his breakfast and having no lunch. It was full of tiny seeds, too many to count. He had bitten into its tangy-sweet softness, enjoying the delicate crunch of the minute seeds against his teeth, and feeling their graininess on his tongue. Well, that was seeds for you – not much on their own, but impressive if you had enough of them … a bit like his fish scale collection. The stars were the same. One on its own wasn't much … but together! *"So shall thy seed be."* The seed of Abraham – the same *"as the stars."* The stars in the dizzying heavens, which made him feel so – tiny and alone …

With a sudden queer jolt Dan remembered the Rabbi's sing-song words droning nasally in the scented hush of the little synagogue, "We are the seed of Abraham …"

"If we are the seed," he whispered, " then I am one of the seeds! I am a little seed myself! Not much on my own … but nor is anyone else! But all of us together …?"

Dan dropped his bowl and ran up the tall hill at the back of the house. From there he looked down across the basin of the sea lying flat and black within its encircling dark hills. A few boats were night fishing, Dan could tell by the double golden flares which were torch flames dancing with their reflections in the water.

To the right were the lights of Tiberius, full of rich Romans with good oil to burn, but they didn't count, lights or no lights. Invisible on his left hand was the town of Magdala and just below him through the scrub was the cluster of mud houses in the little village by the sea. It had sprawled up untidily over the years like a fungus patch; too unimportant even to have a proper name and just called Banayim, the Dwellings. But Dan knew that all around the Sea of Galilee and beyond there were other dwellings, towns and villages everywhere – there would be home lights and fires flickering, even if he couldn't see them. People and their families and their lights, all across the land ... Above were the stars, fiercely bright – and below, the softer, duller stars of earth – the hearth fires of the Jews – the seed of Abraham. Dan suddenly held his breath – feeling for the first time one little piece of the invisible puzzle of life, softly and gently and perfectly, click into place.

He – Dan ben Ammiel, the shepherd's son – yes! – if he was *one of the seed* – he was *someone*, he was *important* – oh, not on his own, but as a tiny piece of the whole thing! The whole thing needed each of the many tiny pieces or it couldn't be a whole thing. What the whole thing was all about he didn't know yet. But he would find out yet! He wanted to shout – oh, how he wanted to shout! He wondered if Johanan knew about it, if Ammiel knew ... he wanted to ask a hundred questions ... and he wanted to hug his new knowledge to himself. He had come to it on his own, and it was precious. Dan's head felt light and his feet had wings. He bounded down the hill bursting with something too big to contain.

He rushed back into the hut, snatching up the dropped bowl from the mint patch on the way and pounced on Aunt Etta, tugging her sleeve impatiently as she spun her distaff, which jerked out of rhythm, the thread lurching and untwisting perversely.

"Sing, Aunt Etta! Sing! " he begged joyously. "You too, Uncle Bukki!"

"What *has* got into the boy?" Etta wondered, but she was so glad to see him well and full of life that she laughingly began a favourite song without question, wagging her distaff to mark the time.

"*Oh Praise God in His Sanctuary ...* " she began obediently in her synagogue voice.

*"Praise Him in His heaven of power ... "* Dan burst in loudly and less melodiously, banging the empty bowl for the beat.

*"Praise Him for His mighty deeds – Praise Him for His sovereign strength ..."* Aunt Etta rejoined more naturally, firmly rescuing the tune.

Dan pointed to Uncle Bukki expectantly.

*"Praise Him with a bugle blast – praise Him with lute and lyre,"* growled Uncle Bukki, despite himself.

*"Praise Him with the drum and dance!"* piped Dan, drumming on the table and dancing around the room. *"Praise Him with the strings and flute!"* He strummed the straws of the worn broom.

*"Praise Him with resounding cymbals,"* sang Aunt Etta, snatching up her coin purse and jingling it vigorously.

*"Praise Him with the clashing cymbals!"* roared Uncle Bukki, vigorously denting Etta's copper pot with her best ladle.

*"Let everything that breathes, Praise the Eternal!"* they finished triumphantly, drumming and banging and jingling everything at once, and holding the last note for the sheer pleasure of it. From outside came an unexpected reprise sung in a high, quavering voice.

*"Ha–le–lu–jah ...!"*

They stopped breathlessly. There was a perfunctory rapping, and the latch of the door lifted. The flame of the lamp flopped about in a sudden draught, sending their shadows lurching across the wall like drunkards – as Old Caleb stuck his face around the door and grinned at their flushed faces.

"Well, well – a pleasant thing it is for a man to hear his friends so cheerful and praising the Eternal!"

"This is a late visit," said Bukki suspiciously, ignoring Caleb's pleasantries. To Bukki, the loftiest psalm would never be more than a cheerful outlet for a good mood, and he hadn't exactly thought of it as Praising The Eternal.

"Yes, a very pleasant thing!" Caleb continued rather hesitantly. "Would this good cheer stretch to hospitality – for an old man whose daughter needs his bed for unexpected guests?"

"Who needs his dinner, you mean," said Uncle Bukki rudely. "Extra Pressings up to her usual company style, I see. Haw! Haw!"

A hardened old shepherd who slept in wind and rain on stones would think nothing of giving up his bed. They knew that, and Caleb knew they knew. His daughter's conduct shamed him, but only Bukki would draw attention to it so unkindly. He flushed. Aunt Etta stood up, habitually ignoring Bukki's bad manners the way she ignored the twinges in her back.

"Come in at once, Caleb, and welcome!" she said briskly. "You come on a good day! We've eaten, but there's plenty of fish in the pot yet. You must have Ammiel's bed tonight and take Dan to him tomorrow. It will save you the extra walk in the morning."

She took the lid off the pot and nodded to Dan to fetch a plate. Caleb hungrily watched her serving the fragrant fish.

"You're a good woman, Etta!" He eyed her speculatively. "A lonely man would be glad of a wife like you."

Etta held up her flat wooden spoon warningly.

"If you dare to propose to me again, you greasy old woolbag, I'll turn you out this instant …"

Dan wriggled close to the old man, ignoring Uncle Bukki's snorts of laughter.

"Look at my black eye, Caleb! Look! Johanan said it was an ostrich egg ..."

"Look at it? Trip over it, more likely ... what have you been up to? And who's Johanan?"

Dan took a long breath. For someone more used to listening, he had an awful lot of talking ahead of him. He had to tell Caleb all about today's accident, and Johanan and the house with an upper room by the sea. Tomorrow he would have to tell his father the whole story again. And he must find Johanan and talk to him about the stars above and the lights below, and being one of the seed and a part of everything, and find out what *he* thought. And soon he would go with Ammiel to Asa and Helen's and there'd be even more to talk about. And find out about. And think over. Dan felt that his life was suddenly becoming very busy and unexpectedly full of words.

## Chapter Six

OLD Caleb and Dan were awake long before the sun. It took them two hours to reach Ammiel's flock, which was already busy cropping grass and nibbling bushes when they arrived. Ammiel took one look at his son and gave a shout of laughter.

"Son, your phylactery has slipped!"

Dan felt his eye gingerly. "I think the commandment inside this one is – Thou Shalt Look Where Thou Art Going."

The tale was told over their breakfast of bread, salt and cold fish – a great treat – and Ammiel winced and grinned in all the right places.

"This boy and his kindly cousin – who were they?" he asked, but Dan hadn't heard the family name.

"Aunt Etta knew them, I think," was all he could say.

Aunt Etta had decided Dan would have to miss out on the fish soup that day. She had packed clean clothes, a bone comb and a small phial of rosemary-scented oil. In the bottom of the satchel was another small parcel wrapped in soft leather. There was to be no delaying of the business – a message had already gone to Asa, so Ammiel and his son would go to Anna's parents at once. If Asa agreed to the match, then the betrothal would be made official at once. It would all be rather disappointing for those who wanted a proper betrothal feast at the parents' house. However, Ammiel would not take time from the flock for this tradition, and Etta was aghast at the thought of travelling so far and in such a hurry. Celebrations would have to wait for the wedding itself, and that was something for which even Ammiel would have to find time.

Caleb grumbled in his beard.

"A hole-and-corner way of getting married!" he protested, but Ammiel just laughed.

"I don't think Asa and Helen will mind – and the wedding will follow soon enough."

After inspecting the sheep, Ammiel clapped Caleb on the back.

"Two days, Caleb – by then the flock will need to move on, and I'll return, God Willing, a bridegroom in prospect! Then Dan can take the news to Etta, and I can stop all this coming and going and get back to my sheep."

Caleb raised his shaggy grey eyebrows expressively.

Ammiel laughed again.

"You're thinking of Etta – and the wedding – but that's women's work and still a long way off. Summer shearing comes first or we can't pay our taxes. That's a lot of work before the rains come. And you know I always patch and re-lime the walls in Spring so Etta's kitchen corner is brightened up. That comes first. Only afterwards will I submit to her fussing."

Caleb grinned. "You think so?"

Knowing Aunt Etta, Dan privately agreed with Caleb's doubt that it would be so simple.

"First we have to see what Anna's parents think," he said cautiously.

"Let's go and find out," said his father.

"A bridegroom needs a friend for that," offered Caleb rather hopefully, thinking of the gifts of food which might come his way as the go-between. Ammiel pretended to consider, then shook his head with a smile.

"Sorry, Caleb. I think an old widower with a boy at foot should be brave enough to make his offer for himself. Anyway, it's a very long time since I've seen Anna. Of course it's her father's decision, but still, I want her to meet Dan … Mind you, that black eye may put her off a bit … maybe I should leave him behind …?"

He chuckled at their expressions, then shouldered Aunt Etta's bulky bag. It was lighter now, with Caleb's provisions removed and safely stowed in a little cairn of rocks. With a gentle farewell tweak of the Queen of Sheba's ears, Ammiel and Dan set out for Cana to the west.

As they walked, Dan wondered whether he should ask his father about the seed of Abraham and what it all meant. But there had been something special about that crystal moment under the stars, and he felt reluctant to expose it in the common light of day, lest it should somehow fade. He would ask something else.

"Abba?"

"Mmm?"

"What *are* the stars?"

Ammiel looked at Dan with fond exasperation.

"Hi-yi! boy! That's a hard one for a man so soon after his breakfast!" He scratched his beard and squinted thoughtfully.

"Solomon probably knew. The wisest man of all time, you know, ought to have known. But he didn't say so."

Dan grinned. "What about wise Daniel?"

His father shook his head. "Who knows? Maybe the scribes who learn all the holy scriptures for us? What does Moses say about it? Or have you forgotten synagogue school?"

Dan thought. *"In the beginning God created the heaven and the earth ...?"* he said hopefully.

Ammiel snorted. "We all know that! We want something about stars, boy. What else is there? *And God separated the light from the darkness ...?"*

Quickly Dan joined him in the recitation, *"and God named the light Day and the darkness he named Night!"*

Ammiel shook a stone out of his sandal and twitched an eyebrow. "Well, now we've got *Night*, at least, so we must be closer."

Dan muttered through the next verses under his breath. "There's the firmament bit ... h'm h'm h'm ... *made a division between the waters which were under the firmament from the ...* h'm h'm h'm ... *and God named the firmament Heaven!"* He finished triumphantly and flashed a look at his father.

"Very good, son!" Ammiel said drily. "Now we're right back to where we started – *in the beginning God created the Heaven and the Earth!"*

"Oh!" said Dan, crestfallen.

He looked up and caught his father's twinkling eye and they both burst out laughing.

Ammiel reached out and tugged one of Dan's scruffy curls affectionately.

"Don't give up yet – there must be something. I don't know much scripture, son, but my father always said – *Surely the* LORD *God will do nothing, but he uncovers his secret unto his servants the prophets.* Now *that's* from the prophet Amos."

Dan asked admiringly, "Your father was a scholar? I thought he was a shepherd like you."

Ammiel rumbled in his beard.

"Yes, he was, a shepherd, and no scholar! There's a family story behind that quotation!"

"Tell me!" Dan begged, but his father shook his head.

"That's a tale for a winter's night when your beard grows. But I'll tell you this – my father's name was Amos, and so was his father's and his father's before. May they rest in peace." He laughed, incongruously.

Dan was entranced. He had never thought of his long-dead grandfathers as having any sort of names of their very own.

"Why weren't you called Amos too?" he asked wonderingly. "Or me?"

Ammiel chuckled again quietly to himself.

"Ah, that's too close to the story! Mustn't spoil it. Go on with Moses and find the stars, if you can. So far, we've got to God creating the heavens – twice!"

Dan took a swipe at a saltbush to aid his concentration. It was so long since he'd been to school. He frowned, sniffing the pungent leaves as he fingered them under his nose. Herbs! Now he knew what came next …

"… *the earth brought forth grass and* **herb** *yielding seed after its kind and likeness* …" he said rapidly. "H'm, h'm … h'm … *let there be* **lights** *in the heavenly firmament* …!"

He skipped a little in excitement.

Ammiel gave him a slow grin. "Ah, perhaps *now* we're getting somewhere!"

Dan ignored him, gabbling the next verses to himself. " … h'm … h'm h'm h'm and – God – made – the TWO GREAT LIGHTS!"

Ammiel nodded. "Go on."

Dan needed no encouragement. *"The greater light to order the day and the lesser light to order-the-night-and-also-the-stars!"* he finished breathlessly, with a whoop of triumph.

Ammiel thumped his shoulder approvingly. "I knew you'd get to it at last!"

They stopped under a wild olive, grateful for the shade. The sun was almost at full heat now, and they were thirsty. Ammiel leant on the trunk and stretched his hairy legs into the dappled sunlight with a contented sigh. He took a good pull at the water bottle and handed it to Dan. He watched the boy's smooth tanned throat jerking with each gulp and asked casually, "So, what *are* the stars, then?"

Dan choked, spluttered, and nearly dropped the water. He looked at his father with water running down his chin. "I remembered all the creation verses up to the stars and didn't find my answer!"

Ammiel rescued the water bottle and stowed it safely in his satchel.

"I know. Sometimes we try so hard to find answers we forget why we want them."

He settled himself more comfortably for a nap.

The hot air wafted around them, and the light shimmered through the leaves. Ammiel yawned like a sleepy lion.

Dan scrambled onto a twisted root beside his father, and picked at the bark thoughtfully. "Father, is there always an answer for every question?"

Ammiel considered.

"No," he said finally. "Not always. Not for now, anyway."

"Why not?" Dan dared to ask, holding himself very still as he felt again that slow, new, faint stirring of awareness within. Answers!

His father settled his body more comfortably, and replied, almost to himself.

"Because there must be something more, something still to know, something to strive towards – or there'd be nothing left for the Resurrection."

Dan released his breath gently. Oh! Resurrection – another thing he had to know more about! He looked at his father with questions in his eyes – but Ammiel's own eyes were drooping.

"A little sleep, now," he mumbled sleepily, "or you'll be stumbling later …"

Dan made a pillow of his satchel, lying down thankfully. He had been up before the sun, and walked for miles. His thoughts circled lazily around their conversation about the stars, and cobbled themselves together into a silly running rhyme about the greater light which was so bright and the lesser light to order the night, and also every flickering star, but no one knows just what they are ... It chased itself around his head, rather annoyingly, as he lay dreamily, gazing without focus through the misty screen of eyelashes ... drowsily watching the sun flash sparks through the gently moving dark leaves above him. *Bits of sun, falling through chinks in the darkness ... the greater light which was so bright, through the dark night ... the lesser light ... flashing and winking bits of sun – like dancing fire sparks at night ... just like each flickering star and we don't know what they really are ...* Dan's sinking eyelids flew open. He sat up and snatched at his father's arm in the grip of a startling thought.

"Abba!" he cried. "The stars!"

Ammiel, who had slipped quickly into deep sleep, was rudely jolted awake. He growled crossly.

"What! Can't a man have some peace in his old age?"

Dan shook him exultantly. "The stars, father!"

Ammiel opened one eye. "What! Still the stars? What about them? Is it night already? Did I oversleep?"

"No! No!"

"Oh, good." Ammiel shut his eye again.

Dan shook him again. "But I know what they are!"

Ammiel sighed and struggled up to a sitting position.

"Of course you do. You are my wise Daniel." He yawned, then relented, seeing Dan's eager face. "What are they, son?"

Dan wondered at a sudden feeling like a sob which rose in his throat. He swallowed it impatiently. "I think they are bits of the sun!"

Ammiel looked at him with interest. "Bits of the sun?"

60

"Yes! Just like the sparks of our fire are bits of fire which escape! You don't see them in the day, only at night. Well, the stars are like that!"

"I see."

"Yes! Because the greater light is the sun, and the lesser light is the moon which is a *steady* light, and even if the stars are a lot *lesser* than the moon, they still sparkle like the sun, don't you see?" Dan finished in a confused jumble.

"Ah! Well! You could be right!"

Impressed, Ammiel put his arm around his excited son, whose dark eyes were sparkling too. "Then what about the moon ?"

Dan wriggled impatiently. "I don't know yet."

But for the moment, Dan could forget the moon. He was already thinking of something else. *As the stars, so shall thy seed be. So the seed of Abraham is to be just the same as the stars. That's right. And the stars are like the seed, and I'm one of them … and that's right. So, if the stars are bits of* **the sun** *… ,* he thought cautiously – but could get no further. He tried again. *If stars and seed are people, then we seed, we stars, would have to be like the sun. So who would be the sun? Is there anything in the Promises about the sun?* He sighed, suddenly daunted. Each answer only created another question.

Ammiel heard the sigh and gave him a sympathetic squeeze. He pushed him gently down and tucked the satchel under Dan's head.

"You have many good thoughts, Dan. The bump has not hurt your mind, at any rate." He lightly stroked the purple bruise on Dan's forehead, and added thoughtfully,

"I think you must go back to school very soon. You will hear better answers from scholars than a shepherd. But now you need some rest."

Soon Dan slept, not stirring even when a family of earwigs crept over his toes. Two hours later, a tremendous sneeze in his ear woke him with a jump. A slender olive leaf had floated down from the tree and gently tickled Ammiel's nose. Dan rummaged hungrily for their food, all thoughts of the starry heavens forgotten. He and his father strode on their way, chewing bread recklessly and dates carefully as they went — and having a competition to see who could spit the stones the furthest.

Just outside Cana they halted by a stream, which staggered down the slope like the sprawling town itself. With many grumbling references to fussy aunts and sisters they splashed off the dust and sweat of the journey, changed into the fresh tunics from their bag and tugged the wide toothed bone comb through their curls. Rolling his eyes, Ammiel rubbed a few drops of rosemary-oil into his auburn beard and hair, sleeking it into submission — screwing his nose up the while and making Dan laugh at him. He wiped his fingers on Dan's head for good measure, and his son sniffed the spicy scent with satisfaction. When they had finished, they gave each other sidelong looks of admiration. They really did look a handsome pair. Ammiel straightened his shoulders, puffed out his chest and took Dan's hand with determination. It was sundown.

They threaded through the cluttered streets of Cana, past the blind beggar on the last corner, and knocked at the gate of Asa and Helen's courtyard just as the first lamplight began to glow from the windows.

# *Chapter Seven*

DAN'S memories of that night were a confused mixture of unfamiliar sights, sounds and tastes – a roomy courtyard, the edge of an accent decorating Helen's voice and crisping her words, the top-to-toe welcome of spiced oil on his scalp and cool water for his dusty feet – a good meal – spiced meat and delicious honeyed sweetmeats with a perfumed flavour – the buzz of adult voices in the courtyard lulling him to sleep despite his determination to be a man and stay awake to hear the business. He was desperately curious to see Anna, but of course, she would not be present while the menfolk discussed her future. That was for them to decide. Or was it? Dan had heard that the Greeks did things differently. But – Anna was only half Greek, after all. Dan's eyes drooped as the shadows danced in the lamplight which crept around the open doorway. What would she think of living with Aunt Etta and Uncle Bukki – or Dan himself? Was it true that second mothers were kind at first and then turned bad tempered? Dan yawned. His own mother had been sharp tempered enough, after all ... The shadows loomed larger – tangled in the dark bars of his eyelashes – and dissolved into dreams.

In the morning, gritty grey light, unfamiliar walls – the clatter of dropped sticks, the protest of a startled chicken, a girl's giggle in the courtyard – then a cool touch on his cheek and a voice he remembered.

He looked up sleepily and saw a tall woman leaning over him, unusual eyes smiling from under straight brows.

"Shalom, Dan. How is your poor head today?"

He blinked at her and struggled to sit up.

"Johanan's cousin!"

She smiled again. "Yes."

Dan was confused. "But – why – what are you doing here?"

Gently she lifted the hair away from his bruised forehead, looking at it critically.

"My name is Anna," she told him casually. "I am to be your new mother."

Dan lay back, staring at her. An odd spreading feeling began in his stomach and pushed its way up through his throat, and into the back of his head. He took a deep breath and blew it out again to ease the pressure. Anna waited silently as Ammiel came and sat beside them.

Dan looked from one to the other. He felt the peculiar feeling gradually contract and settle somewhere into a new certainty, leaving the shadow of the sensation in his chest. Relief stung his eyes.

"Good," he said, wondering why his voice wobbled.

Ammiel pulled Dan to his lap and hugged him warmly.

"Anna is a brave woman, Dan. Marrying a man with such an ugly son."

64

He pointed at Dan's black eye. Anna laughed, shaking her head at him. Dan responded by pummelling his father's rumbling chest in protest, and Ammiel chortled as he wrestled back. It was not a very clever joke, but it felt good to laugh together and the odd tension was broken.

Suddenly Dan was struck by such an exciting thought, it sobered him at once.

"Oh – what about Johanan! If Anna will be my mother, will Johanan be my cousin too?"

Ammiel rolled his eyes and looked at Anna for inspiration. She nodded.

"In a way. He'll become part of your family as well," she replied. "He was here yesterday but went to the other side of town to pay respects to some friends of his mother's. I'm sorry you've missed him, but he'll come back with me to the shore house by new moon, and you can visit him again."

Dan's face lit up. He scrambled out of Ammiel's arms.

"Truly?"

Ammiel handed Dan his coat. "Truly. And with Asa agreed to the match, I suppose your Johanan is almost part of our family already." He scratched his beard. "How strange it was that you should meet both Anna and her cousin when you did – and not know who they were."

Struggling into his coat, Dan protested, "But she was gone when I woke. I never heard her name from Johanan, and Aunt Etta didn't tell me."

Anna remarked, "Etta can keep a secret in her left hand, and her right hand know nothing of it. She will have had her reasons."

Ammiel looked at the lump on Dan's head. "No doubt, but it's unlucky you should meet because of an accident! I hope it was not a bad omen."

Asa entered the room in time to hear these words. He clapped Ammiel on the back and said, "Nonsense! A good omen, if anything, eh, my daughter? A blessing! You were there to mother the lad already!"

Anna nodded. "Yes, father. God's good hand was surely in our meeting."

She left the room quietly, and Ammiel got up to follow her.

"Hurry and wash, boy. The contract will be written at once, then we must be away."

Dan hugged his knees. Yes. Asa was right. God's blessing was in their meeting. After all, Dan was part of the seed of Abraham, part of the promise and so was Anna. So was Johanan. So was Ammiel. God was watching each one of them, along with all the hundreds of other seeds. *"I will bless them that bless thee"* ... *that means me too, because I am part of the seed. Well, I suppose Anna and Johanan really blessed me when they helped me that day. So God would bless them too. If we go on blessing each other, Dan thought carefully, then God will go on blessing us!* That was a very good thought.

The morning sun was pale and soft as Dan stood in the shady courtyard watching a scribe drawing up and witnessing the document of betrothal. Despite the early hour the neighbours knew what was in the wind, and readily crowded in to watch, happy to be part of the occasion. Naturally they had all heard about Samuel's boy bringing Ammiel's message to Asa, and gossip had been confident of the outcome. Why, Asa might be a well-off merchant and Ammiel a shepherd, but he was a good shepherd, with a good name, and successful in his own quiet way. And Anna had been an old maid quite long enough. Likely Asa would be glad to marry her off to her old playmate and take away her reproach. And the boy needed a mother. Yes, it was a good thing. They shuffled expectantly, quietening to watch the simple ceremony.

Ammiel motioned to Dan, who was holding the soft leather parcel Etta had packed the day before. Carefully he unwrapped its folds to reveal a delicate length of silver mesh hung with five silver pieces. Etta had polished it to a fine shine, and the precious metal winked in the sunlight as Ammiel pinned it to Anna's veil with surprising dexterity.

Dan looked at the coins lying across her tanned forehead, and suddenly remembered … the rhythmic chinking sound they had made when his mother kneaded dough … the way they flashed in the lamplight at night … the sting of slapped fingers when he reached to touch them …

Asa put Anna's hand into Ammiel's and handed him the document, saying, "Brethren and friends here present, bear us witness."

Ammiel took Anna's large strong hand into his own larger, stronger paw, as gently as if it was something delicate which might break. With the other he held the parchment high in a hairy fist, cleared his throat and announced in a clear voice, "Anna, daughter of Asa ben Nahath, and daughter of his wife Helen of Philippi – by this document you are betrothed to me, in accordance with the laws of Moses and of Israel."

"So be it," responded Anna quietly, dropping her eyes to meet his.

"Amen," Asa and Helen agreed.

The neighbours clapped and cried out blessings, and crowded and fussed, and hugged and kissed Anna, Ammiel, Helen, Asa, and anyone else in sight. Dan was kissed and clucked over and squeezed into bewilderment. Then, as if by enchantment, the women produced food from baskets and napkins, and suddenly everyone was eating and drinking, talking and laughing. Helen's little servant maid Rhoda carried trays and looked shyly at Dan from under her lashes. Dan pulled a face at her, which made her giggle. It was the same giggle he'd heard earlier in the day. Dan supposed that it was she who had dropped the sticks and startled the chicken. Perhaps she'd dropped the sticks on top of the chicken – now that would have been worth seeing! Dan's wide mouth curved in a grin as he thought of it. He caught Anna's eye and she smiled back. Asa watched them and exchanged a satisfied look with his wife.

Despite Ammiel's intentions of avoiding a fuss, Helen had been too quick for him. She too had been sure of the outcome of Ammiel's earlier message, and had no intention of being unprepared to make it a festive occasion. Ammiel was not a wealthy or learned man such as they had hoped for Anna in her younger days. And a second marriage could be difficult where a child was involved – this her parents had seen for themselves. But Helen knew her daughter's heart, and Ammiel's character, and was content. The marriage would be a good one, and the contract deserved celebration, even if but for a couple of hours. So the neighbours were ready, and the food prepared and the rejoicing was whole hearted. Songs were sung, toasts were drunk in good wine, dancing circles scuffed up the dust, the old jokes were given a good airing. And Ammiel and Dan were still able to start their journey home before the sun grew too hot, spilling out of the gate with the cheerful neighbours, who loaded them with good wishes and pressed packages of food into their hands as they melted off to their own houses.

"So much extra for two men who are already warmed and filled, eh, Dan?" Ammiel commented happily, clutching his little pots and parcels with a comical air. On an impulse, Dan, with a mere glance at his father for permission, skipped over the street and placed his own load at the feet of the blind beggar.

"What's this?" the man spoke sharply, lifting his head suspiciously. He had little reason to trust small, darting footsteps.

"Food," Dan said simply to the disfigured face.

The beggar rubbed his eye bandage in astonishment and eagerly explored Dan's offering, sniffing hard.

"Honey cakes? Nuts? Lentil paste with herbs? Smoked fish? What, no pot scrapings?" He laughed suddenly, sensing Dan's embarrassment.

"We have too much," Dan replied awkwardly, not being used to beggars with a sense of humour.

The beggar sighed.

"Celebration fare – and too much of it – what an affliction to rejoice in! Truth, this is too bountiful for me as well, but it will be shared – and may the Eternal reward you, young man."

Dan scampered back to his father and was rewarded with a warm smile.

"There's still plenty to take home to the others, isn't there, father?"

He took his father's outstretched hand and shouted back to the beggar,

"Shalom!"

The beggar raised his hand and nodded. As Dan and Ammiel turned the corner, they saw him already shuffling briskly down the street, the food scooped tightly into a fold of his tunic. Dan wondered about him for a moment, but the ugly scarred man was soon forgotten as they climbed the slopes of the hillside to the main track.

Dan walked the rough path with Ammiel quietly. There was a lot to think about. Tumbling about inside him was amazement mixed with gladness. Amazement that the kind giantess of the sea shore was actually Asa-and-Helen's Anna! Gladness that she was the woman his father had chosen to join their family. There was amazement that Anna and her father actually believed that the Master of the Universe, the great Creator God, had blessed that peculiar accident with Johanan. And bubbling underneath was a gladness in *understanding* about being part of the seed, and about blessing each other – and being blessed because of it. All in a dizzying circle. Dan thought daringly that if God was blessing them – then – then … something new and good would happen, and go on happening. He was sure of it.

Ammiel looked down at the black curls steadily moving along beside his elbow.

"On the way here you were full of questions, boy," he remarked.

Dan swished at a fly and flashed a smile. "Now I have to think about the answers," he replied.

"Which answers?"

Dan considered. "A lot of different answers. But here is another question. When will the wedding be?"

70

" Well, if I was a young man, and Anna a young girl, the wedding would be in about a year. But Anna is an older bride than usual and I'm an older groom. So Asa is glad for the wedding to be very soon – after the shearing, as I asked."

"Why?"

"Because he's waited too long for grandchildren. At his age the days are longer, but they fly faster. Anna should have married years ago, but somehow she missed out."

Why did she miss out?"

Ammiel waved his arms in mock exasperation.

"All these questions! What, are you a Rabbi to ask such questions with so many answers? The family went to Greece in her younger days, which took her out of the marriage market for a while. They didn't want her marrying out of Judea and living so far away. When they came back – well, she was getting older, her mother was afraid of a bad match, her father was too choosy … and the men didn't like those unusual eyes of hers. Or her size!"

"Do you?"

Ammiel chuckled. "I've always liked Anna, from the time we were children. And I was bigger than her, then!"

"Are you a good match, Abba?"

Ammiel roared with laughter, shaking his golden red curling beard violently.

"No! And Yes!"

Dan looked at him impatiently. "What does that mean? No, and Yes?"

Ammiel snatched at Dan's hand and squeezed it in a friendly fashion.

"It means, my son, *No, I'm not a good match*, because I am not important, clever, learned or rich. And *Yes, I'm a good match*, because I am a strong healthy man with my own flock, able to provide for my own family, and under bondage to no man. And Asa knows I will treat his gentle daughter with respect and friendship."

He laughed down at Dan. "And of course, I must be a good match, because I don't mind that she's taller than me, and also because I have a fine son already! So Anna need not fear how many daughters she bears me."

Dan swung his father's hand happily at this reply, but did not laugh. Something else was on his mind.

Ammiel continued with enthusiasm, "We have a busy time ahead of us, Dan. You, me, Bukki and Etta. There's a lot to do, and shearing is nearly upon us. We must enlarge our house. It was one of Asa's conditions. Anna has a good dowry, but I must provide a good house. It is a very fair match! So a little building is another thing we have to do before there can be a wedding. Our humble house must stretch a little for my new wife and, if God wills, a bigger family."

"I liked their courtyard," said Dan. "A courtyard is a good place for friends."

His father laughed.

"Well, let's have a courtyard then, now that you're gathering new friends to put in it! You know, I had always thought to add another room or two when I grew richer … I had seen myself as another Jacob, with a dozen children … But life has a way of tripping you up … and suddenly there was no need. Until now."

It was not until they were nearly at the meeting place arranged with Old Caleb that Dan asked the question which was worrying him the most.

"Abba – what about poor Aunt Etta – and Uncle Bukki?"

Ammiel glanced looked at his son's shadowed face. He caught the boy to him in an impetuous hug.

"Ah, my little Dan!" he said gratefully. "You have the right heart for a man! Of course they will live with us, just as they do now. Where else would they live?"

Then his mood changed. He squatted down before Dan.

"But why, 'poor' Aunt Etta, son?" he asked quietly.

Dan looked at him straight.

"I know, Abba," he said steadily. "I heard. I know about Aunt Etta's back. And what will happen to her."

"Hii-yii!" a quavering voice floated on the breeze. Old Caleb in the distance was waving to them. Ammiel raised his arm in reply, but made no move. He blew out a long, slow breath and tugged Dan down to sit beside him. They leaned against a still-warm rock and stared at the darkening sky.

"H'mm. So you heard a lot on that night," Ammiel said thoughtfully. "Yes, it is a terrible thing for my sister. But you see, Dan, now we need not worry about Aunt Etta. She will have my accomplished wife to care for her as she becomes more crippled. And in God's good grace, our children growing up to love her and help her. So we can praise God for the blessing Anna will bring to our family!"

"God be praised, Abba," said Dan gladly, relieved. "And Uncle Bukki?"

Ammiel sucked his upper lip and blew through his exuberant moustache.

"Ah! Bukki! Your mother's brother is family still and we are all he has. It's good to have a man in the house when I'm away, you know. No doubt Anna will manage him as well as Etta does."

He sprang to his feet and pulled Dan up with an easy movement.

"Who will reach Caleb first?" he cried and ran. Laughing and protesting, Dan scrambled after him and they reached Caleb together, panting and glowing in the quick sunset.

"Well?" asked the old man eagerly. "Is the thing settled?"

Ammiel grabbed Caleb and swung him off his feet and around in a dizzying circle.

"Settled!" he shouted happily, as Caleb bellowed in fright. "Start saving your appetite, old man! After shearing – the wedding feast!"

He dropped Caleb on the ground, laughing, and the three of them linked arms and began to dance and sing as the sun plunged behind the hill.

*"Hi-yah! Gal-i-lah! Lovely daughter of the hill!*
*Hi-yah! Gal-i-lah! Lovely as a birdsong trill!"*

The stars blinked awake. The sheep lifted their heads curiously but without alarm.

The men sang louder, with Dan's voice skipping over them in a counter melody.

*"Lullah la-la la-la lala lu lah*
*Lu lah la la lu-lu-lah!"*

Dan warbled the refrain as they roared on happily about lovely Galilah.

*"Ga-li-lah! Ga-li-lah!"*

Their feet stamped the rhythm heavily but Dan felt light all over. Surely the blessing – the *something new and good* – was beginning already.

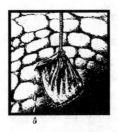

# Chapter Eight

ETTA lifted the heavy water pot from her shoulder and poured it into the larger storage jar, wondering when Dan would return with news. She smiled to herself. How she would have loved to have seen the boy's face when he realized that the woman at the shore was none other than Anna bath Asa herself – not to speak of the surprise to Ammiel! It would be a fine time when they could all exchange their stories. Yes, she had stored up much delight for the future by slyly holding her tongue! *If only it be that Asa approves the match* ... Her back ached, but there was still the bedding to bring in from the bushes where it was draped to freshen in the hot sun. Etta put the pot down with a heavier thud than she intended and tried to stretch, even as Dan bounced through the door and flung his arms around her.

"Shalom! Aunt Etta!"

"Hi–yi! Careful, boy! You'll knock me over," she remonstrated, smacking his rump playfully. "So long a walk, and still so much energy – how I envy you! Now! What is the news of your father?"

Dan felt very important to be the bearer of the news. He strutted about the room and cleared his throat, in imitation of Zaccheus, the richest man in the synagogue. A very small synagogue in the poorer quarters of Magdala, it must be admitted, but still it gave old Zach self-important airs.

"Asa has agreed to the match!"

"Aahhh!"

With a long sigh, Etta sat down suddenly on a stool. Dan looked at her with concern.

"Are you crying, Aunt Etta?"

She sniffed and shook her head and laughed.

"No, not really … God be praised, Dan!"

She raised her hands expressively.

"God be praised for His mercy!" she repeated fervently. "A wife for my brother, a mother for my nephew!"

Dan tugged her sleeve. "And someone to care for you, too Aunt Etta."

Etta looked at him sharply.

"Aye, to care for me in my old age, perhaps, eh, Dan?" She changed the subject, chuckling suddenly, "And did you get a surprise when you met her?"

"Yes! You knew all along! Why didn't you tell me *she* was Johanan's cousin!"

Etta's dark eyes crinkled happily in her brown face.

"What is life without some mystery and surprises? It's not often I have the chance to keep a happy secret to add spice to life! And what if the match had not been agreed to? So – I said nothing ahead of the time … and you like her, do you, Dan?"

"I like her. And I like Johanan. Anna says he'll be my cousin too!"

"He will that," said Aunt Etta reflectively. "A bit of a scamp, Johanan, so Anna says. You'll be seeing a bit more of him, no doubt. I'll have to watch he doesn't lead you into mischief. What about the wedding?"

"Not till after shearing, father says. And we have to build another room first."

Etta nodded. "I expected that."

Uncle Bukki shuffled in. "Expected what?"

"Asa has agreed to Ammiel taking Anna," said Etta firmly, sensing trouble. "And so we will be building an extra room. And at once, too, before it's too wet."

Bukki tightened his lips.

"Extra room, extra work," he grunted.

Etta blew out her breath disgustedly as she rounded on him.

"What is this? *Extra* work? How is that possible when you do no work to begin with, can you tell me?"

Bukki ignored that and reached out a brawny hand for water.

"This house was good enough for my sister, may she rest in peace," he said resentfully, slurping water from the dipper. "No extra rooms were built for her."

He dropped the dipper carelessly back into the water instead of hanging it on the side of the pot.

Aunt Etta's habitual wisdom deserted her. Such good news, *but can this miserable Bukki rejoice for the man who supports him uncomplainingly?* She forgot Dan was listening, and blurted out the thoughts she had never voiced, a stream of buried resentment of her own.

"Indeed this house was *not* good enough for your sister, Bukki ben Bezaleel, as she herself often said outright, *and* in front of her hard-working husband and innocent child. And *may she rest in peace* now truly, poor girl, for it's more than she was content to do in her lifetime … and while you think so touchingly of the past you do well to remember that no extra rooms were built for her because your father believed that her beauty was dowry enough to catch a man …"

"As it was!" interrupted Bukki proudly, knowing Etta had always been plain.

But Etta paused only for an angry breath and finished recklessly, "… despite the obvious fact that beauty buys no bricks – *and* because nobody expected that her house would be cramped by a fat, lazy brother who didn't earn his keep!"

Bukki flushed a dull red.

"You take up a pretty wide space yourself, Etta," he growled slowly. "And how much of your keep will *you* be earning when you're hobbling around like old Zillah in the market, champing your dribbling jaws and groaning to lift your head?"

The vision was horrible, and Etta paled. Dan flung himself between them, shouting.

"Stop! Stop!" he cried. "This is supposed to be a happy day!"

He pushed past them, tears starting down his cheeks, and fled outside.

Feeling sick, Etta drooped over the small scrubbed table, and held her head in her hands. Her bones were too slow and painful for her to run after Dan. But perhaps he was better left on his own. She had caused his distress, after all.

"Two selfish old fools, to be fighting like children!" she said bitterly. "Spoiling a blessed day with borrowed pain from past and future! Bukki, I was wrong to speak as I did."

She looked up wearily – it had been a hard thing to say – but with a thud of the door, Bukki was gone.

Dan tried to lie quietly, staring at the sky on the hill where he had been so filled with wonder that special night when the stars and the seed of Abraham took on new meaning. He tried to recapture the good feeling. It didn't come. He squirmed. Too much was happening. Suspense, and happiness, and relief, and wondering, and then suddenly all this ugliness bursting into his excitement. His stomach hurt and his head ached. Uncle Bukki being nasty at times was something he was used to – that was just how he was. But for Aunt Etta to be cruel to Uncle Bukki – that was new, and unsettling. Dan shook his head and jumped to his feet. His special place couldn't bring him peace today. He jumped off the brow of the hill, and landed awkwardly.

*Whenever you jump off something you always go **down**,* he thought, distractedly, rubbing a bruised knee. *What if you could jump off – and go up, floating **up** away from your troubles …?* He scudded off down through the rocks and made for Banayim and the sea.

What had happened to that wonderful promise of yesterday, when he and Caleb and Ammiel had danced so joyously under the stars, an old man, a boy and his father, all men together, singing about a woman? That glowing sureness of feeling strong and blessed … that the next day would be even better … where did it go?

It was a hot run and his chest heaved, but he had not outrun his pain when he finally reached the shore. He kept running, past the houses – into the water – splashing through the shallows, and dived. The sudden chill made him gasp, and he thrashed and flailed, shouting with the cold, until he felt calmer.

*What if he was a fish? Surely fishes didn't have uncles and aunts to worry about.* He held his breath and wriggled to the bottom, opening his eyes. Cloudy water swirled lazily with sand. Threads of brown weed waved peacefully. Broken shells glinted in the hazy greenish light. Dan's body bobbed to the surface. He took another breath and plunged down again. A tiny blue fish sparkled by his wrist, chased by a silver bubble which escaped Dan's mouth as he pouted his lips for a fish-face. He tried to lie still on the sea bed, arms outstretched, suspended, watching. The cloth of his tunic moved lazily after his body. Tiny bubbles were trapped in the fine dark hair on his brown arms and freed themselves to spring dizzily upwards. But again Dan's body floated up to the surface. He stood up, blowing out and dragging a deep breath. Down he went again. And up.

He lay back and floated, lazily moving his feet. It had been a long walk from the sheepfold, and his early morning energy had vanished in the unkindness of the hut. Now he was weary. The sun was glowing hotly in the sky and Dan's face was tingling as it dried. Overhead, a pair of gulls drifted on invisible currents and mewed to each other peevishly. Imagine floating on air! How did air hold anything up at all? Even a leaf? But it did.

Dan experimented. He took a deep breath in, and his chest rose up in the water. He let it out, and his body sank to the eyebrows. Yes, air had something to do with floating – in water, at least, and so maybe something to do with flying too. Perhaps seagulls held their breath as they flapped? The thought made him laugh underwater, and huge bubbles burst from his nose and

82

mouth. Gasping a little, Dan broke the surface and rolled on his back, drawing in another long breath, once more feeling his chest rise in the water. It was quite uncanny, once you began to notice it.

Dan turned over to float on his face, and stared at the drifting sand in the silent, tranquil world below. He had made another discovery. Two discoveries. The first was that *under the water, everything else seemed to vanish*. It was a different sort of place altogether, with its own dreamy ways. You couldn't worry or be unhappy or even feel very much at all when you were in a world where you couldn't hear properly, or smell or taste or breathe. You could only feel the water blanketing your skin, and see hazily, and hear muffled noises. Coming out of the water into the quicker, crisper world above was like coming alive again.

The second was that *no matter how hard you tried to stay down, you just kept coming back up to the air again*. Of course, Dan knew that sometimes people drowned. But while you had a chest full of air you would float up, every time. Dan thought about jumping – from a table, from a rock, from a tree. You always fell down to the earth. *On land we fall down. Back to where we started. In water we fall up – back to where we started!*

Why? Dan puzzled over this for a while. He wished Johanan was back at his Uncle Joseph's house, the house Dan could see from the beach. He had a lot to talk over with him.

Dan was getting cold and his eyes felt rough, stinging from being held open under water. He waded out of the shallows, with his clinging tunic heavy, dripping and slapping his thin legs. Dan pounced and rolled onto his stomach on the stone-sprinkled sand and heaped it over himself, embracing its gritty heat. He scooped up a pile to rest his chin on, and lay there comfortably, luxuriating in the contrast of hot crunchy powder and cold clammy cloth on his body. His chilly fingers were white and pulpy at the tips from the water, and Dan poked at them with lazy interest. The ragged nails were unfamiliarly clean, and turning blue at the base. Tiny grains stuck to them like coarse salt on peeled garlic. Some were black, some red or dull brown, some white, others translucent like salt itself. He touched it experimentally with his tongue, and then spat.

Dan narrowed his eyes and observed that the grains were all different shapes, too. Squinting so closely made his eyes ache. He closed them slowly and felt the wind finger his cold wet hair. It tickled, and when he scratched the back of his neck, the sand rasped on his soft skin. Dan laid his sand-bearded cheek on his arm and drifted off to sleep.

He woke feeling chilled. His tunic clung like thick wet moss, furred with sand which dropped off in clumps as he moved. Dan stood up, cold and scratchy, and ran back to the sea, holding his breath for a final plunge. He knew what Aunt Etta would say if he brought half the beach home with him. He scrubbed off the sand which plastered him as best he could, and shivering a little, wrung out his clothes and hitched up his damp tunic as high as was decent. He felt cold and clean, and now he could look sideways at the angry scene of that morning. Aunt Etta must have been very cross with Uncle Bukki to be so rude to him. *But maybe it served him right.* Anyway Uncle Bukki's sulks wouldn't change anything. *And he can't stop the rest of us being as happy as we like*, Dan thought defiantly. *And he can't stop God blessing us either!* Now *this* was a striking thought!

Dan jerked the water out of each ear in turn and grimaced. He hated that warm squirmy feeling when the last bit of water trickled out. He wriggled a finger in his ears vigorously, as he thought about Uncle Bukki for a bit longer. Uncle Bukki didn't seem to want to bless anybody, even though he was a Jew and therefore supposed to be a seed of Abraham. Dan tried to work it out. He squatted down, and poked random holes with his finger in the sand.

*This* was Uncle Bukki. *This* was Aunt Etta. *This* was Dan, and this Ammiel, this Anna, this Johanan ... Dan drew lines radiating out from each person except Uncle Bukki. Lines from one touched others. *This is everybody blessing everyone else ...* He looked critically at his drawing. *Now they look like a lot of suns, or stars.* Except for Uncle Bukki, who still was just a blank hole in the sand. Dan stared at it for a while. If Uncle Bukki didn't want to bless any other seeds of Abraham, then he wouldn't be blessed himself, would he? He wouldn't become *as the stars*! Dan jumped up. To be one of the seed of Abraham, and not to be blessed! Was it possible? Hastily he smudged out his diagram with his foot. Poor Uncle Bukki!

He ran past Johanan and Anna's shore house, wishing they were back. He would go there as soon as new moon came. He didn't know enough. The more answers he found the more questions came with them. Nobody seemed to give him answers which stayed answered. It was such hard work trying to find them on his own.

He jogged through Banayim without seeing the narrow streets, feeling very confused about Uncle Bukki, who didn't want to bless anybody, not even himself half the time. Bukki the Unblessed! Dan suddenly felt very sorry. No wonder he grumbled. No wonder he sulked. He didn't know what it was to feel blessed, to be happy. Perhaps he didn't know enough about the Promise to Abraham, just like Dan only a few weeks ago. But of course he must! He was a grown up, and they were supposed to know everything.

Dan was ravenous by the time he reached home. Aunt Etta hugged him tightly, and in the fuss of explanations and dry clothes, they said nothing of the reason he had left. Although she was anxious about the effect of Bukki's words about her and old Zillah, Etta was relieved to see that Dan was cheerful again. No point stirring things up again just now. She would probe him gently later. Bukki was out somewhere on his own, and just as well.

Dan wolfed the bread and oil Aunt Etta set before him, and winced when he cracked sand between his teeth.

Aunt Etta pulled his curls apart and frowned.

"Outside, my boy," Aunt Etta ordered him. "Wash that beach out of your hair before the fishermen cast nets in it."

Dan shook his head and sand pattered onto the table.

"Such tiny bits," he said thoughtfully. "So tiny they get into everywhere, but all together they cover the bottom of the sea! How many grains must there be in the whole world, Aunt Etta?"

Etta flapped him outside with a towel.

"How should I know, nuisance? The rabbis say there are as many stars as there are grains of sand, so count the stars one night and then tell me the answer yourself."

Dan clutched the towel and obediently dipped his head in the washing pot. Suddenly he jerked it out and knelt there with soggy curls streaming water down his face. Of course! The promise to

Abraham again – *"I will multiply thy seed as the stars of heaven, **and** as the sand on the sea shore".*

"Dan, what are you playing at?" came his aunt's warning voice. Dan hastily ducked his head back into the water and rubbed it energetically, blowing bubbles all the while.

*The stars and the sand were the same thing.* They were all describing the seed of Abraham. The stars were all lights in the darkness, maybe bits of the sun, shining with honour, and all looked the same … but perhaps the sand told him something new. He thought of all the hundreds of grains, and how each one was a bit different to the next. Dan toweled his head mercilessly, till his black curls were matted. He raked his fingers through them, tugging at knots and pulling faces, but thinking hard.

*We're all different,* he thought excitedly. *Altogether we are the seed but we are still each ourselves. All together we can be heaped into hills or make a seabed … but each of us is still just who we are.* Dan tried to imagine his family as grains of sand … *Perhaps Father could be a rough red grain of sand … Aunt Etta probably a fat round one, Johanan is a sharp yellow one … h'mm … maybe I'm a knobbly brown one, and Anna is a long smooth white one – no, striped!* he mused with a grin, thinking of her eyes … For a while he was lost in fascinated speculation. *Uncle Bukki? … well, now …* ! Dan tried to see Uncle Bukki as a grain of sand, but all he could think of was a rather cross little crab.

He ran back into the house. "Aunt Etta? What is sand made of?"

## Chapter Nine

"AUNT Etta didn't know," said Dan to Johanan as they hauled rocks together. "I've been wondering about it ever since. What do *you* think sand is?"

Johanan wiped his sweating face. "Who knows? Who cares?"

"But I do care," said Dan. "I want to know things."

Johanan grunted as he picked up yet another everlasting rock. He whisked his foot away carefully as several shining brown scorpions scuttled out into the light.

"God made it that way. Like leaves. Or ants. Lots of little things bunched up together. All the same."

"But it's not all the same," persisted Dan. "It's all slightly different."

"Leaves are too," panted Johanan. "And ants. You know – Husband Ant. Wife Ant. Baby Ant. Maybe even Rabbi Ant …"

He struggled with his last stone and dropped it gratefully on to the wooden sled.

The boys put the rope around their waists and began pulling the sled back home, where Ammiel had marked out walls for not one, but two generous rooms which doubled the size of the house. The courtyard he had promised Dan was created in the space between the old and the new. Already the black basalt foundations had been laid and the walls had grown to knee height. Ammiel placed the heavy limestone rocks carefully while Bukki filled in the gaps with smaller pieces and chips, tapping them into place with a mallet and growling whenever he hit his thick fingers.

Though grander than the original mud brick house, the new rooms were to be plain enough, and Ammiel did not use a stone mason. A hired hewer roughly shaped the biggest stones, bare back glistening almost black in the sunlight, face and leather apron smeared with dust. He nodded to the boys as they delivered their load.

"These are good stones, lads, but small."

He scooped up a rock with one huge hand, juggling it a little as he eyed it critically, and hit it hard with his blade. The side sheared off, leaving a straight edge.

"Good for fitting around a window, though," said the hewer, tossing it gently to a heap of similar rocks. "But keep your eyes out for the big ones. We'll need a lot more yet."

Johanan pulled a face and rubbed his arms.

Anna and Etta were arguing over where a connecting doorway should be and making jokes about it.

"It should be here," said Etta, tapping the spot with her foot. Anna shook her head.

"No, Etta, that's too close to the lower level with the animals. Come winter, if I walk through there in the night I may slip and maybe land on a goat."

"No, you won't," said Etta calmly. "Bukki sleeps in the *other* corner …"

90

The women laughed and laughed until they were out of breath. Dan had never heard Anna really laugh out loud and long before, and stood entranced. It was the most extraordinary sound – tumbling along with upward skips like a gurgling bird with hiccups. It was so funny that Dan rolled his eyes at Johanan and couldn't help a snort of laughter himself. Johanan shrugged and rolled his eyes in turn.

"Always sounds like that," he apologised with a grin.

Meanwhile, the women returned to their argument. Etta said nobody had ever fallen off the ledge since Dan was a baby and liked to cuddle up with the orphan lambs. Anna said that was because there was no extra doorway there to stumble through in the dark at the time. Etta said sarcastically that maybe the animals could have the higher level and then there'd be no danger.

"What – us to eat and sleep in a sunken living room?" Anna's shoulders began to shake. "So in the night a goat can drop on *us* instead?" And they were off again, giggling like girls.

They recovered to find all the menfolk, hot and tired, looking at them rather coldly.

For once Bukki spoke for them all.

"Glad this is all so much fun for *some* of us."

"Then stop now," called Etta, unrepentantly cheerful, waving a dipper of water. "The sun is high – time for food, drink, rest!"

Everyone stopped work thankfully. Bukki threw down his tools rather petulantly. The hewer grinned and rubbed his dusty hands. Dan and Johanan stretched their aching backs like old men, but Ammiel whooped and leapt over the low wall like a boy.

The men splashed their faces and hands in the washpot and sprawled in the shade of the spreading acacia tree beside the house.

A favourite place for eating and resting, its bark was thickly criss-crossed with silver tracings, and clusters of snails huddled in the crook of every branch. Weary birds, creeping things and insects all found the tree a haven in the heat of the day, mice and lizards darted in and out of the roots, and bats drooped there in the night like malformed fruit. Occasionally a snail – or a bird dropping – would fall into a dish and the food would have to be thrown out, but it was a small risk for the pleasure of such shade.

Etta uncovered a basket of new bread and Anna produced a large dish of pickled vegetables. Ammiel bowed his head.

*"Blessed art thou, Adonai our God, King of the world, who causes to come forth bread from the earth. Thou our Shepherd, lead us beside still waters, and show us thy Messiah. Amen."*

Anna leaned towards him as she handed him the bread.

"You have added to this good prayer, Ammiel, and made it even better. I can see you appreciate the psalms of David as much as you ever did."

Ammiel nodded. He tore off a piece of bread and heaped it with pickles.

"Such good food, Anna," he said thoughtfully, "and I don't have to beg for it like so many! I am grateful. But I am beginning to think that a man needs more than his daily bread. He needs hope. Does it please the Almighty to see hunger and sin and despair in His land which once flowed with milk and honey?"

He motioned for the dipper.

Anna poured the water and watched him swallowing. His luxuriant auburn beard moved rhythmically, and as he tilted his head back to catch the last drops, the hidden place under the chin where his beard thinned was exposed, white skin contrasting with the deep tan on the rest of his throat. He put the bowl down with a thud and caught her looking. She flushed a little.

"I see, so you pray for stillness," she said, as if there had been no pause, "and you pray for the Messiah. Forgive me asking what is in your mind concerning these things. What are the still waters, and why do you say "show us" Messiah?"

Dan nudged Johanan, and they both listened hard. They might hear something new about Messiah! They ate quietly and tried not to look at Ammiel in case he declined to answer a woman about such things. But Dan's father had forgotten their presence, and was thinking only of Anna's readiness to ask him. He looked at her hesitantly.

"I am ashamed to tell you, Anna, that I do not know exactly. I feel more than I can explain. I am not learned, but the stillness of the waters, it seems to me, is not the stillness of stagnation, where water is bad, but of a clear pool of peace. Such as where the shepherd who wrote these words, could safely water his flock."

Anna took the dipper and ladled water for Etta.

"Yet how lovely it is, that here the shepherd David speaks as if he himself were a sheep."

Ammiel nodded vigorously.

"Yes! *I may be a shepherd of sheep*, he seems to say, *but the Lord himself is my shepherd*. So we the Lord's people need Him to shepherd us, to guide us, to those still waters of peace."

Bukki champed away at his pickles, a shred of dill dangling from his lip like a green feather. "You look peaceful enough already!"

"Yes, as a man I am, God be praised, but as a nation we lack peace," Ammiel gave him a sober look. "So what can we do but pray for it? Pray for still waters, for peace – for all Jews, all Israel, our nation! As well as for ourselves."

*Aha!* thought Dan with a spurt of gladness, *there it is! There's Ourselves, and All-of-the-Selves which is all Israel. Father must understand about the seed, and the stars, and the sand, too! I should have asked him before.*

The hewer had also been listening as intently as Dan and Johanan, who dared not interrupt.

"Not much hope of peace with the Romans around, is there?" he said dubiously. "Do you really think praying – just words to the sky – will make a difference?"

"Words to the sky!" Aunt Etta burst in rather indignantly. "Does a lost lamb just bleat to the sky? Of course not! It bleats to its dam!"

"Or its shepherd!" flashed Johanan, suddenly seeing the point and unable to keep silent any longer. "Baa! Baa! Save me! Save me!"

Dan pinched his leg warningly and Johanan subsided at once.

"It's the same," replied Ammiel, twinkling at Johanan. "It cries to its protector – whether dam or shepherd. If the lamb cries not, it is already marked for death. How can I find her unless she cries to me? If a lamb cries, it may be heard, and may be saved."

Etta nodded.

"You are right, Ammiel. If we are God's sheep, we must cry too. So we pray. For help."

"And to keep hope alive," added Anna softly.

"Hope of what?!" grumbled Bukki, growing tired of all this theology. "We are not lost! We are Jews – who go straight to

94

Abraham's bosom when we die. Why talk about saving, and crying?"

So rare was it to hear Bukki talking of scriptural matters that the others sat with their mouths open, wondering what really went on inside his head. Bukki swelled a little at all the attention.

"Since we are saved already," he persisted, "why talk about hope? Hope of what?"

Ammiel shook his head.

"Bukki, I can't believe you don't mention the Messiah. He who will gather all Jews together from the dispersion! Who will restore righteousness to the land! Messiah – the Hope of Israel!"

"Do you pray for the sun to rise?" demanded Bukki crossly. "Messiah is promised, Messiah will come – sometime! That's all. No point praying about it. Unless you want God to change His mind about when it happens."

Etta was speechless before this uncharacteristic and dubious eloquence, but Ammiel looked at Anna and raised a quizzical eyebrow. She gave him the ghost of a smile.

"Pardon me, my dear Bukki," she answered gravely, "I do believe prayer is to change *our* minds, not the Creator's."

Bukki didn't meet her eyes, but he looked intently at the top of her head.

"Nonsense," he rumbled, braving interruption from his brother-in-law. "How can it change *us*? Prayer is to give thanks or praise and ask for things."

Bukki wiped his mouth with the back of a hairy hand and eyed the hewer significantly in the hope of impressing somebody. He

95

added boldly, "Messiah is a certainty, not something vaguely hoped for. So why call him the Hope of Israel?"

*Yes, why?* Dan thought urgently. *Why is he the Hope?*

The hewer coughed and looked uncomfortable. This wasn't his idea of mealtime conversation. "Well – surely – he's our hope of deliverance from the Romans, isn't he?"

Anna adjusted her slipping veil calmly and exchanged a glance with Ammiel. He gestured for her to speak.

"Messiah is our hope of life eternal," she answered Bukki. "Forgive me for the contradiction, but Abraham's bosom is not."

"Learned men say so – I've heard them many times!" Bukki justified himself.

The hewer agreed, "So have I – but then – I don't understand half what they say."

Ammiel leaned over and slapped him appreciatively on the back with a roar of laughter. "Well, here's an honest man! I agree with you, friend! What do you say, Anna?"

Anna looked directly at the boys, knowing they were hanging on every word they heard.

"I think we must be careful of confusing *truth* with mere *illustrations* of it."

Dan knew he would have to think that over later.

"I think you duck the question," sniffed Bukki, who didn't understand her answer.

Anna looked at Ammiel apologetically, but he squeezed her hand encouragingly.

She continued carefully, "You ask why we call Messiah 'the Hope of Israel', since his coming is a certainty. It is because this hope is for more than a righteous King to rule our nation. It is because it was promised in Eden, that he would crush sin and death itself. This means people will live for ever and not die. What greater Hope could we look for?"

Dan wanted to stand up and shout "Amen!" but Bukki glanced at Anna dismissively. It was important to keep females in their place, especially if they knew too much.

"Women don't understand about these things," said this unlearned man to the educated woman opposite him.

"Perhaps, Bukki," said Anna submissively, touching the silver coins on her forehead in an unconscious gesture, "that is why I asked my betrothed husband the question."

Johanan gave Dan a delighted dig and Dan hugged himself as he saw Bukki's slightly baffled expression. Bukki wasn't sure whether he had won that point or not. With what he hoped was a dignified snort, Bukki shook his head sadly, brushed crumbs off his stomach and strutted off to relieve his feelings in various ways, which began with his usual scratchings and belchings.

Ammiel took a deep breath and blew it out with satisfaction. Johanan took a quick gulp of water while Dan stuffed a big chunk of bread in his mouth and chewed frantically, as they waited breathlessly for the next person to speak.

Finding her voice at last, Etta said drily, "What was the question? I think it walked off with Bukki."

Anna gave Etta the crooked smile which in a man would have been a wink, and repeated,

"Why does Ammiel pray, *'Show us thy Messiah?'*"

In his suspense, Dan forgot to finish chewing his mouthful. More answers! And all he had to do was listen! He swallowed the lump of bread whole and the bulge pained his throat all the way down and made his eyes water.

*Come on, Abba! I want to know your answer!*

"*Show* us thy Messiah," echoed Ammiel, wiping the bottom of the pickle dish with a crust and chewing thoughtfully. "I pray to be shown, because I know so little. I do not know what or who to look for. I know he is to be our King. But will he come with trumpets? Or as my shepherd king David – hunted in the mountains gathering the outcasts of Israel, until his time came to take the crown?"

Johanan blinked and Dan's neck prickled – what? Messiah hunted? with outcasts? Never! But Ammiel looked up at Anna and down to Dan, frankly.

"I pray to be shown," he added, clearing his throat, "because I am afraid I will not know him when he comes."

There was a moment of silence.

"*Show us thy Messiah,*" suddenly repeated the hewer, emphatically. "That is a good prayer. Yes, a good prayer."

He raised his arms.

"Show us thy Messiah!" he called loudly.

Spontaneously the others held up their hands too.

"Show us Thy Messiah!" they all cried gladly. "Amen!"

Shepherd, stone hewer, women and lads together laughed for sheer joy of the daring words to pray. The laugh died down but a droning snore buzzed in the heat from the cool side of the house where Bukki had escaped.

Etta shrugged expressively, unwrapped a napkin full of fresh figs, and handed them round to huge grins. They were all thinking of how much Bukki loved figs. Soon the fruit was devoured, and the women retired, leaving the men to sleep under the tree till the noon heat was over and work would begin again.

Dan's head was humming with the glory of knowing more. Surely knowledge was a blessing, too. He turned over each new fact and laid it away like treasure in his mind. Later he and Johanan would talk everything out and put things in order. As he had hoped, Dan had already found Johanan was a good companion for talk as well as play, and his laconic comments said as much as many words. Dan happily drifted off to sleep with the others, but when he woke still felt hungry for information about something he couldn't quite remember.

It wasn't until evening when Ammiel had paid the muscular workman his wage for the day, that Dan remembered what he wanted to know.

"Please wait," he begged as the man gathered up his cloak and tools. "I want to ask you something!"

The hewer shook his head wonderingly.

"I never knew such a family for asking questions and arguing about answers!" he said, wrapping his tools in his leather apron. "Why ask me? I don't know anything about the scriptures! Now where's my best chisel gone?"

Dan looked up.

"Anna's found it over there. Here she comes."

He hurried on with his question.

"Do you know what sand is made of?"

The man considered.

"Well, I don't know. Sand is just sand. You get a piece of sandstone, it's made up of sand, really, all stuck together. It breaks down easily. So I suppose sand could be made of crumbled sandstone."

"But which came first, sand or sandstone? It could be either, couldn't it?"

The man scratched his beard and screwed up his face thoughtfully. "That's a hard one. I can't tell you."

Anna handed him the chisel, and he took it with a nod, wiping it carefully on his tunic, and strode off. Dan watched him go, disappointed. But Anna had heard Dan's question.

"Sand is made of many things, Dan," she said.

Dan looked up quickly. "Yes?" he said eagerly. "Do you know about it?"

She nodded.

"Imagine Aunt Etta grinding wheat and barley and corn … all together with a pestle and mortar. The sea is the pestle, the sea-floor is the mortar. Rock, seashells, stones, bones, crab shells … worn away, pounded and ground up together by the waves. Smaller and smaller until all you have is tiny crushed fragments. That's sand."

"Yes!" said Dan gratefully, remembering the different colours and shapes of the grains on his sodden fingers. "Yes, I can see that now. But – there's so much of it!"

Anna agreed.

"That's a lot of rock, shells and bones, isn't it, Dan? But I suppose ever since creation, the sea has just kept grinding more all the time, very slowly, but surely."

She called to Johanan, and they set off for Banayim.

That night Dan dreamed of the sea relentlessly creating sand, more and more, like flour creeping out from under a millstone. Heaping up on the beach, caking itself into sandstone, piling up on the sandhills, spilling over into Bayanim, sifting over the house on the shore, burying the rooms while Anna cried for rescue from the top floor, and Bukki laughed like a hyena in the hills, and he and Johanan dug helplessly to save her, till the house collapsed and Anna's face was buried for ever …

He woke with a gasping shudder, and an unpleasant prickling all over his skin. He crept out of his blanket without disturbing Aunt Etta and looked out of the door for the comfort of the stars. In the moonlight the half finished walls were forlorn ruins.

## Chapter Ten

ANNA and Johanan had left the house by the shore. Helen was not well, so Anna had sent Johanan back to his mother in Jerusalem and returned to her parents' house. Dan felt there was rather a gap somewhere without them. Johanan had run over to help with the building whenever Anna could spare him, and he had livened up the process for everyone … a melon carefully caked in clay to look like a rock, which splattered messy juice and pips everywhere when Ammiel hit it with an adze … a wooden cup with a tiny hole just below the lip line, which dribbled water onto a puzzled Bukki when he tried to drink from it … a plate of goat droppings solemnly handed round as olives which earned him a smack on the ears from Aunt Etta … an impossible knot learned from the lake fishermen which cobbled up the end of the hewer's tunic to his sash and forced him to remain with his loins girded for far longer than he wanted … but nobody could deny Johanan knew how to work hard too, and somehow he got away with it all … The memory of his exploits kept Dan amused even after the heavy building was over, and he and Bukki worked alone on the finishing off.

Then there was the fun of his birthday to remember too. On Johanan's last day, Dan had turned ten. Anna and Aunt Etta had packed the two lads off with a glorious picnic, and they had spent the whole day at the beach – talking, laughing, arguing, swimming

– and even begging a trip in a fishing boat with the noisiest fishermen on the lake – the ben Zebedees, who joked all the time and bellowed at each other equally loudly whether roaring with laughter or impatience, and who presented Dan with one small fish for each of his ten years. It had been a wonderful day, even if half of Dan's lunch had ended up in the lake during a sudden squall. And what a hilarious fish supper afterwards, when they had driven the women to distraction with boyish nonsense! "Playing giddy goats!" said Aunt Etta, trying to sound stern, and rejoicing to see her boy so happy. Yes, it was very quiet without Johanan around – even a little dull.

Dan eyed the new work appreciatively. The old part of the house was built of mud brick, with a roof of woven branches and reeds covered with beaten clay. Dan and Ammiel – and supposedly, Bukki – were constantly re-rolling the roof and patching the walls, as the rains tried to wash them away. There was a shallow curve to the roof to shed the rain, and it would not bear much weight. But the long new room running off at right angles to the old, was built all of limestone on its basalt foundation, and had a strong roof of wood beneath the packed clay coating, which Ammiel had extravagantly coated with lime plaster. A low parapet on the top and a sturdy ladder meant that the roof would be used as an outdoor room. What luxury! Dan ran up and down the ladder a dozen times for the sheer fun of it until Aunt Etta reminded him he had a job to do up there. The old clay roof needed attention too, before the rains, and this year it was getting more than mending and re-rolling.

So Dan obediently crawled about on top of the old section with his heavy wooden bucket, happily slapping thick whitewash – another luxury – over the freshly rolled surface, and anticipating the pleasure of sitting under the shade booth which Bukki had agreed to build over in the corner of the new roof. It was the only part of the building process which seemed to spark his interest, but *Uncle Bukki knows how to make himself comfortable*, Dan grinned to himself. He knew Aunt Etta hoped Uncle Bukki would complete it before the wedding so she could show off their nice new house to all the guests who would pack into the long room for the feast.

The second new room for Anna and Ammiel was smaller and formed the third side of the courtyard. This was another luxury, but of course it would be used for a guest chamber when needed. With his unusually small family circle, Dan had little experience of overnight visitors, apart from old Caleb and Marta. He thought it was very grand to have such a special room ready to receive people like Anna's parents – and perhaps Johanan as well.

"Mind you have finished that whitening by the time I come back," warned Aunt Etta from below, lifting her waterpot to her shoulder. It now was too awkward to carry on her head as she used to.

"Bukki!" she called. Where was the man? He was becoming a very shadow – too much of him around at night and not enough during the day, Etta grumbled to herself.

"Bukki?"

Bukki was nowhere to be found, and the sycamore tree behind the house, where he had been grinding lime for the whitewash, sheltered only abandoned tools, lumps of white rock and pots of burnt shells.

Hi–yi, that man! Well, if that roof wasn't good and finished before the rains, Etta knew where Bukki would sleep if she had her way – right under any drips!

Etta missed Marta at the well that morning, but that was no surprise, and she didn't need the Dabab to tell her why. Half the women were hurrying through their task to get back to the village and cluster around and into Marta's house.

"She's been in strong labour only a few hours, and no doubt many more to come," sighed Rachel, nodding happily as she slopped the water into her bucket, and wishing she could be part of both the crowd at the well and the house at the same time. "May the good Lord preserve her! Of course, her own mother died when she was born … no doubt she'll be remembering that and adding fear to her pain …"

"She's a sensible, healthy girl," said Etta sharply, "too sensible to have been listening to your dismal croakings about dying in childbirth all these months … and she has her mother-in-law with her, a good woman with a kind manner and plenty of experience."

Rachel gave her a patronising smile.

"Well, Etta, you are right to be hopeful. Of course, had you buried three children, as I have, you might think differently."

She trotted off to a more appreciative audience at Marta's house.

Etta also wasted no time in collecting her water, but looking at the crowd around Marta's house as she passed, she knew she would not go in. It was a time for friends who were fruitful wives and mothers, with knowledge, advice and shared experience. Much as Etta was liked, she was unmarried and childless – a withered vine – and therefore not a woman of any great standing. Should anything go wrong – God forbid – there would always be some who would whisper of her bringing bad luck into the birth room.

Marta's husband, Ittai, with a distracted air, was walking rather dizzily around and around a tree before the house. He saw Etta and rushed up to her.

"Etta," he said hoarsely. "Etta, my poor Marta. And none of these terrible women will tell me anything."

"Poor Marta, nothing," said Etta briskly. "The more tears, the more laughter. She will be a happy woman before the day is out, please God."

Ittai tweaked his beard in anguish.

"I never knew the sun so slow – Marta only woke me at dawn, and that Dabab keeps reminding me it could be two or three *days* for a first child!"

Suddenly there was a little movement among the women crowded around the door, as a low wailing came keening through the air. Ittai shuddered, but Etta patted his shoulder reassuringly.

"That's not Marta."

She put down her heavy pot as an unhappy woman ran from an alleyway and pushed into the crowd, pulling at their clothes and begging with tears.

"Is it true a child is born here today? – oh, calamity! Oh, woe to the mother! See, here is my veil – wrap him up! Please, take it, and hide him – or let me wrap the baby and take him away! I will tell no one, I promise!"

The women shrank from her clutching fingers and scolded her roundly, pushing the distraught newcomer hastily out of their midst.

"Marah All-Alone! What are you doing here? Get away, you madwoman! You will bring the evil eye on us all, and bad luck to this house … Cover your head and go at once!"

Ittai shivered and plucked at Etta's sleeve helplessly.

"She will bring bad luck to my darling – please, Etta, get rid of her!"

"Marah!" Etta put down the heavy jar, held out her arms and called. "Marah! Come here to me, my child."

Marah All-Alone wrung her hands and her black, deepset eyes looked around unseeingly. She stumbled as the women behind her shoved anxiously.

"Give me the baby," she whispered. "I will take better care of it this time!"

She held out a grubby veil imploringly, tears pouring down her face.

Ittai quickly sidled off, but Etta approached Marah with soothing words. She coaxed the woman gently, stroking the wild hair from her face where it stuck wetly to her cheeks.

"Marah, Marah, Marah … the babe is not yet born … but it will be taken good care of … Do not distress yourself, my child. All is well. All is well."

She scowled at the other women over Marah's shoulder and turned her back on their curiosity and disapproval. Carefully pulling the veil free from the grasping hands she settled it over the woman's head in a motherly way. Marah became suddenly quiet, unresisting.

"Come, dear, walk with me a while."

Etta put her arm around Marah's waist and drew her away, wondering what demons had been torturing this strange woman since she last knew her. Like herself, Marah was unsought, unmarried, childless. She had lived for many years at Magdala, but oddly, nobody knew much about her history except for the gossip which passed as fact ... a rich but pious father, a tragically leprous mother and a mysterious broken betrothal. At thirty five she was not yet an old woman, and still handsome in a faded way.

Etta felt a pang of guilt. Marah All-Alone had nobody – nobody to love, nobody to worry over – no little Dan, no protective Ammiel, not even a lazy Bukki to drive her to distraction. For the first time, Etta felt oddly grateful for Bukki. She tried to think of something normal to say to her old acquaintance. She spoke cheerfully.

"It's a long time since you've visited from Tiberius ... I heard you had – some troubles ..." Etta mentally kicked herself. *Why not just say 'I heard you were possessed with a devil!'* she told herself sarcastically.

But Marah wasn't listening. Her face was white and strained under its tan.

Etta tried again, more gently.

"Marah, my dear, you are suffering in some way. Can you not tell me what is wrong?"

The woman twisted her fingers anxiously and drew an uneven breath.

"Wrong, yes, oh very wrong ...!" she muttered. She stared at Etta curiously as if awakening from a dream. "I ... I ... something ... I can't remember," she stammered uneasily. She touched the tears on her face and looked blankly at her wet fingertips.

From among the knot of women by the door a came a muffled murmur … a sharp cry followed by a short silence … and then a burst of delighted laughter from inside the house. Etta and all the others froze in astonishment. It was Marta's laugh! A woman to laugh at such a time? Suddenly there was a tiny cough and splutter, and an unmistakable squalling cut through the air like a rasp. Jaws dropped and eyes widened in shock and envy.

Ittai plunged into the crowd and dived through the door without waiting for the midwife to call him. There was a pause of several moments before he bounded out through the surprised and chattering women – shouting and leaping about like a madman.

"A son! Praise the Eternal, a lusty son! Three hours of labour only, and behold a son! a son! and my wife is in there laughing!" He disappeared again.

Laughing! Rachel, who had predicted suffering and doom, was shocked. Laughing? Laughing! Well!

Etta's heart lifted in happiness and she breathed, "Praise God!" even as she felt Marah All-Alone stiffen at the child's cry. She glanced at her quickly. The deepset eyes had glazed over again and she was muttering savagely to herself, twisting her veil, tugging her hair and shaking her head as if to jerk it free of an unbearable fetter. Etta was baffled. She patted the woman's nervous hand encouragingly.

"Marah? Hush now, Marah, hush! – all is well! Marah dear – a boy has been born. He is safe and well, and so is his mother."

Marah stopped tossing herself around instantly.

"Safe," she shuddered. "Safe."

With surprising strength she snatched Etta's arms in hard fingers and dragged her down behind a bush, whispering urgently in her ear.

"Are we observed? Did anyone hear you? You said the babe is safe ... but tell no one!"

"Yes," said a baffled Etta, her back hurting as they crouched together, making little sense of Marah's words. "Yes, the babe is safe and well and so is his mother."

She saw the words calmed Marah still further, and repeated them more firmly, feeling the biting fingers relax on her arms.

"The babe is safe, Marah, the babe is safe and well, and so is his mother."

"Safe," sobbed Marah, dropping her clutching hands from Etta's arms and covering her face. "Both! God forgive me!"

She cried stormily for several minutes and suddenly, to Etta's confusion, slumped to the dirt and seemed to fall deeply asleep.

Etta struggled to her feet, exhausted and cramped, rubbing her bruised arms. She looked helplessly upon the unconscious woman at her feet. A clear young voice spoke at her elbow.

"Is Marah All-Alone a madwoman?"

Six year old Huldah, fat baby sister on her hip, had been jostled out of the group at Ittai's, and sought other excitement. She looked calmly down at Marah, seeing the deep fingernail prints in her now relaxed palms, the bitten lips, the dust mingled with tears which formed muddy streaks on her face, the tangled hair caught in the thorny embrace of the bush.

Etta sighed and tried to stretch.

"I don't know, Huldah. Something is wrong with her."

111

Huldah smacked her sister's sticky fingers as they tugged joyfully at her hair.

"Naughty girl, Tirzah. Don't pull hair. Marah All-Alone pulls her own hair, doesn't she? My mother says she has a devil. What do devils do really?"

Etta felt rather put on the spot by the question. She answered evasively,

"I think she is very unhappy. Perhaps that makes her strange."

Huldah shifted the heavy baby to the other hip, automatically shooing away a buzz of flies which clustered on the dimpled, dribble-wet chin.

"My mother said she got a fever in Tiberius and ever since she's had a devil. You should see the way she stares at Tirzah. My mother says we have to keep away from her."

Etta gave her a level look.

"Is that a fact. Well, Huldah, go you and fetch your mother and tell her to look to the poor woman when she wakes. Perhaps give her a mouthful of wine, and a cold wet cloth for her neck. Then somebody needs to watch her until she comes right again. But I must get back home."

Huldah nodded and trotted off, baby and all, towards the crowded doorway behind them. Etta draped Marah's veil carefully to shield her from the sun and the thirsty flies which clustered at her pale lips. There was no more she could do.

*Lord of the universe, help this Thy daughter in her distress.*

She was walking stiffly back to her waterpot – but stopped in her tracks.

A sudden, and unaccountable commotion coming from Marta's door! Someone was shouting at Ittai to get out, Ittai was roaring that there were too many women in his house, the midwife was babbling something unintelligible, and Marta's voice cried out urgently – Etta went pale – it was not unknown for an apparently healthy child to die suddenly after birth ... let alone the mother! But no – she could hear the newborn squawking and spluttering again resentfully. But why all this noise and fuss just when the mother needed rest and quiet! They should be tending gently to Marta, watchful for the afterbirth, salting and swaddling the newborn, putting him to the breast – humming to him, murmuring blessings, and quietly praising God, not honking and cackling like a lot of geese! Tired as she was, Etta had to find out what was happening. Something must be terribly wrong! She glanced apologetically back at Marah – well, she would come to no harm while she slept so deeply. Determinedly she followed little Huldah as fast as she could go.

Dan scraped the bottom of his pot of whitewash and wriggled his aching shoulders. Why was Aunt Etta taking so long at the well? And where was Uncle Bukki now the whitening had run out? Dan wiped his sweating face and looked longingly at the corner of the roof which awaited Uncle Bukki's promised shade. "He'd better hurry up," thought Dan. Only a couple of days after the next sabbath they would rejoin Ammiel to begin washing the sheep ready for shearing, and there'd be scant time for booth building, no matter how badly Aunt Etta wanted one.

The summer shearing was a time of hard work, but everyone helped, even the grudging Extra Pressings, Caleb's tight-lipped daughter. It was more enjoyable work than the earlier clip at the end of winter. The wool was cleaner and less matted, and washing it was welcome work in the hot sun. The winter shearing was a cold and miserable affair in comparison. But winter or summer, the sheep had to be washed first. The cleaner the sheep, the whiter the wool, the more the money, after all. And with new rooms, and a wedding feast, and new clothes to celebrate, even Dan knew the importance of more money.

He scrambled down the ladder and trotted around the back of the house which was still shaded from the morning sun. He sat himself in Bukki's favourite place under the young sycamore, picked up the stone pestle and began pounding lime in the mortar.

It was tiring, and Dan envied the lazy snails sleeping in their shells among the bark. A spider spun industriously on a trembling leaf, two mice chased each other under a twisted root, and a family of sparrows quarrelled above his head. Dan yawned. The work was monotonous. No wonder Uncle Bukki was having a rest. Dan squinted at the sun and suddenly thought of Aunt Etta, remembering how she had lifted the tall jar to her shoulder and not her head. Perhaps the waterpot was too heavy. *Perhaps she's dropped it and has to go back. She would be ashamed.*

Carrying water was women's work, not for boys. Dan pounded on determinedly. *But if Aunt Etta can't do it, and Uncle Bukki is gone, how will the water get home?* Finally Dan talked himself into it, stopped the heavy pounding with a good excuse, and ran off to look for his aunt. He was half way to the village when he spied her coming slowly along the track.

Etta saw him first, and her eyes were bright with their unshed load of mixed emotions. Little Dan didn't need to know about the strange behaviour of poor Marah All-Alone, who was still asleep or ill or possessed, or whatever it was, and goodness knew

114

there'd be enough gossip about that going around soon … but there was still the news from Ittai's to tell. She put down her heavy jar and waited while he scampered up to her.

"Well, Dan! Have you finished your whitewashing?"

Dan nodded vigorously, too out of breath to ask why she'd been so long. Etta dug in a pouch at her waist and produced a small chunk of honeycomb from a folded fig leaf.

Dan swooped on it with delight and crammed it into his wide mouth at once. Aunt Etta's raisin coloured eyes crinkled with pleasure.

"A treat, eh? Can you guess where it came from?"

Dan shook his head, his mouth blissful with wax and honey, not willing to risk losing a drop of it in speech.

"It's a little gift – from a very excited Potter Ittai – to celebrate the surprisingly easy – and surprisingly swift – birth of his firstborn son! God be praised …!"

Dan nodded his thanks, allowing the last glorious drops of sweetness to spread over his tongue and wash around his teeth. Saving the wad of wax in his cheek to chew later, he shut his eyes and swallowed slowly. He opened them to see his aunt waiting patiently and hastened to correct his lapse of manners.

"God be praised," he repeated dutifully, digging wax out of a back tooth and sucking his finger.

Aunt Etta smiled and after the various shocks of the morning, a few weary tears brimmed over after all, as she produced a second piece of honeycomb and waved it tantalisingly in front of his sticky lips.

"… *and,* fast on his little red heels, a *daughter!*" she finished, triumphantly. "God be praised!"

Dan gobbled the morsel directly out of her worn fingers like a greedy lamb.

"God be praised!" he agreed indistinctly, with a grin.

## Chapter Eleven

AS Dan had feared, and Aunt Etta had expected, Uncle Bukki did not finish the booth before shearing. He had begun it, very slowly, after reluctantly completing the roof while Dan laboriously finished whitewashing the walls. Whitewashing – ugh! thought Dan ever after. It was tedious work without Johanan around. Dan found it hard to picture his lively friend meekly returning to school. He wished he could join him far away in Jerusalem, where the rabbis were supposed to be extra wise and clever. For the first time Dan was glad Ammiel was thinking of sending him back to school too, even if it was only to the small synagogue where there were mostly younger boys and the teacher was bad tempered. But perhaps the long walk to Magdala would be worthwhile after all. He didn't miss the sharp rap on the knuckles with the rabbi's stick when he got his sums wrong, nor the sleepy hot mornings where they drearily chanted portions of the Torah which seemed to be long dry songs without meaning. But he wanted to hear questions and answers – whether his own or someone else's, it didn't matter.

Dan was beginning to feel more than ever that there was too much in the world for him to understand on his own. And there was always that niggle about the Messiah. How frustrating, praying with his father "show us thy Messiah" and not knowing more than scraps about him! Johanan knew more than Dan, but not a lot

117

more. He could quote some scriptures about Messiah, but they didn't tell the boys what they wanted to know. Who was he? Who is he? Or who would he be? How would they know him? Ammiel himself had said he was afraid he wouldn't know him when he came, so how was Dan supposed to know? What would he do? What would he want? Surely a rabbi would have some clear answers – clearer than Ammiel's, clearer even than Anna's. But the shearing was upon them, and a wedding to follow, and schooling would have to wait.

Dan looked down into the drying valley filled with sheep, goats, shepherds and a few dogs milling around the deep brook at the bottom. The animals had been washed early in the day and were now being penned. Dan's lips twitched – Uncle Bukki had slipped that morning while struggling with a very large ram in midstream. Both of them came up bellowing and bucking, and shedding great gouts of water everywhere till Dan was in kinks of laughter. He wished Johanan had been with him to share the fun. Anna would have enjoyed it too. Her peculiar gurgling laugh would have bubbled out irrepressibly and made him laugh all the more. But Anna was not here, and she was not laughing at anything. Her mother's illness lingered, a wasting sickness which neither Asa's expensive doctors, nor Anna's careful nursing, could slow.

Dan scrambled down the slope and joined other shepherd lads in the water, where they were damming the stream into a pool for the women to wash the fleeces. It looked like delicious work in the heat, but the water was very cold and Dan's toes soon went numb. The heavy stones were hard to handle with chilled fingers – which continually were being squashed and nipped when somebody shifted a rock without warning. Dan yelped and shook a suddenly-bloodied thumb when Samuel's burly son jammed an extra large lump into a gap before Dan had time to move his hand.

118

"Sorry, boy," the young man grunted, and kept working.

Dan winced, wondering why cold fingers hurt more than warm. He sucked off the salty blood and found his thumb surprisingly clumsy in his mouth. After all those years of sleepy and satisfying thumb-sucking, it was a curious sensation.

The pool was finished. The lads splashed out, shivering, scattering to rejoin their own shepherds on the baking ground, and the wavelets on the new dam rocked to and fro. Dan watched them as they giddily rippled and finally calmed. Only the overflow moved, brimming lazily over the rock wall and lifting floating debris to toy with on the way downstream. The pool was flat, clear – the water-polished stones at the bottom looming deceptively close when once you peered beneath the shallow mirror of the surface, where the hard blue sky and a lost cloud or two were drowning. Ah, the shepherd's psalm! How real it was. He leads me beside the still waters.

Then there was Ammiel's daily prayer ... "lead us beside still waters" ... Anna's question ... "What are still waters?" ... and his answer ... "it seems to me ... a clear pool of peace ..."

The breath of a hot breeze wrinkled the water and rustled the reeds. The pebbles below blinked and lurched.

"Dan!" shouted a voice.

Dan started from his daydream, waved in response, and scampered downstream to where the men were separating the sheep from the goats. From this distance they all looked the same, but as they passed under each shepherd's rod he counted them off and diverted them to separate pens fashioned from rocks or thorn bushes. Ammiel was one of the few shepherds who had no goats in his flock. They were good leaders for the more docile sheep, but often troublesome. Unlike Ammiel, Samuel actually preferred goats and had more of them than sheep. He was a progressive man who had two trained dogs to help him and Dan marvelled at the way they worked, laughing to see them scrambling up and running over the backs of the animals when the way was blocked. Now that was one thing not even a shepherd could do!

"Dan!" Ammiel called again rather sharply, and Dan shouted back quickly, "Here I am, Abba!"

He heard a snigger from an older boy and blushed a little. Perhaps he was a bit old still to be calling his father "Abba". He ran even faster to where Ammiel was sharpening his shears. He felt the grimness in his father as he rejoined him, panting, and looked up at him hesitantly.

Ammiel glanced at Dan and his expression changed. He threw down his whetstone impatiently and blew out his breath, striking himself on the chest in exasperation. Suddenly he pulled his boy to him in rough reassurance.

"No, Dan, you have done nothing wrong," he said gruffly. "Ah, Dan, my little son – life is so short – so short, and full of the unexpected."

Dan was thoroughly confused.

"Abba?" He gave himself a mental jerk. "Father?" he corrected himself.

Ammiel gave him a twisted smile.

"Samuel's boys have brought me bad news from Cana …" He sighed and did not continue.

Dan's heart grew still. He dared not ask.

Ammiel snatched up the whetstone again and struck sparks from his shears, so sharply and swiftly did his strokes fly.

Suddenly he became aware of Dan's tension and again made a gesture of impatience.

"Dan, I am sorry! My head is full of wool today! Fear not, Anna herself is quite well!"

Dan relaxed.

"It is her mother, Helen. She is sinking so fast under this wasting sickness, that it looks like the wedding will become a funeral."

"Oh." Dan paused, shocked, then ventured to ask, "So ... what about ... the wedding?"

Ammiel tugged his beard and absently snipped a chunk of it with his newly sharpened shears. He had lopped off three fingers-worth of it before he seemed to notice what he was doing. Dan boldly took the iron shears from him and rubbed them pleasurably with an oily rag. They were precious tools, he knew. He squeezed them shut experimentally. It took both his hands, but he liked the thin swishing sound as the blades slid over each other like metal feathers furling together.

"The wedding?" he prompted, releasing his grip with relief. It would be a long while till he had such hands as his father, able to click and crunch shears open and shut all day without fatigue.

Ammiel stared at the coppery coils in his palm and poked them about. He slipped one over his finger like a ring, eyed it critically and sighed.

"Traditionally nothing should stop a wedding, not even death. It is bad luck. Life must be affirmed. *Le chayim!* But my poor Anna! How can a wedding be truly joyful when such sadness is so close to the heart?"

Dan considered, carefully laying down the shears in their cloth. He said tentatively, "Would not a happy time be a comfort?"

He picked up some of the severed beard, and draped a piece of it over his upper lip thoughtfully. Ammiel looked at the bright new moustache decorating Dan's dark young face and chuckled in spite of himself.

"I don't know, Dan. Do I want my wife to come to me veiled in tears of mourning? I think Anna must decide for herself. She will in any case consult her father for his wishes. But if she wants to delay the marriage so it must be. Sometimes tradition must wait upon common sense. Praise God, we are old enough to please ourselves in this matter."

Ammiel rubbed the wiry whiskers into fragments and blew them away like chaff.

He stood up decisively, taking the shears from his son, touching the edge of the blades exploratively with the ball of his thumb.

"I have recovered myself, Dan. Now you can stop looking at me anxiously, and we will work hard together."

The two of them moved to the makeshift fold and Ammiel said,

"What say you, my Dan? Shall the Queen of Sheba be first?"

Dan's grin answered him, and Ammiel called her lovingly, raising his voice above the din of bleating animals and the workers around them, in his distinctive buzzing cry.

"Come to Abba, my Queen ... Queen of Sheba, come to Abba. Come and get your long hair cut. You have been a Nazirite long enough! You will be the most beautiful bald sheep on the hill. You will set the fashion! Come, my lovely Queen ..."

Dan slid the gate open as the Queen of Sheba lumbered out, and jammed it back into place with a peg, as Ammiel fasted his big hands into her shoulders and neatly sat her on her haunches. She sat there indignantly, so much like a fat woman in silent outrage that Dan couldn't help laughing, though he was careful not to do it in her face. Ammiel sheared quickly in quiet concentration, punctuated with a murmured apology whenever he nicked her delicate skin. Dan darted to dab each quivering spot with astringent paste almost before it could bleed, and soon forgot to laugh as he watched with unending fascination the astonishingly clean inner wool parting to reveal even purer skin, deep below the thick matted surface.

"Isn't it beautiful!" he said admiringly.

Ammiel grunted in agreement. "Dogs are the opposite," he said, wiping sweat off his face with his forearm. "They can look clean on top, while dirty on the skin. That's why I don't like them."

He finished turning the heavy animal this way and that, flipped her over and pushed her into the holding pen. "Good girl, Sheba."

Dan scooped up the wool and whisked it up the slope to where the still pool was now unrecognisable. Twenty women were chattering, laughing and gossiping, churning up the water as they bobbed up and down on wet knees atop flat rocks, squeezing and flailing the dirt from masses of wool of many colours.

Extra Pressings was there, working with the same grim determination which characterised her penny pinching. She eyed Sheba's pale wool calculatingly and with a glint of satisfaction in her flinty eye. Good and white. Higher value. Ammiel bred lighter animals whose wool dyed well, trading darker stock with Samuel who sold to a different market. She pounded and thumped the fleece in the pool, skinny arms wasting not a movement.

"So, young Dan – what about the wedding, with Anna's mother so sick?"

Dan blinked, not knowing what to say. He had only just been discussing this with his father, feeling like a man as they talked so confidentially ... and yet, here it was ... a thing the women knew! The younger girls giggled expectantly.

"I don't know," he answered reluctantly. There, that was safe to say, at any rate. They could hee-hee-hee over that, if they liked. Those girls would giggle at a chicken scratching! He ran off to fetch the next fleece.

Behind him the women slapped the wet masses of wool on the rocks with their powerful arms, flailing out the excess water, sending spray leaping into the air to form fleeting rainbows in the sparkling sun. The pungent odour of wet wool and sheep dung hung about them.

Samuel's mother waited till Dan was out of earshot.

"All that work building a new house, you know. Do you think Ammiel can afford it for his rich new wife?"

Extra Pressings smacked Sheba's wool a little harder than necessary against a rock.

"Ada, you're a terrible old gossip," she said sniffily. "It's not a new house at all, it's just two more rooms. Why, I believe our own place is bigger. And his new wife isn't rich."

"She is so, too!" spluttered Ada indignantly. "Her mother brought a good dowry to that marriage, and still has a family of consequence in Greece. And Asa makes a lot of money importing fancy wares from Philippi and thereabouts. Don't tell me Anna's not rich!"

Limping Bethany, an eager little woman with a twisted foot, nodded as she hobbled over to lay her wrung out fleece in the hot sun.

"She's got money behind her, there's no doubt, but you wouldn't see her splash it about. She doesn't behave like a rich woman at all."

"Though she's not mean," piped up a younger girl, careful not to emphasise the 'she' in front of Extra Pressings. Respect for elders was always possible in speech, if not in thought.

Limping Bethany's cousin Noadiah interjected, "Money from Anna has nothing to do with the new rooms anyway. Ammiel had to pay for that! Stone, too – and a hired hewer!"

Ada shrugged, "He's got enough, you know. He's a hard working man, not stupid, and has a good flock. He's just been thoughtless since his wife died, man-like. He could have built those rooms a long time ago if he'd thought about it."

Extra Pressings' mouth seemed to taste vinegar.

"I doubt it. I believe he's only begun to work really hard since she died."

Ada opened her mouth indignantly, but before she had time to retort, Limping Bethany sighed sentimentally, "Burying himself in his work to drown his sorrow …!"

Ada snorted sarcastically.

"Burying and drowning! – what – in sheep?"

She glanced up to see the reaction, but though the younger girls next to her tittered, an aloof expression from the other side of the pool said plainly that Limping Bethany chose not to hear that comment. Ada continued more loudly.

"But in any case, what you say is not fair. Ammiel was *always* a hard worker!"

Extra Pressings narrowed her eyes as she stood up with her stringy bared arms full of sopping fleece.

"Well, perhaps he gives that impression," she said grudgingly. "Of course, he couldn't have built up that flock half so well over the years without my father's great experience."

Beside her Noadiah hooted as she plunged her plump elbows deep into the pool.

"What – so you're proud of poor old hired Caleb now, are you?" she chortled. "Will you promote him to your best room, since you have even more house than Ammiel to spare?"

Extra Pressings looked down on Noadiah's shaking back with disfavour. Calmly she opened her arms – and heavy wet fleece fell with a squelching thud. The women shrieked with delight as Noadiah pitched face first into the pool.

"Oh dear," said Extra Pressings politely, with her first tight smile for the day, and holding out a bony hand to help. "I am so sorry."

Noadiah, gasping under an enormous soaking wig, staggered up, wailing and scolding, grasped the proffered hand with both of hers, and unexpectedly jerked hard. With a squawk of surprise, Extra Pressings hit the water with a satisfying splash. The other women screamed louder than ever in enjoyment until the men hard at work glanced up and roared with laughter at the commotion while the children danced about excitedly and giggled and squealed. Finally, tempers cooled, order was restored, the women wrung

126

out their robes as best they could and kept on working in a dignified silence, broken only by titters from the others. The heat shimmered over the water, and privately both women were glad enough of their wet clothes.

Naturally the silence was for form's sake and didn't last for long – there was far too much to talk about. Marta of Banayim's twins – what an extraordinary thing that was – such a fast and easy labour! They discussed it enviously and in detail. Of course, of the shepherds' group only old Etta had been on the spot, but the Dabab had been there too! And women's language had its own power of sketching a detailed scene with few strokes – so naturally they soon almost believed they'd been there themselves. But for once none of them veered off into their own oft-told birth stories, because that happy day had brought even more fresh food for discussion – Marah All-Alone, for instance. Even Potter Ittai's improper behaviour at the birth was left untasted to the full.

Had any of them heard more about Marah? Such a strange woman who seemed to have no past before she came to Magdala years ago with her quiet old father. Now it was obvious past mere gossip – that the fever she took in god-forsaken Tiberius had left her possessed – definitely! – and in such an odd way. She had become a wanderer, with an uncanny ability to turn up wherever a woman was in labour, be it miles away. Surely this power is witchery? She would haunt the house and beg with tears for the newborn until assured that all was well and led away. Sometimes she was perfectly normal but often she was tormented by some demon or other, and would mutter savage things and beat her breast. It was a dreadful thing to see her, and women shut up their children when she appeared, not liking the avid looks she gave them.

"But really, she seems harmless, for all that," said Etta's voice firmly, so close behind them that the women jumped. They hadn't heard her approach.

"Well now, Etta, we all know you're softhearted," said Ada good naturedly, sitting back on her heels and rubbing her knees. "But you've no cub of your own to protect like a lioness, and even Dan's too old to interest poor Marah."

Etta settled herself on a clump of spiky grass. It was softer than a rock, at least. "Even Dan" indeed! There was no 'even' about it. Dan was her baby as much as Ada's brood were hers, and maybe even more so because he was all she had. But what could Ada know! She hadn't walked in Etta's sandals all these years. For all this indignant reaction, Ada's tactless blunder was forgiven almost instantly, but Etta thought about her comment.

"How old is too old to interest Marah?"

The women considered, glancing at each other for enlightenment. Finally tawny-haired Leah spoke up from the other side of the pool where she was nursing her eighteen month old. She swung the chubby brown feet playfully in her free hand even while she answered thoughtfully, "School age, I think, from what I've heard."

They all thought about it, as they pounded their wool. Extra Pressings had her own ideas.

"I think she has lost all the money her father left, perhaps gambling in Tiberius, and she has gone mad because of it."

Despite the seriousness of the subject, there were a few suppressed smiles at this revealing comment. Leah's sister-in-law dismissed it more openly. She said carelessly,

"Childless women often become baby-hungry when the manner of women is passing from them. And some become quite touched in the head. Everyone knows that."

There were a few apologetic glances at Etta, who simply agreed this was so, even while doubting the explanation. Marah All-Alone was middle-aged, to be sure, but not old yet.

Limping Bethany rubbed her deformed foot gently under her skirts. Thank God! She was not barren.

Etta got to her feet stiffly and returned to the shade of an acacia tree where the women had stored their supplies. She began unpacking bread and fresh figs from a basket. The sun was getting high and soon the men would want to eat and rest. Dan had been a big help in fetching and carrying. She called him over one more time.

"Find your father, Dan, and Uncle Bukki if you can see him anywhere. Tell him the food is ready for them and Caleb too. I doubt Extra Pressings will have brought much for the old goat, and he is always so hungry."

Dan's eyes glinted.

"Me too, Aunt Etta! And won't he enjoy the feast when we have finished shearing!"

Etta laughed.

"He will, that … and won't we all be glad when the work's over! A time for rejoicing indeed, my little man."

Dan squirmed.

"I'm not so little any more, Aunt Etta. But can you tell me if we'll be rejoicing with a wedding as well – or not? Everyone is asking about it now, even the women."

Aunt Etta raised her untidy eyebrows till they disappeared into her veil.

"Even the women, eh, Dan? Even the women! My, my, it seems you're not so little any more, as you say! Well, the answer is, I don't know either." She sighed and combed Dan's curls with her blunt fingers lovingly while he waited expectantly. Finally she said, "The fact is, your father is leaving it up to Anna, but my guess is, that for a while at least, there will be no wedding."

Dan's face fell, but somebody else seemed to think it was good news. There was a satisfied chuckle from behind them, and a jug shaped head poked around the tree trunk.

It was Uncle Bukki.

"No wedding, eh?" he said, with a snaggle-toothed grin, and waggled a slack winebottle at them. He tipped his head back and squirted a stream of wine into his mouth from the leg of the goatskin. He gulped and belched.

"No wedding!" he repeated happily. "Haw! Haw! A more comfortable house, and no wedding after all. Haw! Haw! Haw! Now, Etta, where's the food?"

Dan and Aunt Etta looked at him. They looked at each other. Aunt Etta drew a sharp breath but Dan reached out and touched her hand even as it knuckled her ample hip in readiness for an outburst. He suddenly thought of the picture he had drawn in the sand by the sea. Everyone blessing each other, and being blessed. Uncle Bukki could not be one of them. Poor Uncle Bukki – but he couldn't stop them being happy if they wanted.

"Don't, Aunt Etta. It doesn't matter."

And Dan ran off to fetch his father.

## Chapter Twelve

DAN crouched over the dirty brown foot in his lap, scowling at a tiny thorn in his big toe, as he dug at it with a bigger thorn. It had been a thorny week, one way and another. Dan had lost count of the number of times he had run his foot into one of the prickly walls of the sheep pens as he ran errands, chased runaways, scooped up piles of wool and goat hair, or carried water for the thirsty men.

*Ouch – got it at last!*

Scrambling to his feet, Dan jogged down to join the other lads at the washing pool. It was a sad sight now. Dirty wool-fat glued dead insects and bits of grass to the rocks – greasy hair and wool of every colour from white through browns to black was caught in crevices, and grey scum from the women's blocks of lye soap made a sullen edge around the dull water spilling over the brim.

The boys jumped in, making the biggest splashes they could, and with plenty of shouting, shivering and shoving, began to pull the dam apart, making a competition of tossing the rocks ashore. Samuel's muscular son won easily, throwing even the heaviest stones a good body length further than anyone else. The water flung itself over the breaking wall, helping the task and tumbling the smaller rocks away downstream. Soon the pool was no more,

131

and the brook went hurrying on its way uninterrupted until next season.

The work had been heavy, but at last it was done. Scoured, dried and bundled, the wool was ready for sale. Most would be sold straight away, but the some of very whitest and best would go to the fuller. Carefully bleached and shrunk, and no longer oily, it would repay the extra expense by fetching a high price. It would comb out and spin into fine strong thread, dye well and be painstakingly woven into soft supple cloth. Dan remembered the light woollen gown which Anna had worn for the betrothal. Wouldn't it be funny if the wool for her dress had come from one of Ammiel's sheep without any of them realising it. And just think – perhaps the Queen of Sheba had worn it first! … laughing over this idea Dan wrung out his wet tunic and ran off to find Aunt Etta.

Aunt Etta was up on the hillside under the biggest tree, busy with the rest of the women preparing food, keeping a watchful eye on a simmering pot, patting dough between her palms, and blowing the fire in her little clay oven all at once. She hailed Dan thankfully and set him to tending the oven.

"More thorns, Dan, this fire won't last long enough to heat the clay."

She spun the dough expertly on the back of her knuckles, calculating how much more bread she had to make, and clicked her tongue.

"Why wasn't I born twins, like Marta's babes!" she lamented. "I need extra hands."

Ada cackled as she tested a pile of eggs in a bowl of water.

"You'd be in a fix if you were like Marta's twins, Etta – boy and girl! Would you be a man?"

The younger women gasped at this scandalous thought, but Etta merely snorted,

"Sometimes I would, sometimes I wouldn't!"

Ada clicked her tongue as she fished out an egg which bobbed in the water.

"That scoundrel Hanoch gives me three bad eggs in the dozen. Break them over his miserable head I will some day!"

Etta tried to stretch and winced. Ada looked at her sharply.

"That back of yours, Etta, giving you more trouble by the day …"

"Ah, well, backache's a woman's lot," piped up young Naami complacently, stretching her bones easily and hefting a stocky toddler to the only space on her lap not occupied by a baby-in-waiting. "The lifting, the bending, the carrying, the child bearing … yes, we all suffer …"

Ada and Etta caught each other's eyes and exchanged the glimmer of a smile.

Leah looked at the heavy child and shook her head warningly.

"You'll be suffering a lot more yourself, girl, if you don't stop dragging that lazy boy of yours around now you have another coming so close. Make him walk and don't baby him."

Naami hugged her child defensively and ignored Leah.

"Have you seen Marta's babies lately?" she asked Etta. "Are they pretty? They do say one twin always gets all the looks. And has she enough milk?"

Etta gave it as her opinion that they were equally handsome and that Marta was producing copiously and doing wonderfully well, with her delightful mother-in-law to help, and Ittai's gentle consideration sparing her any trouble.

This was all a bit too much to swallow, and as each woman fitted this information around her own ideas, she privately whittled it down to a more believable size. Likely poor Marta was dragged to death, and quarrelled with her mother-in-law when nobody was listening. As for any young man being gentle and considerate with a house full of screaming babies … it simply wasn't natural. Likely the potter was out as often as he could be, or maybe he was just soft. There were men like that … but who ever got one? There was a collective sigh.

"I knew a young tradesman like that once," said a visiting grandmother dreamily. "A room full of noisy children, a distracted mother cooking, and he with a colicky baby laid over his knees, rubbing its back with one hand while he sketched a pattern for my new table with the other *and* listened to what I said, what's more."

"A paragon indeed," laughed Ada. "Paternal love, or politeness to his customer?"

The grandmother smiled and shrugged.

"Well, perhaps politeness … he was not the father, just a big brother, I believe. But so nice to see such a real *dodi* like this – yes, a nice change from those who have no respect for the home. And he got the baby's wind up all right! Half its feed came with it – sour as cheese – straight down his legs into his sandals, and he only laughed."

The women all chuckled. Leah, whose husband went out drinking every time the baby was teething, and had not called *her* *dodi* for months, smiled tiredly. After all, did this 'darling' of an

134

eldest son actually have any responsibility? Worry, that's what made a man short tempered, not just lack of sleep.

"Aunt Etta, the oven's ready," said Dan resignedly. How the women chattered! And they didn't talk about anything interesting at all. He raked the ashes out of the cavity and reached for the plate of dough. Aunt Etta was busily chopping onions and sniffing desperately.

"You're a good boy," she said, blinking through onion tears. "A blessing to my old age, eh?"

Dan patted the thin slabs on to the hot clay dome and watched them carefully, quick to turn them over as soon as they were dry and browning, and soon began to build a good pile. He thought of folding the warm pieces, scooping up delicious mouthfuls of the stew which simmered nearby, the juice soaking into the bread … his mouth watered. Despite the everlasting sameness of the female talk washing over him, the smells and sly tastings of any feast preparation were worth being around for – there was always a stray morsel or two going begging. Dan was becoming wise to the fact that a young boy who was polite and helpful and kept his mouth shut, came in for a bit of absent-minded petting from the women. He may as well make the most of the extra treats before they realised he was growing up fast.

The provisions were ready, the men and boys joined their families, the blessing was given, and the shearing feast began. The food was good, the wine was good, it had been a good season, praise the Eternal! A pomegranate sun plummeted down behind purpling hills, the fires flickered up into a glowing circle. With the eating and drinking of course there must be stories! The men vied with each other to stretch belief in their exploits, remembering past

135

seasons and disasters overcome, telling ever bolder tales of fighting marauders and performing miracles with slings and arrows, rescuing animals from precipices, and crevasses – from floods – fires – wolves! bears! lions! and eagles! … until finally Ammiel's solemn fantasy of snatching a ram from the jaws of a whale which had accidentally swum up a creek from the Great Sea convulsed everyone until they ached.

One by one the men and boys brought out instruments – a harp, some pipes, and the girls their tambourines and finger cymbals. A thin old voice began – Madai, the oldest shepherd in the group – with a long note calling all to sing and rejoice, and a dozen bass voices rumbled in reply, followed by a flurry of rapid chanting from the women as they tumbled their notes into the song with their strong nasal voices. The children clapped, the women chinked their instruments, the breathy wailing pipes brought the hair up on Dan's arms, so eerie and mournful was it. Even Uncle Bukki had got hold of a small drum and smacked it fervently only just off the beat. The joy and triumph of a successful season broke out in song after song. The shepherd psalms, songs of love, songs of worship, songs of loss, silly songs which made them laugh …

Dan's favourite was the Wolf and the Sheep, where the men roared, "I am a sheep, see my skin, I have wool like you, open the door!" and the women twittered back, "You may wear wool, you may bleat, but underneath we see claws and fangs! We will not open the door!"

The girls sang with simpering faces, the older women with grim relish. Dan couldn't help laughing to see Timid Tobiah, a hireling of dubious courage, rolling his eyes bombastically and growling bravely in the song while his stout wife sang the answers in a mock-fearful voice which was almost as funny.

Then there was the dancing – oh, the dancing! The women in their circle with the girls, the men in their own with the boys. Was ever anything so delightful as the dancing in the firelight, the flickering shapes and deep colours, the intricate changing patterns of flowing forms, the glint of bracelets and flash of smiles, the circling and stamping, the advancing and retreating, the finger shaking and head tossing, the arm linking, the breathless singing and the helpless laughing when you forgot the steps! They danced up all their happiness and gratitude, they danced down all their private pains and worries, they danced all they knew – dances of praise, dances of story, dances which linked them with all the Shearing Feasts of the past, right down to King David's shepherd days and beyond.

So they wove their traditions tightly around them with their bodies and their voices, and glowed with the warmth and assurance. They danced the water dance, with its exuberant lone male voice lifted up in counterpoint to a difficult rhythm, gleefully answered by the cry of Mayim! from the dancers. They danced a shuffling rippling dance where each held the shoulder of the one in front, flowing along behind each other like a living frieze until they broke their hold to punctuate the music with fierce syncopated claps. And finally they danced the only dance where the men and women mingled – the dance of The Victory, telling of the men returning from war.

Dan watched with a heart full enough to burst, as the men and women whirled around in their double layered circle. The women held out their skirts and minced towards the centre and back.

"How fared the battle?" they trilled.

The men shouted and put their hands on their hips, strutting and swaggering triumphantly towards their women. Dan was tickled to see out of the corner of his eye, Uncle Bukki strutting unsteadily and singing all by himself, apparently dancing and bragging to a tree.

"The Lord gave us victory! We were fearless in battle!" the men sang boastfully, and they swung the women round first this way, then that, before joining hands to weave the circle into a lilting chain of movement.

Dan caught his breath to see Ammiel dancing The Victory with Etta, his white teeth flashing in the rich depths of his beard as they sang loudly together. How strong and handsome his father was. And how brave was dear Aunt Etta!

Etta shuffled and held her skirts out with the best of them, despite her bent stance, and as they linked arms in the final steps, only they knew how heavily Ammiel's broad arm supported his older sister. The tambourines gave a final shimmer, the drum a final thump, the reedy piping trickled out breathlessly as the chorus ended, and the dancers stood about laughing and panting.

"You should have been dancing this with Anna," smiled Etta's lips, but her eyes said,

"Glad I am to dance one last festival with you, brother."

Ammiel answered both as he kissed her brow respectfully.

"I know, sister."

They flopped down beside Dan, whose eyes were shining with excitement. He jumped into Ammiel's lap happily and snuggled up for warmth.

"Abba, Aunt Etta – that was such fun – did you see Uncle Bukki dancing with a tree?! And did you hear Extra Pressings clapping out of time?"

Ammiel scratched Dan's head affectionately and drew a satisfied breath.

"Ah, it's good to feel heart, soul and body all shouting praise together, Dan! I'm glad Bukki was enjoying himself harmlessly – and don't you laugh at Caleb's daughter. It's good to hear her clapping at all!"

Aunt Etta reached over and smacked Dan's leg.

"And don't let her hear you call her Extra Pressings, you impudent child."

"Why, Aunt Etta, she's proud of the name!" said Dan, astonished.

"That she is!" wheezed Caleb's voice in his ear. "Proud of her saving ways, she is indeed, and glad others know it."

Aunt Etta flapped a hand before her nose as Ammiel urged Caleb to sit with them.

"You smell very strange, Caleb," she complained, and Caleb broke into satisfied chuckles, nodding and smoothing his hair self-consciously. Ammiel sniffed him experimentally and roared with laughter.

"Etta, not only has Caleb washed specially for the feast, he's anointed his hair and beard with a pomade."

Dan wrinkled his nose.

"What is it?"

Caleb stroked his beard happily.

"It's spikenard. I got it from a bazaar in Nazareth last year. It was very cheap, too."

Beautiful spikenard, with its purple flowers and dusky foliage, and sweet herbal scent? Dan had smelled it at Asa and Helen's house, and it didn't smell like Caleb.

Ammiel grinned.

"I'll wager it *was* cheap! Poor Caleb, you should have been more careful. Haven't you ever heard the saying *'Does anything good come from Gentile Nazareth?'*"

Caleb rummaged in his scrip and pulled out a little clay pot with a wax stopper.

"Here it is. Don't you like the smell?"

Etta opened it, stuck her nose in it and sneezed.

"It's gone bad, you poor silly Caleb. Can't you tell? If there was ever spikenard in this tub of lard, which I doubt, it's gone rancid long since, and there are dead beetles in it too."

Caleb looked downcast.

"I don't smell things as well as I used to."

Dan was sorry for him.

"Never mind, Caleb, I don't care about your pomade. Have you had good things to eat and drink tonight?"

"Oho yes!" Caleb cheered up, giving his stomach a loving pat. "I have indeed, and I haven't finished yet. Praise God, here am I, only an old hireling, yet feasting better than Herod himself."

Ammiel clapped him on the back.

"It's a good feast indeed, my friend," he said with a grin. "A good season too. And Caleb, you are only a hireling by circumstance, not by character. You're a good shepherd who deserves a feast – which is more than anyone would say for Herod! You care for my flock as if it was your own. May your conscience always keep your sleep sweet and your food tasty."

It was a rare moment. Caleb beamed as Etta, in silent concord, handed him the wine.

"Good friends are a blessing from the Eternal," he saluted them happily. "A blessing from the Eternal."

"Aye, Caleb," responded Ammiel frankly, "a blessing to be among friends, and men of good will. Praise God, and blessings and peace to us all."

They raised their cups and drank with contentment.

"Blessings and peace to friends and men of good will!"

The night was quietening down. The numbers of those awake were dwindling, as children and the weariest adults, or those who had drunk the most, fell asleep. Uncle Bukki was already snoring in his blanket. The shepherds took it in turns to watch the newly shorn sheep, now folded for the night, but guarded by the many fires which lit the scene with a ruddy glow. Dan lay on his back, blinking at the clear stars in the soft black sky. So many! *So shall thy seed be.* Did Abraham ever really try to count them? Dan felt dizzy at the thought of attempting it. But he was too full of stuffed dates, cheese, watered wine, bread, stew, almonds, raisins, honeyed figs … and a dozen other delicious things … he couldn't even remember all his own questions, let alone think about answers … he closed his eyes with a contented sigh … *not tonight …*

Then … a quavering hum … Caleb … humming to himself, as he often did. It was usually rather a cheerful drone. Dan's mouth twitched and he mentally began sorting through the limited number of tunes Caleb attempted … perhaps it would be *"Galilah!"* again. Caleb liked singing about beautiful and happy women, perhaps because he didn't live with one. But this tune was different, and as Caleb's humming firmed and grew clearer, Dan opened his eyes and tried to place the song.

Caleb was oddly caught up in his strange tune … he began to sing words. Dan raised himself on one elbow and looked at him. Caleb's voice had never sounded so – so – so, well, what? Clear? Tuneful? Strong? He wasn't singing loudly, it was just …

"Beautiful!" Etta whispered in astonishment to her brother. "But what is he singing?"

Ammiel shook his head and touched his lips. "Ssh …"

Caleb's eyes were shut and his head was tilted to the stars. His corded throat vibrated and his wrinkled jaw was relaxed as he sang, not the tight little quaver of his usual style, but with a younger voice which seemed to be singing from deep within him. As Dan watched, open mouthed, a tear slid from beneath Caleb's sparse eyelashes and coursed its way down his leathery cheek.

Quietly and surely the haunting melody floated out, unusual, ethereal, with words so strange and beautiful they gave Dan an odd shiver.

> *"Kabod! Kabod!*
> Glory! Glory! Glory in highest heaven!
> Glory! Glory! Glory to God most High!
> *Kabod! Kabod!*
> Glory to God in the Highest."

142

"*Shalom! Shalom!*
Peace! Peace! Peace be on earth.
Peace! Peace! Peace toward men of good will.
*Shalom! Shalom!*
Peace and goodwill for mankind."

As Caleb sang, Samuel and Ada slid out from among their sleeping children and crept over to join them. By the time Caleb's voice died away, Limping Bethany's menfolk were also crowded silently round.

Caleb opened his eyes and looked at them all, seeming confused. He dabbed his face with his sleeve and said simply,

'Hi-yi! brethren – I was very far away. I did not mean to wake anyone."

Ammiel touched his arm.

"Caleb, old friend, this was an unusual song, with great power to move you. In all the years we have been together I have never heard you sing it before – and never have I heard you sing with such a voice."

Caleb nodded.

"I thought I had forgotten it. And yet tonight my heart was opened – and your words lit the flame of memory … and I felt a great longing to sing it again …"

"But where did you learn it? And what is it about? Is it a psalm?"

Caleb looked confused again.

"Sit down, Caleb," said Etta gently. "It seems to be some mystery."

Wide awake now, Dan joined in the group around the old man.

Caleb was not used to being the centre of attention. He shut his eyes apologetically. As they waited, the tension faded from his face, and he said at last, in a whisper,

"It was such a night as this ..."

## Chapter Thirteen

WHAT was – *the night like this*? Another shearing feast? When was it? The questions were respectful but came crowding in. Caleb held his head in his hands, eyes still closed as if he feared to open them and let the images in his mind escape him forever into the night.

"It was long ago – during the first census ordered by Caesar Augustus … and what I can recall is like a campfire in the mist … dreamlike … and yet strangely the song is clear … somehow it went into my soul … and tonight, it poured out like a river of life to my old bones …"

Limping Bethany's husband shifted impatiently but Samuel held up a warning hand, and Caleb continued cautiously feeling his way through his memories.

"My friends," he said apologetically, "I was like you, then … Yes – a man in my prime – hard to believe, that you will grow old like me, but so decrees the Master of the Universe, eh? A man in my prime," he repeated the words lovingly, " – and a flock of my own, you know. Oh yes, I once had a flock of my own – not large, but it was mine, and I tended it like a Jacob. Sleep often departed from my eyes too, but there was no miraculous increasing of the flock for me, quite the opposite. But it was enough to support my family ... until ... until ..."

Caleb stopped and cleared his throat. He opened his eyes and glanced about nervously before shutting them fast again. He took a breath and said quickly,

"My daughter was very young then – and not yet surnamed Extra Pressings. Just my little Keren she was, already bossing her two brothers and scolding any waste of food."

He twisted his hands together.

"My wife and sons drowned when an old well collapsed, and I took heavily to wine." He compressed his lips and dropped his voice. "Yes. I became a drunkard."

Dan's eyes were round in horror. For the tragedy, not of death, but of life. Old Caleb, a winebibber? A shambling, mumbling, shameless drunkard? Surely not! Etta, who had been about to offer him another drink, hesitated uncertainly. Ammiel patted Caleb's shoulder encouragingly.

"You didn't make up this song while you were drunk, I am certain!" he prompted.

"No," said Caleb slowly, "only – the song – I heard it not long before that terrible day which brought such darkness into my life ... and so I cannot tell how real my memories are. You see, there are – gaps."

"What do you mean, gaps?" Dan asked anxiously.

Caleb looked guiltily at the young face which watched him with unhappy eyes.

"You have seen drunkards, little Dan. They are not a pretty sight. They walk as if tossed on the sea – and many times fall – and strike their skulls unknowingly. So it happened with me, and there are memories knocked out of my head, both good and bad. I do not remember my eldest son's face, nor yet my wife's – yet I recall my younger son as if he stands before me now, though his name escapes me." His voice faltered. "And there are horrors of those wine-sodden nights – monstrous things of vision – which I see in my dreams yet, all too clearly …"

Samuel handed Caleb the wine unflinchingly and glared at his wife's murmured objection.

"Well, you're no drunkard now, old man. So drink this, take courage, and tell us what you remember. Let us decide how real it is afterwards."

The others nodded impatiently.

Caleb swallowed obediently and continued urgently, the words tumbling forth as if long rehearsed, and waiting a long time to be said.

"It was as I said, such a night as this – I was south of Jerusalem then, with other shepherds on the slopes outside Bethlehem Judah – all of us returning to our birthplace for the census, you know. Tales were retold of boyhood, and family, and old friends, but I had no patience for such memories … for a young man dreams of his future, not the past, eh? I was thinking of my pretty wife at home with my little family … Yes, though I have forgotten her looks, I remember she *was* pretty, and thank God for that at least. Imagine that, friends – old Caleb was young Caleb then, with a pretty wife who loved him! Ah, it was a long time ago …

" And so there we were – in the temple field at night, with the sheep and lambs, the goats and the kids, to be carefully protected and nurtured for sacrifice – an honoured job for a shepherd indeed … and we sat around the fires with our shared memories and private longings … and whether I was indeed dreaming, or the thing has gone from me, I seem to remember an echo of thunder and a feeling of confusion … a noise like the fading of a distant shofar … perhaps it was but a cry from the shepherd on the watch-tower – what it was I cannot swear to, but then the memory blazes up clearly like a new-fed fire! Ah – it was then, *then!* – just on a night like any other – that the breath seemed to stop in my throat – and suddenly all around – above – beneath, and through our very bodies, the song burst upon us and drowned the darkness in light and our souls in fear …"

Caleb was trembling – Dan was hanging on every word – Ammiel was transfixed – but –

"Bethlehem Judah?" loudly broke in Ephraim, Limping Bethany's husband, with a sudden laugh of recognition. "The Census? Of course! Why, I know this one! It was doing the rounds of the lowlands for years in my father's time."

Ammiel frowned at him, but Ephraim stood up, shaking his head with amusement. The spell was broken, and Caleb looked up, painfully dazed.

"*Angels* singing, eh? That's it, isn't it? Angels of heaven singing, and heard by mortal men – not the learned and the wise or the priests of the law, but by ignorant shepherds in a field! And a baby Messiah born to young peasants, squalling among the chickens and cows!"

"Yes, yes!" answered Caleb, his mouth dry. "So it was!"

*Messiah? A baby Messiah?* Dan's mouth was already open, so he shut it and held his breath. *What does Caleb know about the Messiah – and why hasn't he told us before?!*

Ephraim patted Caleb on the back in a friendly fashion.

"You had me taken in at first, old man. You've put some very pretty music to the best legend of our trade for a long time, and improved it handsomely. What a tale! And so beautifully embroidered, too! I didn't know you had it in you! Well done."

Chuckling he drew his sons and brothers-in-law with him, and left the small circle of light. The others were silent, waiting.

Caleb looked up at last. Only Ammiel, Etta, Asa and Samuel were there. And Dan.

"You see," he said humbly, "the story is not new, though I have rarely told it. It was wondered over, and talked about, and laughed at, then hated, more than a generation ago. At the last I mistrusted what had happened myself, though the song haunted me somehow. But it was just days later when my dear wife and sons were killed, and part of me died as well. I found comfort in the strong drink which dissolved painful life into mere dreams ... and my punishment is now, that the dreams are confused or forgotten. My weakness bereft me twice over – with so much of the precious past lost to me! Even today I cannot remember their names without my daughter reminding me." Caleb seemed unaware of the tears on his rough cheek, which glittered redly in the firelight. They were part of the old story, and came without bidding.

Ammiel, who remembered his own beautiful wife with clarity, put a gentle hand on the old man's thin shoulder, his eyes filling with sympathy. How dreadful to forget beauty and happiness! How dreadful to forget old joys which sweetened fresh sorrows! He could not speak.

As for Dan, he could not move, frozen with the terrible thought – *Would Abba ever forget my name?* Surely it was not possible, no matter how many blows to the head, or how much wine! But then, Ammiel would never turn to strong drink ... would he?

149

Nobody spoke. Their silence was respect.

Caleb continued almost as if to himself;

"Only that strange and glorious song remained in my head and would not leave me, not even in my worst moments. I felt – perhaps foolishly – that God was holding me with it, like a leading string. There was a terrible, shameful time when I woke to find my beloved flock mauled, my small daughter afraid, cold and hungry, and three days missing from my life." He sighed. This was one memory all too clear, and which still hurt. But there was no point in stopping now he'd come this far. He stared at his dirty feet and finished the tale.

"I gave up my wine, sold my sheep and sent little Keren to her grandmother. I came north then, cursing the drunkenness which fogged my memory. Since then I can neither fully remember, nor fully forget ..."

"You can't forget something which never happened, father," said a crisp voice, as Extra Pressings stalked up angrily. She had heard the laughing comments of Ephraim and his family as they wandered back to their own campfire. She grasped Caleb's arm firmly, jerking the forgotten wine from his hand, and pulled him to his feet.

"You've heard shepherds telling stories and singing wild songs so often on so many befuddled nights, that you believe they really happened to you! That's what happens to men who drink too much. You know I've told you not to repeat that story – it only makes you ridiculous."

Caleb looked stricken.

"I was there," he whispered to himself, shaking his head. "I have muddled it somehow, I know ... I don't remember all we did and said … but I was there … and they sang … it was glory … and beauty … such rare beauty! … it happened …"

Dan looked up and plucked desperately at his sleeve.

"I believe you, Caleb," he said breathlessly. "I want to know more …"

Extra Pressings stamped her foot and raised a warning finger.

"Don't you dare encourage him!" she snapped. "Do you think I want him in his second childhood ahead of time?"

She hustled him off.

The adults looked at each other, and Samuel whistled.

"I'd forgotten the story myself," he confessed. "The shepherds in the field, the angels singing. Of course, some peculiar tales went around about all sorts of things, during the Census. Folk from all over the empire, cramming back into their home towns, bragging or slinking according to how life had treated them – and there was a lot of gossiping, reshaping ancient scandals and folk lore, swapping stories …"

"What about the Messiah?" begged Dan.

Samuel scratched his neck apologetically.

"The story goes that angels told the shepherds that Messiah had been born in a stable, and the men found the babe as they were told …"

"They *saw* him?" squeaked Dan. "They actually saw the Messiah? What then?"

Samuel shrugged.

"They saw a newborn baby, anyway."

"So it was said," corrected Ada. "but *they're* not hard to find. Not even in a stable. The towns were overflowing during the Census and more than one babe was born in the very street. And a newborn wouldn't have much to say for itself, would it?"

Samuel shook his head.

"Not much to brag about after singing angels, hey? But who knows? Maybe they'd all been drinking too long, maybe Caleb was already a drunkard, his poor head confused even before the angel of death struck his family. Who can say?"

Ada looked after Extra Pressings with dislike.

"No need to shame the old man before his friends," she said crossly, before she and Samuel returned to their fire.

Etta had been silent a long time but now she unfolded her arms and said, "Well?"

Ammiel stared into the fire in consternation.

"Do you know, Etta, I had never heard that old legend? Though of course there were other Messiah rumours not long after …"

Etta glared at him. Ammiel gave her a reassuring nod and continued without a break, "But then I've never been that far south. I wonder Caleb has never spoken of it before. We have often talked about the Messiah … and he never once said a thing about angels in a field …"

Etta looked grim. "Hardly surprising, is it? Extra Pressings bites his head off, and others laugh at him. And Messiah rumours are not always – well received …"

It was Ammiel's turn to glare at her. She finished unperturbed, "And he said himself, it's a long time ago and his own memory is

152

unreliable. I'd say he has done his best to forget the whole thing, whatever did or didn't happen."

Ammiel looked distressed.

"He said tonight his heart was opened, and my words reminded him … and now he has been made unhappy because of it … it's not right."

He looked at Dan, who was hugging his knees fiercely.

"Dan, you said you believed him. That was very kind and brave of you."

Dan looked up into his father's puzzled eyes.

"No it wasn't," he said stubbornly. "I do believe him. He wasn't lying."

Ammiel put his arm around Dan's slim shoulders reassuringly.

"No, no, my Dan, nobody really thinks he was exactly lying. But even Caleb said he was not quite clear about what happened, so how can you believe him?"

Dan leant forward and poked the fire suddenly. Sparks flew up and winked out of sight.

He looked at his father stoutly.

"Caleb can shout *Mayim!* in the water song chorus. He can croak out *Galilah!* and a few other songs, when he doesn't forget the words. And he can keep time. But, father, even Uncle Bukki can sing better than him!"

Ammiel stared. His arm slid forgotten from his son's shoulders, as in something like awe he finished Dan's thought aloud …

" … yet tonight we heard him sing like a priest, and saw him weep for the beauty of it!"

There was silence as the three of them searched each other's faces.

Etta bit her lip.

"Oh, Ammiel!" she breathed. "When and how could the old man ever learn such a thing! ... could it really be from the lips of angels?"

Ammiel scrubbed his ragged beard unthinkingly, muttering almost to himself.

"If this is so, if this was true! Can it be? – that the truth has been lying naked before our generation and we have been too blind to see it! Too deaf to hear? Thousands of years – the waiting – the praying – the promises – now?"

"It has to be *'now'* some time!" urged Dan. "Why *not* now? Whenever it happens it will be a 'now' for *someone*. Why not us?"

"But – but who could expect a peasant Messiah, and an infant at that?"

"A babe! A babe!" Etta was trying to think it out.

"Of what use a *babe*?" Ammiel shook his head in agitation. "And a *peasant*? He is to be royalty! A Prince – a King!"

Dan was beside himself with frustration. This time he would keep asking!

"Who is Messiah supposed to be, father?" he cried. "A man like you? Or Abraham? Or King David?"

"Oof – a lot better than me! Like King David, I have no doubt," said Ammiel affectionately.

"King David – the shepherd king? Isn't a shepherd a *peasant*?"

Ammiel blinked, and half laughed, then stopped.

Dan ploughed on. He was going to get answers this time!

"*What* is Messiah supposed to be, father?" he demanded again. "Is he really supposed to be a man? A man like you? A man like Moses?"

"Aye, son – a *man*, like Moses! – with strength and power! A man like Moses to save his people, to redeem the land, to give us back the Kingdom of God ..."

Dan sucked in a huge breath and jumped to his feet, his eyes glowing.

"A man like Moses? What! Like *Baby* Moses in the Bulrushes?"

He snatched up a stick and gave the fire a savage whack. And another. And yet another. Hardly able to stop – beating sparks from the coals – he thrashed out his exultant words –

"*How – else – can – a man – come – unless – He – is born – somehow – somewhere – to someone – first?*"

"Hush, Dan! Hush!" cautioned Aunt Etta automatically, though the back of her neck was prickling.

"Hush?" Ammiel dragged the boy down and smothered him in a half-angry embrace. Hasty tears sprang to his eyes. "Oh Etta, he should shout it to the world! Of course a man has to be a baby before he can be a man. Of course he does! Of course! What did we think we were waiting for?"

"We are still waiting!" Etta reminded him shakily. "Who has heard of him since? And what has he been doing all this time?"

Dan struggled free from Ammiel's smothering grip, and spat out two stray curly whiskers impatiently.

"Maybe he's been doing the same as me," he offered excitedly. "Growing up."

155

"Growing up," repeated Ammiel flatly. "Somehow I never thought he would need to grow up. Why didn't I? Or that he wouldn't be the Messiah *until* he was … But what does it mean?"

Etta shivered. Ammiel put his arm around her.

"You mustn't get cold, Etta, it's bad for your back." He pulled a blanket up around her tenderly as if she was no bigger than Dan, instead of a stout old woman.

"What does it mean?" she murmured, snuggling the harsh wool gratefully around her neck. "Perhaps something obvious. We've missed the obvious all along, after all …"

Ammiel threw another blanket around Dan.

"The trouble with the obvious is that it's never obvious," he muttered.

Dan gripped his arm and shook it, feeling light-headed.

"Isn't it exciting that our very own Old Caleb saw angels! I want to know what they looked like! And he actually saw the Messiah! Before anybody else in the whole world!"

Ammiel scratched his head.

"That's the part which beats me! A common shepherd like myself …"

Etta trod on an escaped ember which was trying to start its own little campfire beside her foot. She rubbed it out absently.

"For shame, Ammiel! After Dan's reminded us of where King David came from, you call yourself common? And are you the only shepherd ever to pray Show us thy Messiah? Perhaps Caleb did once too – and what are prayers for if not to be answered?"

Ammiel looked at her admiringly.

"Etta, that speech was worthy of my Anna."

"Oho – *my* Anna, now, is it?" Etta said under her breath, knowingly.

Ammiel heard, but ignored it. He was still wrestling with the whole matter.

"Well let me think ... shepherds in a field ... that's normal enough ... then angels tell them Messiah has come ... so strange and wonderful! ... yet still a baby ... has to grow up ... first ... but a generation later, we have still heard nothing ..."

"This boy is not hampered by adult notions," said Etta slowly. "He has already led us so far by his questions ... ask another question, Dan."

Dan tucked his feet inside the blanket and tried to calm himself enough to think. What with the feasting, the singing, the dancing, the angelic song, Caleb's history, and the bursting glory of this new knowledge – it was almost too much! So many nights and days he had crept like a snail towards understanding ... and suddenly there were too many answers all at once ... and too many new questions along with them. He breathed in, as Ammiel breathed in before praying. *Please, God of Abraham, help me ask the right questions!* He breathed out slowly, wondering with a far-back part of his mind, at the oddity of asking God for the questions, instead of answers. But – if it led to the truth – perhaps it didn't matter which came first.

"Do you have any more to say about this, my Dan, my little Daniel?" Ammiel asked him gently.

Dan nodded. It had taken some sorting out, but here it was.

"Father, don't you remember when we were building the new rooms? Anna asked you about that prayer 'show us thy Messiah'

157

… and you said, you were afraid you might not know him when he came. You said *'Will he come with trumpets? Or as my shepherd king David – hunted in the mountains gathering the outcasts of Israel, until his time came to take the crown?'"*

Etta and Ammiel exchanged startled looks.

"You *said* that," persisted Dan. "So doesn't that mean you *didn't know* how he would come? *Will he come with trumpets … or as my shepherd king David …*"

Ammiel gnawed his fist.

"I did say that, Dan. I did. But, God forgive me, it was half conceit – I was thinking of the words, the ideas, not of the reality."

Dan wriggled impatiently. Etta grasped her brother's arm suddenly and spoke rapidly, leaning forward in the fading firelight, and her face so eager that she looked almost young again.

"Out of the mouths of babes! I see what Dan means – it answers your question! What is the manner of his coming? … What if it's neither with trumpets nor as a fugitive …? But *announced ahead of time* while still a mewling babe! … To warn us that the time is at hand … to warn us – to prepare for the coming! What of *that*, my clever brother?"

Ammiel drew in his breath.

"Aye, Etta, I see your point! I have always thought he would burst upon us – like Caleb's angels – I never expected *them* as heralds, to be sure, unless to show Messiah in glory with an unbared arm to deliver Israel! And yet I still didn't expect him to come in my lifetime – I thought I did. But I see now I didn't. Does that make sense?"

Dan sighed. It didn't. Not to him. He changed tack.

"If they really saw the Messiah when he was just born – how old is he now?"

"Well, I don't know – the year of the census …" Ammiel snatched up a stick and scratched some numbers on the ground, muttering to himself, but Etta was there first.

"Almost twenty nine," she murmured, smiling inwardly to see Ammiel's laborious calculations. Imagine trying to keep up with old Zaccheus and his ilk at the bazaar if she had to do it that way!

Ammiel finished his sum and nodded, snapping his stick distractedly into pieces.

"So, *if* the baby the shepherds saw *was* the Messiah, and *if* nothing has happened to him, then – "

Dan clutched his slipping blanket in dismay.

"Happened to him! Nothing can have happened to him, father!" he protested, "not with angels and promises and things all waiting!"

"The faith of a child!" Ammiel berated himself, dropping his broken sticks on the fire. "Of course nothing can have happened to him – and nothing will! But listen to how we talk – as if it's all true beyond a doubt!"

"How can it be only half true?" Etta wrapped her blanket tighter. "It's true or not."

"Ammiel?" a gravelly voice hailed him quietly from the shadows, and they all jumped. It was Ammiel's turn to watch the flock. He nodded, and turned to Dan.

"Tomorrow we get Caleb away from his daughter, and hear all he has to say, muddled or not! And you must take word from me to Anna as soon as possible! She must know all of this, and have something to say about it. She has a clear mind, and an education. I am impatient to hear what she thinks!"

Dan nodded.

"You do believe it's true, don't you, father?"

Ammiel picked up his sling and blankets, tossing them over his shoulder.

He kicked the coals of the fire back into place.

"Watch this fire, Dan – you could have set the hills alight earlier ..."

"Father?"

Ammiel relented. He bent down to hug Dan fiercely and said in a low tone,

"My son! I want to believe it more than anything! That's all I can truthfully tell you."

"And if it's true, father," Dan insisted, almost choking with excitement, "where is he now? And *who is he*?"

# Chapter Fourteen

DAN was sure he would be awake all night with questions buzzing around his head like wasps, but he sank quickly into a dreamless sleep, and woke so suddenly just before dawn, that he felt the night had passed in a mere blink. Even Aunt Etta was still sleeping, and Ammiel had not finished his night watch. The hillside looked grey and dreary in the early light, as if the colour and life of the night before, like flames, had faded to ashes. But Dan's thoughts were as clear as the crisp morning air. He rubbed the sleep out of his eyes and scrambled out of his blankets with one purpose in mind – to find Caleb.

He picked his way past sleeping families, and exhausted fires. Asleep, everyone looked the same. *Perhaps it would feel like this, to be the first person on resurrection day!* It was a thought which lifted the hair on Dan's neck. A baby woke with a hungry squawk and made him jump. Its sleepy mother gathered the infant into her robe with one practised movement. Dan grinned as the wail choked off into a satisfied snuffling. Babies, lambs, they were all the same. *All bleat and belly!* Aunt Etta would say. He hoped nobody else had heard. It suited him better to have everyone asleep.

Dan's heart gave a thump of relief. There was Caleb – awake and shambling off to a clump of broom bushes. No Extra Pressings in sight! Dan ran lightly to join the old man.

"You're up already!" Dan whispered as Caleb glanced over his shoulder.

"Aye." Caleb spoke grumpily. "Old men and babes wake early."

"I had to find you, Caleb," Dan persisted, timidly. "I need to know things."

At last Caleb sighed and turned around with weary eyes.

"All these years I held my peace – I should have held it longer."

"No!" protested Dan. "Father thinks if it's true we should shout it to the world!"

Caleb's eyes flickered.

"Does he now?" He looked about him cautiously. "My daughter sleeps heavy, but she will wake soon, and I care not to have the edge of her tongue again." He paused, shame-faced. "She means well ..."

Dan, who had been agog at the disrespect Extra Pressings showed her father, answered carefully, "She doesn't want you to be laughed at."

"That's right," Caleb nodded. "Very proper feeling for a daughter, eh? But if you have questions, ask them quickly where we won't be disturbed."

He took Dan's small paw in his knuckly hand and trotted further away from the sleepers on the hill down to the pile of rocks by the brook, which had formed the dam only a day before. The two of them knelt and drank the cold, dark sweet water which slipped silently past. Rubbing their wet hands over their faces,

162

they huddled behind the rocks just as the sun shimmered above the horizon and tinted them with delicate colour. The dawn pipings and twitterings of waking birds had begun already, and soon the hillside would begin to stir with wild life underfoot and busy insects about them, and the shepherd community would be bustling again.

Dan wasted no time.

"What did they look like?"

Caleb hugged his knees and rocked himself a little. No use pretending he didn't know what the boy meant.

"I am remembering what *I believe* I remember, you know," he said cautiously.

Dan nodded impatiently.

"And of course, it was night, and our eyes used to the darkness. When you stare at a fire in the dark you see nothing for a while but a green flame blinking ... So it was – I was dazzled by the sudden brightness, and the singing dazed me more – it was like nothing I'd ever heard – so rich and sweet and pure ... and ..." he spread his arms in a billowing movement "... and *huge*!"

"But when you *could* see?!"

Caleb's voice hushed to a whisper and his eyes filled unexpectedly.

"*Light* – spun all round them like morning mist ... They were creatures of light, boy. Creatures of light, who shone like sunlight on water ! Young men ... with beauty in their faces and joy in their voices ... Aye, Dan, their very robes glowed – and there were hundreds of them! Hundreds, singing one to another and answering in exultation! At least, so I thought, until my senses began to swim ..."

"What else?!"

Caleb lifted his face and stared with unseeing eyes at the pink dawn staining the clouds.

"I was stumbling with the others towards the town ... they were in haste, half dragging me as I limped with a broken sandal ... just on the outskirts ... I hit my head hard on a low doorway ... there was warmth in the cave, the smell of animals, the smell of blood and birth, a dim rush light ... shadows ... a feeding trough hewn out of the rock wall ... and a new-salted infant bundled in it like a lump of winter barley cake."

"What did he look like?" Dan demanded breathlessly.

Caleb shook his head.

"All newborn babes are alike. Crumpled. Cross looking. Snub noses. You know."

Dan didn't. He urged, "Can you remember anything else?"

"An exhausted girl, limp in her husband's arms. Too weak to hold the child, perhaps."

"*Was* it? Was it ... ?"

"I believed it was, then. Well, we all did. We all knelt, and the girl wept to see it."

"Don't – don't you believe it any more, Caleb?" Dan asked tentatively.

Caleb sighed and buried his face in his knees.

"I don't know," he answered hesitantly. "All I know is, I saw the angels and their song entered my soul. I believe that, all right. Peace to men! Glory to God! Ah – what a thing to believe in, eh? Then somehow I was worshipping a baby in a hovel, with an idea in my muddled head about the Messiah. What happened next is

– not there any more. Someone once told me we spread the story to all who would hear … all who bought our lambs at the Temple … perhaps we did … I suppose we did … but it has long since been blotted out for me … they say we told folk that just before the chorus of angels a single angel had actually spoken to us – saying we would find the Messiah newly born in the Bethlehem stable."

"Do *you* remember that?"

"No, only the song of peace and glory. And a crowded cave."

Dan sighed.

"Can't you remember anything else, really?" he begged.

Caleb scratched his balding head and inspected his dirty fingernail thoughtfully.

"The babe sneezed," he offered at last. "Yes, that's right. It sneezed!"

He chuckled at finding this long lost fragment in his mind and dusted it off delightedly. "Yes," he repeated. "Sneezed. *Tchi!* Just that."

Dan tried one more time.

"Who were the parents, Caleb?" Caleb looked glum.

"I don't know." Then he looked at Dan speculatively … "But I do know this – the town was Bethlehem in Judea. Bethlehem Ephratah – eh? Where I was born. Where everyone else there was too, for that matter, being the Census and all. Where this child was born. And – where *King David* was born – now, what do you think of that?"

"I'll tell you what I think of it!" hissed a voice behind them. "I'll tell you!"

Dan and Caleb looked up, startled. They hadn't heard her glide up behind them, but she was there, with sallow face and biting her lips till the blood came. She thrust her writhing face into theirs, grinding the words out through a ghastly bitter smile.

"I'll tell you that because of your drunken tales, rumours flocked together and roamed the land seeking what they might devour! Rumours of David's descendant! Rumours of Messiah's advent! Rumours of Israel's King! Rumours – speculation – evil, careless talk which made the countryside hum – loud enough to be heard in the palace!"

Dan and Caleb quaked, staring at the apparition before them. She tore her hair and spat,

"Heard by Herod, no less! Heard by the king so suspicious of plots he would murder his own wife, his own sons, to stay on the throne!"

Her voice cracked, and she stamped her foot impatiently. "How did such a man deal with such rumours, eh? *How?*"

She snatched Dan up by his hair and shook him. Dan, petrified, cried out and clutched his painful head, casting a mute appeal to Caleb for help, but the old man sat mesmerised, his mouth quivering. The woman put her panting lips close to Dan's ear and whispered hotly,

"Does your mother love you, boy? Are you her *dodi*, her darling, her only one? Would she die for you?"

"My mother's dead!" Dan gasped, trembling, eyes wide in terror.

With a wail she dropped him and let her arms hang loose.

"Dead! Aye – dead!" she whispered brokenly, her eyes dark and glittering. "So were they all! Every one loved and the darling of its mother! Little ones slapping happily at the breast, bonny boys

chewing their fists, stumbling toddlers laughing to be chased …
but it was no game! The children spitted on swords and the breasts
running with blood … blood!"

Tears ran freely from her eyes, but she did not sob. The silence
with such tears was unnerving. Caleb swallowed painfully.

"The slaughter," he acknowledged reluctantly, his voice a mere
croak. "What a time for my own miserable life to begin again …
The slaughter of the babes …"

"And mothers," the woman said huskily, slowly pulling off her
veil. "And the mothers who took the blade first … and the fathers
and sons who fought for their lives and their names to continue
in Israel …"

Her hair was filled with earth. Dan felt his tongue stick to his
teeth and his heart was racing.

"It was not – our – my – doing!" stammered the old man. "That
was later – there were foreign men – signs in the sky – men of
learning – from the east – they came to Herod –"

The woman laid her veil on the ground and carefully scooped
earth into it, breaking into dreary weeping at last.

"He would have dismissed them!" she sobbed, patting the dirt
into shape. "Surely he would have dismissed the ramblings of
Gentile seers! But he had already fretted and fed on your lies for
so many seasons! And all Jerusalem rife with speculation – talking
of a Messiah – a new king of Israel – with true royal blood … to
half-breed Herod of all people! To murderous, suspicious, evil
Herod …" Her voice died away, exhausted.

Caleb scrambled to his feet cautiously, pulling Dan with him, and
began to inch away. Kneeling, the woman wrapped the earth shape

tightly in the cloth and lifted it tenderly, cradling it in her arms, singing a quavering lullaby through her tears. Her sleeve fell back, revealing long ugly scars. She seemed to have forgotten them. But Dan's nerveless feet tripped and the woman looked up sharply. Caleb's trembling arm tightened round the lad's shoulders and Dan felt as if he would never breathe again.

"You never asked my name!" she accused them angrily.

"Pardon us, lady," said Caleb humbly. "Who are you, and what is your name?"

The woman sank back to the ground and broke into fresh sobs.

"I am all mothers, all grandmothers! I am all sisters and all daughters! I am Rachel!"

She unwrapped the veil and laid her cheek on the earth within it, crying horribly with huge gasping sobs. The dirt spilled out from the cloth in her hands, and as it fell she shrieked in agony and pounded her fists on the ground.

"Run on, Dan lad," said Caleb unhappily as they stumbled off as fast as they could.

Dan felt tears spring to his own eyes.

"I can't," he gasped, "My legs won't work!"

Suddenly his knees trembled so badly he crumpled to the stony ground. Caleb patted him awkwardly on the head.

"It's all right, boy," he encouraged him. "Here's your father coming …"

Dan looked up with wet lashes, which he scrubbed at hastily with his sleeve. Not only Ammiel but half a dozen others had been roused by the screams and commotion and were running towards them. Ammiel reached them first and swept them aside from the knot of people as it straggled past them. The woman on the ground sprang to her feet with a bitter cry and took to her heels, wild hair streaming behind her, crumbs of earth flying from the snatched veil. Swiftly she disappeared. The hubbub of surprised voices was left behind as Ammiel carried Dan in one arm, with the other around Caleb's shoulders.

"A crazed woman!" Caleb said, shaking himself like a dog out of water. "I don't know where she sprang from! But she heard us talking about the Bethlehem angels, and it set her in a sudden fury."

"About the angels?" Ammiel asked, surprised.

"Aye," answered Caleb in a low tone. "She claims such tales prompted Herod's terrible purge. Ah – I should have held my tongue! She must have suffered greatly, and the memories haunt her. She is quite gone – snarled and spat and nearly tore poor Dan's hair out of his head." He hung his head in defeat. "That story brings me grief every time it's told. I will not tell it again."

He looked nervously around for his daughter, but Extra Pressings had been kneading her dough when the cries were heard, and she wasn't leaving it for Samuel's dogs to bolt behind her back. She'd hear all about it in time. And what's more, there was no sense leaving three half baked cakes to burn in the fire and waste good barley meal, just to go chasing sensation. She looked at Caleb almost approvingly when she found he had brought the story to her first-hand before anybody else. And the cakes just nicely cooked to go with it. A satisfying economy of time and trouble, and no waste of food either. Caleb looked at her with relief. Give him a scold rather than a crazy woman any day. At least she was predictable.

"I'm all right now, father," said Dan, wriggling, but Ammiel carried his son all the way back to Etta, holding him more closely than he needed to.

"The lad's had a shock," he told her soberly, and Dan found himself rolled in a blanket and leaning back in his father's arms being fed hot wine-and-water sweetened with honey. The warmth stole through his stomach and finally reached his cold feet and hands and by the time Ammiel had sketched the tale, Dan had stopped trembling and piped up with the more graphic details Caleb had left unsaid.

Ammiel chided him for hounding the old shepherd so early.

"You should have waited till I could hear him too," he said, "and perhaps you would not have been accosted by wandering madwomen."

Aunt Etta gave him a barley cake and handful of dates.

"Eat this, boy, and try to forget about that poor woman Rachel. I have not heard of her before, but I doubt she would have harmed you more than pulling your hair."

She paused, wondering if she should say more. *Hi-yi! The boy can't be sheltered forever from the world's misery.* With a glance at her brother, she went on matter-of-factly,

"Poor Marah All-Alone is also stormy and anguished by turns but it quickly passes." *Yet another one crazed over babies!* she thought wonderingly. Still, perhaps it was to be expected among women, and this woman had reason enough, poor creature. One's secret despairs could become overwhelming. *Aye – let it be a lesson to you, Etta!* she warned herself. She went on, more gently,

"There are many such folk troubled by passionate spirits in this world, Dan. It's a sad affliction, and frightening if you've not seen much of it. It must have been a nasty moment for poor old Caleb too, though of course he's tough as old Hanoch's chickens."

Dan put down his food untouched.

"Caleb – and the angels! It *was* real. But the woman mixed it up with Herod and the blood of babes. I thought it was her madness talking, but Caleb knew about it too. You haven't told me anything about that."

Ammiel sighed and exchanged a look with Etta. So much for their earlier caution.

"That's one I do know," he admitted reluctantly, "and all Israel knows it, though it's not really for the ears of children. A while after the Census, learned men came to Herod the Great. They said they had read signs in the heavens that the King of the Jews had been born. You can imagine Herod wasn't very pleased – you see, Dan, he was merely of Idumean descent – not anything like real royalty, or even a pure Jew, come to that – and wildly suspicious of anybody taking his throne."

"She said that too."

Ammiel nodded.

"Herod called the scribes and asked them where the scripture says that the Messiah will be born."

"It *says* where?" cried Dan.

Ammiel looked guilty.

"Why, yes, my son. Did I never tell you that? When he found out it was Bethlehem Ephratah, he had all the babies in the whole area killed. Not just male babes, either. Even Pharoah was more merciful than that, eh? It was a black and tragic time, and he was hated more than ever."

Dan kept very still for several moments. The now familiar creeping glow of knowledge and surety which had been stealing over him subsided, leaving him with a sinking fear.

He looked at his father with wide eyes.

"Then even if Caleb has forgotten bits, his story is quite, quite true! The Messiah was born in Bethlehem Ephratah. The scripture said he *would* be. The angels said he *was*. The shepherds *saw* him. The clever men saw the *signs* in the sky … King Herod *believed* it – and *killed* him …"

He clutched Ammiel's rough coat accusingly.

"You said nothing could happen to him! Oh, father – what if the Messiah has been killed!"

Dan was tearful in good earnest now. The long night, the early morning, the thrill of Caleb's story, the savage unpredictability of the woman Rachel – and now a tragic ending?

Ammiel folded Dan to his chest, smothering him with auburn beard, and shook him to and fro. Etta watched him thoughtfully. The man was getting softer in his old age. *Or was it just that his heart is opening wider with resurrected thoughts of Anna?*

"Oh you poor silly Dan! Where's my wise old Daniel now, eh? How could our Messiah be killed! All the waiting and watching, as you said yourself? For nothing? Is God good or not? Would He permit that?"

"Messiah has his work to do, Dan," said Aunt Etta firmly, tossing a handful of dates into his lap. "Delivering Israel! Giving us our King at last! And I should think, if there's any killing to be done, he'll be doing it to someone else, not any wicked old Herod killing him, child or no. Now you eat and cheer up."

172

"What about our King David, Dan?" laughed Ammiel, smacking Dan's knees for emphasis. "Don't forget all the stories you know about him! How many times was he trapped? How many times did he nearly get killed?"

Dan sniffed and pushed away the tickling whiskers around his face with his fingers.

"Lots," he answered reluctantly, combing his fingers through the wiry hair.

"Who saved him? And stop tidying up my beard."

"God, of course." Dan inhaled the rich toasty smell of beard and gave it a final tweak.

"Well, you foolish Daniel you – which is a contradiction – if God kept rescuing a grown man because he was anointed to be King … sit up, you great nuisance … how much more is he going to rescue a helpless child who is anointed to be the most special King ever?

Dan sat up and began to nibble his dates cautiously.

"That's a good thought," he admitted. He stopped. "But …"

"What else?" Ammiel asked, rolling his eyes at Etta.

"*Was* it Caleb and his friends' fault – Herod killing children?"

"No," answered Etta and Ammiel together firmly.

"If angels told them about the Messiah," said Etta briskly, "then you can be sure God meant people to be told. Killing innocent children through fear and spite – that's on Herod's wicked old head alone. Well, he's dead now and if anyone tells me he's in Abraham's bosom it's more than *I* can stomach. Now, Dan, Sabbath tonight and much to be done. Time to put your questions in your pouch and pay attention to your father."

173

Ammiel bundled Dan out of his lap and refused to listen to any more.

"I know, I know! – we don't know how he escaped Herod, and we still don't know who he is, where he is, or when we will find him. But we already know a lot more than we did yesterday, and we all have our work to do. Even if Messiah steps out from behind that tree this very instant, we have to break camp and clean up – the sheep still have to be grazed and watered, bread baked and fuel gathered. So to your chores, boy and after the Sabbath you're going to Anna, as I said. Not just because I need an answer about the wedding, but the family must hear Caleb's story! Even with Helen so sick, this will lighten their eyes."

"She will be excited, won't she, father?"

"You can be sure – " began Ammiel, but Aunt Etta interrupted, peering with great interest at a stir down the hillside.

"Well, well – there's little Naami going off with her husband, panting and groaning and looking sorry for herself. He's sat her on the donkey and is carrying that heavy lump of a child himself. Wonder of wonders! And about time too. And there's her mother huffing and puffing along behind them, giving orders and looking important."

Ammiel and Dan exchanged long-suffering looks.

"Aha!" said Etta, with satisfaction as she interpreted what she saw. "That's it – she's in labour! A little early, according to her calculations. Not that she's ever been good at arithmetic, mind you. She suffers for it at the market, poor girl. It's my opinion this child is late. Anyone could have told her the head dropped a full week ago. God be merciful to her now her time's come – she's a good little mother, if over-indulgent, and deserves another son. Luckily they don't have far to go – she'll be home in less than an hour, that's a comfort. Well, I wonder if Marah All-Alone will be waiting on her doorstep, poor woman, ready to beg for the child."

Ammiel looked startled.

"Do you mean to say, Etta, that Marah already knows? That she has become some kind of unholy seer?"

Etta nodded.

"Somehow, she does. Walks miles and turns up at the right place at the right time. It gives you the chills to see it – but just seems to be one of the devils driving her."

Ammiel shivered.

"I don't understand it. I can see wolves in the dusk and lions before dawn, but this is beyond me."

The sun had scrubbed the sky clean of grey and pink and flooded it with a watery blue which was deepening moment by moment. Dan stretched himself luxuriously and then scurried with a good will to break camp. Families were moving off before the day grew hot. The men were loading the wool on donkeys and carts for market. Ammiel had already carefully weighed out the best fleeces for the *Reshith* – the first of the fleece, as the rabbis required. Ten Galilean shekels' weight was the minimum prescribed by the Mishnah and Ammiel stuck to the letter of the law. Had he been able to oversee the fleece actually getting as far as the temple, as he said apologetically each time, he would have given more. As it was, he atoned for this Pharisaism by paying the tax at both shearings.

It had been a wonderful Feast, capped with the drama of Caleb's story and mad Rachel's appearance, to make it truly memorable. What a shame Naami hadn't started her labour a day earlier –

there would have been even more excitement and celebration if a son had been born during the feast as well. Even so, here would be plenty to re-live during the long winter nights. *If only I could talk it all over with Johanan!*

Ammiel, Caleb and the flocks moved on. Etta took leave of her friends, while Dan managed to find Uncle Bukki under a rocky outcrop, where he was sleeping off a bad headache. Finally they were back home, unloading their bundles in the newly spacious house in time for the noonday rest. It felt quite strange, as if it wasn't really theirs, thought Dan, when he woke – *as if someone might come home and ask us all to leave.* Aunt Etta would not allow any spreading of their belongings from the old part of the house. She had said that the new rooms must remain empty for Anna to arrange with her own things as she wished when the time came. Dan picked up a stick and wandered through the vacant spaces, poking idly at the many tiny cobwebs which were decorating the corners. The busy spiders would have to find somewhere else to live. A chorus of geckos crouching on the beams vied with noisy swallows under the eaves to drown the chirping of the cicadas in the bush outside. A sparrow hopped through the window, cocked his head on one side and hopped off again as Dan shooed him away. These were Anna's rooms. They had better be lived in soon or they would become a menagerie! He wondered what they would look like when she had finally married his father and moved in. Anna was used to a low bed – with cushions! How would his father like that? Or perhaps Anna would be the one to change, and accustom herself to a mat on the floor like the rest of them.

How wonderful to be entrusted with telling her such important news about Caleb's story, and the birth of the Messiah – for surely it was true! Dan knew she was clever, and had read books – and Ammiel hoped she would have a lot to add to what they knew.

176

*What about Johanan! I wish I could tell him everything, but he's so far away in Jerusalem.* Dan had a sudden inspiration. *Perhaps Anna can help me write to him!* A real letter, like the one Dan was taking her from Ammiel, with Anna writing down all the things he wanted said. The next time someone from Anna's house visited her Aunt Mari, they could take the letter! Johanan could read it, and maybe answer it – then they would all be able to think about the exciting ideas together, even if apart.

Dan skipped up the ladder to the half finished booth on the roof, wishing he could somehow shout to his friend from the house top and be heard up in Jerusalem. He leaned over the parapet to get that daring fizzy feeling in his toes which came from being up so high and looking down so far … and then remembered he was supposed to be hauling in a generous supply of dried cow dung for Aunt Etta to cook with while he was gone. It was an easy job, though, and with good pastures attracting the cattle drovers of late, and the summer heat, there was plenty to be found ready-baked on the slopes outside Banayim without having to go further afield. Yes … he'd have everything else well finished by the Sabbath at sundown. Then the day after that, he'd be off to Asa and Helen's. He slid down the ladder happily enough, but then remembered something else and pulled a face.

Uncle Bukki was to be his travelling companion. And Bukki wasn't any more pleased about it than Dan was.

## Chapter Fifteen

AUNT Etta woke Dan much later than she had intended for the journey. She had struggled to the well for news and water, very early. She did not admit to having only partially filled her jar.

"Come on, boy, the sun will outrun you today," was all she said.

Dan and a frowzy, reluctant Uncle Bukki were almost ready to leave, before she spoke again.

"I'm preoccupied this morning," she apologised to Dan's puzzled face. "I'm worried about little Naami. There's still no news and it's been two days. And the Magdala midwife sent for early this morning ..."

Dan remembered.

"Did they really find Marah All-Alone on the doorstep?"

Aunt Etta eased her bulk onto a stool and put her elbows on the table.

"Not exactly," she said uncertainly. "But she was loitering on the edge of the village all day, and never once spoke. At sundown she suddenly left without a backward glance."

Aunt Etta shook herself. *What – are you a superstitious pagan now, Etta?!*

"Perhaps Marah is getting better," she said cheerfully. "Or she had another mother to chase elsewhere. Well, I will say another prayer for Naami and one for Marah too. Now, have you got that letter safe, Dan? Bukki, is the stopper tight on that jar, and did you pack that lovely bit of new fleece for Helen?"

"Stop fussing, Etta," said Uncle Bukki impatiently. "It's here all right."

Dan hugged his aunt. "Be good while we're gone!"

Aunt Etta aimed a swipe at his ear as he skipped laughing out of her reach.

"Such cheek from a puppy! I shall sit here like a great lady without you two to plague me for food and tax my patience all day. Marta's Ittai has promised to run over each day to see all's well, though I suspect it's so he can brag about his twins to a captive audience. Now go, and Godspeed. And be sure you pay my respects to all at Asa's house. Bukki?" she beckoned hastily.

"What now?" said Bukki in an exasperated voice as she drew him aside.

"Bukki, they are cultured people at Asa's," Etta murmured hopefully.

Bukki grinned, his nose hairs bristling over his moustache.

"Don't worry, Etta. I'll see that Dan behaves himself."

This was not what Etta meant, and Bukki knew it. He strode off in a good mood, with Dan waving goodbye as he followed.

From the door, Etta watched them take the west path and as she turned to go back inside, saw to her surprise Potter Ittai coming up the track from the village. His clay-smeared clothes showed

180

that he had come straight from his wheel. He was a bit beforehand with his attention, Etta thought, until she saw his face and knew, even before he finished the customary greetings.

"Marta thought you'd want to know at once," he began heavily, but Etta didn't need any more. The tears were already flowing, her knuckles already knocking rhythmically on her chest.

"Oh, poor Naami! I feared as much! Poor little Naami! And poor Thaddeus! Alas, alas for their little one, unsalted and unswaddled! Was the poor babe a son or daughter?"

Ittai thought guiltily of the recent easy birth of lusty children to his laughing wife and how they'd triumphed over the Dabab's fears. He shook his head as his eyes filled.

"Yes, poor little Naami, indeed," he said with a catch in his voice. "But Etta, it is Thaddeus who has lost all", he said soberly.

"No! Oh, no! No!"

"And no-one will ever know whether he lost a son or daughter. The child was never born."

" Ai! Ai! Alas, my sister! Alas, my young friend!" Etta mourned. Her body drooped sadly. *So it is, so it was, so it ever will be*, she thought despairingly.

"So young!" she protested with a catch in her voice. "The poor, dear girl! Too soft with her boy, but a good mother, and never one to talk behind her hand. A good girl, kind and loving. Only two days ago we were talking at the Feast! And such a little time since we were dancing at her wedding, such a little time since we were sending gifts for the birth of her son!"

*Aye, and I said the same when Dan's mother died. How much more shocking is death in the young. And death at a time meant for new life!*

Ittai made a restless movement. He had something on his mind. He blurted out,

"Marta and I were so greatly blessed, you know, Etta! I didn't appreciate it till now. A first birth, so swift and painless and twins too – a birth in ten thousand, the midwife said – all happy and healthy, praise the Eternal! I said it then, and often, but not with such meaning as I will say it now. I will say it with all my being from now on! Praise the Eternal!"

With a full heart the young father tore to the top of the hill behind the house and it burst from him in a loud urgent shouting that startled birds from the trees and conies into the rocks.

"Praise the Eternal for His goodness! Blessed be the Master of the Universe! Thanks be for His mercy!"

He came back, panting, and a little shamefaced. Etta looked at him with silent compassion as he picked up stones and flicked them forcibly at the large rock which sheltered Etta's herb patch.

"And yet I feel – somehow, unworthy, to be thanking God at a time when another man is struggling to accept a cruel thing at His hand. It could have been me wailing and beating my breast! Instead there was I strutting around with pride, as if I had anything to do with Marta's miraculous delivery! It was enough to tempt God, yet He left me unrebuked. But now ... well, Thaddeus is a man dazed. He dares not curse God, but he is out for Marah's blood."

The stones cracked sharply against the rock, one after the other.

"Marah? But it's not her fault!" gasped Etta, moved to speech at last.

Ittai shrugged and having relieved his feelings, flung away the remaining stones and dusted his hands.

"No one can deny the woman has an evil spirit, and she was lingering about the village the day before. Thaddeus swears she put the evil eye on his wife. He thinks if she had stayed around like she did for my Marta, the mother and child would have survived."

Etta dabbed at her brimming eyes with the hem of her veil.

"What? Does this make sense?" she protested in astonishment. "Does she cast out evil at one moment, and cause it the next?"

"I don't know, Etta. None of it makes sense to me. But the man is beside himself, the little boy screams for his mother, and they wash her for burial as we speak."

*The bridal, the birth and the death! Oh, the bridal, the birth and the death!* The words keened in Etta's head. Yes, it was life. Yes, death was part of life just as much as birth. *Obviously! But what comfort is that when you meet it? Or when fear lurks in your heart?* Oh, what was in store for dear Ammiel and Anna? *When her turn comes, she won't even have youth on her side,* thought Etta numbly. Not that youth had helped Naami. *Poor child! Poor girl!*

Etta struggled to her feet.

"If you can walk slowly, I will go back with you."

"That's good, Etta," said Ittai approvingly. No wonder Marta enjoyed her friendship. She might be just an ancient virgin of no great reputation, but you could talk to old Etta properly, and you didn't have to say everything twice. Why, it was as good as talking to a man.

"Marta can cry on your shoulder while I get back to my clay and you can prepare funeral food together. Thaddeus will be glad of your respect for his wife, and another voice among the mourners shares the load of sadness in a small village. There won't be time to gather many from round about before the burial. It will be just before sundown tonight."

Etta understood. After all, it was the height of summer.

"Stay the night with us, Etta, and I'll carry your water back here for you in the morning."

He picked up the carrying jar, noting with surprise that it was only half full. He looked at her shrewdly.

"It will be a full jar, too."

He tipped it into the main pot and swung it by the handle while Etta bundled up the bread she had baked that morning. No point leaving it or tomorrow it would have to be soaked. She added to it a handful of fresh dates for Marta, a bag of lentils for the funeral meats, and her cloak. Summer or not, any night could turn cold, and her bones ached so quickly with it. Her back turned, Etta struggled to balance the shame of the young man knowing her weakness, against the relief of his help. She faced him again, with a wry smile.

"You're a good man, Ittai."

And so Etta left the house on the young potter's arm, and the rooms were emptier than ever.

Uncle Bukki remained in surprisingly good humour for a long while after his parting comment to Etta. Every now and then he would remember it and laugh again. Soon he began to whistle as he stumped along. It was a widely sung tune, known almost everywhere as a very rude drinking song, but Dan wouldn't know the words, and the tune was good to tramp to.

"Uncle Bukki?"

184

"H'mph?"

"Uncle Bukki, will you teach me to whistle?"

Uncle Bukki looked down in astonishment. He couldn't remember Dan ever asking him to teach him anything before. He never considered that it was perhaps because he had nothing worthwhile to teach him.

"Why?" he asked.

"Oh, it sounds so good, and it looks so easy! But I can never get it right. It would be fun. And I could show Johanan when I next see him."

Uncle Bukki plumed himself a little.

"It's not everyone can do it," he said knowingly. "You have to have the right knack."

"Tell me, please."

"Well, there are several methods," said Uncle Bukki importantly. "You can whistle through your teeth or through your lips. Show me your teeth."

Dan obediently bared his teeth. His uncle peered at the gaps calculatingly and shook his head doubtfully. He must be seen to have special knowledge, even if he had to make it up.

"I don't think you can do it through your teeth until they've grown properly. Why they're only halfway down!"

Dan immediately felt ashamed of his half grown teeth, but persisted, "What about the other way? My lips are all right, aren't they?"

Bukki frowned at them.

"They're pretty *wide*," he said grudgingly, "But I suppose they'll do."

185

Dan grinned, pleased.

"I've got the lips all right. So what do I do next?"

Bukki considered. How on earth did you whistle? He just did it without thinking. He frowned as he whistled, trying to work it out.

"Watch me … and copy."

Dan pursed his lips and blew. Just air. It was like the time he was being a fish underwater in the sea. Blowing bubbles. He blew until he was dizzy. At last –

"No good," Bukki shook his head. "You can't just blow like blowing out a lamp."

He whistled a bit more, as Dan scrutinised him so closely that he tripped over a rock.

"Sort of a kissing face, only tighter?" he suggested, and tried again. The resultant noise had no polite name. Bukki roared with delight and Dan laughed so much he had no hope of pursing his lips again for quite a while. Finally he calmed down enough to attempt it once more, vocalising in his eagerness.

"Stop that silly 'oo-oo' noise! Use less breath," instructed Uncle Bukki sternly. "You only need a bit."

Dan tried again. And again. And – "I did it!" he yelled, capering about. "Listen!"

Another thin weedy note trickled out of his lips.

"H'mph!" said Uncle Bukki, unsure whether he should be proud of his teaching methods, or resentful that Dan had got it so quickly. Dan solved the problem for him.

"Thank you, Uncle Bukki! Now I can whistle! Thank you!"

Bukki bridled a little with pleasure. He must be a good teacher. He set about informing Dan how to strengthen the notes and make a tune. Meanwhile Dan experimented for himself with scant attention to Uncle Bukki's advice, and so got along very well.

The unexpected discovery of a mutual interest made the weary walk far less unpleasant than either of them had anticipated. Uncle Bukki's shambling gait was not graceful, but covered a surprising amount of ground, and the day did not drag as Dan had feared. Bukki was quite cheerful all morning, and only subsided to his usual moroseness after their very welcome midday sleep. He was never his best when first woken. This Dan was used to, and did not mind. The journey was long, hot and hilly, but not as far as the distance Dan had walked with his father from the sheep grazing grounds so many weeks before. It was yet light as they descended from the fresh, gusty chalk ridges into the humid valley, still faintly green as summer's end drew near, and where the glaring white and brown roofs of Cana spread like a crop of mushrooms in a field. They had made good time, to the surprise of them both, and there was yet an hour till sunset.

Dan had been practising so assiduously during the day that his nose felt funny, and his lips and cheeks were aching, but he was determined to have the skill to show Anna – so by the time they rounded Blind Corner and came upon Asa and Helen's house, the boy was whistling jauntily. Alas, it was still Uncle Bukki's drinking song, but Dan only knew it was great fun and he'd got it right at last. With the journey's end, and good food and rest within reach, Uncle Bukki mellowed enough to be humming along, though he had sense enough not to sing the words, and Dan felt very clever to be forming such a musical accompaniment. So proud of his accomplishment was he, that he would not let Bukki knock until they had finished their verse, and he began another even as

187

Bukki's hairy knuckles hammered the door. The little servant girl Rhoda unlatched the gate, recognising Dan with a shy giggle, and ushered them into the courtyard beyond while she went to fetch her mistress.

A tall sun-darkened man with waving black hair and a very straight nose, his jaws clean shaven like a soldier, was sitting under a tree, mixing coloured pigments on a wooden tray, and scowling at the results. He looked up and scowled even more. Dan stared at his bare face curiously, and his joyous whistling died away. Bukki scraped his manners together with an effort and introduced himself, with most of the proper salutations, to the stranger.

"So you're Bukki, are you?" the tall man answered without enthusiasm, wiping paint from a small flat stick and rubbing it with a rag. "And I suppose this is Dan?"

Dan nodded apprehensively. Who was this beardless man who knew his name?

"Where did you learn that tune, boy?"

Dan pointed mutely to Uncle Bukki, who shuffled his feet anxiously.

"Do you happen to know the words?" The dark eyebrows were raised enquiringly.

Dan shook his head. The owner of the eyebrows turned his penetrating gaze on Bukki.

"Just as well – for both of you," he said drily. "I would find a new song if I were you, boy, and quickly. Maybe even before you find your voice."

Dan gulped nervously, but Bukki coughed angrily and was about to retort, when an amused voice called to the tall man, "Loukanos, are you being impolite to visitors again?" and the equally tall Anna appeared through a doorway, silver coins on her forehead winking in the light. Dan looked at her gratefully as she held out her hands to him.

"Dan – my dear child, what a surprise! How good to see you! And Bukki! Shalom, and welcome to our home! Blessings and peace! I hope I find you well." She looked about expectantly. "No Ammiel?" Quickly she added, "Is he well? And Etta?"

"Shalom, Anna," said Bukki gruffly, rather relieved. She should see he had manners too, even if this odd fellow in her courtyard didn't. "Thank you, I am well, and so is Dan." He cleared his throat. "Etta is well also," he proceeded laboriously without seeing her tension, "and so is Ammiel ... Er, Praise God," he added dutifully, and felt he had excelled himself.

Anna relaxed and smiled at them, but her face was pale and weary.

"Come in and wash your feet – you must be very tired after your long journey. Tired and hungry. Father will be honoured you have come so far to visit. You will forgive us being quiet and simple in our entertainment, I know. The doctor has decreed that mother must have peace while she is so ill."

She caught Bukki's faint expression of concern as he was reminded of Helen's illness.

"It is not contagious," she said gently.

"What, am I invisible?" said the shaven man irritably. He made a fierce dab with a small brush at a parchment weighted with stones which lay at his feet. Dan was intrigued to see he was creating a picture. A picture! A dozen puzzles crowded to his mind, starting with "Thou shalt not produce any likeness ..."

Anna suppressed a smile and beckoned him forward.

"I beg your pardon – I thought you had already introduced yourself before I came out." She put a hand on Dan's shoulder and gestured to Bukki politely.

"Bukki, this is Loukanos the Greek, a painter, of Philippi."

She looked down at Dan with her steady gaze. Dan looked right back at her extraordinary eyes. Yes, they were as odd as he remembered them. One hazel, one brown. She smiled at him.

"Dan, this is your future uncle – my half-brother."

## Chapter Sixteen

DAN and Bukki both revived considerably after a refreshing wash and a fine supper. Bukki thought momentarily that if this was what Anna meant by simple entertaining, then perhaps she might not be a bad addition to the household after all. Rhoda waited on them, smiling shyly at Dan, who stared rather enviously at her front teeth, which were large, white and fully down, though he was sure she couldn't be much older than he was. His tongue explored the latest tender gap in the back of his mouth and felt the four sharp tips of a double tooth just breaking the surface. He wondered whether Rhoda had all her second teeth through, and if they irritated her too as they grew. Maybe it was different for girls. Dan didn't know much about girls. When he came to think of it, he didn't know much about boys either. Except Johanan. It had been a long time since he was at school with boys his age. Though he had been quite content with his adult family for so long, for the first time Dan was conscious of a sudden pang of loneliness.

"Tired?" Anna had heard his quiet sigh.

Dan sat up straighter.

"No!" he answered quickly. He was determined not to fall asleep as he had the last time, and miss all the conversation. Besides, he had a mission to fulfil.

Asa had encouraged but little talk during the meal.

"Eat first!" he told them hospitably, waving his hand at the beautiful dishes before them. "It is only bad news that cannot wait, and anything else is the better for savouring at leisure. And I would keep things quiet in the house for the sake of my wife. The doctor has ordered it." He smiled a little to himself.

"It's only good sense," growled the gangling Loukanos, bending his sleek wavy head over a bowl of soup. Bukki watched him and thought that maybe there could be some sense having no beard to get in the way when you were really hungry. Dan watched him too, wondering why he was so surly. Why, he was as bad as Uncle Bukki! *Are all grown up brothers bad-tempered in their sisters' homes?* he asked himself, fascinated.

The meal over, they retired to the roof top, where the air was cooling quickly, bringing a welcome freshness after the hot day. Helen remained in her sickroom, but Anna told Bukki she was sure her mother would be glad to see him and Dan for a short time in the morning.

"It's when she feels the strongest," approved Asa. "Now, up here we will not disturb her rest, so tell us, Bukki, all your news."

Bukki rubbed his stomach, which was feeling rather tight and uncomfortable. It had been an interesting meal, but – a few unusual flavours. Greek herbs, perhaps? He wasn't sure about this foreign style food and hoped he wouldn't have a bad night of it.

"My brother-in-law Ammiel sends us to you with a question, and a message," Bukki began, then hesitated. He rarely had to convey formal messages, and couldn't remember which way round was the proper way to put things. Well, as long as they all got said!

"He sends you greeting, blessings and peace, and wishes you good health," Bukki plunged on, suddenly realising that should have been said first. "He regrets not being able to come in person or sending notice of our coming. He was impatient to send us even sooner, but after the Shearing Feast was the Sabbath."

"The Shearing Feast, hey?" Loukanos gave a wolf-like grin. "I know what they can be like. Is that where Dan learned your song?"

"Stop it, Loukanos," said Asa. "Well, Bukki, perhaps I can guess the question. Have you come for my decision about the wedding?"

Bukki nodded. "I have." He was relieved the formalities were over.

Asa gestured to Anna. "It is yours entirely, my daughter. Your mother and I will respect it, whatever it is. I know it will not be made lightly."

Anna's eyes softened as she reached out to squeeze her father's hand.

"You are very good to me, father. I have indeed given it much thought and prayer. Bukki, please to tell my betrothed that I am his whenever he wills. His wishes must override my own and if so, I will gladly follow them. But for myself, I believe our celebrations will be the happier for knowing my mother is *out of danger.*"

Dan's mouth drooped a little even while Bukki smirked in relief.

"A very devoted daughter," he nodded to Asa. The attractive vision of Anna's "simple" meal had long since faded in a growing stomach ache. Etta's plain fare would do him for a while yet, even if there was a bit less of it. A man of his age needed to watch his comforts and not put a strain on his system. And meanwhile, he would enjoy having a room to himself. It was all nonsense about Etta keeping the place half empty for this woman to fiddle about with! And he wished he hadn't eaten so many spice cakes.

"You do all realise," Loukanos broke in bitterly, "that mother is probably dying. That it may not be a question of her ever being out of danger."

Anna said something to him sharply in Greek, and he held up his hands depracatingly.

"I'm sorry. I apologise. Of course it is in the hand of the gods, and who can tell if they may be gracious? There seems to be little that medicine can do, that's all."

Asa looked at him with a hint of reproof.

"A very good physician once told me that in the most severe cases, a cheerful spirit and a positive outlook could work miracles. Would you not think it is just as important for those around the patient to take the same attitude?"

Loukanos rasped a thumb across his chin impatiently. The sound entranced Dan. It was the sound of Aunt Etta scaling fish.

"Physicians will tell you many such things when they are powerless. Perhaps it's to remove the failure from themselves and blame the patient."

"No, no, Loukanos," protested Anna. "It is a true saying. You know it is."

The thick eyebrows darkened.

"Maybe," he said grudgingly. "But far harder to do than to say."

194

Anna laid her hand on his arm.

"Of course it is. Of course. But the Eternal knows our fears and our sorrows. He will sustain us."

Loukanos shook her off and got to his feet.

"Oh yes, how could I forget your everlasting "Eternal" ..." he turned and smiled mirthlessly. "Did you hear that? I think I made a joke! It's good I can find something to laugh about at such a time. Oh! I'm sorry – did I offend you? Or your god? You know, the Greek gods have a much better sense of humour."

Asa shook his grey head sorrowfully.

"Ah, Loukanos, Loukanos! You are in much pain. But beware you do not hurt your mother by saying such things in her hearing."

"Me! Hurt my mother! Zeus grant me patience!"

And he made to storm downstairs. Anna leapt to her feet with surprising agility and snatched at his sleeve with another rapid torrent of Greek. He answered, and there was a swift exchange between the two of them. Finally he took a deep breath and sighed in defeat.

"Father, your pardon. I am behaving very badly, and before guests as well. It is an insult to your hospitality, and I ask forgiveness."

He sat down again, glancing at Anna as if to say, "Will that satisfy you?"

She nodded at him gratefully.

Dan had been open mouthed at this exchange. He had never seen Anna so fiery. As for Bukki, he thought of Etta's parting plea, and was very tickled to see that arguments happened even among "cultured people". That was one in the eye for Etta!

Asa waved his hand dismissively.

"It is forgotten. It is a difficult time for us all."

"And especially for you, father!" said Anna, pointedly looking at her brother.

Asa patted her hand.

"Yes, my dear, but we all love your mother very much. And don't forget – Loukanos has known her longer than any of us!" He tried a laugh, with only partial success. He passed a hand across his eyes, looked up and smiled determinedly at Dan and Bukki.

"Let us come to the rest of your business! There is a message, you said."

"Yes," Bukki could not resist a rueful shrug. "But Ammiel entrusted it to the boy."

"Dan? Tell us, then, my child," encouraged Asa.

Dan wriggled with importance, and pulled out the piece of leather which had cost Ammiel much labour to cover with writing.

"There is a letter too," he said. "From my father to Anna. But he said it must first be given to her father to read."

"Naturally," beamed Asa. He called for Rhoda, who obediently brought up a whole menorah and lit all the wicks. Dan looked at the extravagant sight with delight. Never had he seen so many lamps together, and the light was bright and clear as two full moons together. Asa ran his eye over the parchment.

"What is this? Arithmetic? *25 fleece to fuller Timna. +18 Zaccheus, +15 Nazareth Simeon … −2 Caleb …* ? Surely a riddle to tempt Samson! And so faint – it's very hard to read …"

Dan blushed.

"Father reuses his parchment all the time. He had a good ink by mistake once and that bit never washes out. The letter is underneath ..."

Everyone laughed, and even Loukanos allowed himself a small twitch at one corner of his firm mouth. Asa rolled up the letter and tapped Dan under the chin with it before handing it to Anna.

"Well, Dan, my eyes are too poor to read much by lamplight. I think Anna can read it first after all."

Anna took the letter, which had no salutation, and read it aloud.

*"The time of the first Census. Angels told shepherds that Messiah was new-born in Bethlehem. My hired man Caleb was there. He saw them and heard them. Dan knows his story. Sages from the east believed it. Herod believed it. Remember the slaughter of the babes. I think it may be true. He would be a man grown now. Has his time come? Talk to Dan. Tell me what you know. Tell me what you think. My respects to Asa. My prayers for Helen. To you – my ..."*

Anna stopped.

"My what?" Loukanos peered over her shoulder, but she rolled the sheet up smartly, and handed it back to Asa. They looked at each other wordlessly.

"Well?" Loukanos demanded. "What is this all about?"

Asa pulled the skin open and read it again, forgetting his sight was poor. In a slightly breathless voice he read the whole as if Anna had not done so first.

*"The time of the first Census. Angels told shepherds that Messiah was new-born in Bethlehem. My hired man Caleb was there. He saw them and heard them. Dan knows his story. Sages from the east believed it. Herod believed it. Remember the slaughter of the babes. I think it may be true. He would be a man grown now. Has his time*

*come? Talk to Dan. Tell me what you know. Tell me what you think ...*

"Bukki, what do you know of this?"

Bukki chewed his bottom lip rather crossly. It had been a long journey to go chasing old folk tales!

"I don't know much about it," he growled. "Old Caleb was telling his stories while I was – ah, asleep – at the shearing feast. Etta and Ammiel got very excited about it and insisted we come to tell you."

"What do you think about this?" laughed Loukanos.

Flattered to be asked, Bukki looked a little superior.

"More Messiah fever, I suppose," he said grudgingly. "It breaks out occasionally. *The time is coming! The time is near! Woe to the wicked! Joy to the faithful!* Never happens, of course – everything always goes on as it always has. I don't take much notice. But Ammiel wanted you to know about it – and he had to know about the wedding anyway, so here we are."

Asa looked at him thoughtfully.

"You don't believe it, then. You have no faith in the Messiah?"

Bukki wagged his head solemnly.

"Of course, I believe it will happen some time! I'm a Jew, aren't I? But I'm not having faith in anything till I see some proof."

"H'mm," commented Loukanos sardonically. "That's an interesting definition of faith."

Bukki shrank back a little. How could he forget the vigorous Messiah discussions during the building of the new rooms! Did he really want to go through more smart debating with this unusual family? The Greek would be an unreliable ally, too. He straightened

198

up and said solemnly,

"I have my own beliefs, and I let others have theirs. I prefer not to argue about religious matters. It only brings trouble."

"Have you ever argued about religious things, Uncle Bukki?" Dan couldn't resist asking in amazement.

Uncle Bukki looked wise. "Have I! When I was only about your age, boy, I was actually arguing in the Temple!"

Loukanos choked suddenly. "And about what?" he demanded rudely. "The price of doves?"

Bukki dropped his thick eyelids and looked suitably modest.

"Your little joke, of course. Why, about the Messiah! Yes, indeed. I was there with my parents – your grandparents, may they rest in peace, Dan. And there was a lot of Messiah talk at the time then, too … much workings out of time periods, and great excitement … and so forth … And one ancient old woman even claimed to have seen him! Senile, I suppose. Again, it came to nothing. So you see, I have heard it all before."

The vision of Uncle Bukki as a young boy arguing intelligently in the temple itself was almost too much to grasp.

"With whom were you arguing?" Asa was entranced.

Bukki remembered even yet his sulky demand that his mother stop gossiping about Messiahs, prophecies and rumours and take him to the bazaar, right now! Well, that was an argument. Bukki rubbed his ear meditatively, as if he could still feel his mother's smack.

"Two adults," he replied casually. "Even then I believed it was not true, and had my say. But it taught me that peace was more important than personal opinions."

He rubbed the other ear. His father had a heavier hand than his mother, too.

Asa, who found Bukki's piety deeply suspect, reached forward and took Dan's hand.

"Are you still awake, lad? Are you able to tell us your story?"

Dan was very much awake still and waiting nervously to do just that.

He told them all he could remember – everything he had heard from Caleb himself, everything the families of Ephraim and Samuel had said, everything Ammiel and Etta had discussed, everything Caleb had answered him with the next morning, and even most of what the unhappy madwoman Rachel had said. And in remembering the tale, he forgot other things which would normally have bothered him. He forgot that he was only a boy, and that a circle of adults was listening to him in perfect silence. He forgot that Uncle Bukki didn't believe it. He even forgot the sarcasm of that alarming pagan Loukanos. And when he finished, he looked at Anna.

"Father said you are educated and have read many things, Anna. He said you would have something to say about it."

Loukanos gave a short bark of laughter.

"My sister has something to say about almost everything," he said. "But she's not the only educated one in this family. Would your father be interested in what I have to say about it?"

"I doubt it," said Asa warningly. "Loukanos, do not make fun of this boy, and do not attempt to confuse him."

"Ah!" said Loukanos dismissively in disgust. "I won't interfere! Perhaps I envy his ignorance."

"Perhaps you do," said Anna quickly. "And I envy his passion for knowledge."

Bukki uncrossed his legs restlessly and crossed them again the other way. These two Greeks, envying this boy? It was more than he could fathom.

Asa shook his head as he looked from Loukanos to Anna and back again.

"Sheathe your swords, for pity's sake, you two, and let us have some peace. Has nothing changed since you were children?"

To Dan's surprise, both of them smiled.

"Pax!" said Loukanos regretfully. He got to his feet. "I'll leave you to talk religion. I have to check on our mother."

"And then will you be – painting?" asked Anna cautiously.

"Yes," he answered shortly. "Don't wait up for me again, will you? I may be hours."

Dan and Uncle Bukki exchanged a rare look between them. What an extraordinary man! Who could be painting in the dark?

Suddenly a yawn overpowered Dan, who gulped it down as hard as he could.

Asa's lined face looked at him with respect.

"Dan, thank you for bringing us your amazing tale. Such a young lad, but you have told it with care, and no doubt, faithfully. Your father should be proud. You have given us much to think of, much to be excited about. But you will now be off to bed, I think."

Dan looked dismayed, but Asa was firm.

"Father is right," agreed Anna. "This is too big a matter for us to quickly form an opinion! We will be talking till very late. Come, Dan. I promise I will tell you everything I can in the morning."

Asa looked at Bukki, who was not likely to add much to their discussion.

"My friend, I think you also may wish to retire? Rhoda will give you some wine to take away the stiffness of your journey, and may you rest well."

Bukki nodded, mightily pleased to avoid a lengthy and dry dispute over dusty old scriptures, during which he would be expected to know things and be polite and interested. He thought a little wine would be very helpful indeed, thank you, and good night.

Long after the rest of the house was dark, a lone torch flared above Asa and his daughter on the rooftop, still talking out in low and animated voices the single part of that evening which was worthwhile in their eyes – Dan's story.

## Chapter Seventeen

ASA pulled at his bottom lip meditatively.

"Well, daughter! Your Ammiel sounds very excited about this. But, as he says, it is not a new story. It spread around the countryside and caused a stirring in many hearts at the time. As a matter of fact, your mother and I heard it ourselves before we returned to the Land, but after the first spark of interest we paid it little attention. Nothing came of it after all, and there are always those unfortunates who imagine visions, in every place you go."

Anna sighed.

"Yes, father, I know. Depending on the grace of their families they set up as mystics or end as scavengers in Tophet – or even bound in chains. Horrible! Do you remember that poor wretch who terrified us several years ago when Uncle Joseph took us across the Lake?" She shuddered. "He was like a vision of Hades! I had nightmares for weeks."

She ducked as a swooping owl plunged past in pursuit of small prey which scuttled through the light spilling down into the courtyard below. Above the torch-head, moths and mosquitoes danced unconcerned around the steady flame.

Asa patted her hand and chuckled ruefully.

"Joseph and I were pretty shaken ourselves, I don't mind telling you. And didn't your mother give us the edge of her tongue for taking you on men's business! Still, we made some good connections there, and I still get a beautiful dye from that smelly little skew-eyed Jabir."

Anna returned to the subject.

"Father, did you and mother not think it was unusual for a group of men to claim the same vision?"

"Well now – let me think. The talk went around ... we heard it and wondered ... but now that you ask me, I don't believe we really thought that far at all. Certainly we made no attempt to investigate it for ourselves. How do you get to the source of common talk? Of course for a moment we pricked up our ears ... we felt that tingle of anticipation ... Not just ourselves either ... many devout friends felt the same ... after all, we were all of us waiting for the Messiah, as we have done for thousands of years, eh? – it is the focus of our religion to wait for him ..."

Anna broke in. "Ah! – I think you have said a profound thing, father! Perhaps it is true that – *waiting* for him is so deeply entrenched that we are not open to actually *finding* him. All our thoughts, our rituals, our prayers – are centred about his *absence*, and none about his *presence*! Could this be a reason why the shepherds' story fell to the ground even though it was followed by the claims of the eastern sages?"

"It could be," Asa replied slowly. "Yes, my daughter, perhaps it is true we think more of his absence than his presence. Is it because we never really believe strongly enough that his presence will come in our own day? I know we say 'the time is at hand' but even the saying itself has become part of our culture, and has lost the power to move us. And we become wary of Messiah claims because they have always proved false. So we become even more wary ... and so it goes ... You know, even when we were back in Philippi we heard about the peculiar visit of those Persians. They had actually come to Herod with gifts for the new King of the Jews! Oh, what poor judgement! They were lucky to get out of the country alive, if they ever did."

"So because the earlier story of the shepherds seemed to have no substance, you dismissed more easily that of the Persian sages? You didn't think they were the more likely to be true because of being from two sources which could never have colluded?"

"Possibly ... but ... I've travelled a lot, Anna," Asa shifted his shoulders defensively, "and I know that politics and king-making is a dangerous business, and that foreigners have their own odd ways of achieving their ends."

"Politics? Let's examine that, then. *Were* they emissaries of a government, father? Whose government? And why would any government want to worship any newborn prince of any poor nation crushed beneath Roman rule? To what purpose? Unless they were mad visionaries too, or equally mad mystics, the thing makes no sense. King-making I can understand ... but in someone else's country?"

Asa held up his hands in protest.

"Stop! You rush me! So many questions at once! Am I on trial here?"

Repentantly Anna lifted his turban and kissed the bald spot on her father's head.

"Yes, dear father, you are indeed on trial for the crime of never discussing this with me before."

"Ah, my daughter!" Asa settled his turban with a sigh. "How you torment me. Have you no respect? How should I know what to discuss and not to discuss with a woman? Many a time I have talked to you knowing full well you sit there saying Yes Father and No Father, and inside your head were shopping at the bazaar …"

Anna burst out laughing, and the liquid notes bubbled up the scale, making the old man chuckle. He shook his head.

"Where you get that laugh is beyond me. How *do* you produce that sound?"

"I don't produce it. It is a gift," she answered cheerfully. "A compensation for my bad singing."

"Aye," smiled Asa. "Your children will be chanted or whistled to sleep, I declare." He sobered suddenly. "That visit may have been from peaceful mystics, Anna, or it may not, but look at the results – it did not bring peace, but a sword. If any family had been foolish enough to put up their child as a pretender to the title of Messiah they certainly paid for it."

"Wait, father," said Anna, lifting a finger. "With respect, I think you are talking in circles. The visit of the sages was a surprise, was it not? Before that there were no 'pretenders to the title'. The mass execution of babies was the result of the sages' demands to see a young King of the Jews. Herod's preventative! Nobody had been parading a child about saying 'my child is the Messiah!'"

Asa slapped a mosquito. "What of the shepherds?"

Anna drummed her fingers. "Even then, surely the same applies. Both times the claims of Messiah's birth came from people totally unconnected, as it were. Let us assume that the shepherd's tale was false. To what purpose?"

"To gain respect? Power? Money? Fame?"

"Exactly ... so why make up such a tale and then not produce the child? If it was a shepherd's child so spoken of, it would be more understandable. But it wasn't. And the family and child remained invisible, as it were. I repeat, if it were false, to what purpose?"

"Yes, I see what you mean!" her father said, looking surprised. "I wonder I never thought of it before! And the Persian wise men!" he continued. "As you say, to what purpose was their interference? Why should they come so far and with such a useless tale, only to disappear? What would they gain? And what connection could *they* possibly have with any family in Bethlehem?"

"You see my point! Had they brought some child with them and claimed he was the King of the Jews ... there would have been a very interesting political situation ... But why bring a false tale? I know Herod the Great was a suspicious man ... but the point is, he believed them."

Asa frowned. "What did you think of Bukki's experience in the Temple?"

Anna laughed. "H'mm! Can you really see Bukki as a youth, being as full of thoughtful questions as our little Dan – and consumed with his kind of enthusiasm for true answers? I think he made it all up."

"What about the ancient old woman who said she had seen Messiah? I wouldn't think Bukki had imagination enough to create her."

Anna pulled her hair back with both hands and scrunched it up off her neck. The cool night air was delicious against her bare skin. Regretfully she let the heavy skein flop down again and sighed.

"I don't understand where she would fit in," she admitted. "Maybe she had visions. Maybe she was a relative of the child the shepherds knelt to. Maybe she was indeed, senile. Still, she said it. Bukki said he was about Dan's age when he heard these things at the Temple ... How old is Bukki?"

Asa gave her a look. "Who can tell with a man like that! Too little work, too much wine ... he's both older, and younger, than he ought to be. I think he was some years older than Dan's mother, but I don't really know."

"So his visit to the Temple *could* have been around or after the Census time, couldn't it? The old woman may have been real after all, but was her claim?"

They sat in silence for a while. Several flakes of burnt cloth floated off the torch in a puff of wind and a sparkle of tiny embers formed a tiny shooting star against the black sky.

"Of course, there was more!" added Asa suddenly. "Remember what Dan said – Caleb mentioned the men of the east – had seen *signs in the sky* ..."

"Yes?"

"The star!" Asa said softly. "Yes, the star! I had forgotten. There was indeed a new star, you know, that year. Very bright and clear. And it moved. Not as other stars move slowly with the seasons, but constantly – with a shining tail streaming behind it – ah, that was something to see! Then one day it was gone."

"Which means?"

"Why, that there *was* indeed a remarkable sign in the sky! How often is such a thing seen? The Persians believed it was the sign of a King, and not any King, but the King of the Jews – and came all the way to Jerusalem. It was a long way to come to satisfy the whim of astrology, was it not?"

"Indeed," Anna agreed, "and if that was all, why bring gifts to a King too young to reciprocate, and unlikely to be useful even if of age! And consider this," she leant forward in her eagerness, "that if the *sages* had come *first*, you could understand some shepherds trying to further their own ends by supplying the missing new King of the Jews, and inventing stories of angelic heralds ..."

"But it was the other way around!" Asa dashed off his turban in his excitement and scrubbed at his head until his white hairs stood out on end.

"Yes!" Anna snatched his hand and began slapping it between her palms fervently. "And what an unlikely story to be believed – a star as a sign of the King? They should have been more careful than that, if the story was a ruse of some sort! What! Coming to *Jews* with *astrology*?"

"The scriptures do not speak kindly of astrology," admitted Asa, rescuing his hand and shaking a finger at his daughter. "I think Isaiah is particularly scathing ..."

Anna nodded, and quoted with a smile, "*Thou art weary among the multitude of counsellors. Now let these astrologers, stargazers, and monthly prognosticators, stand up and rescue thee from all that shall befall thee ... See – they shall be mere stubble, to be burnt up with fire ...*"

"Ah, yes!" Asa was remembering affectionately. "I remember when your mother was converted, how fond she was of that passage, and how she used later to quote it to Loukanos ..."

"Who never took the slightest notice," Anna finished drily. She had fought some hard battles with Loukanos herself when he was first dabbling with his Gentile world.

Asa held his head.

"Ouf! It is enough to make my head ache. The sages came because of a star, because they were star-gazers – yet the prophet condemns it! Was the star of God? Or was it coincidence? And what could they know of Jewish Messiahs and kings after all?"

There was a rustling of clothes, and a wavering light wobbled up the stairs.

"Please excuse me, sir," whispered Rhoda. "My mistress has woken."

"Is she worse?" cried Asa, scrambling to his feet. Anna, who had bounded up in a moment, helped him up.

"No, sir, she says not to alarm you. But she knows you are still awake, and the night hangs heavy upon her. She asked for her son, but he is not home yet. Will you join her, sir? Or shall I stay with her?"

"No, child," said Asa. "You are a good little maid, a hard worker, and need your sleep. Go you to bed, and we will continue our discussion downstairs, with my wife."

He lifted the torch and extinguished it in a pail of sand, and they followed Rhoda's creeping steps down into Helen's room.

"What's this, you disobedient wife?" chided Asa tenderly, leaning over her white face and gently tugging the silver plait lying over her shoulder. "Awake at midnight instead of sleeping healthily as you were ordered? I should beat you!"

Helen stroked his hand and smiled at him faintly. "Black and blue!" she rejoined softly, and the two of them chuckled quietly. It was one of their oldest jests. Anna's eyes filled suddenly. She turned to Rhoda.

"Take your bed into my room, Rhoda. Your mistress will not need you any more tonight."

The girl nodded and slipped away.

"She's a good little thing," murmured Helen. "Now, I know something has been going on … I could hear your voices rising and falling when I woke … you must tell me all about it."

Asa rolled his eyes. "Help me, Anna – it's such a long story now we have teased it all apart!"

Anna tucked a cushion behind his back and settled her mother higher on her pillows.

"Keep your ear out for Loukanos," she warned. "He won't be pleased to hear us disturbing you so late!"

Helen waved her hand dismissively. "I shall tell him it is I who disturb you. The night is long when you are alone."

"Are you in any pain, mother?" Anna asked anxiously.

"No, dearest girl, no pain, now. Just a little tightness in the chest, a little breathlessness, you know. Nothing new. Now tell me everything."

So Anna and Asa told her everything about the purpose of Bukki and Dan's visit, and found clarity in renewing their own questions and answers. Helen, very curious, had a few of her own to add, until a growing wonder flourished out of her original scepticism.

211

"I think this is beginning to make some sense, Asa," she whispered at last. "After all these years of not thinking, this is the first time we have really put all these things together! If these stories were lies, they would make even less sense than if they were true. And yet to disbelieve them at the time seemed the wise thing to do."

"We were beginning to think the same thing," Asa confessed. "It is Dan's – and Ammiel's – utter conviction about the truth of Caleb's angels which has made us re-examine everything in that light. But we had reached the point of puzzling about the travelling star. If the star was a sign from God, why does the scripture condemn astrology? And from whence was their knowledge of any promised King of the Jews to come?"

Helen took a drink of water from the cup beside her bed and screwed up her face.

"Ugh! Rhoda has been putting those horrible herbal drops in my water again! Anyone would think she's trying to poison me. Loukanos bribes her, you know. He has a touching faith in the concoctions of the apothecary … but if he tries to restore me with one more bowl of barley drowned in goats milk I declare I'll stick his head in it!" she coughed suddenly.

Asa and Anna looked away for fear they should catch each other's eye and not be able to laugh. That she was so desperately frail, and still trying to tease them, was very dear of her – and painful.

Helen took a deep breath and sighed. She opened her eyes and said, "I don't like to admit it, but the drops do help. Now let's think about this astrology matter …"

There was silence for several minutes. Helen's lined face smiled at her daughter impishly.

"I know! Let's get Rhoda to kill a chicken so we can study its entrails! Maybe that will give us the answer!"

This time they all did laugh, but quietly.

Helen held up a bony finger. "Perhaps … perhaps it is this … what is the problem with astrology? Why is it discouraged?"

"It is not for man to seek the future," offered Asa, "except where the Master of the Universe requires him to seek. That is, in His holy Word."

"To know too much – or to believe you know – is to discourage reliance on God," suggested Anna.

Helen tapped her teeth thoughtfully. "That is, assuming that astrology is what it claims to be, of course. But it can't be, not totally."

"Not totally? You think it has *any* merit?" Anna asked, astonished. "Mother!"

Helen took another sip of water, too intent on her thoughts to complain of the taste.

"Don't misunderstand me, dear daughter, my pagan past is truly dead. But we are overlooking something. I believe that there are some signs placed in heaven by the Eternal to advertise His purpose. Perhaps at one time holy men were taught to read them."

"On what do you base this?"

Helen took a slow breath. "It is not provable, perhaps," she cautioned. "But I base it on Genesis. '*And God said Let there be lights in the firmament of the heaven to give light on the earth, to put division between day and night; and let them be for signs*, you note how that comes first?, *and for seasons, and for days and for years* …' And also, think of Noah. God placed the rainbow in the sky as *a sign*.

213

We could think – oh! just a natural phenomenon … but no, clearly we are told, it was a statement of intent by the Eternal. Of course, a rainbow is not a star. But anything in the heavens cannot be manipulated by man, so must be of God. And sometimes may be, as it were, His finger, pointing, for those who can read it."

Asa and Anna glanced at each other.

"There may be something in what you say!" said Asa, astounded.

"There may be a lot in what I say!" his wife replied, with a nod.

"Mother, you are a clever woman!" rejoined Anna. "What a wonderful thought! But if the 'star of the King' was indeed for that purpose, how did these wise men of Persia know about it? Or that it would herald a King of the Jews?"

"H'm," Asa rumbled. "I suppose – though I know it's far fetched – is it not possible that knowledge was passed down through a very famous wise man of the east from centuries ago? A man who *understood signs* …?"

"Oh, father! You mean – Daniel the prophet!?" breathed Anna. "But scripture says nothing of that."

"It says nothing of what he ate for breakfast, either," Helen pointed out, "but that doesn't mean he never had it. It could have been as Asa says, but if it is not important for us to know, well of course, it will not be written."

Asa scratched his beard. "Well, I dislike speculation as a general rule, but all this is very plausible. "

"Jeremiah!" said Anna suddenly, remembering. "Oh, father! Mother! I think it must be true! However it was that the sages came to ask of the new King of the Jews, the fact is, they *came*. And *because* they came, all the infants in the whole area were executed."

"Jeremiah?"

"Yes, don't you see? He speaks of the time Israel will be comforted, and gathered together from all lands, how her weeping will turn to rejoicing. Remember? *'The Eternal hath redeemed Jacob and ransomed him from the hand of the stronger one ... they will gather together singing in the height of Zion ... they shall not be sad any longer ... the maiden, the men young and old will rejoice together in the dance ... I will turn their mourning into joy and console them ... and cheer them from their sadness ... the priests and people satisfied with my goodness ...'* Is this not Messianic? All these words about redemption and consolation?" Her parents nodded, but their daughter swept on excitedly. "Now look! A little further on The Eternal says to Israel, *'don't cry any more ... dry your tears'* – because, why? What had happened? The passage before tells it – *'A cry was heard in Ramah, lamentation and bitter weeping; Rachel weeping for her children, refused to be comforted for her children, because they were gone ...'* – and then follows the words about drying tears, reassuring us that she will be comforted at this happy time to come."

"Messianic, no doubt, Anna. But confusing. It speaks of future Israel and dead Rachel in the one breath. How does it relate to Herod? And why Ramah?"

"I confess I don't know precisely – but it points us to the area! Ramah is near Bethlehem, isn't it? And Rachel died *'when there was but a little distance to Bethlehem'*, the city of David, the city where the Messiah was to be born! Why would Moses mention Rachel dying near Bethlehem at all if it wasn't significant?"

"Admitted that it points to a general area where the Messiah is to be born – or where Rachel died – you were talking about Jeremiah's prophecy, not Moses, so exactly what has Rachel's sorrow to do with it?"

"Don't you see?" Anna said passionately. "I think we have to put the two together. It can't be Rachel herself – how could she weep for her dead children, when it was *she* who died and *they* who lived? What happened during the Slaughter of the Babes? Was there not the sound of great weeping throughout Bethlehem, Ramah and all the coasts thereof? When did that ever happen? Little Dan's madwoman has already given us the clue! *Rachel* is a symbol of the mothers of Israel! This Messianic passage prophesies that very slaughter, that weeping!"

"Oh!" whispered Helen, her eyes shining, and "Oh!" blurted out Asa, his jaw dropping.

Anna snatched their hands.

"Oh!" she repeated, her face glowing. "Oh! Oh! Oh!"

And "Hush!" whispered a timid girlish voice as Rhoda pattered into the room.

"Loukanos is coming through the gate!"

Asa snuffed the wick and they crept like the guilty to their rooms – burning with excitement, and realising that sleep would escape them for hours.

## Chapter Eighteen

LOUKANOS and Bukki were both still asleep when Dan crept from the guest room at first light. He had not heard Loukanos come in during the night, and guessed it must have been very late indeed. There was something peculiar about this painter – another mystery to fathom later. Perhaps Anna would tell him more. In the central living room, Anna, wrapped in an embroidered shawl, was bending over a table at the courtyard window, writing by the light of a guttering flame which was fast being dimmed by the grey light from outside. Her dark hair was twisted into a long rope, and fine wisps hung over her face. As Dan's bare feet padded noiselessly over the cool flagstones she laid down her reed pen, sighed and stretched her arms, flexing her hands, and rubbing her neck. She started upon seeing Dan. He grinned, and she shook a finger at him in mock reproof.

"So early! You must be hungry!" she said, careful to keep her voice low, and reaching out to push back the tangled curls from his forehead. Dan rubbed his head vigorously. *Why do women always want to play with your hair?*

Anna seemed to know what he was thinking.

"Just habit," she whispered, laughing a little and pulling her shawl more closely around her. "I used to be always messing or

217

tidying my brother's curls. He hated it too. Now, young man, it's cold still. You sit right here and wait."

She threw Dan a soft striped blanket – into which he curled gratefully – and disappeared briefly, returning with a handful of leftover spice cakes. Dan munched in happy silence but his eyes were brimming with questions. Anna raised one eyebrow.

"Anything you want to know about my family?" she teased.

Dan nodded.

"Tell me about Loukanos!" he begged, with his mouth full. He breathed in a crumb, and coughed. Anna put a finger to her lips warningly and nodded.

"My mother is Greek, as you know. Her family married her to a rich man, who was very much older. He died when Loukanos was tiny. Later my mother converted to Judaism and married Asa, my father. So it was, that when I came along I had a ready-made big brother to annoy. Which was just as well, as, sadly, they had no other children. But Loukanos became a wild boy and left home very young. Some other time I may tell you his story."

Dan's eyes showed disappointment, but Anna would tell him no more. Then she added, almost reluctantly, "We love him, you know, and are proud of his accomplishments. But the fact is, he is a pagan, Dan, despite his upbringing – which pains my mother sadly, and hurts my father's pride. We have not been accustomed to speaking of him to others outside of Greece, foolish though it seems. You are the first – except for your father."

She stood up, pinching out the wick of the oil lamp. The once bright flame had become almost invisible in the greater light of day, and was no longer useful. She looked down at Dan, her pale face weary, and smiled a little.

"Families are complicated things, Dan."

Dan nodded slowly. He would have to think about it. He should ask Johanan about his family. He never had before. Everyone around him seemed to have small families of leftover relatives, stuck together. But he knew "father, mother, and a tribe of children" was how it was *supposed* to be. Maybe … he wriggled out of his blanket …

"Maybe, when you and father are married – maybe we'll end up with nice big proper family like lots of other people, Anna."

Anna laughed, kissed the tip of her ink-smudged finger and tapped his nose.

"God willing, Dan boy. God willing! Come on, I hear Rhoda in the kitchen, and I'm not dressed properly yet. Father will be scandalised. I have to wake Loukanos and attend mother soon, too. She didn't sleep well last night. Actually, none of us did. I'd like to let her sleep, but she has her medicines to take and the doctor insists on routine."

She tilted her parchment to the light. It was dry, so she rolled it up and handed it to Dan.

"A letter for your father," she explained. "Put it in your satchel and we'll talk it over later. You and Bukki will stay tonight as well, so there's plenty of time."

Dan nodded.

"But you haven't forgotten we came about the Messiah, Anna?" he asked anxiously.

"Oh, no, indeed I have not! I have thought of little else, and we were up half the night over it! But we'll speak of that soon, when you see mother."

Dan had one more thing he was curious about.

"Will you tell me about your brother's painting?"

To his surprise, Anna broke into her peculiar laugh.

"Sometime, I promise," she agreed. "But whatever you do, don't ask him yourself!"

She escaped, still laughing, and Dan danced off to the kitchen to tease Rhoda with a lovely brown spotted frog he'd found near the privy the night before, and had kept especially for the purpose.

Loukanos was sitting with Helen, holding her hand, when Anna ushered Dan and Bukki in later that morning. He got up abruptly.

"Don't tire her," he said. "Mother – don't forget your tonic."

Helen, propped up on pillows, terribly pale, and thinner than Dan had remembered her, pulled a face.

"Must I, Louki? It's disgusting, and I'm sure it does me no good."

"Don't be a baby, mother." He dropped a kiss on her forehead and left.

Helen patted a low stool beside her bed. Dark purple stains ringed her hollow eyes.

"Come and sit here, Dan – and Bukki, please take that chair."

"No, thank you," said Bukki, uncomfortable in the sickroom. "I just looked in to pay my respects, and send you Ammiel and Etta's good wishes and – ah, blessings – for your recovery."

"Very kind," murmured Helen, closing her eyes. "Please thank them for me."

220

Bukki gave a stiff little gesture, half nod, half bow, and escaped thankfully. This visiting was a strain on the nerves, as well as the stomach. He'd better go down town and see about some business while he was here …

Dan sat on the stool and wondered at the change in Anna's mother. In the weeks since he had last seen her, she had become almost transparent. She touched his arm.

"Dan, Asa and Anna have told me everything. Thank you for coming to tell us."

"Father insisted."

She nodded. "He's a good man. With a good son. He'll be a fine husband for my Anna. I should have realised it long ago."

"Mother!" Anna spoke warningly.

"It's all right, Anna. A dying woman is done with secrets, after all. You see, Dan, I knew your father wanted to marry Anna many years ago. He never said anything, but I knew. And I knew my daughter loved him dearly. I discouraged him at every turn, and he never dared ask. He knew my foolish pride would never allow it."

Dan's eyes widened. Anna was looking annoyed.

"Mother, is this really necessary?" She patted Dan's shoulder. "Don't worry, Dan, your father didn't break his heart over me. Once he met your beautiful mother he never gave me another thought, I promise you. She was small, and pretty, and utterly bewitching, and I danced at their wedding with a light heart."

"Oh!" said Dan lamely.

Anna laughed at his expression.

"Life is full of surprises, isn't it, Dan? Perhaps mother just wants to let you know that your father and I will be very contented with each other."

She gave her mother a steely look over the top of Dan's head.

"Yes," replied Helen thoughtfully, picking stray grey hairs from her blanket, where they had fallen from her thinning scalp. "But more than that, I want to tell you both that Truth is the most important thing. I hid from it when I was young and married for money. I hid from it when Loukanos left home, and I hid from it when I knew you loved Dan's father. And I believe Louki hides from it yet. You see, I am in a mood to confess!" she smiled apologetically, her thin lips bluish against her ivory teeth.

"You faced it too," reminded Anna gently. "When you embraced the true faith."

Helen raised herself on one elbow with a sudden change of mood.

"This is not mere breastbeating to embarrass the boy," she said crossly. "Dan, I meant to be a good grandmother to you, and now I have no time left. So I am passing on to you all my wisdom in one package while I can – *never hide from the Truth, it's a waste of time and effort.*"

Dan nodded. He had never thought about Helen becoming his grandmother, and caring about how he lived his life. It was a warm thought. Helen lay back on her pillows, her face white beneath the parchment skin, breathing quickly. Anna shook her head slightly and gave her the despised tonic. Helen shuddered.

"I declare that evil Louki stirs my medicine with his paintbrushes," she muttered, and chuckled. Anna smiled but her

222

lips quivered. Dan looked at her enquiringly, but she answered, "No, don't go yet, Dan. Wait."

A tinge of colour returned to Helen's face. She opened her eyes and looked at Dan.

"Now, Dan. I have said, never hide from the Truth. And – praise the Eternal! – I believe you have brought us the most wonderful truth of all ..."

Dan's hands grew cold ... Helen nodded, her jaundiced eyes shining at last. She gripped his arm with sudden strength.

"Yes, Dan. We have been talking and thinking of nothing else all night. Everything you and Ammiel have told us makes sense! And all those rumours which we heard years ago and dismissed, because we all were *hiding from the truth!* We did not see or hear what we expected or wanted, so we did not believe. But now! I believe Messiah has truly come! He is here! He is somewhere, walking amongst us! Grown to manhood and maturity – gathering his power, and ready to reveal himself!"

Dan bounded off his stool and flung his arms around the fragile woman. He hugged her hard, making her gasp.

"Thank you!" he cried jubilantly. "Thank you! At last someone believes it!"

Somehow, even one other person believing, made it more real. Anna's mother laughed a little, kissed him lightly and pinched his cheek, though she drew her breath more heavily.

"More than one," added Anna gladly. "Dan, my father and I are also convinced that your story is real, and true." She was trembling slightly. "The scriptures are plain, the events correspond, and the time is right. Our Messiah is here, at last! There is no doubt!"

Dan hugged her too before he could stop himself.

"Why didn't you tell me this morning?" he accused her.

Anna smiled through her tears. "Father insisted we must give mother that particular pleasure …"

"So we could all rejoice together!" said the deep voice of Asa behind them, clapping his hands on Dan's shoulders. Dan looked up thankfully, and all around him. Such a fullness of heart was swelling within him, such a tightness in his chest and a lightness in his head – such relief and gladness that he snatched Anna's hand, swinging it wildly, and began to sing as he had weeks ago in the dim little house at the edge of Banayim:

*"Oh Praise God in His Sanctuary … !"* Dan stopped, suddenly self-conscious, but Helen's waxy face lit up. People had been quiet and sober around her for so long. It was good to hear some joy breaking out!

"Go on, young Dan – sing up!" she encouraged in a whisper.

Dan grinned and repeated more surely,

*"Oh Praise God in His Sanctuary …"*. He raised his clear boy's voice. *"Praise Him in His heaven of power!"*

*"Praise Him for His mighty deeds – Praise Him for His sovereign strength …"* Asa rumbled melodiously, pointing to Anna …

*"Praise Him with a bugle blast – praise Him with lute and lyre,"* she sang back, a deep voice and slightly flat.

*"Praise Him with the drum and dance!"* warbled Dan, drumming on his knees and dancing around the room as he had before.

*"Praise Him with the strings and flute!"* chanted Helen breathily, twirling her wasted fingers above her grey head, and strumming her thin grey plait in time.

224

*"Praise Him with resounding cymbals,"* Anna tinkled her coin headdress with a finger, laughing at her inability to hold the tune.

*"Praise Him with the clashing cymbals!"* Asa clapped his hands, elegantly hopping and tapping his feet to the rhythm.

*"Let everything that breathes, Praise the Eternal!"* piped up little Rhoda, coming in with a tray, and joining in to prove she knew the words too.

*"Ha-le-lu-jah! ..."* they all sang together. And then because it felt so good they looked at each other and burst out with a final, even louder – *"Ha-le-lu-jah!"*, sinking down on bed, chairs, and floor, breathless and laughing. Dan's heart bounded happily. Why, it was no different to being with his father and Aunt Etta and Caleb or Bukki, after all.

"Where is Uncle Bukki?" he asked while they caught their breath, suddenly feeling they had left him out of something very important.

"He went to the tavern," Rhoda whispered to him, as she slipped out again. She collided with a tall, dark and stormy figure in the doorway, and everyone scrambled guiltily to their feet.

"What in the name of Zeus is all this row?" he raged. "Are you trying to kill her? Get out!"

Dan took one look at the furious face of Loukanos and bolted.

Asa patted his stepson apologetically on the shoulder and blowing a smiling kiss to his wife, pulled Anna out with him before she could open her mouth.

Loukanos dropped to his knees before his mother and laid his slender artists' fingers on her wrist. Helen was panting. He swore, and snatched a phial from her table, shaking bitter drops on to her tongue. Her eyelids fluttered open.

"Don't you say a word!" she whispered. "I have been happier this morning than for a long time! If I die an hour earlier for it, what of it? Messiah has really come, Loukanos!"

He snorted. She twisted her hand around until it was she who had hold of his wrist. She dug her mauve tipped fingers into his fine golden skin.

"Listen to me, Louki. Will you honour a dying wish from the mother who bore you?"

Loukanos set his jaw. "You will not die."

"What, are you God, Louki? Of course I will die. I am dying as we speak. Will you honour my request? Answer me."

A single scalding tear dropped from his deep grey eyes and stuck to the black stubble on his cheek. "Yes, you know I will."

Helen drew a ragged breath and closed her eyes.

"Good. It is this. You will stay with your sister, and give her every assistance until she is safely married –"

Loukanos interrupted indignantly, "You hardly needed to ask me that!"

Helen opened her eyes and looked directly at him.

"I have not finished, son. Until she is safely married *or* until she finds and sees our Messiah – whichever comes first."

"What! Mother, you cannot be serious!"

Helen turned her head. "Ah, Louki! I was never more serious in my life – or should I say, my death …"

"A poor joke!" Loukanos snapped.

She smiled at him tenderly. "You will not go back on your word?"

226

Loukanos bit his lip. "No, but mother, this was a nice trick to play me!"

She picked up his hand and kissed it, laying it against her sunken cheek.

"You think so? But Messiah has come, so she will find him soon. And you will help her. It won't take long. Such beautiful hands, Louki. My little Louki. My baby boy."

His hand slid from her relaxing fingers. The room was very still.

## Chapter Nineteen

"WHAT do you want?" snapped Loukanos. He had been painting furiously on a thin square of wood but now paused to look blackly at Dan. "Have those caterwauling women left yet?"

"The hired mourners are still at the sepulchre," replied Dan timidly. "Anna asked me to find you and ask if you will keep her company when they leave."

"No, I won't." The painter scrubbed at his board with a dirty rag, smudging yellow streaks across red, while Dan peered curiously. "It's a loathsome custom. What good will it do my mother?"

"None," Dan admitted. "But perhaps it will do Anna good?"

Loukanos eyed the lad narrowly and tucked the rag back in his belt.

"You're sharper than you look for your size, boy," he said grudgingly. "But I'm not wailing and beating my breast for anyone. My mother's in a better place, and not suffering – and for all that your Messiah nonsense hastened her death, she seemed to die happy enough. So there'll be no public performance from me."

Dan looked at the angry tears standing in the man's eyes, consideringly.

"These are for myself!" Loukanos said resentfully. "Not for her. For myself. Grief is always for ourselves. We can mourn anywhere! It's hypocritical to screech over a body. But – Anna's a woman, and women are weak." He stabbed his brush into the red ochre on his plate while Dan stood by in silence.

Finally Loukanos shrugged his shoulders in resignation. "I'll do as she asks."

"I'll tell her," Dan answered, and turned to go. He turned back.

"Where is this better place? Where can your mother be, if she is not in the sepulchre?"

Loukanos stared at him, and gave a harsh laugh.

"Of course, you little Galilean, I'd forgotten you are indoctrinated early. Do you really think she is snuffed out, just like that? All that energy, that passion, that humour, that endurance, that *life*? Do you really think that waxen corpse they wound up and carried out is all there ever was of my mother?"

He beckoned Dan over. "What's this?"

Dan looked nervously at the picture.

"Um ... I ... a sunset?"

Loukanos snorted. "It's a pomegranate. Art! In this case, an ordered arrangement of paints, but which depicts life. Just like a body, which reminds you of a living person, see? What does it bring to your mind?"

Dan gulped. It brought to his mind the time he dropped an egg which had the beginning of a chicken inside.

"A painting of a pomegranate?" he suggested untruthfully.

Loukanos sighed.

"What did I expect?" he muttered. He looked approvingly at the painting. "It brings to mind the real thing – a real, fresh fruit, growing and flourishing on a bush, moving in the wind, swelling with the watery pink sweetness of the seed – the bitterness of the rind, the faint spicy perfume, the first time you ate one, the day you tried to count all the pips – or spat them at someone – the worst one you ever ate, the best one you ever ate, and maybe, for a Jew at least, some of the decorations of your worship ..."

Dan screwed up his eyes and thought hard.

"Yes, I suppose it does." *Now that I know it is a pomegranate,* he thought a little rebelliously.

Loukanos grunted. "That's right. That's what it does. So, are all those things real?"

"I don't know what you mean. They were real then. Now they are things which I remember."

The painter dabbled his brush in a pot of water. "Real, unreal ... what does it mean? I'm trying to tell you that while this pomegranate is only clay and pigment on a board, there is a real pomegranate just like it somewhere else."

Really? Dan thought, looking at the drying paint and squinting.

"My mother's body is in the sepulchre, but the spirit of everything she was, lives on. Just like this painting is not a real fruit, but the fruit and its memories are real. Now do you understand?"

Dan squatted down resignedly. Clearly this terrible Loukanos would not let him go until he had made something very simple, into something complicated. Why was he making such a meal of it?

231

"Of course I understand about memories living on," he said rather defensively. "My own mother is dead, and I have memories of her … a few …"

*Only a few … beautiful fragrant hair, a sharp voice, the sting of a slap on his leg …* it was not much to warm himself with.

"I'm not talking about memories. I'm talking about the soul. The essence. The real life which goes on after death."

"Oh. Well, I know Helen – and my mother – will be raised to life in the Resurrection."

Loukanos flicked his brush in his impatience. "How many dead people have you ever seen resurrected?" he jeered.

Dan was startled by his vehemence. "None. I mean, the day has not yet come. But it will – scripture says so."

Loukanos tried again. "What about Abraham's bosom? Even your own people will tell you about the dead going there."

"I … don't know. I will have to ask …"

Loukanos gave up. "Why am I talking to a mere child!" he reproached himself.

Dan felt irritated. "I'm not a mere child," he said boldly, tired of being glared at. "I'm going to be your nephew – *Uncle* Loukanos!" he added emphatically.

Loukanos looked startled – then laughed shortly.

"Ah! The puppy bites! Well, I suppose you're all right, really. Tougher than you look. Get out of this sun, boy, and have Rhoda give you something to drink. I'll join my sister and stepfather at the grave. Ach!" he muttered, "one wailing woman and two pipes is all your rabbis require for a wife, and why that isn't enough for my family I don't know – it's just as well mother can't hear the racket." He dried his brushes and rolled them up in a rag, casting a dark glance at the silent Dan. "I said I'll go! I'll even put up with the mourners if I have to. But – " he jabbed a finger at Dan's chest, "only because I know my mother is standing right now in Elysian fields, and laughing to see how wrong she was all these years!"

He stalked off.

He had reached the gate when suddenly Dan called after him, "Uncle Loukanos?"

"What now!"

Dan ran up to the man who was so unlike his gentle sister, and put out a tentative hand.

"Uncle Loukanos, did our singing really hasten your mother's death ...?"

Loukanos looked at the anxious eyes, and was forced to relent.

"Oh, I don't know!" he admitted reluctantly, clutching his hair in exasperation and dropping his hands wearily. "Excitement was bad for her, and she was certainly excited. But there was really –" His voice suddenly husky, Loukanos cleared his throat and swallowed. "There was nothing more to be done. I hoped mere force of will could keep her alive. Stupid of me. Better she died with a smile. Drop your dramatic bundle, boy. I spoke in hot haste, but now I, Loukanos of Philippi, say – you did not kill her!"

Dan's chest began to heave with relief. Loukanos cuffed his head in a not unfriendly fashion, and loped off.


Dan waited till the urge to sob had passed. The tears in this place were catching! He returned to look again at the painting. It was the first time he had ever seen one closely. *I suppose it could be a pomegranate, if you look at it a bit cross-eyed.* He was disappointed and a bit puzzled. Who would buy a picture like this? And what was all that about Elysian fields and souls and Abraham's bosom? And how could Loukanos say Helen was deaf to the mourners and pipes one minute but laughing the next? More questions to ask … queer ones he hadn't ever thought of himself, and resented crowding in on his careful and laborious plotting of the way things were … and all coming on an unhappy day. After such a wonderful morning, too.

Dan sighed, and a tear rolled out of the corner of one eye before he could catch it. Helen had planned to be a good grandmother to him. How unexpected. He had never known grandparents, and now he had been cheated of them. He sniffed, then brightened as a thought struck him. *Asa can still be my grandfather, at least. I'll have a grandfather, and a mother, and a mysterious uncle!* That would be double the family he had now – no, more! Because there would be Johanan! And Johanan's mother, he supposed. *Nearly three times the family!* And then, Rhoda was another interesting addition, though of course, as a servant, she would not have much time to play. Dan suddenly felt as rich as he had felt poor only moments before and cheered up properly.

He touched a corner of the painting carefully and tried looking at it upside down, and sideways. It was plain that *somebody* knew little about such things – whether it was himself or Loukanos he wasn't quite sure. Probably it was himself, he admitted. And then, as he cautiously picked up the ugly wooden picture, he caught sight of sheets of papyrus beneath it.

Hands! Dan twitched nervously. What was the meaning of this? He looked at them with awe. Hands on their own, without bodies, without arms! Where was the sense in it? Sketched boldly in charcoal, all over the page. Hands which looked as if they were

234

alive enough to draw themselves. Thin, wasted hands, wrinkled but energetic, gesturing. They reminded him of Helen's hands as she lifted them joyously in dancing praise on her deathbed. He lifted the next sheet swiftly. More disembodied hands! With large, thick, hairy, masculine fingers. The next – long, capable, with large knuckles, but tapered, feminine, with a heavy bangle on the wrist. And finally a pair of boyish, slender hands which looked familiar …" Why, they're mine!" Dan gasped, recognising the half-healed scar near the thumbnail, "and these – they are Helen's – and these must be Asa's – and yes! I'm sure those *are* Anna's …!"

Quickly he put the sheets down and covered them with the painting again. Loukanos surely could not paint worth a mite, he was sure of it. But these bizarre drawings – well, the real puzzle was, why was Loukanos painting unrecognisable pomegranates when he could draw like this? Dan shook his head in frustration, and ran back inside.

Rhoda was in the long main room. She was crumpled on a stool with her head on her knees, crying. Dan stopped, and then tried quietly to edge around her into the guest room. Rhoda lifted her head and saw him. She jumped to her feet and a linen package dropped from her lap. She snatched it up and waved it helplessly at Dan, tears streaming down her face.

"A letter – for my – m-m-mistress!" she sobbed. "She – she'll n-n-never read it now …"

"For Helen, you mean?" Dan tried not to look at her swollen eyes, like soaked dates in pastry. Her nose was running. Rhoda wiped it ineffectually with her sleeve and nodded, choking down her tears determinedly.

"Who is it from?" Dan knew it was a stupid question, but couldn't think of anything else to say.

Rhoda sniffed luxuriously. "Parosh the tanner brought it from Jerusalem. He often takes messages for the family. It's from Johanan's mother, Mari." She gulped and blinked at Dan. Her tear-wet lashes clumped together, giving her a strange, spiky look. "Now the master will have to read it instead. Alas! Alas! How sad I am for my dear mistress!"

Dan nodded and escaped thankfully to the guest room.

A strange humming greeted him. Uncle Bukki was sitting cross legged on the floor, with a large jug and several cups in front of him. Humming mournfully, with great concentration he was pouring a wavering stream of barley beer into each cup. From the look of the floor, he had been refilling them for a while. An army of thirsty ants formed an industrious frill on the shores of several small lakes on the flagstones. The room smelled thick, sour, beery.

Uncle Bukki blinked at him owlishly and raised the jug to greet him. Stamped with a taverner's imprint, it was a lumpy creation which would have earned Ittai's scorn, but held a great deal of liquor.

"Me'n my frenz hav'na drink – mem'ry o-o-ova ni-ni-ni-slady!" he finished the unsteady sentence with a flourish. He gave a rumbling belch.

"Rezpec' for-th'-dead!" he informed Dan solemnly, and tilted his head for a long draught. "Alwaysh pay r-rezp- rezp – ix! – par'-me!"

Dan was horrified, but he knew there was not much budging of Uncle Bukki to be done in this state. It answered the question of where Uncle Bukki had been during the funeral, at any rate.

236

He had to get Uncle Bukki out of here or be disgraced before his new family.

"What would Aunt Etta say?" he tried.

Uncle Bukki shook his head and tapped his greasy nose wisely.

"Ssshh!" he reproved.

Dan had an inspiration. He bent close to Uncle Bukki's ear and hissed,

"What about Loukanos? Quick! He's coming! Don't come back till you're sober!"

Uncle Bukki paled.

"Ver' rude Geek man." He scrambled to his feet. "No simf … no simf-smip-simth-pappy!" Hastily he staggered out, upsetting the cups, but hugging the jug to his chest.

Dan watched him go with relief. Then, braving the possibility of finding a sobbing Rhoda in the kitchen, he fetched water to clean up the mess. *Me and my friends!* Honestly! Poor Uncle Bukki – did he have imaginary companions, or did he really think the ants were his friends, or was he being funny? *Who knows?* As he wiped up the unfortunate ants together with the beer, he felt a little sorry for them. Maybe ants had families too. He remembered Johanan saying, *"You know – Husband Ant. Wife Ant. Baby Ant. Maybe even Rabbi Ant."*

Maybe there would be an ant funeral today as well. Dan hoped the room would not still smell of beer when the family returned. It was too bad of Uncle Bukki.

There was a tap at the doorway and Rhoda entered. Dan was glad to see she had washed her face and was no longer crying.

"You are a guest," she said, alarmed. "This is for me to do!"

237

"No," Dan answered. "I didn't want anyone to know. Anyway, it's done now."

Rhoda shook her head at the smeary floor, and took charge of the pail and rags. Wringing the rags expertly, she rubbed and rinsed until the stones were polished to her liking, then opened the shutters, which Uncle Bukki had closed. She took a wide towel and handed one end to Dan.

"Do this!" She waved the ends rhythmically. Dan copied, and gradually the huge fan flapped the stale air out of the room. It was fun. Quite recovered by now, Rhoda giggled.

"That's better! I'll strew a few herbs too. Loukanos will never know. He's very much against beer."

Dan handed back his end of the towel.

"How did you know it was him I was worried about?"

Rhoda gave him a look. "Nobody else would be coming into the guest room. And we all tip-toe around Loukanos."

She folded the towel neatly and left to fetch the herbs.

When she returned, Dan asked curiously, "Why is he against beer?"

Rhoda twinkled at him, snatched up the towel, and hopped up on the stool, draping herself from shoulder to the floor in the long linen cloth. She drew her eyebrows together and looked down her nose.

"Filthy stuff!" she snapped in a deep voice. "Makes you stink! Gives you a belly! Invented by Philistines! Doesn't that tell you something? Stick to wine – preferably Greek!"

Dan rolled about laughing. "That's wonderful!" he gasped.

238

Rhoda jumped lightly from the stool, folded the towel for the second time and hugged it to her chest with a guilty smile.

"Don't tell," she warned with another giggle, and disappeared.

Feeling greatly daring, Dan followed her. There was obviously more to Rhoda than met the eye. He found her in the courtyard, sweeping with a fine twig broom.

"You're always so busy," he said.

Rhoda looked up, surprised. "Of course! What else would I be? Aren't you?"

Dan thought of his own long, carefree days. "Not really."

"What about school? I would love to go to school and learn to read! But of course, that's for boys."

"Anna can read," said Dan, who'd never really thought about it at all.

"Yes, she is educated. But she is not a Galilean."

"Have you no family, Rhoda?"

Rhoda tucked the dark hair over her ears. "Why, yes, I have. I see them from time to time. But we are all working in different places, you see. My mother is a widow, and of course we need to live. I am blessed in having such kind people to work for."

Her eyes filled again. "My mistress was always good to me, though I did not often understand her jokes, and I will miss her."

Dan put his head on one side, considering how different his own life would be if it had been Ammiel who had died, rather than his mother. It was an alarming thought.

"I – I'm not in school," he confessed. "But I want to go back soon."

"Oh, yes, indeed you should!" cried Rhoda eagerly. "There is so much to learn – and so much you can do when you can read and write and calculate! Why, you might become a scribe one day! Such respect they have, and so clever!"

Dan shook his head. "I want to be a shepherd, like my father."

He looked at the things Loukanos had left behind under the shady courtyard olive tree. Rhoda noticed.

"What about a painter?" she suggested, tongue in cheek.

Dan looked at her closely.

"He's – well, he's not very good at it – is he? Or is he?"

Rhoda put a hand over her mouth but her eyes danced.

"It is not for a servant girl to judge," she said primly. She put her lips close to Dan's ear and whispered, "But, no, he isn't!" She giggled, and resumed sweeping.

Dan wriggled a finger in his ear to stop the tickling.

"How does he make a living at it?" he asked cautiously.

Rhoda shrugged. "Oh, he doesn't have to," she answered, coaxing the leaves and sticks into a neat pile. "And he is pleased enough with his own work."

Dan tried another question. "Have you ever seen any of his drawings?"

Rhoda slowed to a standstill.

"Yes, once – by accident," she whispered. "He was angry."

"Why?" Dan moved away from the pile of drawings with an air of carelessness.

"I think they are forbidden. They were frightening."

"Frightening?" Dan's eyes widened in surprise. "What do you mean?"

Was Rhoda frightened by the oddity of members without limbs attached? Admittedly, it had given Dan a queer sensation himself, but ... Well, she was only a girl! *but a girl who is used to Loukanos and his ways* ... so maybe there was more. He would find out.

Rhoda became very busy. She put the broom away and trotted inside, where she began to make a great fuss about washing her hands and pounding stoned dates to a creamy paste. Dan followed her, relentless.

"Tell me about the drawings!" he insisted.

Rhoda looked at him sideways and pounded harder. Dan boldly snatched the pestle out of her hands. She fluttered her eyelids a little in confusion.

"What were they of?" Dan demanded, suddenly feeling masterful. It was a new sensation for him, and not unpleasant.

Rhoda put a brown hand to her slim throat and looked a little scared.

"A person," she confessed at last, glancing up.

Dan handed back the pestle almost in disgust. Not as bad as the hands, anyway. A whole person? What was frightening about that? Forbidden, perhaps, but not frightening.

Rhoda bit her lip and worked hurriedly.

"Cut open!" she whispered quickly, dropping her eyes. "The drawing was of all their insides!"

Dan gaped at her and his skin began to prickle.

There were voices outside and a rattling at the courtyard gate.

"Come on – open up, Rhoda!" Loukanos was back.

241

## Chapter Twenty

DAN had a bad night of it. The burial itself, a solemn and unhappy affair, had been only the beginning. Some hours later, the professional mourners had gone home, but a crowd of people returned to the house with Loukanos, Asa and Anna, and lamented noisily all over it as they shared their mutual loss of a friend and neighbour. It brought back surging waves of shadowy memories which hurt Dan's throat and squeezed his chest. And if the sorrow was inescapable, so was the discomfort.

Dan, as the only male child in the house, was seized upon as an aid to grief. It was rather disconcerting. On the one hand, Asa had sobbed loudly and crushed him to his brawny chest, the ceremonial rip over his heart sprouting thick grey ticklish hairs through the torn cloth ... Anna had wrapped gentle arms about him and bent her head to shed weary tears in his hair ... Rhoda had gone about wetly sniffling and giving him lost looks ... neighbours had patted and stroked him consolingly, and mere acquaintances who were unsure of Dan's position in the family had clutched him and moaned over him as if it had been his own mother who had died. This was all very well, but it meant Dan came in for an unwelcome share of the chief mourners' food. Obediently Dan chewed the plain lentils, round bread and boiled eggs which symbolized life rolling towards death, until his mouth felt as dry as the grave itself. Uncle Bukki, he noticed crossly, had managed to escape this fate by melting into the crowd as a mere acquaintance.

Loukanos had bared his teeth at him in what could have been a smile or a snarl – Dan wasn't quite sure which – while Uncle Bukki, still not sober enough to risk conversation, carefully arranged an expression of pompous importance between his jug ears, sighing heavily and shaking his head whenever there was a lull in the general confusion, and humbly accepting any tasty food or drink pressed upon him.

Dan felt completely rattled by the end of the evening, and very thankful to take himself and his thoughts to bed. He tried to make sense of them, but the vision of Loukanos and his sinister drawings kept looming in the darkness. *What does a person look like when they're cut open?* Dan shivered. He felt very homesick, and wished he could feel Aunt Etta's comforting broad shoulders warm and solid against his. Somehow he always felt safe with her sleeping at his back. He supposed a lamb would feel the same cuddled up to a nice fat ewe. And as for his father … Dan suddenly longed to hear the reverent intake of breath as he began his prayers, and hear the sigh of acceptance as he finished. It was a reassuring sound, quite unlike the fitful snorts and gargles coming from the snoring Uncle Bukki in the corner.

Ammiel was not educated, like Loukanos, or even Anna, and his Aramaic was – like that of most Galileans – crudely spoken, with an accent that was sneered at by southerners – so he told his son. *But he is wiser than them all!* thought Dan defiantly. His father would have answers to all these new puzzles which had put up their unwelcome heads in the last couple of days – or at least, he would aid Dan to work them out for himself. Even Anna had been no help to Dan tonight, and how could he ask her to write a letter to Johanan when she was in such misery?

Dan sighed and turned over, feeling wretched. There were too many things in his head, and not enough people to share them with. He thought of his father again, and Caleb. He was frustrated that the wonderful excitement about the sureness of Messiah's birth had been so quickly diluted by so many tears of grief over Helen. Of course she should be wept over, it was only right. But what a mixture it all was! He sighed again and pulled the blankets over his head. He was worn out. He was restless. He was disappointed. He was excited. He was unhappy. Oh, he was ... not *sure* what he was any more!

A flickering flame wobbled into the room. Dan tried to lie still. Unexpectedly, in the feeble leaping light which Dan could sense through his eyelids, the covers were dragged gently from his head and turned down beneath his chin. Dan froze, his eyes shut, his breath quick and shallow.

"Tcha! Half smothering himself! He'll give himself nightmares," a voice muttered.

Dan felt his wrist being held, and heard a click of the tongue.

"There – nightmares already! Silly boy."

A cool hand touched his forehead. A grunt of satisfaction, and the light wavered away to the corner of the chamber and was extinguished in a whiff of oil.

For a long time all was silence. Dan's heart gradually stopped racing. Clearly Loukanos meant him no harm, though what he had meant at all was baffling. Dan abandoned any hope of understanding that, and cast his mind back to the Messiah question – deliberately recalling Caleb and the astonishing way he sang –

245

the look on his face. He tried to picture what Caleb had seen in the cave, to imagine how he had felt. *Messiah! Messiah!* But the funeral, Loukanos, Rhoda, the drawings he had seen – and worse, those he had not seen – kept intruding. Dan tried to quieten the clamour in his head, and tidy the cascade of vivid images. At last, sheer weariness muffled the voices to an indistinguishable murmur, and the images were dully floating around in totally believable disarray … when something pricked Dan into unwelcome wakefulness again.

He lay staring at the darkness, wondering, listening. Threaded through Uncle Bukki's guttural snores was a soft, smothered, choking sound. Drearily, quietly, Loukanos was weeping.

Despite his lingering tiredness, Dan woke early, yet again. It was always the way when he slept in a different place, for some reason. Today it was hunger which sent him creeping from his mat, a hunger of which he felt almost ashamed in this house of sorrow. It must have been all that funeral food he'd had to eat yesterday … no doubt Aunt Etta would say he'd stretched his stomach. He glanced nervously at Loukanos, half wondering whether he had only dreamt that tortured sound of the night before. Loukanos lay silently sleeping on his back, the shadowy outlines of his face revealing an unexpected resemblance to Helen. In the half light it was unnervingly like looking at her corpse. Dan picked his way past Uncle Bukki's jumbled heap of bedclothes, and slid behind the curtain into the outer room. He made his way to the kitchen without knocking anything over. The household slept still, much to his relief.

Dan tiptoed into the dim room and helped himself to water, wincing as he cracked the dipper accidentally against the rim of the jar. The cold drink helped but he was still desperately hungry. He poked and pried as quietly as he could, and finally discovered some flat bread in a crock. It was already very leathery. He didn't think Rhoda – or Anna – would mind if he ate it. Dan lifted it out and bit hungrily. It was not what he expected.

*What's this?!*

It was the package Rhoda had received the day before, still unopened.

Dan shook his head with a grin, and rummaged deeper in the crock, with more success. Chewing on his bread, he considered the mystery of the letter amongst the bread. Rhoda had been so miserable yesterday, and when Loukanos had bellowed at her to open the gate she had become rather scatterbrained. There had been so many people coming and going and "helping". Either she had dropped it in the dry crock for safekeeping while she was so busy, or someone had mistaken it for wrapped food … whichever it was, it was clear that neither Asa nor Anna had seen it.

Dan tucked it safely in his bosom and bent to replace his cup on the wooden shelf.

"Stop right there!" hissed a quiet voice, and Dan froze. He looked over his outstretched arm at the figure in the doorway, which brandished a grim looking stick. Too short for Anna or Asa, too tall for Rhoda, too thin for Uncle Bukki. Holding his breath, his heart turning somersaults, Dan very slowly straightened up, never taking his eyes off his challenger, who was edging forwards with equal slowness and menacing intent. Suddenly the figure gave a muffled yelp and bounded forward. Dan flinched, throwing up his arms to protect himself – and found himself wrapped in a boisterous embrace, being shaken to and fro.

247

"Dan! What are you doing here! Thought you were a thief! Save the household! Protect the women!" his attacker yapped hoarsely in his ear. Dan gasped.

"Johanan? Johanan!"

Their arms locked around each other, the two boys leapt exuberantly from foot to foot in a brief, delighted, clumsy dance of joy, before breaking off to hiss at each other to be quiet.

"Food!" Johanan demanded eagerly. "Got any?"

Dan nodded and the two of them tumbled out into the courtyard and clambered into the tree, where it was safer to talk, albeit very quietly.

"Whew!" Johanan rolled his eyes. "Scared me witless."

"*I scared you?!* I thought you were going to knock my head off."

Johanan grinned. "Not me. All bluff." He tore off chunks of bread and devoured them diligently while Dan pelted him with questions.

"When did you get here? Are you alone? How did you get in? Why are you here?"

Johanan tucked his mouthful into his cheek and replied huskily, "Just arrived. In strife. Ran off from Jerusalem. Climbed over the gate." He resumed chewing.

"You ran away from home? What, all the way from *Jerusalem*? How? Why? What happened?"

Johanan swallowed the bread and cleared his throat. "Rude to the rabbi."

Dan gasped. "You were rude to a rabbi? Why?"

Johanan took a breath and leaned back against a branch. "A long story. Now your turn. Same questions."

"I came with Uncle Bukki two days ago." Dan hesitated. The reason he had come, was not the reason he was still here. Which should he tell first? He made up his mind.

"Your Aunt Helen died yesterday."

Johanan stared at the rising sun. "Oh."

They sat in silence, while Johanan moodily picked at his toenails.

He said crossly, "I liked her. A lot."

Dan nodded. "Me too."

After a while he said curiously, "What's wrong with your voice?"

Johanan grunted in disgust. "Leaping."

"Leaping?"

"Like a frog. You know – up and down, up and down."

"Oh!" Dan was impressed. He squinted at Johanan's upper lip pointedly, and his friend barked a laugh.

"No whiskers yet. But you wait. I'm going to have the longest beard in town."

"Beards!" Dan grabbed his arm. "There's a man staying here who shaves his off!"

"What – a soldier?"

"No – it's Anna's half-brother – Loukanos!"

"Ah! Long, dark Loukanos!" Johanan looked knowing, and Dan begged,

"What do you know about him? I know he's a pagan. But there's more, isn't there? Did you know he's a *painter*? And he can draw too …"

Johanan shook his head urgently and put a finger on his lips. Someone was coming out of the house.

It was Anna. The boys breathed a sigh of relief and slid down the tree.

She looked up, startled, and pressed a hand to her heart.

"Dan – and *Johanan*? You'll be the death of me one day! What in the world are you doing here?"

The two dragged her to the stone bench under the tree and tried to explain. She looked sober.

"Johanan, rudeness to a rabbi – at your age? And running off from your loving home?"

Johanan blushed and gave her a defensive hug.

"I'm so sorry about Aunt Helen, cousin," he said. "I shouldn't have come here."

"Well, you couldn't have known … and she sank quickly at the end …" Her eyes dimmed a little. "But you have done wrong, cousin. What of your poor mother? You have really gone too far."

"I have," he agreed, as he remembered the long walk and the nights in the open, "But I left her a note."

"A note!" Anna lifted her hands in disgust. "Some comfort!"

Johanan squirmed a little.

Dan said, "Wait! This came from Johanan's mother yesterday!" He tugged the letter from his tunic and handed it to Anna. "I found it in the bread crock earlier. Rhoda must have forgotten it." He added, "It was for Helen. Rhoda meant to give it to your father."

"Ah!" There was silence while she read the letter.

"Well, young man, your mother got your note, and knows you were coming here."

"I told you."

"H'm … she wants us to keep you for a couple of days and talk sense into you before you go home."

"Thought she would."

"She says you've been missing school a lot … and that you will have much to say about it."

"Yes," he nodded emphatically. "Can I have some real breakfast first?"

Anna sighed and folded the letter.

"When my poor little Rhoda wakes and gets the fire going. Not before. She had a tiring day yesterday … as did we all. You are not going to be fussed over. And I want you to remember a few things, cousin – One, this is still a house of mourning. Two, we have guests, and Three, my brother Loukanos is here and not in the best of moods. He came all the way from Philippi for my sick mother's sake, and for my wedding. He was not pleased to find it postponed. And for her to die so quickly was a shock. Though of course, he was glad to see her again before …" She rubbed her forehead tiredly. "I had not known he was coming at all, or I would have sent word … though clearly it would have been too late anyway …"

She shook her head, her words trailing away.

Johanan put an arm round her shoulder impulsively and she looked up, patting his hand.

"Well, perhaps it is good you are here. Loukanos can scold you when he is cross, and the rest of us will escape."

Dan plucked at her sleeve. "You said you would tell me more of his story."

Anna glanced up at the sun which was glinting over the rooftops. "Oh, Dan – I have much to do in the kitchen."

"Please?"

Johanan urged, "Do, Anna. I don't know it all myself!"

Anna put out a hand to tidy Dan's curls, and stopped herself short with an apologetic laugh. "Well, it won't take long in the telling, I suppose, and Rhoda could do with a little extra sleep. You already know my brother lost his father while not much more than a baby. Soon afterwards, little Loukanos became very sick, and all mother's money could not buy a cure. She took him to the shrines of all her gods in vain, until a Jewish friend of hers told her to try the Hebrew God, insisting *He is the Master of the Universe.*

"Mother often told me of the desperate night she took her sickly son in her arms and carried him to a synagogue. It was dark and deserted, but the stars were out, and she took courage. A Master of the Universe, of all those stars? Surely he would find healing a little child a simple thing! She laid him at the closed door and prayed with earnest tears to the God she did not know. The next day, the fever was gone and he was hungry at last. Slowly my brother recovered, and mother was overjoyed. When he was quite well she returned to the synagogue – courageously, in daylight this time – and knelt on the doorstep to thank the Jews' God."

Anna began to laugh quietly, much to the boys' surprise. She explained.

"Inside, a Sabbath service had just finished – and just as she bowed her head, the door was flung open and she was knocked flying – struck almost senseless. Men streamed out of the door and there was such a fuss as they saw this Gentile woman staggering, holding her head and moaning on their sacred steps! Only a visiting merchant from Galilee had compassion. He ran to help her, and heard her story … Well! She converted fully to Judaism, against her family's wishes of course. That was the last she heard of them! But it's a romantic tale, isn't it?"

"And then she met Uncle Asa?" Johanan didn't like loose ends. Anna laughed again.

"He was the Galilean merchant. He settled in Greece for a while after marrying his proselyte wife, and adopted little Loukanos as his own – and then I came along to complete the family."

Dan stood up and stretched happily. It was a good story. But –

"Why didn't Loukanos come with you to Galilee?"

Anna's smile faded. She sighed and rubbed her hands over her face, combing back sleep-tousled hair with her fingers.

"That was years later, when I was about eight years old, and Loukanos was twelve or thirteen. He hated being brought up as a Jew, and wanted to be like his Greek friends. And then to be taken away to some uncivilised Jewish backwater? Never! He jumped ship at Cyprus and ran away to my father's brother who lives there. Yes, Johanan, don't smile – he too ran away, but he was just as wrong as you! Perhaps you are the more wrong, because you believe the Commandments, and he didn't.

"Well, Uncle Joseph did his best, but Loukanos had the bit between his teeth. He ran away from him as well and made his way back to Greece. You see, boys, running away can become a habit. We lost him for years. Mother could never bear to speak of him.

253

For her son to reject the God whom she believed had saved his life ..."

"What happened next?" Dan was amazed. Why, Loukanos had only been Johanan's age! Imagine roaming the empire on your own rather than being safe with your family!

Johanan caught Dan's eye. His recent exploit looked rather petty in comparison.

"Ten years later my parents returned to Greece for a period. Loukanos heard of it from some Jewish friends, and came in repentance to my mother. He had missed her badly, but was too proud to seek her out before. They were inseparable from then on till we returned to Cana some years later. He was pursuing his own dreams of success, and would not come with us, which was understandable."

Dan looked puzzled, remembering the messy painting under the tree.

"Is he successful now?"

Anna gave a wry smile. "Oh, yes, indeed. Very. Except in the one thing which matters. The true Faith." She held out her hands. "Enough delay! I have duties to attend to and again, I am not properly dressed yet." She shook her finger at Dan. "You are always catching me with my hair uncovered and putting me to shame. I was in Greece too long, I think, and grew careless."

The boys took a hand each and pulled her to her feet.

She warned Johanan, "My father will want to speak to you later."

He nodded gloomily, and watched her hurry back to the house.

As soon as she had gone he brightened and sprawled himself comfortably on the warm spot where she had been sitting.

"Now! There's so much to tell!"

Dan nodded eagerly. "But I have to tell you something first! " he blurted out, unable to wait any longer. "Anna and the others already know – but the funeral has spoiled everything – it is this! Messiah has really come! He is here!"

To his astonishment Johanan's face fell a little.

"But *I* wanted to tell *you*!" he cried, lifting himself on one elbow.

"What?"

"Yes! I know he is here!"

Dan was so dumbfounded he could only echo while gathering his wits, "Yes! He is here – somewhere!"

Questions rushed to his tongue and jammed themselves together. He had just opened his mouth to splutter "But how do you know?" when Johanan swung his legs around and sat up straight, his dark eyes glowing. Deliberately he said,

"I know where he is ... and I've seen him ..."

## Chapter Twenty-one

DAN stared at his friend's triumphant face.

"Seen him?" he croaked, feeling more like an echo than ever.

Johanan nodded.

Dan shook his head to clear his thoughts.

"How did you know him?" he demanded. "And why doesn't all the country know of it by now?"

"Look!" Johanan said, "The thing is, he's not what anyone's expected."

"What do you mean?"

Johanan frowned, toying with a broken sandal. "That's why I argued with the rabbi."

"Stop going around in circles."

"I mean, the rabbis say Messiah restores the Kingdom ... puts Jews back where they belong – God's chosen people – leaders of the world."

"Well?"

" ... and he appears in shining splendour to the leaders of his people ..."

"Do they?" Dan recalled Caleb's words … yes, the angels shone in splendour, but not the baby in the cave.

"So they say. But not much about how he goes about it."

Dan was nearly mad with impatience. "Never mind the rabbis! Just tell me the important bits!"

"What if he *doesn't?*" Johanan replied abruptly.

"Doesn't *what?*"

"Doesn't appear in shining splendour. Doesn't appear to the leaders … .."

Dan opened his mouth to reply, then shut it.

"Oh!" he said, almost to himself. *Just an ordinary baby, shown to shepherds.* "Wait – yes! That's right! I don't think he does! I mean, he didn't."

It was Johanan's turn to look puzzled, but he ploughed on regardless.

"What if he just bursts out of nowhere and calls his people to turn to their God?"

"That sounds all right –" said Dan cautiously, "doesn't it? Isn't that what the prophets did?"

"I think so," answered his friend firmly. "So what would you think if you went somewhere and found a holy man, big, strong! – voice of authority, caring for nobody, preaching repentance? Saying *'The Time Has Come!'* Demanding that *Jews* purify themselves?"

Dan swallowed. "Was he – old or young?"

"I don't know – about thirty, I suppose," Johanan was surprised to be asked. "And a voice like thunder!"

258

Dan got to his feet. About thirty! Oh! Could it be? His legs felt peculiar, but he had one thought in mind, even before asking more questions.

"We have to tell Anna!"

Johanan nodded. "And there's lots more to tell. Oh, but I'm tired! And hungry yet!"

Dan looked at him properly for the first time, seeing how dusty and weary he looked. It was a very long tramp from Jerusalem to Cana. Dan had never done it, but he knew it was at least a two or three day journey.

Rhoda pattered across the courtyard, her shadow flitting over the fresh weak light on the paving.

"Will you come in and break your fast?"

Johanan got up gladly, groaning about his stiff limbs, and galloped awkwardly past her into the house. Dan followed in time to hear Anna ordering her cousin to wash his head and hands. *Women and water!* She was as bad as Aunt Etta.

Rhoda plucked at his sleeve, her face flushed.

"Thank you for finding the letter. Yesterday I was so distressed … and my head ached so … I … just forgot all about it. I don't know how I came to put it with the bread."

Dan grinned. "It tasted horrible," he said, and was rewarded with another of Rhoda's giggles. But her heart was not in it.

Anna would not let them talk while eating. Not even about Johanan's Messiah.

"We are all worn out," she said softly but firmly. "I know we have much to tell each other, but it will be better when we are all together and not whispering. The men are still asleep, and must

259

not be woken till they please. Rhoda has even covered the chicken coop to keep the birds silent. Dan, will Aunt Etta worry if you are not home by tonight? I would have you – and Bukki – stay a little longer."

Dan bounced a little with joy. Now that Johanan was here he had forgotten his homesickness.

"She expected us to be away at least four days," he said hopefully. "She said Uncle Bukki would not like to be rushed. Marta's Ittai is visiting her each morning, and father was to be home tonight."

Anna nodded. "Good. I will send her a message with Philip the fishmonger. He deals with the ben Zebedees near Banayim, and will always take a note for a few coins. Today is his usual buying trip and he makes short work of the journey with his donkeys. Let me see … a full moon, so no doubt he'll return tonight to have the fish fresh for early market … That means we'll have an answer before sunrise tomorrow morning. If Aunt Etta says you may not stay, you can still leave before noon and be home at the time she planned."

She yawned suddenly. "I'll have him put the answer under the gate," she said tiredly. "So we don't have to get up with the sun – or stars – yet again! Dan, shall I take back the letter I gave you and send it to your father as well? It will reach him before you do, now."

Dan nodded, unable to speak because her yawn had set him and Johanan off, both. She shook her head at them in sympathy, and then caught Rhoda yawning too. She murmured a word to the girl, and Rhoda slipped off gratefully. With a stack of hot barley cakes and milk inside him, Johanan was already half asleep. Anna shook his shoulder gently.

"It's bed for you, cousin, as soon as you're clean enough. You've been walking for days and sleeping rough for a city lad. We won't get much sense out of you in this state."

She took a basin of water, spread a rough sack over her lap and knelt down to wash his feet. Johanan was startled into wakefulness.

"Anna! That's a servant's job! My feet are filthy!"

Anna looked at him seriously.

"Would you have little Rhoda do it? No, Johanan, I'm doing this in place of your dear mother. You see, I know how she feels, because of our Loukanos. How happy she would be to know you have come safely to those who love you, in spite of your wilfulness! How gladly she would wash your straying feet, if she were here!"

Johanan swallowed something in his throat and was silent. Anna toweled his feet roughly and stood up. Her cousin flung his arms around her waist and hugged her fiercely. She smacked his head lovingly.

"Take my room," she said, pushing him in the right direction. "And take that hollow-eyed Dan-boy with you. I don't want to see or hear either of you for four hours. After that, the whole family will eat together – then talk as much you like. I promise."

The boys knew that tone. They went silently to her room, pulled off their outer clothes and dropped on to her cushioned bed, Johanan without a thought, Dan with a feeling of trespass. He couldn't believe he was so sleepy so soon after getting up. But somehow, the tension of the last few days was draining away, even faster than the questions about Johanan seeing the Messiah were pressing in. Dan hadn't realised how poorly he had slept of late. *What a soft bed!* It was almost as good as Aunt Etta herself. He pulled up the bedclothes, tugging back his portion from Johanan's greedy hunched shoulders. *A sheet! Such luxury!* It smelled faintly of spikenard. Dan sniffed in the clean, sweetly spicy scent and relaxed even more.

*Why do we always get interrupted?* Still, Johanan wasn't going anywhere. There would yet be plenty of time to talk. Already the older boy was dead-to-the-world, exhausted by his adventures and sated with warm food. *How did Anna know I was still so tired?* And the important answers could be explored later in the day, with Asa and Anna to help – despite the unavoidable impediments of Uncles Bukki and Loukanos. Dan removed Johanan's sharp elbow from his ribs, and turned over with a thankful sigh. It had been a good breakfast – more than he would have had at home, where it was taken on the run. In here at least there was no snoring, no stifled sobbing … just silence … Suddenly, he was asleep too.

Anna poured the dirty water away and wiped her hands on the coarse towel. She pulled the letter for her betrothed from Dan's little satchel hanging on a peg behind the door, and scrawled a hasty footnote with a blunt pen and the cheap ink she kept in the kitchen. Gently fanning her page to dry the ink, she looked around the silent house, still dark with its night shutters down. The men had not stirred. Rhoda was curled up in her little cubbyhole in the storeroom, whence Anna had sent her. The boys were sleeping like puppies.

Quietly the tall woman slipped out of the house to Blind Mordecai's haunt on the street corner, She had never seen him sleep. Sure enough, as she approached, his scarred, greasy face twitched in her direction. He knew her steps, her voice, the scent of her garments, and the smell of her food, as he knew everything about everybody.

"Shalom, Anna, daughter of Asa. Alas! for your mother, the kind Helen of Philippi, and may she rest in peace," he said courteously. "Many's the piece of soft-worn linen she gave me." He touched with respect the finely woven bandage hiding his terrible eyes.

"Shalom, Mordecai. It is a sad loss indeed." She was silent a moment.

"You have fresh barley cakes for me, Anna. Such a good smell. Why so early?"

Anna was recalled to her errand. "Will you take word to Philip the Younger before he leaves for the Sea today?"

"The fishmonger? So easy! I'll just follow my nose ..." he cackled quietly.

Anna looked at the ugly damaged face compassionately. The smashed nose almost met his upper lip. She made an effort.

"Don't do that, Mordecai," she responded, knowing his eagerness in trading jokes. "The man is not underground ..."

It was not her idea of amusement, but Mordecai chuckled and wheezed with enjoyment. Retelling it would be worth a few extra pence on market day. She handed him Ammiel's letter and gave the message for Etta, and he repeated it exactly. Anna left him enjoying both his joke and his unexpected breakfast, knowing he was a reliable messenger. He knew his way about the town – well, blindfold.

Wearily she let herself back into the house, glad to have avoided other early risers and their condolences. Suddenly her limbs and head felt as heavy as her heart. All was still deathly quiet despite the brightening sun without. Even Bukki was no longer snoring. Through the dim of the shuttered house she moved softly to the room where Helen had spent so long … the room where her heart and flesh had failed, and her spirit strengthened. It was empty now, everything within it washed and dried and strewn with aromatic herbs, the low bed stripped back to a narrow mattress and folded blankets.

Anna kicked off her sandals and stretched herself slowly on the bed, pulling up a red-brown blanket to her cheek. Her eyelashes trembled as she sensed the aroma of wool stealing with warmth from the auburn fibres. Head pillowed on a cushion, she clasped the blanket in her arms, her eyes staring at nothing visible, and over-spilling with loss.

"Ammiel," she whispered, half ashamed. "Where are you when I need you?"

Her lips moved in silent prayer. Slowly the lines on her forehead melted, the wet-fringed lids drooped gradually over brown and hazel eyes, and she too slept, in sheer exhaustion of soul.


Dan stretched himself luxuriously and rolled on to the floor. The bed was glorious, but sharing it with Johanan was not. At least Aunt Etta didn't kick and twitch. Johanan must have been walking to Cana and back in his sleep. Dan peered out through the shutters. Why it was broad noon! He looked back at his friend, who slept on regardless, short eyelashes flickering. It was tempting to throw open the shutters to wake him, but Dan decided to leave him alone. The smell of food would get Johanan up soon enough. Dan padded out to the kitchen. Surely Rhoda would be up too by now. It was strange to be getting up to eat at such a time … there would be no midday sleep now, anyway! so they could all sit in the cool house and talk properly at last.

The kitchen door was open to the courtyard, the light outside clear and bright, and the air heavy with warmth. Rhoda was listlessly fanning the low fire, her cheeks red. Dan nodded to her and was about to speak when Loukanos wandered in, his hair no longer sleek, but looping in unruly curls all over his head.

"What in the name of Zeus is everyone doing, lying about sleeping!" he complained, ignoring the fact that he had been doing the same. "Girl, did you not wake your mistress?"

Rhoda looked at him uneasily and her lip trembled. Dan came to the rescue.

"We all woke at dawn," he said. "When Johanan came from Jerusalem. Anna made us eat and return to bed. She said we were all worn out. I think she's asleep too."

Loukanos chewed his lip and grunted. "Well, there's some sense in that," he conceded ungraciously. "Sorrow saps the body. What's that about Johanan?"

Dan told him.

Loukanos shook his head. "Young people!"

It surprised Dan that he of all people should be so disapproving. But then, this Loukanos was full of surprises.

There was a hiss of steam as the covered pot on the fire boiled over. Rhoda squealed as a splash of hot water hit her bare instep.

"I'm sorry," she stammered with tears, "I wasn't paying attention ..."

She lifted the heavy pot unsteadily from the coals, setting it down on the hearth with a bang. Loukanos looked at her lean brown foot. "Not fatal," he said, tipping a beaker of cold water over it. He eyed her sharply. "How long have you been sitting over this fire?"

"Not long."

Loukanos reached out a hand and she flinched. He flung his arm down by his side in exasperation. "By the stars, girl! Do I hit children?"

He glanced at Dan, who glared at him.

"What is all this?" Anna entered, cool and refreshed, full of her usual calm resolve. "What are you doing to my good girl?"

Loukanos gave her a brief reply in Greek.

"Oh." Anna sat down and held out her hand. "Come here, Rhoda. My brother will not hurt you." She touched Rhoda's face with the back of her hand and nodded to Loukanos.

"Are you feeling quite well, child? Do you have any pains?"

Rhoda looked guilty. "My head, and under my eyes … since yesterday … but it was not a day to be unwell …"

"I understand," said Anna. "But today you are allowed to be sick. I think you have sat up too many nights with my mother, and I reproach myself. You are a little feverish, but I think it is only a cold."

Cupping the unhappy face, she pressed her thumbs lightly around Rhoda's nose and cheekbones and the girl winced. Loukanos rubbed his hands and said something laughingly to his sister. Anna smiled and fetched a bowl and towel and a pungent plant from the storeroom.

"There is nothing to fear, Rhoda," she said cheerfully. "Loukanos is teasing me. He thinks a good Roman steam bath would cure you. Like most men, he swears that would fix anything. But of course

266

any excuse for a steam bath. I think it's the gossip and the pampering and the food they like more than anything. We'll have to make do with a little bowl."

While she spoke, she poured boiling water into the bowl and crumbled into it a spike of rosemary leaves. Dan watched with interest as she bent Rhoda's head over the mixture and draped the towel over girl and bowl like a tent.

Just then Uncle Bukki came in, and gave a leap of alarm at the vision before him. Little squeaks and gasps came from under the towel.

"It is only congestion from a cold!" Anna reassured him firmly. She looked at Bukki's worried face and relented, extracting Rhoda temporarily from her steam tent.

"Come, Rhoda, you will do this elsewhere. Go to my room, and continue your treatment there. Take plenty of clean rags and keep trying to clear your head. When the water cools, wrap up and lie down. I'll bring you some chicken soup later. If Johanan is still in bed, tell him to get up at once and join us here."

"Drink plenty of water," added Loukanos gruffly, shoving a jug into her free hand.

Rhoda nodded forlornly and disappeared.

From his cautious corner, Bukki heaved a sigh of relief. What with having to associate with pagans, and people dying and suffering from colds and congestion and undergoing strange cures – Asa's spacious house was shrinking too fast for his liking. Johanan's face appeared, bright and energetic as usual, all traces of his earlier tiredness gone, and thankful to find that Anna had already spoken to her father about his unceremonious arrival. Asa followed on the boy's heels, apologising and berating himself for his rudeness in sleeping in.

"Peace, father," said Anna, moving briskly about the kitchen. "Yesterday and today were not normal days. We have all slept deeply. Sleep is a great healer. Now we will do better for it."

The table was spread with good food, much of it thoughtful gifts from neighbours the day before. Loukanos sat with his arms folded, staring at the ceiling while Asa gave the blessing.

"Blessed art Thou, Master of the Universe, who causeth bread to come forth from the world. To Thee creation lifts its eyes, to Thee we turn and are fed day by day. In joy our Increaser, in trouble our Guide, in sorrow our Comfort, Thou art our God and our Salvation. Amen."

"Amen," they responded. Loukanos simply reached out a long hand and helped himself.

The relative silence of hungry eating was brief. Asa looked at the three expectant, impatient younger faces around him and nodded soberly, his eyes still heavy with long weeping.

"Yes, Anna has told me, there is much waiting to be said. Yesterday my dearest Helen was yet living, and I can only thank God for the haste with which He sent us Dan – and Bukki – with their great news. I am so grateful she shared our joy and certainty in Messiah's coming before she died. Dan, you will thank your father a thousand times for me. Now this boy, my sister's son, has incurred wrath because he too shares this certainty. You were very wrong to run away, Johanan," he turned to his nephew seriously, "but now I charge you to tell us all you know, all you have seen, and let us consider this matter further together, as a family."

268

Johanan nodded eagerly, and leaned forward. "I tried to tell Dan a bit this morning," he said. "But I was tired, and hungry, and Anna sent us to bed. Now to start at the beginning. I really have seen him. And asked lots about him. It's the Messiah, all right. Even his birth was a miracle!"

Anna automatically murmured under her breath her mother's saying, "Every birth is a miracle."

Johanan caught it and looked scornful. "Not like that. Not soft women's talk. I mean a real miracle. Against nature."

There was a disconcerted silence. Asa put down his bread in the act of pulling it apart.

"Go on, boy," he said. He looked sideways at Loukanos who was ostentatiously saying nothing. "No one will interrupt you."

## Chapter Twenty-two

BUKKI ducked his head and scratched a reddening ear with exaggerated nonchalance. Talking about religion was one thing, even if it had to be done in such a passionate group, and in front of a man like Loukanos as well. But neither of the words "miracle" and "birth" was a subject Bukki felt comfortable – or qualified – to discuss … especially with a woman present … and to put the two together was not … was not … well, it just *wasn't*, that's all!

Nobody else noticed his fidgets. Johanan drummed his stumpy fingers on the table excitedly. "Against nature, see?" he repeated. "And the best part is, I found out his name – Johannes – so really it's the same as mine! Won't that be confusing!"

"I doubt anyone will be in much danger of confusing you with a saintly deliverer of the nation," commented Loukanos drily.

Asa held up a hand. "One thing at a time. So, his name is Johannes, well, good! We won't forget that in a hurry. *Favoured of the Eternal!*"

He looked around the group, as gratified as if he had chosen the name himself. "A fitting name for our Messiah!"

"Yes, but you know," Johanan added impatiently, "he preaches to everyone – not just us! He calls everyone to turn to God before it's too late – Samaritans, even – and Roman soldiers – anyone who'll listen."

"That's interesting!" said Anna softly. "It reminds me of Jonah … a Jewish prophet with a cosmopolitan message … Now, I wonder what that signifies?"

Dan tapped her and whispered, "What's cosmopolitan?"

"Something which spreads over many countries, Dan, or many races …"

Dan felt something settle gently into place inside him, but he wasn't sure what it was. *Many countries … many races – many stars … many seeds … could it be?*

"Messiah is a seed of Abraham … part of the promises?" he muttered without realising he'd spoken aloud.

"Yes, Dan, most certainly! What are you thinking?"

Dan scratched his head, not exactly clear what he was thinking. "What you said … *In thee shall all nations of the earth be blessed …* Is that 'cosmopolitan?'"

"Yes, it is, Dan!" Loukanos interrupted, looking highly amused, and forgetting to call him 'boy' for once. "Yes, indeed it is *cosmopolitan!* Well, well, well! How about a Jewish messiah who comes to fulfil the promises … and forgets he's exclusive to Jews … and opens his arms to bless all the nations of the earth!" He tipped back his chair and gave a shout of laughter. "That's one in the eye for the chosen people!"

"Softly, softly, Loukanos," his stepfather admonished gently. "Dan is a lad who thinks, and thinks with purpose, on good things. He is young and unsophisticated, and may easily follow a thought down a blind alley. If Jews are blessed, and the heathen respect that, they will be blessed too. *I will bless them that bless thee.* That is what it means."

Uncle Bukki decided it was safe to expostulate. "Don't forget! Messiah is just for the Jews, Dan," he warned, feeling very avuncular and wise. "What would he want with mere Gentiles! ... Oh! Ah, begging pardon ... present company excepted ... or, ah ..."

"Present company *not* excepted, you mean ..." Loukanos was hugely enjoying poor Bukki's discomfort. "Present company being a mere Gentile who himself wants nothing to do with Jewish messiahs, whether real or pretenders."

"Then why," Anna flashed, "is Present Company sitting here to discuss it?"

Her hand flew to her mouth almost at once but the words were said.

Loukanos abruptly scraped back his chair and strode to the door. The others hesitated, expecting him to storm out, but he stopped suddenly, folding his arms, and leant his head wearily against the doorpost. His muscular chest swelled and sank slowly in a long, deep sigh. He turned his head and glanced over his shoulder at the mismatched group behind him.

"It was mother's wish," he told them truculently. "I promised to stay beside my sister until she found her Messiah, or until she married, whichever came first."

He turned back to stare at the glaring courtyard.

Johanan laughed, Dan grinned, and Uncle Bukki looked puzzled. Asa and Anna sought each other's hand under the table, and gripped hard as they exchanged voluble looks. Asa touched fingertips to his lips and Anna nodded almost imperceptibly.

"Good, son," said Asa casually. "It is good that you honour your promise even if reluctantly. Your mother would be proud." There was no answer, so Asa continued offhandedly, "Well now, it is in your own interest for Anna to find him as soon as possible, so let me suggest that you approach the matter without prejudice. Observation, deduction, diagnosis, application ... these are your skills. You apply them to your study of painting, apply them now as a physician would. Apply them to this case despite your disapproval of the patient."

Loukanos scuffed his foot slowly back and forth against the stone doorstep while the family held their peace. He turned abruptly.

"Well spoken, father. No more kicking against the goad, then. For mother's sake – and my own. But I warn you – and Anna – I will be merciless in my haste, and my thoroughness. I will not be recalled once I leave this miserable country."

He threw himself back into the chair and put his elbows on the table. He waved a hand at Johanan. "Continue. Messiah candidate – name, Johannes – Approved of Yahweh –" Asa flinched reflexively at the free use of the sacred name, but said nothing, and Loukanos finished, "... and supposedly a miracle child. Now that sounds more interesting and to the point. Explain, Johanan, or perhaps we should call you Johannes too?"

Johanan's mouth quirked. "Miracle birth – yes – his mother was past childbearing age when he was born."

Loukanos snorted. "Past childbearing! Many a lonely little extra is tacked onto the end of a family through *that* misconception!" He sought Bukki's eye for appreciation of his joke, but gave up as Bukki merely blinked uncomprehendingly.

"Maybe!" Johanan retorted, who refused to acknowledge such a low play on words, even at the expense of being thought unsophisticated like Dan. "But what about when the woman was barren? Never carried – never even conceived? Long past wishing, long past bearing … Husband and wife old … married fifty years and never a flicker of hope?"

"Perhaps that *would* be miraculous," Loukanos conceded grudgingly, "*if* it were true, and the woman's age and infertility not in doubt. But who's to prove it?"

"There's more!" Johanan interrupted. "What about a miracle at the birth?"

"We Jews like our miracles," Uncle Bukki said deprecatingly, with a nervous smile, wishing the miracle would choose a less biological subject for demonstration.

"What else do you know, Johanan?" Anna asked. "Though, if what you say is true, it would hardly need more evidence. Historically, this has been a sign of God's intervention for significant chosen ones – the patriarchs all had barren wives – and think of Hannah and Samuel, Manoah's wife and Samson …"

"No, no, Anna," her father checked her. "Loukanos is right – a miraculous conception is not easy to prove in the absolute, and can only rely on the truthfulness of the couple involved. In the mouth of two or three witnesses a thing can be established, not one. So perhaps it would indeed 'need more'."

Johanan came to almost the last crumb of information which he possessed.

"His father was dumb."

The others were nonplussed, not seeing the point.

"He was!" Johanan assured them. "That is what I heard. And when the boy was born he began to speak."

Loukanos looked at him steadily and cocked a sardonic eyebrow.

Johanan looked back at him crossly. "I meant the father began to speak, not the child!"

His cousin shrugged and admitted, "I suppose that's possible. But not necessarily a miracle. If his wife had conceived so surprisingly, he may well have been struck dumb with a nervous shock, a kind of hysteria … one of those vows you people use to barter with your God."

Dan thought of a pagan Helen praying to the God of the Jews for her sick boy – did she 'barter' for his life? – while Loukanos continued to discount the idea of any miracle.

"Perhaps it was even a deliberate choice to remain speechless, borne out of painful suspicion. Later, the birth of the child, the joy of finally holding a living heir, however dubiously produced … could have quelled his doubts, anger, fears … and he found his tongue again."

Dan, who had understood half of this and Johanan, who had understood most, exchanged disgusted glances. Asa and Anna, who had understood it all, looked frustrated. Uncle Bukki who had understood none, merely blinked again. *Even a fool is counted wise when he keeps his mouth shut*" was one proverb even he knew and had often found useful. Loukanos watched them all, and slapped his palms on the table in a dismissive gesture.

"I see," he said flatly. "You already believe enough to bar the door to doubt."

Asa shook his head. "Not really, Loukanos. But to be fair, we are examining this in a different light to you. You see, we are already confident Messiah is here. We are only trying to determine who and where he is."

There was a moment's silence.

Anna stood up. "Have some more soup, Loukanos. Bukki? Anyone else? This is Old Dinah's – better than any I make, and she guards her recipe like Holy Writ. I must take some to Rhoda. Father, do tell Loukanos and Johanan what the rest of us know from Dan and Ammiel. Then we will all know all there is to know, and things will be clearer."

She poured a bowl for Rhoda and left the room.

"How are you feeling, Rhoda?"

The heavy eyes looked dully up at her. Anna put down the bowl.

"No better?" She felt the damp forehead, and back of her neck. "Come on, lamb, let's get some of this soup into you."

She lifted the girl in the crook of her arm and fed her the soup slowly. Rhoda began to whimper, looking a little green. She gulped.

"I feel …" she was unable to finish as a heaving spasm wrenched her without warning.

"Oh! Oh dear!" she sobbed. "I'm so sorry!"

Anna sighed, and laid her back gently.

"Never mind, Rhoda. I'm sure you feel better now. Maybe enough stayed down to do you good." She wiped the girl's face, gathered her skirts carefully, and opened the shutter wide.

"I'll be back in a moment to clean you up. As soon as I change my clothes."

She let herself out a side door. The wry thought persisted, that evidently it was her year for collecting second-hand meals.

It was some time before she rejoined the group around the table. Loukanos raised an enquiring eyebrow.

Anna replied with a smile.

"A bit sorry for herself, that's all." She sat down. "No painting tonight."

Dan had almost given up trying to work out where Loukanos' painting fitted into the scheme of things. It reminded him there was more to discover later. And what in the world did Anna mean by referring to it just then?

Asa looked appreciatively at his extended family and waved his hands expansively.

"Now we have all shared our information – now we all know what is going on – and the matter fits together better than ever. We have an announcement by angels, the presentation of a child, a heavenly sign, a quest by eastern wise men for the King of the Jews, the wrath of the king, the terrible slaughter of innocent children, and the weeping of the community … foretold by the prophet Jeremiah, and corresponding with the time worked out by the learned from the writings of Daniel."

"A child of promise, born to be King, in the city of David," Anna summed up, pouring her father watered wine, "who would now be around twenty nine or thirty years of age … ready to reveal himself."

"That's what I've been telling you," said Johanan as patiently as he could.

"A long time to be waiting around, wouldn't you say?" Loukanos said drily.

Johanan interrupted so scornfully that his voice squeaked, dropped to a growl and leapt back to a squeak before he finished the sentence –"King David had to wait around – he was thirty years old before he began to reign!"

He clutched his throat and rolled his eyes at Dan expressively. Dan bit his lips and managed not to laugh, but Loukanos didn't even try. He laughed out loud even while clapping his young cousin on the back with a barely sympathetic thud.

Anna patted Johanan's hand and said pointedly, "Loukanos is remembering how badly he suffered himself when his voice changed. You know, there was the time ..."

"Pax, Anna, pax!" her brother said hastily. "I promise to be kinder."

"Be so," she responded warningly.

Asa continued as if there had been no interruption. "And here we have a sturdy young prophet appearing in the Jordan valley, child of a miraculous conception, his birth attended by a miraculous cure, named *Johannes* to signify our God's approval – now around thirty years old and preaching of renewal, repentance and cleansing!"

Loukanos tapped his long fingers together and studied them.

"Given your own criteria, and ready belief in the interference of your God in human affairs, I can see how it may appear plausible to you," he said finally.

Uncle Bukki came to life at this. "Yes, it indeed appears convincing," he said agreeably, eyeing the jug expectantly. Anna filled a cup with the mixture and pushed it towards him with a brief smile. He drank thirstily, but with disappointment, wishing she was not so generous on the water side. Why, it was barely flavoured.

Dan nudged Johanan. "You still haven't told us how you found out about this man," he reminded him.

"Nobody gives me chance!" his friend protested. "It was mother – her friends – a wedding in Jericho. I had to go too – you know, squealing and cackling and Oh-dear-you-were-such-a-beautiful baby-how-you've-grown! sort of friends … suppose they'd be more surprised if I *hadn't*, … when they'd finished with pulling my looks apart … crying over the bride … clucking about the food and clothes … talk started about a prophet. Close by – at Bethabara, edge of the desert. Just appeared one day and started preaching! So soon as we could, off we went to see for ourselves. There he was – preaching, just like they said he would be. And dozens of people, all over the rocks like washday … by the water … listening."

"What did he look like?" Dan asked eagerly. Surely he'd get a more satisfactory reply than Caleb's 'all newborns look alike … ' sort of answer.

"Big – with a voice to match. Thin but strong. Big hands, big bones. Balding forehead, hair in long ropes, bearded clear down to his belly, and tanned as a soldier's boot. Rough tunic, girded up, with a leather belt. Like Elijah, I suppose."

Dan sighed with satisfaction. He had been hoping for something like this – while secretly afraid of a kind of glorified princely Pharisee who would not have time for ordinary 'rough' people – especially uncultured Galileans.

"Nice observations," Loukanos murmured to himself in a surprised tone. "Not bad for a careless lad."

Dan heard it and felt a glow of pride in his friend. Perhaps after all Loukanos wasn't so bad himself, *for a careless uncle* …! Dan was pleased with his mental quip.

"Why was he girded up?" Always after meaning in the small details, Anna was curious. "Was he on a journey? Or working? But you said he was preaching."

"He was. Preaching, I mean. But I suppose he was working too, in a way." Johanan leaned forward, savouring his moment. He had been saving this for effect.

"See, he was baptising people!"

"What?" Almost in unison they all chorused. "What? Baptising?"

Even Loukanos raised his eyebrows – both of them this time, instead of his usual lopsidedly quizzical look.

"That's what I said. Baptising. Hold your breath and push you under."

"Why?"

Loukanos scratched at his cheeks. It would not do to shave during the days of mourning, and his stubble itched. "Mother was baptized, you know."

Asa confirmed it. "Indeed she was – but because she was a Gentile, a proselyte, converting to the faith from her pagan ways. Had she been a captive in war *I* would have shaved her head and cut her nails," he said with an attempt at a smile, "but she was a captive of conviction. Therefore she was baptized to wash away her old allegiances – just as the mixed multitude were baptized with the Hebrews in the Red Sea, and became part of the congregation of God."

Dan, who didn't know anything about baptism, listened with fascination.

"So Gentiles can become Jews? Is that allowed?"

"Of course," Anna gently reproached him. "We are speaking of my mother, remember."

"Yes, yes," said Dan, kicking himself for stupidity. "She was a Greek *Greek*, wasn't she … well, you know what I mean, not a Greek *Jew*, not to start with, anyway …"

"That's right, Dan," Asa encouraged with an approving nod. "She became a Greek Jew when she was baptized. Her Jewishness was by faith, not by birth."

"So are all Gentiles who want to be Jews baptized? "

"Not always. But it is common, yes," Anna said.

Dan propped his chin in his hands and knit his brows at the delicate black patterns on the red wine jug.

"Then why baptize *Jews*? They are *already* Jews. Where's the change?"

Uncle Bukki sighed with relief. Someone was asking the obvious questions, and it didn't have to be him.

Johanan held up a finger and wagged it tantalisingly. "Aha! That's it, isn't it?! Why? As Dan says, where's the change?"

"You tell us, since you have the answers." Loukanos folded his arms. By the stars, it was like drawing teeth, getting anything out of this boy!

Johanan stabbed his finger in his chest. "Here! And here!" He tapped his head. "That's where the change is. The change is – in repentance!"

"Repentance!"

"Yes – that's what I was telling you before you started! The Messiah preaches Repentance. Repent of our sins, great or small.

Repent, turn away, change, leave them behind – and he will baptize you for the remission of sins!"

Asa blew out a long breath, shaking his head and murmuring under his breath. Anna stared at the boy, motionless. Uncle Bukki bridled a little. Sins? Such a harsh word! He'd never murdered anyone. What could he have to 'repent' of? His 'sins' were tiny little grey things hardly worthy of the name. He was – basically – a good – (well, sort-of) person ... Uncle Loukanos was smiling grimly. Dan looked from one to the other, feeling anxious. His world was shifting ground again, just as he had got it stabilised.

"But – but, what about the sacrifices? The temple ... the sin offerings?"

"Where does the law speak of baptism?" Asa joined him, dismayed.

Johanan shrugged apologetically. "It's what he demands," he said. "And he's the Messiah, so can't he demand what he wants? Can't he add something new without spoiling the old? Does the law speak of baptism of proselytes either?"

Anna flashed him a relieved smile. "Right, cousin! It does not. Is it wrong? Clearly not, since it is permitted by the learned. Of long tradition it is held that adding extra rituals respectfully, dutifully and willingly to the law, in order to cover situations which are new or unexpected, is a safeguard of holiness ... and regarded as honourable – not wrong!"

"I see. I see." Asa chewed his grizzled moustache anxiously. "At least, I think I see ... so you think that a baptism of repentance is a good thing ..."

Johanan linked his short fingers together and pushed his hands inside out with a cracking sound. "It's not whether we think it's a

283

good thing … a thing commanded by the Messiah? Of course it's good! And useful! How many people keep running up to the temple to make sin offerings all the time? I don't know any who do, and I live in Jerusalem!"

Poor Bukki had been valiantly trying to follow the thread.

"What's the difference, if you have to keep on running off to be baptized all the time?" he grimaced. "Though it's cheaper, I suppose …"

"I don't know," Johanan admitted. "I didn't think he meant all the time, just once. For the remission of sins, remember."

Dan tugged Anna's sleeve again automatically.

"Remission?"

"Well, sort of – going back, really."

Loukanos overheard. "See here, Dan, if a sick person has a remission of their illness, the illness goes away – they're getting better, understand?"

Dan nodded slowly. "So if you have a remission of your sins, they go away too?"

"Yes, I suppose that's what you're meant to think."

Johanan thought of his dawn breakfast. "Like the dirt on my feet," he suggested. "Anna washed it off and it was gone."

"Yes, but what happens if you pick up more?" Loukanos said slyly.

Johanan stopped himself from pouting just in time. After all, he was not a child any more! "The Messiah will tell us," he said stoutly.

Asa combed his grey beard distractedly with thick fingers. "Yes, lad. We must hold to that. We cannot expect to understand everything at once! No doubt David's reign made changes to Saul's kingdom … this may be the same. And Messiah may require us all to acknowledge our sins and be cleansed before he will subdue the kingdoms before us. Remember Joshua, and Gilgal. The crossing through the water, and the circumcision, the return to the commandments – all this came before the Eternal conquered Jericho."

"A good point, father," Anna said quietly. "A very good point. And here's another to think of. Is not Bethabara of today – strangely near ancient Gilgal?"

Johanan clapped his hands together with a triumphant crack that startled them all.

"What say you of *that*, Loukanos?" he crowed.

# Chapter Twenty-three

AMMIEL noisily splashed his face and hastily mopped it dry. It was good to find the water jar properly full. Ittai had looked after Etta faithfully.

"What think you, Etta?" he nodded towards the closely written parchment on the worn table. "We have to give Philip an answer in three hours."

Etta was seated against the wall, stitching a cover for her new cushion of lately shorn wool. Its springy warmth would ease her back, and she longed to use it every day. She frowned at her polished bone needle, poking at the eye with a strand of black thread. It missed, and she licked the frayed end, rubbing it between her fingers and trying again.

"I think it will do Dan good. He's missed his friend, and it's good for him to spend time with Anna and her family." She glanced up at her brother. "Give him a bit of pampering, even. It won't hurt him." She gave up trying to coax the thread through the needle and sighed. "Will you pass me the wax, please?"

Ammiel handed her the criss-crossed lump of wax from her workbasket on the table, and Etta pulled the yarn sharply over it. "That's better!" The thread slipped neatly through the eye, and she stitched quickly to make up for lost time.

"What a to-do about that naughty Johanan running away from home!" she commented.

"Arguing with the rabbi!" Ammiel shook his shaggy head and sat combing his wet beard thoughtfully, raking the reddish ringlets into smooth ripples. "But, Etta, he is a respectful enough boy in the main, and to disagree with his own schoolmaster is a serious thing ... I don't believe done lightly. So what do you think about his claim to have seen the Messiah? Anna's postscript was so brief, and I wish she had told me more."

"You're lucky to get even that," was Etta's reply. "The woman must be exhausted – Dan and Bukki arriving without warning, and Dan's story, messages from you – her mother dying – the funeral – dealing with this mysterious brother of hers I didn't even know she had, even if you did – and now her outlaw of a cousin turning up on the doorstep as well!"

Ammiel put down his comb and ran his thumbnail over the teeth, producing a musical burr which ended in a snap. "I know," he admitted, picking out the broken tooth delicately. "And her father to care for in his sorrow as well as her own ... Ah, Etta, we should have been married by now, and I could have helped her to bear it better."

"I think she's bearing it very well, by the sounds of things," Etta replied impatiently. "More likely, she needs help to stop all this bearing it so well, and weep freely."

She looked at him out of the corner of her eye.

Ammiel broke another three teeth deliberately and arranged the four bits carefully on the table. He frowned at them moodily.

"It's such a mess, Etta. This should be a time of rejoicing! Our marriage! Our Messiah! I thought when he came all my worldly troubles would suddenly melt like snow. That I would be able to welcome him with singlemindedness – wholeheartedness! And here I find he comes just at the time when all our lives grow so complicated! I am excited – but confused."

Etta tugged at a snarl in her thread.

"Is he the less welcome for that, little brother?"

"No," Ammiel admitted. "It is myself I am dissatisfied with ... I am shocked to realise that suddenly life is moving too fast. I find I have slowed down over the years – and in selfish ways, I think."

Etta picked up a sharp bladed knife and cut her yarn neatly. "Then you must run to catch up. The whole of life awaits – a long and happy life still ahead of you and Dan, and Anna ... and who knows what good and thrilling things with Messiah in the land? Stop moping around and make something happen."

Ammiel flicked the broken pieces away. "How?"

Etta put down her work. "Ammiel, I declare you are behaving like a gangling youth, sulking because you can't have something you took your time about wanting ... at any moment I expect to hear your voice crack!"

Ammiel looked up and laughed in spite of himself, his brow clearing. "I am indeed sulking, Etta. I never would have believed it of myself – and at such a time as this! I deserve to be stood in a corner by my big sister. Perhaps I should ask her what to do next?"

"Go to Anna, of course." Etta stitched furiously. "Stop this tedious business of unsatisfactory letters and postscripts and find out things for yourself. Find the prophet Johanan saw and decide if he is the Messiah or not! The shearing is over, the wool is fetching good prices, the flock is healthy, it's too early for lambing …"

Ammiel got up and stroked her bent head affectionately.

"I see you have it all worked out," he said thoughtfully. "But who will tend them? This will not be a mere two or three days away. If I am to find the Messiah, and somehow lighten Anna's load – though I know not how I can do that except for removing her two unexpected guests – it will take time."

"If you want to go, you will find a way." Etta was uncompromising.

Ammiel took down the lamp from the polished shelf which was Etta's favourite.

"Caleb is as reliable as myself," he admitted. "But he will need either one man, or two boys to help him if I am to be away any length of time."

"What about Eli, Samuel's oldest? He's a good lad, strong, a dead shot with the sling, and keen to learn more about sheep. He's a fine one with the goats, but Samuel's got plenty of other sons to help out, and his mother told me the boy needs more challenge, something new. They don't want him getting bored and troublesome."

"That's one boy. What about a second?" Ammiel carefully filled the lamp.

Etta watched him twist a few straws into a taper and light them at the tiny fire on the hearth. "Isn't it about time Bukki earned his keep?" she said grimly.

"He's more trouble than he's worth as a hired hand, Etta," Ammiel grimaced. "I simply wouldn't trust him. And in any case, he has more use here around the house. Limited, I know, but he's a man about the place. You must make him do more."

Etta looked scornful. "Oh yes?"

"I'm serious, Etta." Ammiel lit the lamp and looked at her. "He should carry the water, for a start."

"Can you see him doing a woman's job?" Etta made no attempt to pretend it was getting beyond her.

"I will tell him," Ammiel said soberly. "I have not been fair to you, in being easy with my brother-in-law. I thought I was helping him, but it has only encouraged his indolence. He will have to pull more of his weight."

Etta couldn't stop a sudden snort of laughter.

Ammiel met her eyes and chuckled. "I know, I know – in that case he should be very helpful! As for a second boy, well, I don't know."

"Dan is ten years old," Etta pointed out. "Time he either went back to the School of the Book, or began learning his trade."

Ammiel groaned, and shook his head to clear it. "Was ever a man so indecisive!" he chided himself. "I used to make decisions so quickly, it was so easy. Now I seem to see so many outcomes for every choice, I can hardly make up my mind to do anything."

Etta looked at him penetratingly. "Uh – huh," she nodded knowingly, and packed up her sewing. The light was now too poor for close work.

"What does that mean, pray?"

"It means you are waking up, little brother!" she laughed, and would not say more.

The rest of the evening passed too quickly for Ammiel, but by the time Philip the Younger's steps were approaching the door, he had finally made up his mind, and was ready.

"I will return with Philip to Cana this very night. If Asa approves, I will take his nephew safely back to Jerusalem, and then seek the new prophet for myself. Dan will come with me. It will do the boy good to see the Holy City and the Temple. Bukki I will send home to be useful to you. On the way he can find Caleb, and Samuel and give them these letters. Samuel's not much of a reader, but Eli has had seven years of schooling, and can read for Caleb too if need be. Old Caleb must find an extra boy himself if Eli is not free to help, but I think he'll be willing enough. The sheep have been lately moved and will not need a new fold or special tending for a week yet. Will you be anxious if I leave this very night? Otherwise I will go tomorrow."

Etta shook her head. "There's no need to delay further, and you will have a faster journey with Philip. Dear young Ittai has taken it upon himself to visit me for the next few days in case you were delayed, so I will be well shepherded!"

"My blessings on his head!" Ammiel said gratefully. "He is a good man indeed."

There was a heavy knock at the door. Ammiel opened it cheerfully.

"Come in, Philip! It is I who will accompany you back, and not merely a message, if you will accept me as a fellow traveller. Come in and take some hot soup to set you on your way. The nights are growing cold."

A distinct aura of fish accompanying him, Philip entered with a long face.

"Blessings on your house, Ammiel," he said rather crossly. "And God be with you, Etta."

"And also with you," she replied, handing him the soup she had ready by the fire. "Not a good catch?"

He shook his head.

"Terrible! Blessed be God who brings forth food for all the world," he added carelessly to the soup. He slurped noisily while Ammiel winked at Etta over the irony.

"I could have brought one donkey instead of four!" Philip grumbled between gulps. "There'll be a beast for you to ride yourself, Ammiel, one to spare, and a swift journey for both of us. No doubt it's the weather, or the moon, or something equally ridiculous. If Zebedee's boys weren't catching, nobody else was, that's for certain."

Ammiel turned swiftly as a sudden thought struck him.

"Oh, Etta! Why don't you come with us!"

"What? Cana – and Jerusalem? Now? How could I! What of Bukki?"

"Bukki can shift for himself! You can ride one of Philip's donkeys!"

Philip nodded gloomily, though his eyes glinted. "I won't charge you much."

Etta's eyes shone. "Oh, Ammiel! To see Jerusalem after all these years! To search out a prophet – maybe find the Messiah! But I will drag the journey down – it is so far … I am so very slow."

"How often do we look for prophets or Messiahs together – as we used to play when we were children? It's been a good season, Etta – I will hire a beast of our own! What say you to that?"

Etta threw her old arms around him as spontaneously as a girl, tears in her eyes, even as Philip asked in bewilderment, "What's all this about prophets and Messiahs?"

"Plenty of time to talk on the journey!" Ammiel was in high spirits. He pulled a burnt stick from the fire and swiftly scrawled a message on the door for the faithful Ittai next morning, while Etta fastened her cloak, found her coin purse, and crammed some more food into the satchel. She quickly filled a slim flagon with watered wine, stopped it firmly, and snatched up a few spare garments.

"I'm ready!" she announced breathlessly, while Philip stopped in the act of fishing out juicy lumps from the bottom of his bowl, amazed.

"Was ever such a woman!" he said admiringly. "Ready for a long journey in such a short time?"

Ammiel lit a spare lamp, fastened the shutters and doused the fire. "Like most women, she can always be ready in a moment when she wants to be," he grinned. "Etta, you'll want to wash the bowls before we leave or they'll have to be broken by the time we get back. We'll pack the donkeys while you do. Then we'll be off for adventure!"

Happily Etta poured hot water from the blackened clay cauldron into her empty soup pot and scrubbed dishes energetically. Luckily Philip had the last of the soup, and there'd be no waste. Jerusalem! Her! Etta! It was years since she'd seen the Temple! Oh, it would be a welcome relief from the drudgery and drama and sadness of recent days, and no mistake.

Outside, Philip pushed at a reluctant animal. "Get over, you useless beast of a Balaam's ass! What is the matter with you?"

Far away in the moonlight, a pair of wolves set up a dismal howling on a stony hillside.

The donkey honked a protest and shifted its feet nervously.

"Well fed wolves, you old donkey, you!" Philip told his beast impatiently, rubbing its prickly nose automatically. "At the end of a long hard winter you can worry and not before. Now get over!"

He tripped on something soft and muttered to himself.

"Bring the light, Ammiel, will you?" he shouted.

Ammiel held it up and uttered a sharp exclamation.

"A woman!" said Philip. "And not a sound from her … She'll have a bruise or two from being stepped on, poor creature. My fault. But, so still – is she dead?"

"No. She's breathing, but unconscious." Ammiel held the lamp closer, and sighed.

"Marah All-Alone."

Etta, hurrying joyfully out of the door, heard, and stopped – suddenly, wearily, conscious of the aching bones she had forgotten for a few excited moments.

"Bring her inside."

Quietly she took off her cloak and met the consternation on her brother's face.

"Go, go, go!" she said, waving her hand. "Jerusalem and the Messiah are eternal. They will wait for me – unlike Philip's fish – or his donkeys for that matter! Give me the lamp. Mind you send word when you can!"

Ammiel looked at her brave face and enveloped her in a lingering, warm embrace.

"Many sisters have done virtuously, but thou hast excelled them all," he said lovingly, with a gentle kiss on both the plump weathered cheeks. She returned them heartily.

"Dearest Ammiel! Go with God, my brother. Give my love to Dan – and my condolences to Anna, her family, and the Temple!" she called as she waved the men off.

She watched them melt into the shadows, and shut the door. Then she turned and patiently relit the fire. Kneeling beside the dishevelled woman on the floor, she covered her warmly. Rare tears of disappointment dropped like rain onto the filthy face.


Under the bright full moon and a host of brilliant stars, Ammiel and the fishmonger Philip jogged on through the black and white landscape to Cana, arguing over the likelihood of Messiah being already in the land. Finally they lapsed into silence, wrapped up in their own thoughts.

"Will you pass the rest of the night with me?" Philip asked as they plodded through the pre-dawn streets.

Ammiel paid him with thanks and shook his head.

"I'm used to the open!" he declined, sliding from his donkey. "I'll wait at Blind Corner, near the gate. Rhoda is always up early, and I can catch her attention without rousing the whole house."

Philip nodded and put the coins in his purse with satisfaction. He would have plenty with which to regale the market in a few hours – news, at least, if not fish!

Ammiel found Blind Mordecai's corner.

"Peace, friend," he said. "I wait here for Asa's household to wake."

"You have travelled with Philip," said Mordecai, nostrils twitching and holding up a hand to stop further speech. "Philip was to bring only a message back to Anna, not a man. And not a man with the smell of sheep on his garments. So you are anxious to see her and share what cannot be satisfactory in mere writing …"

He smiled knowingly and lifted his hands. "Greetings, Ammiel! You are welcome to share my mat. Your Anna is good to me, like her mother was, may she rest in peace. I wish you both joy."

Ammiel shook his head in disbelief. "A man of cunning!" he congratulated him with a smile, and wrapping his legs in his coat, settled down to wait in silence. Soon he had slumped down in sleep and for a long time the men were motionless.

Blind Mordecai woke from the light doze which was the nearest he ever came to sleep, and felt lightly and carefully over the features of the man sleeping beside him.

"A handsome man," he told himself, gently counting the coins in Ammiel's purse. "And richer than one would think, or prudent for a forthcoming journey, or carrying a bride price … or perhaps ready to buy his bride presents … well, Kind Helen's daughter is a lucky woman to find such a man – or indeed a man at all at her age …"

He sighed, and tucked the purse back in Ammiel's belt, unaware that Ammiel, still breathing very regularly, had opened his eyes and was watching every move.

First twitching, then yawning loudly Ammiel demonstrated that he had woken. He sat up slowly, and carefully pulled his purse open.

"Give me your hand, friend," he said to the blind man. Baffled for once, Mordecai held out his hand curiously. Ammiel closed the sensitive fingers around a coin.

"An honest beggar, even a curious one, deserves reward," he said quietly.

Blind Mordecai faced him for a moment in astonishment, and then his scarred face split into an enormous smile. Ammiel chuckled, and the two men leant against the wall, laughing quietly together, as the sun flung its first beams over the rooftops.

## Chapter Twenty-four

"IF!" Johanan's mother said sternly, knitting her tilted eyebrows – "If!" She held up a forefinger warningly and jangled the silver bracelets on her creamy gold wrist. "If I hear one more sound out of you boys this night, across my knee will you go, big as you are!"

Dan's startled face nearly undid her, and she dropped the heavy curtain quickly before she gave herself away.

"She won't do it," whispered Johanan comfortably. "Never does."

"Are you sure?"

"Yes – but we'll hear about respect and the fifth commandment and what the law commanded for disobedient children all tomorrow morning. Not worth it. Goodnight."

"Wait!" hissed Dan. "What did the law command for disobedient children?"

Johanan stuck his head out of the blankets and solemnly intoned, "St-o-o-ning!"

"Oh!" Dan thought about this for a while, but Johanan was sublimely untroubled, so it did not seem to be a serious threat, at least for the moment.

He listened to the hubbub of adult chatter on the other side of the doorway. Anna's voice was too low to pick out, but he could hear Ammiel and Mari laughing over something. Loukanos' crisp tones came through the warm sound, and Dan decided it was just as well it was not he who was quietening them. He would always keep his word, Dan was sure of it. A gecko ran up the wall and lay upside down on the ceiling, emitting a plaintive wail as if mourning the death of the mosquitoes and moths he was gobbling. Dan knew from experience this could keep him awake all night, and tried mentally to smudge it into the general hum from the next room. He hoped Loukanos wouldn't think the gecko's noise was caused by them, or there might be trouble. He looked over to Johanan suspiciously, and was reassured by the peaceful face. He lay down, not noticing the sleepy grin lurking as the boy opened his lips to add a few extra notes to the gecko's grief. But Johanan was genuinely exhausted, and soon the gecko hypocritically lamented alone.

As his friend's breathing slowed and became regular, clogged with an occasional half-snore, Dan stretched out on the unaccustomed bed, not sure whether he liked it or not. It was far softer than Anna's, which had been soft enough to be luxurious but not stifling like this. And what about fleas? Aunt Etta always held that mattresses held droves of them. Dan scratched himself at the mere thought. Sheets again, and supple blankets, and a springy wool-stuffed pillow which made his face hot and gave him a neck-ache. He pushed it off the low bed and rolled over. The worst of a bed – even a whole bed to yourself – was that you ran out of it if you rolled too many times. Already his knees were poking out. He turned on to his back and wriggled his shoulders into the mattress.

It had been a long journey – the longest Dan had ever made, and every day a revelation. The jolting of the patient donkeys had taken some getting used to, but it was good to be able to ride when your legs were tired of walking, even if it did peculiar things to your stomach at first. He smiled to himself as he remembered the moment when Ammiel had astonished them all by marching in to the house in Cana. Anna had turned pale, Bukki red, and Asa had looked so funny with his jaw dropped and the big bristly moustache fringing his open mouth like grey creepers around a hillside cave. Loukanos, who had opened the gate to Ammiel as he left on another of his private errands, had missed quite a sight.

Surprised as he had been to have Ammiel turn up so unexpectedly, Asa had been thankful to hand Johanan over to his care, vastly relieved to find such a reliable way of getting his irrepressible nephew back to Jerusalem. What had been even more unexpected was the reaction of Loukanos, who had insisted that he and Anna went as well.

"It's an ideal opportunity," he said firmly. "With all of us investigating together, we'll find your Messiah faster than working alone, and then I can get back to Greece."

To his step-father he said privately, "If I can force Anna to leave you for a little while, she will realise you are capable of managing your own affairs without her. Otherwise, the longer she delays, the guiltier she will feel about deserting you, and the wedding will be put off again … and so it will go on. And if there is no Messiah after all, I will never get home."

Asa looked at him gratefully. "Ah, you're a good man, Loukanos. It is a wise plan, and takes care of my worry about Anna. I don't want her here clucking over me when she should be making a family of her own."

"She's afraid you will sink into deeper sadness."

Asa shook his head. "She suffers too – and you – as well as I. It will not make my pain less if she prolongs her own, and she's waited long enough for happiness. You must leave the moment this mourning week is over. As for me, praise God the memories of my lovely Helen are sweet, with not a drop of bitterness. They will keep me warm enough until I have grandchildren to kindle new flames in my heart." He paused, adding, "Speaking of which …?" and looking enquiringly at his step-son.

Loukanos shook his head emphatically, and Asa shrugged with a smile, even as he sighed. "Yes, I know! You are too busy – your work must not suffer – you want a paragon who does not exist – and she will want one too – so there is an end of it …"

Loukanos made a comical grimace and looked up from his sketching. "I see you have not forgotten all my excuses! But we Greeks have other ways of achieving immortality besides begetting whole tribes of children to keep our names alive …"

Asa patted his shoulder affectionately. "Yes, yes, so you say. But there is nothing new under the sun, and many great achievements rise and sink without trace in the ocean of history. Meanwhile, we will agree to disagree. You will permit me to hope for grandchildren from either of my children, and I will remind you of the fact that none will bear my name and make me immortal." He glanced at the page before him. "Whose hands are these?"

"Johanan's. Neat and nimble, unusually short fingers, wide palm. To me, the hands of a good workman – made for honest service. Yet he's very sharp too, no mere plodder. I like the lad – I think he'll have an interesting future."

"Speaking of service – Old Dinah will housekeep for me. She's quick and clean, and I can trust her not to torment our Rhoda. How is the child?"

"Much better. Eating garlic and onions dutifully and drinking water like a fish. She's obedient all right. Put her back to work tomorrow before she gets lazy."

And so it was decided. Anna's protests went unheeded. When the seven days of mourning were completed Old Dinah was installed in the kitchen where she proceeded contentedly to drive Rhoda to distraction with her chattering. It was Rhoda's private view that work was done just as well without a constant stream of unwanted information about a fellow-servant's children and grandchildren, all of whom seemed to be virtuous, handsome and talented beyond bearing. Old Dinah, on the other hand, seemed to feel that talking was as vital as breathing, and worked all the better for the rhythm of her words.

Asa had kissed his family – both existing and prospective – all round, and determinedly sent them off with blessings, instructions, messages, warnings, food, money, and hired animals. Blind Mordecai heard the eager bustle, and seized on scraps of information like the beggar he was. Messiah, eh? About time too. Not that it would help *him* much, though some said when the Kingdom was restored the lame would walk and the blind would see. Yes, it was in the prophets, *but I'll believe that when I see it!* He was amused by his own black humour. *Ah, rumours!* How many had he heard over the years while ignorant passers-by assumed his mind was as useless as his eyes. He chuckled to himself as he remembered the visit some years ago of the confidential-voiced woman they called the *Dabab*, come to see her relatives. The woman was a constant stream of loud gossip which he could follow round the streets like a bad smell, and the way she mixed up information about people she didn't know was an entertainment all its own.

The journey had been long and full of intense interest to Dan, who had never travelled so far in his life. Ammiel and Anna between them had turned the way into a continuously unfurling scroll of history which Dan hoped he would remember. Meanwhile, he was sure his head would rattle if he shook it too hard. It was humbling to realise that Johanan seemed to know everything already.

"He's been to school for years – and in Jerusalem," Loukanos had reminded Dan with a quiet grin, seeing his admiration. "He *ought* to know his history. Even I know it from synagogue school in Greece. It's no glory to him, really."

Dan, who thought it was, looked unconvinced.

"It's my fault you don't know more, Dan," said Ammiel regretfully, bare legs striding freely beside the dusty donkey. "It's back to school for you as soon as possible. But in the mean time, this is a grand way to learn."

Now this, Dan could agree with.

But three solid days of steady walking and absorbing tales from ancient times were plenty. He was glad they had taken the shorter route through Samaria instead of crossing to the east of Jordan. Neither Ammiel nor Anna gave any serious consideration to the idea of skirting Samaritan territory, even though the more particular Judeans might regard it as not strictly "clean". Quite apart from the inescapable fact of Loukanos, the idea of any Galilean trying to avoid Gentiles was rather absurd. *Though are the Samaritans exactly Gentiles, in any case?* Dan scratched his head over that one. Despite worshipping at Mount Gerizim instead of Jerusalem, they accepted the Law of Moses, and waited for a Messiah. It was a puzzle to Dan, who decided it would have to wait for now, and mentally added it to the ever growing pile of "things to find out about".

And so they walked south from Cana, through Cana, through Sepphoris, curving round to Nazareth, where Etta had years before bought the little wooden shelves she prized so much. Ammiel knew the shop by its quizzical sign *Ben Netser* and made them wait while he looked inside to buy Etta a particular gift.

Johanan slipped off to find his mother a peace offering in the shape of a trinket from a coppersmith's stall in the next street, while Ammiel took his time choosing his surprise for Etta. It was not a kitchen item but a stick with a curved handle for her to lean on. The heavy set young carpenter watched with satisfaction Ammiel's fingers appreciating the smooth shining wood.

"Thy rod and thy staff comfort me," the shepherd murmured. "Well, let's hope this cut down crook comforts you, Etta."

"It will," the man told him. "You see, it is better balanced than a crook or a staff – it has an extra curve here to support the weight closer to the body. Thus, she can lean her palm on the handle without straining her wrist or fingers by gripping a straight shaft."

"A nice design," Ammiel approved. "You're a smart man."

"Not me." He wiped a oiled rag neatly over the handle and eyed it critically. "My brother. He has a knack of finding a particular use for odd bits of wood most of us would discard."

"Jacob!"

Ammiel looked up as a thin muscular man in a sacking apron appeared from the back of the dim, fresh smelling workshop, face screwed up, feeling his way with one hand and pressing his streaming eyes with the other.

"Jacob – help! Both eyes at once! And it's pine."

Jacob winced sympathetically and turned around to see his brother about to walk into a tall rack of wood. "Wait!" he cried and leaped to stop him, smacking his own face into a plank which wobbled off the top and crashed to the floor.

"Ow!" he yelped and stood clutching his eyes, thereby mirroring the thinner man in front of him. Ammiel looked from one to the other, at first with consternation, then with a grin. He replaced the plank carefully.

"Jacob?" blurted out the other man, blinking furiously on the tears pouring from his scarlet eyes and groping frantically.

Jacob began to chuckle, despite the pain. "Sorry!" he said, his bulky shoulders shaking. "I can't help you get sawdust out of your eye – I've got a great plank in my own …" He rubbed his thick eyebrows and groaned dramatically.

Then suddenly there were two of them laughing, and, as Ammiel joined in, three.

"Here," he said, still grinning, "let me."

He took the tear-blinded man by the arm and led him into the light. Borrowing a fine handkerchief from Anna, Ammiel wet the corner, and gently coaxed sharp specks out of the inflamed eyes. Dan slid off his donkey to watch, giggling to see his father's mouth drooping open in sympathy as he cautiously dabbed at the quivering eyeballs. The man stood perfectly still till he had finished, then the curling dark beard split in a big smile. He pulled a coarse cloth from his belt, flapped the sawdust off it at arms' length, and blew his nose, mopping the tears from his smeared cheeks. He looked with pleasure at his rescuer, bloodshot eyes crinkling at the corners.

"Ah! Relief at last! Thank you, friend! Thank you! Green pine's the worst to have stuck in your eyes and I seem to have rubbed it in! Jacob and I usually perform this service for each other, but as you see …"

Jacob poked his head out of the door. "Don't worry about me will you? Knocked senseless, that's all …" He pointed exaggeratedly to his reddened forehead, but it was clear he was not really hurt, and his brother merely laughed, patting his back in equally exaggerated sympathy.

"Poor old Jake."

"Maybe you'll get two black eyes," piped up Dan from his own experience. He had sidled up close to watch the eye operation.

"If I'm lucky, eh?" Jacob grinned. "Me with black eyes, my brother with red. Won't we be a pretty pair? Now, don't forget your auntie's new stick." He handed it to Dan, who caressed it respectfully.

"Nice and shiny smooth!"

The thin man smiled as he helped Dan up on the donkey, though his eyes were still bleary. "She won't want splinters in her hand, will she? But you may need to shorten the length from time to time, if she loses height faster than the tip wears out."

He glanced at Ammiel, who nodded, looking a little blank as he took the reins. "Did I tell you my sister's affliction?" Suddenly he snapped his fingers and clutched at his purse. "Ach – memory! I'm getting old! With all this, I've forgotten to pay you!" He tugged it from his girdle.

The workman glanced curiously over Ammiel's head to the beardless Loukanos, who was muttering exasperatedly in Greek with Anna, and obviously impatient to move on. Fine woodshavings danced springily in his own sooty beard, which twitched with a faint smile while he tightened the knot at the back of his dusty headcloth.

"What price a physician's fee?" he said lightly. "To help a man to see, is surely worth as much as to help a woman to walk."

"Aye," Ammiel responded, laughing. "But I hold that brotherly kindness is free, or we can expect nothing from God. And a workman is worthy of his wages! I don't know if it was you or your brother who made those old shelves my sister prizes yet – but they were worth the price, and so is this stick. Here is your money, and you'll get no haggling from me."

"I made them," the tradesman nodded, flipping the coin expertly to Jacob, who caught it with an appreciative grin and disappeared. "But it was my father who taught me all I know."

"As I will teach my boy, eh, Dan?" Ammiel slapping Dan's shoulders affectionately. "Well, we must be off."

"He is already well taught, friend. Let that thought comfort you."

The lean man was swallowed up in the dusty shadows of the fragrant workshop, and the party moved on, with Ammiel humming jovially, Anna daintily refolding her handkerchief, Dan rubbing the smooth roundness of the wooden handle against his own smooth round cheek, and Loukanos muttering darkly about the familiarity of tradesmen.

"But I am a tradesman of sorts myself, Loukanos!" Ammiel protested mildly, breaking off his wordless song. "And all Galileans are brothers, after a fashion. Why not be friendly?"

Loukanos twitched his shoulders. *"He is already well taught, friend!"* he mimicked the rough Galilean pronunciation. "What would he know?"

Anna gave her donkey a kick as the animal tried to walk sideways to investigate an interesting vegetable stall nearby. "He would probably know how to flatter his customers, eh, Loukanos?" She kicked harder. "Unlike some people, who think it beneath their dignity. Here! Stop it!" She dragged at the donkey's head to no avail.

The greedy animal's thick hairy lips were nibbling curiously at a feathery pile of scented anise. The scraggy stall holder leapt up with howls of outrage and thumped the donkey on the nose even as it sank its yellow teeth into some succulent grapes and nudged a pile of melons which toppled over and bounced and splattered all over the ground. Ammiel jumped to the rescue, grabbing the donkey's tail and pulling. Anna dismounted by the simple expedient of putting her feet down, and stood tugging the halter with all her might and muttering fervently in Greek. Ammiel shouted, Anna's Greek became more voluble, the stall holder babbled excitedly, the donkey protested loudly, then Johanan rounded the corner and bounded into the fray joyfully jangling his newly purchased bunch of copper bells, startling the poor donkey further and getting his feet trodden on for his trouble, while a vocal and appreciative audience gathered gleefully to watch the fun, snatch up the damaged fruit and add to the noise and confusion.

"What was that about dignity?" Loukanos shouted from a safe distance, while he and Dan laughed till they cried.

Dan grinned happily to himself under the sheets as the memory tickled him again. That had been the funniest day of their journey, and had kept them all laughing as they picked their way carefully down the steep hill from Nazareth, over the slopes and across the green Plain of Esdraelon, where gnats danced in scintillating clouds, frogs sang in the marshes, and you might see a hoopoe flapping overhead at the end of its summer holiday.

Dan whistled merrily whenever he had the breath for it, proud of his accomplishment, and extending his repertoire of tunes rapidly – though careful to leave out Uncle Bukki's disreputable drinking song. Johanan joined him, finding whistling far more reliable than singing at present, and a nice pair of pipes they made of it together. When Loukanos was in a good mood he told them funny moral fables by the wise Greek slave Aesop. Dan had never heard such things before, and was rather surprised at Greeks having any moral tales at all to speak of, but by the way Ammiel and Anna exchanged comical glimmers when they thought the boys weren't looking, it was obvious they knew them from way back. The fables were entertaining enough, and made a light splash in the depths of history poured out by Ammiel and Anna as they walked through the land which was in itself a tale written by God's hand.

It was Ammiel's intention to stick to the main trade routes where possible, but he would deviate a little if he thought they might miss a special sight. He pointed out to the boys the grand swelling of Mount Tabor which rose in the distance to their left.

"A perfect rallying point for Deborah and Barak's army, eh? You couldn't miss it!" he said. "And a bit further south from there you'll find Endor."

"The Witch!" cackled Johanan, clanging his bells and pulling a hideous face at a laughing Dan. "Aha! Beware! The Witch of Endor! Aha!"

Anna cocked an amused eyebrow at Loukanos, who was wearing his Very Patient face. He seemed to find the age Marta had labelled "All Hair and Horseplay" very trying, though he ought to have understood it better than anyone, she thought drily. Perhaps she wouldn't ask him for his opinion on the true nature of witchcraft, not right now, anyway. As for Ammiel – he seemed to enjoy romping just as much as the boys. She looked at his sparkling brown eyes and wild red-gold beard tossing in the wind. This must be the first time for years the man had been free from the immediate care of his flock. She breathed a prayer of thanks for Caleb.

Bypassing Nain and Sulem, the small party travelled on, past the Esdraelon township and into Ginae, where they spent the night. After supper, Anna took the boys to the roof of the town's rough travel shelter and pointed out distant black peaks to the east.

"Mount Gilboa."

The boys looked at each other while a lonely night bird cried somewhere in the darkness. A place of tragedy!

Anna murmured, almost to herself,

"The beauty of Israel is slain on the high places – how have the mighty fallen!"

The opening words of Song of the Bow. Would the boys know it?

"Tell it not in Gath," Johanan responded soberly. "Proclaim it not in Ashkelon's streets, lest Philistia's daughters rejoice and the uncircumcised exult."

"Oh, mountains of Gilboa, let no dew or rain fall on you, or your fields of sacrifice," said Dan breathlessly, thrilled that he knew it too.

311

Johanan nodded and picked up the next line, "For there the shield of the mighty was defiled and Saul's shield cast away, as if he was never anointed."

"From the blood of the slain and fat of the mighty, the bow of Jonathan did not turn back, nor the sword of Saul return empty." Now Ammiel had joined them and his arm went around Dan's shoulder. Anna's moonlit eyes caught his and he touched her cool fingers, nodding encouragement. Together they recited the next lines, lingering over the words,

"Saul and Jonathan were beloved and beautiful in their lives, and in their death they were not parted."

"Swifter than eagles! Stronger than lions!" Johanan struck in eagerly.

Anna smiled at him. "Oh daughters of Israel, weep over Saul," and there was a queer little catch in her voice, "who clothed you in scarlet luxury, putting gold ornaments on your garments."

"How have the mighty fallen in the midst of battle! Jonathan is slain on your high places!" the others responded, and waited for her answer.

"I am grieved for you, my brother Jonathan. You have been a delight to me," Anna said softly, putting her free hand on Johanan's shoulder. He patted it affectionately.

"Your love for me was wonderful," replied Ammiel gently, his arms now firm around Dan and Anna both. "Above the love of women."

The mood of the starlit night was strong, and every eye and heart was warm and full. They all took a steadying breath for the last lines – but a cool dry voice finished for them –

"How have the mighty fallen! And the weapons of war perished!"

Loukanos was there in the shadows, resting his elbows on the parapet. The spell was broken. Dan looked up at the dark face as he leant over the edge and just caught sight of a sparkling drop like a falling star vanish into the unseen void below.

# Chapter Twenty-five

JOHANAN turned over with a grunt. "What?" he demanded clearly, startling Dan awake again, just as he was beginning to drift off at last. He was about to reply when Johanan murmured something which might have made sense if arranged in a different order. So he was still asleep after all. Dan thought he sounded rather like Uncle Bukki after too much wine – or beer. Outside a torch flared past, with a group of men arguing noisily. There was a rattle of bolts, and an irritated householder yelled for quiet.

"What are you? Samaritans?" shouted the angry voice, and a burst of derisive laughter answered. The voices swept on and out of earshot, while a door banged crossly over the way and the bolts rattled furiously.

Samaritans! Well, Dan had tried his hardest to see what made them different, but they seemed to act just like anyone else, despite the ferocious hatred traditional between them and Jews. After leaving Ginae on the second morning, Ammiel's party had struck directly into Samaritan territory – across the ridges and right through the city of Samaria itself. Dan studied the people covertly, but except for the absence of Pharisees, could see no obvious deviations from normality. He would have to talk this over with Johanan as soon as they got a chance. Of course, he could ask the

315

grown-ups, but it was good to have some ideas of your own worked out first.

After all, as Dan and his family had passed on from the city Samaria, and through Marbartha, they had Mount Ebal behind and Mount Gerizim before them! The sacred mountains of Cursing and Blessing! Were Samaritans cursed? Unclean? If so, then why did they have the Mountain of Blessing in their land?

He was puzzling over this when Ammiel told them to picture the ancient tribes of Israel chanting the Cursings and Blessings as commanded by Moses – six tribes on one mount, and six on the other – and their mighty chorus of voices filling the plain between with the solemn words of God. Loukanos wasn't interested in ancient curses or blessings, but interrupted to explain why each tribe could hear the other from so far away.

"It's a natural amphitheatre," he said. "Land shaped like a huge bowl – holding the sound like a dish holds water. If you ever get the chance, you'll see plenty in Greece, built on the same principles. A man down in the centre can whisper, and still be heard by a man sitting right up at the top."

"They could get the chance in their own land, too," said Anna coolly, "if amphitheatres were ever used for a worthier purpose than coarse entertainment. There *have* been one or two modern innovations in the Land since the Flood …"

"Oh?" her brother answered politely. "So you're proud of these base innovations? Or not?"

Anna tried to frown at him, but couldn't help seeing the ridiculous in her contradictory position, so the moment ended in laughter all round. As they trudged on to Sychar and the territory of the Patriarchs was all about them Dan was astonished to realise how much important Jewish history had happened in despised Samaria. Something had gone wrong somewhere, he decided.

Loukanos spluttered resentfully when Ammiel insisted on a detour to Jacob's Well, but as Dan and Johanan drank the cold earthy water with reverent delight, Ammiel and Anna exchanged satisfied smiles. It had been a long day, but the autumn weather was fine, and with the patient donkeys to carry the heavy bundles, they had pushed on determinedly until the Judean border was reached at last. And so the second night was spent once more in Jewish territory, at the town of Lebonah. Even Johanan slept dreamlessly that night, and not a single sleepy mutter or snort from his friend broke Dan's sleep.

Cockcrow on the third day saw them striding out resolutely. The lush plains were behind them now. Fewer were the busy fields and orchards, white with grain and fragrant with the last of the summer fruit, fewer the clustered housetops thickly spread with drying figs. Dan thought half-guiltily of Aunt Etta managing this vital task without him, but knew she and Marta would share the labour. There was a tremendous rushing sound above as a stork flapped its way before them, flying high with emphatic strokes as if to lead the way. Ahead the ridge route of the dry mountains of Judea beckoned them onward and upward. Johanan and Dan demanded a competition to see who could spy the most animals. Johanan counted more wild goats and asses, Dan saw more snakes, desert rats and lizards. Ammiel once glanced back and caught sight of a lioness and her half grown cub stalking a panting oryx as it fled over a nearby hill, its long striped horns tossing like a double whip over its heaving flanks ... but he forbore to mention it to avoid alarming Anna, merely feeling for his sling out of habit, just in case. Loukanos, surprisingly, was more interested in noting birds than animals, and was quite proud of his growing list of

317

eagle, stork, vulture, crane, owl, quail, partridge, and raven. Johanan and Dan remained unimpressed, pointing out that they were all too common to notice, and most could have been seen at home. Anna meanwhile contented herself with pretending to count camels whenever a caravan passed , while privately watching out for scorpions, admiring Ammiel's easy stride and keeping an eye on the boys.

On to Bethel – which to Dan meant chiefly the intriguing story of Jacob's Ladder – and Ramah – the home of the prophet Samuel – with Jerusalem drawing ever nearer ahead! Dan had always assumed the whole of the Land was like his Edenic native Galilee, but the landscape here wore a sterner look, and the further south they went, the more austere the country. Ammiel remarked thoughtfully that he wouldn't like to lose a lamb among these hills, that he wouldn't!

The donkeys picked their way along the rocky track, and nobody rode, though a noisy group ahead of them did, their animals driven up the steepest slopes with prods and kicks, and scarcely visible beneath fat women, petulant children and bulging panniers.

Ammiel tapped Dan on the shoulder.

"A righteous man respects the life of his beast, Dan – or any beast, for that matter, not just his own. You need to treat a dumb animal with wisdom, you know. Push it too far, and you've lost it. It can't be reasoned with."

Up ahead, an overburdened animal sat down abruptly and refused to budge.

"See what I mean?" Ammiel chuckled.

Dan thought he did. The whole family shouted and smacked it with sticks and threatened and cursed, but the donkey remained unmoved. What was one more blow after so many? At least it was able to rest. The woman and two children on its back scrambled off in disgust, and after a few triumphant brays, the donkey got to its feet again and scampered off ahead with the irritated family yelling in pursuit.

Anna turned to her cousin, her unusual eyes twinkling.

"Looks like this animal has some wisdom of its own after all."

Johanan grinned. "Pity it's not Balaam's ass! I'd like to hear what it would say!"

Loukanos gave a snort. "Nothing polite, I'm sure!" and soon they were all helpless with laughter. Again.

They had laughed so much on that trip, Dan thought happily, snuggling deeper into his blankets. Despite Helen's death – or maybe even, because of it? Maybe it was a very good thing to laugh after so much sadness. "A cheerful heart is the best ointment!" Aunt Etta always said. Whatever the reason, Dan suddenly felt *sure* again, all through. It was hard to describe what this sureness was. But it had to do with the blessing – the 'something new and good' which he had been certain would come to his family. He remembered how this sureness had been shaken several times when things went wrong – *but it's still there!* he told himself. *I must remember that, when things go wrong again. Because they still do – maybe they always do. But the really big things, the really good things – the Promises, being the Seed, being Blessed, and now even The Messiah – they don't change.* Dan rolled over suddenly and stared into the blackness, feeling wide awake.

"Of course they don't change," he whispered, and his mouth widened in a huge grin, snatches of forgotten half-listened-to synagogue prayers crowding back to mind from some dormant spot. "*O Eternal, who changes not ... Thy goodnesses are at all*

319

*seasons ... Thou, Adonai, who endures for all time ... Thou art He, forever and ever ... from generation to generation ...* Because *God* doesn't change! And the really big things, the really good things – are all *His.*"

Hugging this new revelation to himself, Dan curled up into a ball and mentally danced along the final part of their memorable journey. Their intended route from the mountains of Ephraim would have taken them over the Valley of Jehoshaphat, past the ancient Royal Tombs, and so into the bustling bazaars of the city's northern quarter. It sounded exciting enough to the boys, but at the last came an unexpected change. Ammiel, succumbing to a sudden urge for the dramatic, had decided that Dan's first view of the sacred city should be unforgettable. He should not come across Jerusalem as a city of markets – he should see it as the city of the Temple! Nothing could be as thrilling as the spectacular Eastern entry. Yes, the unnecessary detour would take longer, but Ammiel knew Dan would treasure the glory of the moment. Cautiously he broached the matter with Loukanos.

"There is not much of lasting pleasure a man can give his son in these days of high taxes and uncertainty," he confessed apologetically, while Anna and the boys were out of earshot. "But nobody can tax or steal such a wonderful first impression. If I can show him this, it will be his forever. We began so early this morning there is time yet. If you wish to take Anna directly to her aunt's house, we will not be more than a few hours behind you."

To his surprise, Loukanos smiled, white teeth flashing in the shadowy stubble which lightly sketched the neat shape of his normally invisible beard.

"A hand can only hold the temporal, while a mind can hold the eternal, eh?" he commented. "Do you know, my artistic sense

320

agrees with you. The city will jump out at him like a vision if he comes on it suddenly, and he will indeed never forget it. And I approve heartily of Herod's architecture. I suppose there's no point in separating our party now. We'll stay together."

"Thank you," said Ammiel simply, very gratified. "To be in the company of his new family will make it even more special."

Loukanos flung him a warm look, opened his mouth to speak, shook his head and strode on to catch up to the others, leaving Ammiel wondering, but content.

So from Gibeah they turned to the east as if making for Jericho, down over the backbone of the ranges to Bethany, with Johanan saying 'not long now' till Dan grew tired of racing to each new vantage point and back in disappointment.

When they reached the little village, Johanan pestered Anna for food.

"You're a positive hyena, Johanan!" she protested. "You've done nothing but howl for food since we left, and it's not more than an hour's walk to your house now. What's your excuse this time? If it's good enough, I'll relent."

"Two excuses! I'm a growing lad!" he grinned. "And Bethany is the House of Dates, you know! Better eat some – just out of respect!"

It wasn't particularly funny, but somehow they all found laughing easy – especially with the end of the journey in sight. Anna obediently handed out dates, they each took a pull at the water bottle, and at last began the final ascent to the city of the Kings.

The broad road wound up the steep slope, a rough white girdle embracing the hill called Olivet, where refreshing gardens enveloped them in leafy splendour, and the white dust settled quickly. The pocket of cool air was layered with elusive smells – tangy, pungent, earthy. The olives which named the mount shimmered in dusky green and silver, gnarled trunks twisted into the rocky soil along the terraced hillside. Ancient figs splashed their huge leaves against the sky like pale green hands hailing the travellers, and tall palms tossed shaggy heads high above myrtles, pines and cypress trees. Small knots of people sat and talked or walked in the soft green shadows. Johanan grinned at Dan's face.

"Better shut your mouth, Dan," he warned. "You might swallow a fly and be unclean till evening!"

Dan turned his head this way and that. He had never seen such a place. He looked again – and he had never seen such phylacteries! A Pharisee stood a little way off, with his eyes and arms raised, pale lips murmuring prayers in the depths of his flowing beard, enough leather thonging on arm and head to hold a dozen phylacteries in place, even bigger than those he wore. And what a depth of blue to his skirts! Dan dared to wonder if even the high priest would look more impressive.

Ammiel laughed at the wonder on his son's face, and caught his hand, beginning to recite,

*"I was glad when they said to me, Let us go up to the house of the Lord! Our feet stand within thy gates, O Jerusalem!"*

*"A city compacted together – where the tribes go up, the tribes of Israel ..."* Anna rejoined, her light veil flipping dizzily in the late afternoon breeze.

*"... Obediently to give thanks to His name!"* continued Ammiel, cocking an eyebrow expectantly at Dan, *"for there thrones were set for ... ?"*

322

*"Judgement!"* crowed Dan. The meaning of his own name! And perfectly placed in a psalm of Ascent.

Johanan jumped in front of them and held out his hands like a choir master, risking his uncertain voice with a clear opening note.

*"Pray!"* he sang in invitation. *"Pray for the peace –"* His face lit up with relief as the note held true – and they chorused at once, Anna quite flat, as usual, Ammiel in his rich bass, and Dan piping the treble,

*"Pray for the peace of Jerusalem – may they prosper who love thee!*

*Peace be within thy walls! Prosperity within thy palaces!"*

Anna impulsively turned a happy face to her tall brother, and he shrugged goodnaturedly.

*"For the sake of my family and my friends,"* he sang suddenly in a beautiful firm voice, shocking them all into delighted silence. *"For their sake I now say, Peace be within thee!"* He shut his mouth with a snap, turned his back and became very busy with the donkeys.

Dan and Johanan jumped around excitedly, while Anna's eyes suddenly filled. Ammiel squeezed her hand and muttered, "He sings better than you, anyway!", making her laugh again, and the four Jews sang the final line of the psalm together,

*"Jerusalem! For the sake of the house of our God, I will seek thy good.*

*Jerusalem!"*

They had just sung the last words when the road suddenly turned, and there it was.

Jerusalem – so close it seemed you could reach out a hand over the ravine of the Kidron and touch the very houses of the priests.

And there – Mount Zion, with Herod's palace spread where once King David lived! But the road dipped, the city hid momentarily behind a hill as if in shyness for being so suddenly surprised – Dan raced ahead to an unobstructed point where the road swung over a breezy ledge and there it was again, the whole of it, spread out before him, shining in the late afternoon light.

He stood there, gazing. Ammiel put an arm around his slight body, feeling it tremble a little. For a while neither of them spoke. There was a crunch of powdery gravel, and Loukanos' voice behind him, amid the slowing footsteps of Anna and Johanan.

"Even I, Loukanos of Philippi, will admit it is an extraordinary city," he casually said, to no-one in particular.

Dan had thought about Jerusalem a hundred times and never imagined what he now saw. What a marvellous, crazy, daring and fantastical place for a city! It was a complexity of deep valleys and dizzying towers, stern forts, massive walls, airy aqueducts, vertiginous bridges, dazzling white houses clinging determinedly to terraces, perilous steps and steep streets, pristine palaces, shining brass, glossy marble, stern gates, inviting porticoes, gorgeous gardens splashed about here and there – and across an amazing viaduct over the ravine – oh! the Temple! At last – the Temple!

Dan's eyes darted greedily, almost despairingly. There was too much to take in, too much to remember, too many details! But off to one side of the city, he spied an amphitheatre. Dan's lips lifted in a half smile. He knew how *that* worked, at any rate.

He looked up at Ammiel with a deep breath and hugged him tightly. Ammiel squeezed back and screwed his fist into Dan's hair, tugging it gently to and fro. They both laughed, because there were no words, and Ammiel knew that the gift he had given his son that day, would last all his life.

The images swirled around in Dan's head as he lay drifting finally towards sleep, rolled up on the awkward bed in the unfamiliar and luxurious room. The final congested city walk to Johanan's home in the central, bustling Tyropoen Valley area was too much of a blur to recall. (Had he ever thought *Cana* was a busy place?) And the polished way people spoke – all neat and clipped! The phrases they used! The way they dressed! The way they moved! Only the beggars looked familiar. With all that was so new and overwhelming, Dan found it hard to remember that they had come, not to see Jerusalem in all its bewildering intensity, but to find a lonely prophet nearby, in a mere oasis of the Jordan, in the stark wilderness of Judea.

## *Chapter Twenty-six*

TO the boys' great impatience, it was two full days before they were able to set out for the Jordan. Sabbath would fall on the evening after they arrived, and Ammiel wanted them to spend it in the Holy City. Not only this, but Johanan's mother was so happy to have her son safely home that she insisted on a celebration for the repentant runaway, forgetting the fact that the night before she had threatened to beat him for his escapade. Delighted to have the company of her three extra guests, she arranged a special Sabbath meal to which she summoned her close neighbours.

"I know how anxious you are to see the prophet for yourself," she beamed. "But it will be good for you to hear what others say about him before you go, and believe me, Jerusalem is buzzing with talk about it. You can't go far on the Sabbath anyway, so make yourselves comfortable in the meantime."

The servants worked steadily all the next day, preparing for the holy day which would come with nightfall, and as Dan continually jumped out of their busy way, he remembered the shepherd's wives and daughters preparing the shearing feast, and his part in it. How Aunt Etta would have loved half a dozen servants to do the tiring work which took her so long! *Well, maybe her new stick will help a bit.*

327

Loukanos washed and shaved with evident relief, and then disappeared with his bulky satchel. Ammiel and Anna spent hours in conversation with Mari, while Johanan showed Dan around the streets near his house, and pointed out his synagogue school from what he hoped was a safe distance.

"We won't go any closer just now," he said cautiously, peering round the corner of the wall. "I have to make my peace there before I go back."

As he spoke the door opened, and a stream of boys poured out into the street.

"Hey! Isn't that Johanan?" a young voice shouted, pointing their way.

Johanan turned around, grabbed Dan's arm and bolted in the opposite direction.

"Don't let him catch us," he puffed, his feet pelting down the pavement. "That's Heber ben Heber – sanctimonious little snob!"

He jerked Dan into a narrow street hung about with cloth, where near-sighted men sat cross-legged, chattering and stitching patiently.

"Aha – you're back, Johanan," croaked a voice close by. "Being chased again? In here, then!"

Pulling Dan with him, Johanan dived under a voluminous awning of striped stuff, from which emerged the torso of a dark little man who was sitting on a small table, smothered in cotton.

"Don't move!" he hissed.

Dan sat rigidly inside the stuffy light-filtered walls of the makeshift tent, while running feet and aggressively shouting young voices approached and faded quickly into the distance. The cotton was lifted, and a gentle wizened face appeared, upside down.

"Come on out, then, and introduce your friend," it chuckled.

Johanan laughed and scrambled out. Dan found that the Street of the Tailors was a favourite bolt-hole for his friend, and a useful place in times of trouble. So, it appeared, was the Braziers' Bazaar. The Bakers' Street was a favourite too, for different reasons. Dan munched happily on a delicious crust, crescent-shaped and sesame-topped.

"You've got a lot of useful friends!" was his comment.

Johanan laughed again and licked crumbs from his sticky fingers.

"Just as well – I've a lot of enemies! Well, one, but he has lots of friends, if you see what I mean."

"You mean Heber ben Heber? Why is he an enemy?"

Johanan trotted back home, Dan following at his heels.

"Silly, really, you know. My family's rich, his isn't – that's one reason. But there's more to it. His father's a great scholar – a proud, dedicated Pharisee. Knows Targum, Midrash, Halakhah, Haggadah and the rest – so he's really a Somebody, see? Much more important than a rich man – even more than an ignorant priest."

"An ignorant priest? Can there be such a thing?" gasped Dan.

"Of course!"

They were home now, and Johanan banged on the gate, which was opened by an old servant with kohl-rimmed eyes and arthritic hands like claws. Johanan nodded cheerfully to her as they passed and the glimmer of a smile flickered over her wrinkled face.

"I still don't understand," Dan persisted. "Why would having such a dedicated scholar for a father make this Heber hate you?"

Johanan clattered down the stone steps to the kitchen in search of more substantial food.

"Because Heber the father expects him to be the same, of course. And because Heber the son isn't! He's got the pride bit all right, but not the dedication. He's lazy – doesn't care a fig about the scripture himself, for all his posing and finger-wagging. Never pays attention in school, won't learn, and is always in trouble."

He turned and winked at Dan. "Whereas Johanan ben Marcus, of no religious importance whatsoever, loves it, and never forgets a thing."

"Ah!" said Dan, enlightened at last. Now it made sense.

He pricked up his ears as a far off eerie note punctuated the air.

"Sabbath approaching," said Johanan. "Listen – there'll be two more."

It was the warning call – three trumpet blasts from the temple. There was a moment's flurry in the kitchen as the servants half-guiltily scrambled through their remaining tasks. All work must stop to avoid risking an encroachment on the Sabbath which was still a few hours away. The family made their final preparations. Everyone washed, and changed their clothes, even Loukanos, who came home almost too late with an oddly smeared robe, and looked grim. Dan looked at the reddish-brown streaks and held his peace. Probably he'd been painting more hideous and unsuccessful pomegranates.

The servants had taken all the food to the upper room where guests were entertained. Joining them was Pagiel, a thoughtful old man married to brisk Hannah, with three tiny daughters clustered around her skirts, childless Shimon and Jemimah from next door, and intelligent, peculiar Nathan Hill-and-Dale from over the street whose mood could lurch from gaiety to silence in a snap of the fingers. Mari lit the sabbath menorah. Shefi carried washing bowls and cloths. Dan and Ammiel looked at the many beautiful dishes – which had been placed in hot clay ovens and straw-boxes to keep warm since the first trumpets – and exchanged glances. Certainly Aunt Etta never carried things this far! They dipped their hands in the bowl Shefi offered, and did their best to unobtrusively follow the correct handwashing movements of their more sophisticated neighbours. They dried their hands carefully and took their places with relief, just as sunset fell.

The second triple trumpet-call which marked the commencement of the sacred day, floated through the window grating and there was a moment's hesitation. The house was Mari's but a widow could not lead the blessing in the presence of men … Johanan was too young … and the nominal head of the house was therefore Loukanos, who was a Gentile – an unbeliever! Had he not been family he would not even have been at their table. Perhaps, would Ammiel … ? She gave him a helpless look, and Ammiel smiled at her, gesturing to old Pagiel in an instant.

"Please, sir, to take the head of the table, and ask the blessing."

"Nicely done," Loukanos murmured in his sister's ear. "Your shepherd has instinctive breeding."

The blessing was asked, the Amen fervent, the meal was delicious and the Sabbath songs sung gladly. Dan watched Loukanos with sly interest. He did not join in the Amens, nor the psalms, yet Dan, sitting beside him, could feel a rhythmic

331

vibration – and was sure he was humming under his breath the melodies once learned as a child.

As for the discussion about the prophet, the whole matter was rehearsed over and over again. Johanan and his Galilean party were convinced he must be the Messiah – the native Judeans were more wary, and Loukanos kept his opinion to himself. Finally the only agreement they could all come to was that a prophet he definitely was, but as to being the Messiah – each man must decide for himself. As they retired for the night, Johanan muttered to Dan, "I feel like the wicked in Nehemiah's day!"

Dan looked at him with great interest. "You do?"

Johanan rolled on to his bed and said glumly, wishing, *"Oh that the Sabbath was over!"*

Dan laughed. "One more sunset, then we can go! Tell me again everything you remember about that day you saw him – and then let's talk about Samaritans!"


In the morning, all except Loukanos went to the synagogue for Sabbath service. The rulers in their fine robes and prominent black phylacteries sat in the front seats, nearest the niche where the scrolls were kept, the most respected of them sitting by the platform with the reading desk. Seats of honour indeed, and old Pagiel sat with them, facing the congregation with the other scholars. Johanan nudged Dan suddenly and with a fleeting grimace pointed out Heber the learned – frowning at his fidgeting son, who was staring at the ceiling and yawning already.

Dan, Ammiel and Johanan themselves sat amongst the more humble back seats, dressed in their best clothes, and with unusually clean fingernails. As Dan listened to the opening benedictions, he couldn't help thinking of the small dim building at Magdala into which the worshippers could scarcely fit. Anna had told him – hard as it was to believe – that Jerusalem had *hundreds* of synagogues, of every imaginable size, and for Jews of every nationality! So there must be tiny synagogues here too – but this was not one of them. He glanced up to the spacious women's gallery where airy motes drifted hazily on ribbons of sunlight. Amidst the press of women Anna smiled at him from behind the railing, silver coins glinting in the shadows of her veil. The Shema began, and Dan brought his attention smartly back to the scribe chanting under his prayer shawl.

*"Hear O Israel, The Lord thy God, the Lord is one. Love the Lord thy God with all thy heart, all thy soul and all thy strength."*

The building might be bigger, the people grander, but the service was the same.

*"God does not change,"* Dan reminded himself happily.

Loukanos was not to be seen the whole day and returned late at night. However, true to his promise, he rose with them all very early on the first day of the week, and together they retraced their steps in pre-dawn light over the hill of Olives, down past Bethany, down, down to Jericho and the Jordan valley. It was a stiff walk of some hours, but they all – except Loukanos – were fresh, and the road was, after all, downhill for most of the way. Mari had declared she would not go at this time, and only urged that Ammiel keep a close eye on her son, but it was difficult when Johanan kept running ahead like an antelope. At length he promised to stay with them, and so they were all together when they turned a bend in the road to see below the narrow Jordan flowing sluggishly between its stony banks.

The slopes were filled with people of all descriptions who had evidently been there for a while, judging by the baskets and bundles, and the young children settled among the rocks with older ones to watch them. Men and women, shy girls and larking boys, tradesmen, servants, scribes, rich and poor – even farmers, freed by the seventh year resting of the land to attend to less temporal needs. Palms rocked overhead, low sprawling shrubs and grasses bent over the eddying brown waters, bulrushes trembled and water-reeds waved with the movement of the stream which chattered busily around the smooth rocks and little pools. It was an oasis of green on the edge of a glaring wilderness which stretched whitely into the distance, a comfortless expanse of jumbled stone hills, frowning ledges, meagre scrub, looming rocks, and sombre caves hinting at unseen dangers. The eye instinctively dismissed this deceptively lifeless scene to focus on the living river, and so it seemed that this reviving fragment of scenery stood alone, unrelated to anywhere else, a place out of time.

Standing on a half-submerged rock in this place of contrasts was the man Johanan had described days before.

Dan, Anna, Ammiel, stood very still, their hearts pounding. Was this – was *he*, the Messiah? – the shadowy Redeemer promised for thousands of years, since the world began? Suddenly here, a living, moving, breathing man who stood right before them? In person! – standing on a rock, his bare feet lapped with muddy Jordan water – thinning black hair ruffled in the breeze? It was too tremendous a thing to believe!

Dan's mouth was dry and his knees suddenly trembled. Ammiel gripped his son's hand in a sweaty palm until it hurt. Anna's fingers dug into Ammiel's arm. Johanan stared excitedly, while Loukanos moved forward like a stalking lion, with slow deliberation and watchful eyes.

"Big – with a voice to match. Thin but strong. Big hands, big bones. Balding forehead, hair in long ropes, bearded clear down to his belly, and tanned as a soldier's boot. Rough tunic, girded up, with a leather belt. Like Elijah, I suppose."

So Johanan had described him, and here he was, in the flesh. Tall, lean, muscular, and with deeply olive skin, the man called Johannes looked over the crowd, his dark intelligent eyes lined from years of narrowing against desert glare. He opened his mouth and spoke.

"The time has come."

He did not shout or bellow, but his voice was indeed huge, and resonated powerfully across the water, to be heard clearly on each bank.

"The day is at hand, and in His graciousness, God tells you so plainly. Warns you. Calls you. Repent while there is time."

"You said that yesterday!" came a scornful cry from the crowd on the far side, shocking Dan's family out of their trance. Dan flinched nervously, but the inhabitants of Judea were bolder, and had seen many zealots come and go.

"I said it yesterday," the tall man answered deliberately, "And I will say it today. And tomorrow. All the past has been leading to this moment – and the time is here. Today, and 'today', and yet another 'today' and suddenly your opportunity will be gone, because you will be dead in your sins. Prepare now! Prepare for the times of refreshing from the Eternal! Prepare and repent so you may be ready for His blessing!"

Ammiel, Dan and Johanan scrambled down the bank until they were sitting on a rock at the water's edge. Anna and Loukanos followed carefully but stayed on dry land.

"The times of refreshing!" Ammiel murmured under his breath, his breath coming quickly. "Yes, how long have we waited for this!"

"How do we prepare?" cried an eager voice. "What are we to do?"

The man on the rock turned to a younger man in a simple white tunic, who stood ankle deep, a little apart from the crowd.

"You can only prepare yourself. Your own heart and mind," he told him. "Repent of your sins – be baptized."

"Yes, yes, a ritual, I understand!" said the young man, his eyes shining. "Purity is before all! So first the soul must be purified by righteousness, and then the body purified by water!"

Johannes squatted down and beckoned him closer, and the young man waded through the cold shallows, lifting his tunic to keep it dry. Ammiel, Dan and Johanan listened avidly.

"Fallen man cannot attain purity – or righteousness – on his own," the prophet said quietly. "Baptism is not about cleansing a righteous body. It is about admitting unworthiness. I give you baptism to wash away sins."

"But I avoid sins!" protested the young man. "And all impurity! I am scrupulous about it! I am an Essene!"

Johannes shook his head regretfully. "I thought so."

He watched the young man disappointedly splashing back to the bank, stood up and said to the crowd,

"Demonstrate true repentance – then you may be baptized for remission of those sins which you have hidden for so long in your hearts – as well as those you have committed outright! Which of you will become a people prepared for your Lord? Whether priest or pauper, you are all called to repentance. All called to be his special people!"

"We are Jews!" an old man cried fretfully. "We are already special people."

"How special?" Johannes asked quietly, spreading his hands in appeal. "How different from the rest of humanity? How sanctified in the heart?"

There was a moment's silence. Ammiel gripped Dan's hand, and Johanan's feet curled in fierce concentration.

"What are you?" Johannes asked, raising his voice a little. "A merchant? Then do you give fair measure? Just weight? Exact change? Every time? How sanctified are you – yourself! – not the nation! – to your God? Are you prepared to meet your God should you die tonight?"

The old man shuffled and melted back into the murmuring crowd.

Suddenly there was a little commotion on the other bank. A very fat man thrust his way through the people and waddled to the water's edge, his cheeks flushed, and elegant curled moustaches shining with oil above a ringleted beard.

"I'm a merchant too," he panted. He swallowed hard, and continued desperately, "And I have given many a short measure!"

Dan watched with his mouth open as the merchant shuffled deliberately into the river, his beautiful embroidered hems and expensive drapery soaking up the cloudy water. The man bobbed and splashed his way determinedly to the dark prophet, who slid from his rock, striding through chest high water to meet him. He held out a hand, and the fat man grasped it thankfully, his chins barely above the surface.

"I am a sinner, Baptist!" he stammered, struggling for a foothold on the treacherous pebbles beneath. "I go to the temple, and give alms to acquire merit – but in my heart, and in my head, I sin even while withholding from evil."

"Yes," answered the prophet intently. "That is where sin begins."

"But I repent of it!" the fat merchant gasped, the sodden ends of his moustache drooping out of curl and deftly painting oily slicks on the lurching water. "Today I change my practices! Today I ask for the baptism of remission of sins! Today!"

A light transformed the tall prophet's dark expression, and he flashed a huge, frank smile right into the shivering man's tense, blinking face.

"Today!" he repeated joyfully. He lifted his head and the vibrant voice rolled across the water. "Today if you will hear his voice, harden not your hearts!"

He turned back to the man before him. "What is your name?"

"Moshe ben Rimmon."

"Moshe ben Rimmon, by commandment of God, I baptize you for the remission of your sins."

He put his large hands on the fat shoulders and pushed. Moshe ben Rimmon sank obediently from sight, to re-emerge a moment later like a whale, blowing, gasping and spluttering. He embraced Johannes with ferocious thanks and staggered to the bank, his prosperous stomach creating its own bow wave as he lurched

338

forward on each step, finally tripping as he stubbed his toe, and fell on all fours in the shallows. He scrambled up again. The gorgeous coat was smeared with mud. He had lost a fine leather shoe. His dripping hair was flattened away from its bald patch and stuck out over one ear. His beard was kinking up into a frizzy mess. And he was radiant.

Loukanos and Anna stood aside in silence as he passed them, shivering still, his lips stiff with cold. He paused before a yellow-skinned, thin young girl who sat at the edge of the crowd begging, her deformed arms held out by force of habit. With a sudden effort, the merchant Moshe twisted his heavy body out of the expensive sodden coat and stood in a wet sleeveless indoor robe, gooseflesh pricking his flabby naked arms. He placed the heavy garment gently on the outstretched twisted limbs.

"It will dry, you know, my dear," he said apologetically, and disappeared through the thickening crowd in the direction of Jericho.

# Chapter Twenty-seven

FOR the whole day, Ammiel, Dan, Johanan, Anna and Loukanos stayed to listen and to watch. The fat merchant's was the first baptism they saw, but there were many others who walked out of the crowds and down into the water. Dan thought Johannes looked like a shearer dipping the sheep before shearing. Johannes the Dipper. The idea was intensified in his mind as the rocks and bushes began to be spread with wet garments, like the clean fleeces around the women's washing pool on the Galilean hillside.

"Notice his hair?" Johanan nudged Dan. "Long as a woman's."

Notice? Dan had been fascinated from the start, and rather worried. "Why?"

"Probably too busy living a Godly life to have his hair cut," replied Loukanos casually, suppressing a grin at Dan's perplexity over this apparently contradictory answer.

"What do you mean?'

Ammiel stared at the Baptizer as he realized what Loukanos meant. Suddenly he smiled at Anna in delight. "Yes! Look, Anna, he has twisted his hair into seven locks, you see. I believe Loukanos is right – and Johannes the Baptizer is a Nazirite!"

Anna's lips parted in admiration.

341

"Then he is a separated one, indeed. See, Dan! He shuns wine because only in God will he find delight … And because he himself is a vine, patiently producing that which will delight the heart of his God, do you see? And he has no regard for losing manly pride by his long hair, because it shows him to be a bride to the Eternal. Is that not beautiful?"

Dan and Johanan were relieved to hear this explanation, as it made the prophet even more likely to be the Messiah. But Dan determined to ask a great many more questions about Nazarites on the way home. He had only seen one or two in his whole life, and at the time, had been too ignorant to seek explanations.

At midday Loukanos reminded them of the basket Mari had provided, and made them sit in the shade and eat. The food was beautifully prepared but not one of them could have said what he was eating. The long-haired Baptizer did not eat or rest. He walked the banks talking to the people, and many clamoured to him with private questions.

"His answers are all one," said Ammiel intently to Anna. "Baptism in repentance for forgiveness of sins. And living a Godly life."

Loukanos squinted at the river, where Dan was making a small collection of the loveliest smooth stones he could find to take back to Aunt Etta. She already had a jar of all the shells he had brought her since he was small, and it was nearly full. On wet days they would sort through them, exchanging their memories. Now she could begin a pebble collection, and Dan would recount his adventures as they enjoyed them together.

"He's quite an Elijah, isn't he?" Loukanos glanced at his sister. "And not once this morning have I heard him quote a sage or rabbi, or even mention the Mishnah. Now that's a refreshing change. Never have I known a holy man take a step without tripping over a thousand precedents. I wonder what your rulers will make of that?"

"They won't like it much." Johanan had the experience to know. "The most learned scholar always cites his authority from someone else."

They fell silent. This was worth thinking over. Surely it could only mean a greater authority than the sages … or a fraud. But Johannes the baptising prophet asked nothing for himself, so what would be the point?

Anna fanned herself with a fallen palm frond, watching Dan scurry up the short slope towards them with his treasures clutched in his folded hem.

"He says nothing of the law, but goes direct to the heart of it. Fear God. Do good."

"A lot easier to remember!" a panting Dan piped up with a grin, tipping out his collection for her to admire. "And simpler too."

"Aye," Ammiel answered soberly. "The law is our teacher, but Abraham did without it, did he not?" He fingered Dan's pretty collection absently, clacking the stones together in his large hand.

"Doing without the law!" Johanan was shocked. And yet, what Ammiel said was true.

"Nobody is suggesting we do without the law!" Anna assured him hastily, retrieving the heavy pebbles from Dan's father before he could begin absentmindedly tossing them away. "Only that the spirit of it should not be forgotten." She stroked the coloured stones approvingly and handed them back to Dan with a smile. He screwed them up tightly in a cloth from the food basket, and stowed them safely inside his tunic where they made a comical bulge.

"There's plenty who have forgotten it," said Loukanos grimly, "who would obey nit-picking nonsense about straining water, but refuse help to a wretched slave who dared break a bone on the Sabbath." He looked up and started suddenly. "Well, would you believe it! There he is now!"

Johanan looked up too and blinked. "*You* know Heber?"

A group of richly dressed men had picked their way down to the river where they stood with their arms folded, and Pharisee Heber from the synagogue was one of them. They argued grimly among themselves, shook their heads, and expostulated. Heber urged them forward.

"It will be a meritorious act," he assured them, coaxing. "Repentance is approved of by God, and besides, you see how this people looks to us to lead the way. If we hold back from this harmless ritual, which clearly the common folk have embraced so heartily, we give the man more power by contrast. If we take part, then he will be seen as being one of us, or under our jurisdiction as it were, and when his influence wanes, we will be still as we were, in the sight of these ignorant people."

"Wise words, rabbi," eventually came the murmured acquiesence, and they moved forward to the bank. Ammiel rubbed his chin thoughtfully, Dan tugged his father's sleeve with wide eyes, while Loukanos' eyes narrowed. Johanan and Anna stared, expressionless, at the men, who were carefully removing their beautiful long outer robes.

344

The Nazirite lifted up a frail old man from the water and helped him to the bank. Then swung around to face Heber's party, and held up his hands.

"Stop," he said quietly. "For what reason do you come to me?"

"Why, baptism!" said Heber with an expansive smile, conscious of his audience. "We agree with this concept! We encourage our flock to take part!" He lowered his voice. "Of course, it is a mere formality, but formalities are matters we understand well. So here we are, and repenting of any trespasses we may inadvertently have omitted to atone for, which can be but few, we join with you in this pleasing symbolism of renewal."

"Vipers," commented the Baptizer, softly.

Heber stared. "I beg your pardon?"

"Yes, vipers." He spoke as if to himself. "A brood of them – with poison in your mouths."

"Did you say vipers?" gasped the Pharisee. "Meaning, us?"

"I did. What has lit the fire under your nest? Who has warned you to flee from coming wrath?"

"Well!" spluttered the rabbi. "It is you who has been preaching of judgement, and urging this baptism! And now you turn us away with insults? Whom do you think you are?"

The prophet's eyes gleamed.

"Let me ask you this – who do you think you are?" he enquired steadily.

Their tongues loosened at last, the outraged men all answered at once, each man's angry words tumbling over the others'.

"We are elders of synagogues!"

"Pharisees! Men of understanding!"

"Learned men! Spiritual leaders of this people!"

"Who can trace their ancestry back to Abraham himself!"

"Possessors of his virtue through lineage!"

"Assured of salvation!"

"Then why come to be baptized?" came the cool response.

The people, some shocked and some delighted, crowded around closely to listen, cutting off the indignant men's retreat and pinning them in front of the Nazirite's uncompromising gaze. Obeying a sudden impulse, Loukanos sprang to his feet and pushed in among them, relishing the prospect of a lively debate, and on the lookout for flaws in either argument.

"We are true children of Abraham!" Heber repeated proudly, looking at the crowd for support.

Astonishingly, the ghost of a smile flickered across Johannes' face.

"Of Abrahamic ancestry?"

Suddenly Loukanos knew what he meant and gave a shout of laughter.

"So was Ishmael!" he called to the Pharisees mockingly. "So were all the sons of his concubines whom he sent away!" For the moment, he had forgotten this was not a Greek forum.

The people gasped. Heber and his companions started with outrage, but seeing it was not a Jew who had spoken, they quickly ignored him, shuffling as far away from this unmannered, shamefully shaven Greek as they could conveniently manage with the pressing crowd. Pharisees did not argue with Gentile dogs! The Baptizer glanced interestedly at Loukanos, who was suddenly disgusted with himself. What did it matter to him who won the argument, anyway? Besides, this zealot needed none of his help.

The rich voice rang again. "What price your lineage indeed, you Pharisees? Would Abraham recognise you, as his children in faith and deed? I tell you that the God who made man from dust can raise up children to Abraham out of these very stones. You are part of a rotten tree bearing rotten fruit, and the axe is already being swung! Show me evidence of your repentance in deeds, not words. Till then, baptism will only make you wet sinners!" He turned his back on them and waded back to the rock in midstream.

Heber shook his fist.

"God will punish you for this insult!" he shouted furiously. "By what right do you talk to us in this way? You know nothing of the mysteries! Nothing of the traditions! Is salvation a thing the unwashed rabble can understand?"

Johannes turned around and looked at the men and women who were pushing into the water with intent faces, conscious of their past, anxious for their future. He smiled, sadness and triumph mingling on his dark expressive face.

"No, not the unwashed!"

He slid into the water and grasped the first pair of hands which were outstretched eagerly.

*What do you come here for? … What is your name? … I baptize you by the commandment of God for the remission of your sins …*

So the ritual continued.

Loukanos rejoined the others, looking a little cross with himself.

"Fiery words, Loukanos!" Ammiel said admiringly. "But true – and you made a very good point!"

Loukanos threw himself down on the ground and rummaged in the basket.

"Well, Anna knows – I can never resist a good argument. And I had my reasons for annoyance with that nasty piece of work, Heber. Here, Johanan, have you eaten all those date balls? You're a very Ostrich, boy!"

His nephew opened his mouth to ask again how Loukanos could possibly know Pharisee Heber, but spying a spare date ball which had rolled unnoticed out of the basket, he pounced on it, and his teeth were stuck together for the moment. Meanwhile, Loukanos found a few sweetmeats the boys had overlooked and with his mouth full remarked, "I like the man's wit. Raising up *banim* from the very *abhanim* … building up *those which are built* – from *things* which build! Very neat. Wasted on most of them, of course."

"Teacher!" called a voice from the awestruck crowd. "If we repent – if we are baptized, what then? What should we *do*?"

"The spirit of the law!" answered the prophet, pushing back stray wet strands from his high glowing forehead with strong bony fingers. "Think of it! These days we no longer sit every man under his own vine and his own fig tree – so you may not have fields with corners to leave the poor, but do you have more than you need? Share it! Share your clothes, share your food!"

Ammiel shook his head at the sinking sun. "None of us wants to waste time going back to Mari's tonight but we've left it a bit late to start looking for shelter … if I'd thought of it sooner we could have tried over in Bethany itself, though I doubt we would have found any. Remember how crowded it was as we came through the other day. Anna, I'm afraid it means a night among the rocks."

348

"If I'm to be a shepherd's wife, it will be good practice," she said cheerfully. "And it looks like we'll have plenty of company."

Around them, people were unrolling blankets and kindling small fires from carefully guarded embers. It was not cold, and few had food to cook, but a fire kept away marauding wild animals, smoke discouraged mosquitoes, and the friendly light would be appreciated once the blanket of darkness smothered the day.

Dan and Johanan, who had been eagerly swarming over the immediate countryside, came back to report to Ammiel.

"We've found a nice deep cave all by itself over there. Can we sleep in a cave? Please? Smells a bit, but we don't care." Scarcely waiting for an answer, they scampered off downstream to show him.

Ammiel followed their trail obediently to investigate, and plunged into the shadows after them, sniffing loudly. He shook his head.

"Not this one. Firstly, it's too small for us all, and secondly you're not staying here on your own after I promised Mari not to let you out of my sight. Most importantly, the smell – see those droppings? They're fresh. And that fur? And freshly chewed coney bones? Madness! Come on, lads, it's too close to nightfall for us to be—"

A mewing sound squeaked at the back of the rocks where it was darkest.

"Out!" Ammiel snapped at the boys.

"What?" stammered Johanan, but before Ammiel had a chance to reply a sharp hacking snarl rasped the air and a slinking dark shape was silhouetted against the mouth of the cave, its long slender tail lifting and twitching menacingly.

349

Thrusting the boys into the rock face, Ammiel flattened himself against them.

"Keep still!" he hissed.

Their faces ground into the sharp chalky surface, the boys hardly dared to breathe.

Dan's eyes were screwed shut, his lips twisted painfully on a gritty lump which was crumbling sand into his open mouth, sudden sweat prickling his armpits, his father's weight crushing him. Ammiel was fumbling at his belt, elbows jolting the breath out of Johanan as he hunted frantically for the sling he was not wearing. The wildcat spat again and her eyes flashed as the kittens mewed demandingly.

Everything happened in a heartbeat. Ammiel leapt towards the snarling beast, roaring and waving his arms, but the wildcat in vicious fury sprang for his face – just as Dan wrenched his cache of stones from his bosom, and darting in front, hurled them with all his might. The creature dropped in midair with a scream, twisting round and lashing her long tail as she fell with the heavy stones scattering at her chest. In a flash Ammiel whipped off his cloak and flung it over her head. She fought her way out in an instant, but it was long enough for Johanan to scoop up the struggling kittens and pitch them straight past her, far outside the cave where they squalled lustily in the scrubby bushes. The outraged mother darted after them, coughing and screaming her anger and distress. Ammiel snatched up the cloak, roughly bundling the boys out before him, and they all ran into the sudden twilight, stumbling over the rocks and back to the slate coloured river which lapped idly at their feet..

For a moment nobody said anything. Ammiel was puffing, his moustache lifting lightly on each breath – Johanan methodically washing his hands of blood drawn by needle-sharp claws and teeth – Dan was giggling a little hysterically, not feeling at all like laughing but doing it anyway.

"I have just three things to say, " Ammiel said at last when he'd caught his breath, unexpectedly beaming at the boys. "Firstly, is anyone hurt?"

"No," said Dan, his giggles subsiding suddenly.

"Not much," said Johanan, wincing with the sting of the water. "Tiny scratches, is all. They were too surprised to fight."

"Good. Secondly – don't ever blunder into strange caves like that again! Dan, my son, you should have known better, at least. And thirdly – I'm proud of you both, and thank you heartily. Quick thinking, acting with courage – you were real men."

He extended his arms and clasped them both warmly by the shoulders. They all laughed with relief, then Ammiel said with a lopsided grin, "I've just thought of another question. Do we tell the women? Or not?"

Johanan and Dan looked at each other, considering. They grinned back at Ammiel.

"Not!"

Together they made their way back up the river towards the spot where Loukanos and Anna, like many others, had made a fire in a protective circle of stones. There was Loukanos, dark against the dimming sky, skilfully fashioning a rough shelter of palm leaves over thin boughs leant on a tall rock. No doubt it was to keep the night dew off his sister. He would hardly trouble for the rest of them. Johanan was impressed. He had no idea Loukanos was so practical. But then, a boy who'd run away across whole countries, must have learned a few tricks about sleeping rough.

"What about the mother?" Dan asked before they came within earshot. "Do you think I hurt her?"

"Yes," his father answered frankly. "She probably has broken ribs, at least. But I don't think the kittens were hurt. Baby animals are tougher than they look."

"Will she die?"

"It's possible – and yes, if she does her little ones will probably die too. They're only a few weeks old. It's a shame, Dan, I know, she was only protecting her young like I would my lambs. But there wasn't much else for it. If I had not been stupid enough to forget my sling I would have killed her myself. As it is, she may be all right – and I am thankful for your bundle of stones and the quick wits of both of you! Otherwise I would have had my arms and maybe my throat laid open. I am only ashamed I was such precious little help."

Dan thought of his father shielding them with his body, and springing at the savage wildcat with nothing but bare hands and the strength of his lungs. It seemed to him this was nothing to be ashamed of.

## Chapter Twenty-eight

THE wildcat adventure could not be kept from Anna. Despite the firelight her sharp eyes noted the marks on Johanan's hands, and even as Loukanos raised his eyebrows enquiringly she spoke.

"Have you been fighting with a thorn bush, cousin?" she exclaimed, and so the truth had to come out. His protests ignored, Johanan had to submit to having his hands bandaged for the night in a pungent mixture of olive oil, mashed garlic, and a little myrrh Loukanos dug out of his satchel, and which, he said, he had been carrying for emergencies. The next morning, Johanan inspected his wounds lovingly. Loukanos looked over his shoulder.

"Keep an eye on them," he said casually. "They can turn nasty in a hurry."

"How do you know?' asked his cousin. "Ever been bitten by a wildcat?"

"Not me," said Loukanos. "But I've seen unfortunate people who have. Did you say these were just kittens?"

"Still on milk," said Ammiel, and Loukanos nodded, losing interest. Around them folk were eating a leisurely breakfast, and stretching cold and cramped limbs into life.

"There he is!" someone called, and the familiar figure in its rough camel hair cloth appeared from the rocks into which he had vanished the previous night. Soon the banks were once more clustered with hearers, and the voice began again to lift up its message in the wilderness. Dan, who had been wandering around listening to other conversations among the rocks and bushes, came stumbling back, looking stricken. He clutched at his father's sleeve.

"Father, I've just discovered something terrible!" he croaked drily. "The prophet Johannes is a Levite!"

Unhappily, Dan related what he had heard. Yes, he was a Levite! To be precise, his father was a Levite, of the course of Abijah. This meant that he was only nominally a priest through the vicissitudes of necessity after the Babylonian exile, and not even of Aaronite descent himself. Johannes' mother, on the other hand, was from the family of Aaron. A noble lineage, no doubt! But how could he be the Messiah, if he was not of the tribe of Judah! It was a terrible blow.

"I should have known he was a Levite!" Johanan chided himself rather sarcastically. "Soon as I heard that voice! He'll be a beautiful singer, too – you can tell."

He nodded at Dan's puzzled look. "A good singing voice – one of the most important requirements of a Levite, the rabbis say. No, I'm not joking!"

Anna tried to find comfort in the words of the Messianic psalm – *"The Lord has sworn and will not repent – thou art a priest forever after the order of Melchizedek ..."*

"The psalm says clearly Messiah is also to be a priest," she reasoned. "Would not that indicate he may be a Levite?"

Loukanos frowned. "Your reasoning's driven by your desire," he pointed out. "This argument is most unlike you, sister. There's a massive flaw in it."

354

"Show me."

Loukanos sighed. It has been a long time since he'd been forced to think about the Hebrew scriptures. "Look, Melchizedek was before Abraham, wasn't he? Therefore he had no tribal affinity, was not of Abrahamic descent, and, if you like, not even Hebrew."

Johanan scowled at him. He didn't like. Trying to get rid of Abraham again!

"So think about it carefully," Loukanos was relentless. "A priest forever *according to the order of Melchizedek* can't have *anything* to do with *any tribe in particular*, not even Levites! Melchizedek was a priest outside of that system. That's the sort of priest your Messiah's supposed to be."

Ammiel looked troubled. "And everywhere else definitely says he is a descendant of king David – so that's that."

"Maybe we just don't understand it properly?" suggested Dan. "Sometimes I think something is wrong just because I don't understand it all yet."

"That's just possible," Loukanos conceded. "But don't think I'm not as keen as you for this man to be the one you want. I have a life to get back to, after all!"

The others cheered up. Maybe it was just possible, as Dan said, that there was something missing in their understanding. Something which would make it all come right. Something which would make the rough man in the Jordan their Messiah after all.

A quiet word from Ammiel had Loukanos obligingly accompanying the boys to the bank, leaving Ammiel and Anna sitting at the spent fire. There were hundreds of people around, so propriety should not be offended, and Loukanos had little time for

Jewish scruples anyway. Even Asa did not insist on Anna covering her face at all times, though it was lightly veiled today among the crowd. Let the two of them talk without an audience for a change!

Ammiel was grateful for the rare opportunity, but suddenly he was not sure how to begin. He picked up her lean brown hand and turned it over, gently pressing the long palm experimentally with his rough thumb.

"So soft," he said musingly. "You will spoil these hands, as a shepherd's wife."

"Oh, a Greek tragedy," she answered, laughing. There was a pause.

Well, Anna," Ammiel tried again, "it seems you are no worse for your night in the open."

Anna's eyes danced mischievously.

"As children, my naughty brother and I spent several illicit nights camping out in woods and fields," she confessed. "We had a few private adventures of our own which our poor parents never knew of." She looked more sober. "Thankfully none involved the dens of wild animals!" She shuddered a little. "When I think of what might have happened …!"

"It didn't," Ammiel replied quickly, glad of the opening. "But it did remind me that life is very short. It could have been a lioness, not a wildcat. And here we are in this place, seeing such amazing things, and hearing such a powerful message … such a stirring call to our faith! … and calling to us *"Today is the time!"* reminding us that no man can give a surety for his tomorrow …" He paused, and Anna waited, her eyes downcast, her hands clasped around her knees. Only the travel-stained toes, clenched in the sturdy sandals which showed under her blue hem, betrayed any tension.

356

"Anna, with very good reason, and so short a time ago, you wished to defer our wedding. May I ask if you still feel the same way?"

She lifted her eyes at last, and the bottom lashes were glistening.

"No, I do not. But ... forgive me ..."

Ammiel reclaimed her hand. " For what? Delaying the marriage? It was right at the time. Forgive you for changing your mind? Not when it is what I want!"

Anna whisked away the traitorous tears. "Forgive me rather for my frankness," she murmured, "while I confess my inability to choose between you – and my father's needs."

Ammiel smiled slowly and triumphantly. "Anna, you cannot be everywhere at once, and your father had a most interesting talk to us before we left. Yes, all we men of the family together!" he continued, unconsciously leaving Bukki out of his mental family image. "Asa implored us to help you see reason."

Anna was baffled. "He did?"

"You see, Anna," the shepherd persisted earnestly, "in losing his dear wife, he wants even more for his daughter to bring him new happiness, and not to delay. Can you understand that, my very clever Anna?" Ammiel patted her unresisting hand gently, toying with the bangles on her narrow wrist. She dropped her eyes again and tucked her feet under her robe.

"Of course," she said huskily. A pause, then, "I think I have been a little blind."

They became aware that the sounds of babbling water, the continual murmuring voices below – threaded through with the Baptizer's vibrant words – and the wind in the palms above were blending into a musical richness – a swelling of melody from many throats. Somewhere, somebody, in the fullness of their heart, had begun to sing, and the song had seeped through the bystanders until the shallow valley was pulsating with the beauty of the psalm. The sober notes rolled like a wave along the river.

> *"Adonai is merciful, compassionate and gracious*
> *Slow to anger and generous in kindness.*
> *He will not always chide*
> *Nor be angry forever."*

And like ripples dancing over pebbles, came the brighter assurance:

> *"He has not dealt with us as our sins deserve*
> *Nor rewarded us the measure of our iniquities.*
> *But as the height of the heavens above the earth*
> *So great is His loving kindness towards those who fear Him."*

*"Kindness towards those who fear Him!"* Unexpectedly joining the refrain came the deep voice of the Baptizer, whose strong bass rang out among the lighter voices. As Johanan had gloomily predicted it was indeed beautiful.

> *"So far as the east is removed from the west*
> *So far does He remove our transgressions from us!"*

The powerful notes vibrated with joyous conviction.

Suddenly, Ammiel stood up, pulling Anna with him, and sang out the response with all his strength in an outburst of feeling,

> *"Yea, like a father has compassion on his children –"*

Dan heard him and looked up, waving with a happy face as he caught his father's eye, and joined in with the rest in his still childish voice:

358

*"So the Eternal has compassion on those who fear Him!"*

*"Compassion on those who fear Him!"* Johanan's husky tone repeated bravely with only a momentary fracture on the highest note. Anna did not trust herself to sing, but she hummed with a greatly contented heart.

The singers on both sides of the bank, the singers yet in the water, and those at its edge, melodiously completed the majestic words of the psalm, and its burden was the same as that of the solitary Johannes, the Levite, the Nazirite, Baptizer, and Prophet – flowing into his preaching as naturally as winter snow into the rivers of spring.

*"Man is grass, his days are fleeting.*
*Bless the Eternal while there is time.*
*All creation performs His will.*
*Obey Him, thank Him, give Him the dominion!"*

The shepherd stood with his bright curling hair radiant in the sunlight as the last notes of the many-chorded voice faded ... and with renewed vigour, the Baptizer continued his message. The people in the crowds chattered or argued, or listened in silence, while the beggars industriously worked the fringes. They gathered thickest where the wet folk scrambled up the bank, full of happiness and good intentions.

Ammiel watched his dark young son below, who was listening to the preacher with his elbows propped on a warm rock, and idly fishing out a new stone collection for Aunt Etta from the shallows during the baptismal lulls. Loukanos and Johanan traded arguments nearby. He looked down at Anna, who thoughtfully stood beside him on the lower side of the slope, creating the rare illusion that he was taller than she. Together they watched the crowds as the intense man below moved among the people, talking, teaching, warning, answering, questioning, and always performing the compelling ritual of baptism for those who were sincere. A strange, bloodless rite, no busy formal rote of complicated piecemeal washings with poured water and basins and towels – just a simple and moving act, this grim plunge below the water – with strong undertones of death – which appeared at first glimpse to be an attempt to drown the submissive suppliant.

"You know, Anna – I have many sins to repent of – sins I hardly knew as such at the time."

"Yes? So have I, Ammiel. So have we all."

Ammiel cleared his throat. "Yes, to know the law, is to be aware of continual sin. For me, some of them were over you."

Her eyes flew to his in alarm. "Oh – no – I don't need to know – I don't want to know!"

He shook his head. "Pride was one, Anna. Your mother wasn't the only one who was proud. I know now I could have been more in earnest, I could have fought for you – but I was vain, and too easily rebuffed. My pride was badly ruffled. I can admit it now."

Anna bit her lip and tried to laugh. "And I … I have been lying – for years!"

"Tell me?" Ammiel enjoyed the rare luxury of tilting her chin up towards him for his answer.

"My feet …" Anna began, and her voice trembled, only half laughing.

"Your feet?" Ammiel could not think about feet just now.

"My feet," she said deliberately, and blushing, "did not dance lightly at your wedding …" – at last the admission came – "… I felt I was dancing on sinking sand."

360

Ammiel's eyes been lingering on her straight eyebrows, the silver coins touching them lightly, then her chin, its firm outline softened under her fine veil, her crooked smile, the straight nose – and finally they met her gaze.

"Ah!" he said slowly, and smiled a little. "Two confessions of sin!" The shepherd took her hands. "It is enough. Anna, let them represent all the rest, and let us be free of them together."

"Yes, Ammiel!" she responded, her eyes shining. "And then?"

"And then, we will waste no further time. A letter will go to your father this very night and Old Dinah can begin bossing the life out of Rhoda at once with a hundred preparations."

"Poor Rhoda! And the Messiah? Is this Johannes he?"

Ammiel began to run down the slope like a boy, tugging her with him, laughing, in a flurry of skirts and veiling.

"Why, we'll ask him!" he cried.

Loukanos looked up in astonishment to see his normally sedate sister flying down the hill like the shadow of a windblown cloud. Johanan and Dan both laughed at the sight but were quickly composed again as Ammiel told them what they were about to do.

"You are going to submit to this peculiar business?" Loukanos sounded quizzical.

"It is of God, Loukanos," Anna said determinedly, still panting a little. "And I believe what is peculiar to man, makes perfect sense to the Eternal. After all, the two are directly opposed by nature."

Loukanos rasped his thumb across his bare chin and said nothing.

Ammiel held out his hands appealingly. "Loukanos, this is good for you, do you see? Anna and I want a new start, ready for our new life together. We will marry as soon as we return to Cana, and you will be free to return to Philippi."

Dan and Johanan gaped at each other. This, they had not expected. Dan felt a huge grin wrap itself around his face.

Loukanos looked from his sister's happy face to her betrothed.

"You think this man's your Messiah then?" he asked rather grudgingly.

"We don't know," said Ammiel frankly. "But even if not, he is from God, and we have sins to repent of, forgiveness to ask, and preparation to make for Messiah the Prince. If this Nazirite is the Messiah, we will be ready. If he is not, we have still lost nothing and gained much."

"Loukanos!" said Anna impulsively, clinging to him in a rare moment of appeal. "If only you could believe what you know!"

He shook her off, but gently, took their coats and motioned to her to remove her veil. "If only," he repeated drily. "How simple life would be! Go, then."

He shooed the boys after them. "Go! Don't you want to be part of this celebration?"

Recovering their scattered wits, Dan and Johanan scrambled after the adults, and splashed in up to their knees as Ammiel, holding Anna firmly by the hand, waded into the deeper water. At last it was their turn, and the determined dark eyes met theirs and softened.

"For what do you come?" asked the Baptizer.

"For the baptism of repentance – and for answers," said Ammiel courageously.

Johannes smiled. "Then I will give you answers first. Ask."

Ammiel looked at Anna, and they asked together, Anna in her tension reverting to a slip in Greek.

"Sir, are you the Messiah? The Christos?"

Johannes took a deep breath and exhaled gently, nodding.

"It had to be asked. The answer is for all, not just you."

And so they stood together in the deep flowing water before Johannes, the Baptizer. Ammiel's long golden beard like sundrenched grasses drowned in the river, Anna's dark hair flowing like spilled ink and rippling like a live thing among it. And in front of them, the strong lonely young man with the desert-etched face, lifted his head and his beautiful voice – and they heard the truth at last.

"I am not he! I baptize you with water but one mightier than I is coming. As for me – I am not fit to untie his sandals! He is one who will baptize with the Holy Spirit – with Fire! He will winnow and clean out his threshing floor – he will gather his wheat to his barn. But the chaff he will burn with relentless flame."

There was a great silence. The water gurgled and eddied, rushing on downstream to its salty death and rebirth in sun-spun cloud. Ammiel and Anna stared at the Baptizer, their initial sinking disappointment replaced almost instantly with surging excitement for the extraordinary, compelling and awe-inspiring words which followed. He was not Messiah – but clearly, greater things were to come!

"Who *are* you?" Anna dared to whisper into the silence.

The tall man's chest swelled and sank, his head bent, and against the current, his body was still. He closed his eyes as if gathering strength.

"I am a Voice," he said, softly. "I am just – a Voice."

He opened his eyes, straightening up to address the silent crowd on the banks and unleashed his powerful words across the water.

"I am the Voice crying in the wilderness. *Make ready the path of the Lord!* I say. *Prepare his road!* I demand. *Fill the ravines! Level the hills! Straighten the track! Smooth the way!* Then all mankind will see God's salvation!"

He turned back to the couple in the flowing water before him and said quietly, "That is the truth, friends. Does it set you free of your doubts? Or create more?"

"Thank you," said Ammiel huskily. "The truth always sets us free, I believe."

Johannes smiled wearily. "You are an honest man. And now?"

"We want to be baptized, still." Ammiel looked at Anna, who nodded.

"More than ever!" she said in a low voice.

"Gladly," said Johannes. "What are your names?"

Dan and Johanan watched, forgetful of the chilly water and the sudden gust of wind which ruffled its surface. First Ammiel, then Anna, sank from sight – the golden curls, the swirling dark hair engulfed by muddy water – and reappeared, gasping with cold, and like the fat merchant of the day before, radiant with joy.

Loukanos met them as they splashed to the water's edge and told them curtly to hurry to the fire. Dan crept up and touched his father's dripping beard. He seemed the same person, but the glow in his eyes was new. Ammiel snatched his son and kissed him loudly on both cheeks, unable to speak. Anna was actually chattering – Anna, who never chattered – she was so moved.

"Gone! Oh, Loukanos – all the horrible pettiness and stupidities – the vanity and ugliness of every sin I ever committed or imagined – and the Eternal has blotted them out!"

She hugged him tightly, then Johanan, who wriggled in protest, then Dan, who was too small to get away.

"Now look, you've made us all wet!" Loukanos said curtly. He pushed Anna into the little shelter he'd made the day before and soon she handed out her wet clothes and reappeared in a cloak and blanket. Ammiel also donned a blanket and coat and sat shaking water out of his ears while Anna laboriously disentangled her hair, combing it with her fingers as it slowly dried.

Loukanos, who had become quite bossy, made the two of them huddle close to the fire which he heaped up and soon had blazing cheerfully to dry the damp clothes. The boys had taken an end each and had a lot of fun wringing with all their might until the tunics twisted up into huge knots. Ammiel's was draped on rocks by the fire and was soon steaming nicely and smelling like a sheepfold in summer rain. Anna's wrinkled fine Byssass cotton dress sprawled lazily over the palm leaves of her little booth. There was an air of holiday festivity everywhere. The noon light filtered hazily through the smoke which kept every eye watering. At least, everyone said it was the smoke, but they were all a little incoherent for a while.

Loukanos demanded food and prepared hot watered wine with honey. Dan sipped his eagerly, glad of Mari's generous provisioning, remembering the last time he'd been given this warming concoction. Then he had been frightened, this time he was excited.

"So, as he said himself, the Baptist is not your Christos," said Loukanos at last, when they were all feeling calmer and the bread, smoked fish and pickles had disappeared.

"You don't look exactly crushed with disappointment."

"Yes and No!" laughed Anna. "Of course we hoped he would be, but – but you heard those words! He is a fulfilment of prophecy too – right before our eyes! He is the fore-runner, *himself* prophesied about in Isaiah! And the Christos will soon reveal himself. The Baptist says so."

"Yes!" Johanan said eagerly. "It all makes more sense now than ever, don't you see? The Bethlehem angels, shepherds, wise men – the prediction of the murdered babes – all the stories – everything we talked about in Cana – all still true!"

"Without any complications about fitting Levites into the tribe of Judah," Anna added in an amused murmur, ashamed of her earlier bad logic.

"Our Redeemer is alive today, by all those prophecies and tokens for absolute certain!" said Ammiel emphatically. "Preparing himself for *us*, you see … which is why we have to be prepared for *him*!"

Loukanos yawned and stretched out on the crackling grass, wriggling himself free of an insinuating rock, and flicking away a small centipede before Anna could make anxious noises about scorpions. He had seen the pair of them dried and dressed, warmed and fed. And Johanan's wounded hand was not infected. He could do no more.

366

"Well, as long as you're happy," he murmured lazily, lulled almost to sleep by the insistent low whining of a beggar who was evidently working the hillside somewhere above them. "I'm only thankful that since he isn't the Messiah, you're getting married as soon as we get back to Cana. Otherwise who knows how long I'd be stuck here."

Dan, who had been warmed and fed into drowsiness himself, sat up suddenly.

"Aunt Etta!" he cried. "We must write and tell her everything!"

Ammiel poked the fire enthusiastically, and cheerfully whacked a large cinder which sizzled on his reeking tunic. There was a lightness about him too, which freed his own tongue into voicing his thoughts in an unhindered way most unusual for him. Dan and Anna were equally surprised at how much he and Asa had already conspired together.

"You're a good lad, Dan. Always thoughtful for your Aunty. I'll write the second we get back to Mari's place, and tell her to pack up Bukki and her party clothes, and go straight to Cana – Asa wants the wedding in his house, despite tradition, and Etta's thankful for it. I'll tell her to splash out on a hired donkey and hang the expense! Potter Ittai, Marta and the babes must come too, if they're up to it. Caleb and Extra Pressings and poor old what's-his-name her long-suffering husband – they'll have something to fill their ribs at least – and Samuel's family! And if poor Marah All-Alone's still around, why, let Etta bring her as well and give her something happy to think about for a change! Asa demands a crowd, he told me! We can all meet up there – and then – his eyes narrowed and the happy stream of words stopped abruptly. "What? No! Tell me I'm seeing things! Tell me it's a phantom!"

"By the stars, man!" grumbled Loukanos, rolling over on to his elbows and looking up sleepily. "What phantom?"

"I don't believe it!" gasped Anna, and they all sat up to stare in the same direction.

Dan couldn't believe it either. The whining beggar who was shuffling along in the dust on the ridge above them had a peculiarly recognisable head … like a jug.

It was Uncle Bukki!

# *Chapter Twenty-nine*

HAMPERED by his blanket, Ammiel could only yell.

"Bukki! Bukki ben Bezaleel!"

The beggar lifted his head, and Dan saw to his horror his eyes were bandaged. The man shuffled hastily out of sight. Springing to his feet Dan tore up the hill in pursuit, grabbing him by the arm as he dived behind a rock.

"Uncle Bukki? It is! Uncle Bukki! What has happened to you? How came you here?"

"Oh, ah! – Dan! Is it really you? I thought someone was after me!"

"What do you mean, Uncle Bukki? And what's wrong with your eyes?"

A very dirty, very bedraggled, and (truth to tell) very smelly Uncle Bukki lifted the blindfold and peered out cautiously.

"Are we alone?"

"Yes – sort of. Most people are resting or eating … nobody sees you. But what's happened?"

Bukki pulled off the bandage and blinked. "Ouch – it's very bright." He clutched Dan's arm. "Have you any food?"

"A little …"

Uncle Bukki licked his lips. "Wine?" he asked slyly.

"A splash, that's all – come down – father will be worried."

Bukki condescended to stand up, brushed himself down and followed his nephew rather sheepishly.

"What does this mean, Bukki?" asked Ammiel sternly, but anxiously. "Why are you here – and where is Etta – is she safe and well?"

Bukki shrugged. "I suppose so."

"What do you mean – you suppose so? Where is she?"

"At home, of course," said Bukki crossly. He stuffed his mouth eagerly with sesame bread and chewed vigorously.

Ammiel swept the food aside.

"Not a morsel more, brother-in-law," he said seriously, "until you explain yourself."

Bukki scratched himself and his muddy little eyes darted nervously from Ammiel to Loukanos, who was looking grim. He decided it was prudent to be brief.

"That Marah woman gave me the creeps – weeping and wailing or staring like an idol. Etta treated her like a baby, and a man got no rest, all that prowling around half the night … well, I met a man, see … Tiberius was more lively, with a dice game or two, and a little social drinking. You know, all those soldiers aren't the same – and I learnt to play Basileus, and made a few friends …"

Dan remembered a miserable Uncle Bukki drinking with his invisible friends – or maybe the ants – at Asa's. Did he really have friends? What did they think of him?

Bukki looked at Ammiel's compressed lips and hurried through his tale with uncharacteristic honesty.

"I got drunk," he said, with a gulp. "I won several games of dice – drank it all. I don't know how much. I meant to go back to Etta in the morning – I did!" he said hastily, beginning to feel hardly done by, and infusing a whine into his trembling voice. "But when I woke up I found myself in Jericho – inside a wagonload of carpets – very smelly – dusty – and stuffy – jolting along – and I was very sick ..."

"I'll bet you were!" said Loukanos with relish.

Bukki looked hurt. "Very sick indeed!" he said piteously. "And nothing to eat or drink ... nowhere to stay ... no more money."

He carefully rubbed a tear into his eye. "And the wagoner beat me for damaging his carpets," he finished mournfully, rolling up a sleeve to show the lingering bruises.

Loukanos prodded one with evident satisfaction, making Bukki jump.

"Nice colour!" he commented. "Got any more?"

Ammiel had listened in silence. Now he stood up, tucking his blanket firmly around his narrow hips and breathing deeply. He turned his back and walked off a little way. Dan looked at Johanan, and then at Anna, who was neatly fastening the thin veil back over her face. She shook her head and laid a finger on her covered lips. Uncle Bukki reached tentatively for the wineskin but Loukanos gripped his wrist with the speed of a snake, and gently returned the fat hand to its owner's lap. Ammiel turned his head slightly.

"Anna?" he choked.

She went to him, holding her rough blanket in both hands as if it were a delicate gown.

"Anna – this is horrible!" Ammiel fought for control, staring sightlessly into the distance. "On this glorious day – a new start without sin – and suddenly I am in a rage! My poor Etta! She knows nothing except that the ungrateful fool who was to assist her has vanished into thin air. She will be beside herself! And how is she managing? My new and shining life – scarcely an hour of it, and I want to beat the stuffing out of my brother-in-law!"

Anna laid a hand on his arm. "You are not wrong to be angry with his conduct. But his desertion was not deliberate, and I think Etta will be all right. Come, sit …"

With a sigh Ammiel sank beside her on a warm rock.

"Yes, calm me down, Anna," he muttered unhappily. "You really think Etta – ?"

"Most likely," she responded gently. "Marta would know immediately if she didn't come to the well, and would make it her business to discover why at once. Ittai would soon know or find out about any expeditions to Tiberius, and news of Bukki's gambling would get back in a hurry. There are some times that you can be grateful for a Dabab you know! Etta would put two and two together. Most likely she would know all about it before a day had passed, and Ittai will be sure to keep an eye on her. She may even be relieved – a drunken, miserable Bukki could be better out of the house than in. I doubt she'd worry about him, and she certainly wouldn't worry about herself with Marta close at hand."

"Yes, that's true," Ammiel conceded reluctantly. "But why didn't he send her word – or start back for home at once!"

Anna pulled her cloak tighter as she thought. "I would say his first thought would be for food or wine … and then money or supplies for the journey back, and to Bukki I suppose that meant begging or gambling. Maybe both. Lucky for Bukki he woke in Jericho with a repentant crowd nearby to beg from."

"Obviously working his way back did not occur to him," Ammiel muttered. "Though that's not his talent. Why didn't he think to seek us out in Jerusalem?"

"To be fair, Ammiel – that would be quite a task, would it not? He would not know where Aunt Mari lives. And in any case, I think he would be afraid to face you."

"Rightly," said Ammiel drily. "For him no doubt it was sheer bad luck we saw him among all these people."

"And don't forget Marah All-Alone, who may still be there, and of more help to Etta than we imagine. She is tormented by spells, but in between times merely unhappy, from all accounts. Rather like Bukki, perhaps," she added, surprised by the thought.

There was a pause, and Ammiel took a deep breath.

"Ah, my Anna – heart-glad I am for you, woman! I am in my right mind again – and if I can be clothed in my right garments again too, I shall feel more myself than ever. Come – the moment our clothes are dry enough we'll start back to Jerusalem."

He stood up and pulled her to her feet, adding, "And that letter to my sister will have more than wedding news. How she will gasp over Bukki trying his luck as a blind beggar! Wait!" – and Ammiel was struck by a thought which brought the smile back to his face. "Bukki shall write to Etta himself! She can keep his apology in her workbasket and bring it out to read every time he forgets himself. Most likely it's the only one she'll ever have from him, so she may as well make it last!"

Laughing over this novel idea, they rejoined the others, who looked at them in surprise, and – on Bukki's part at least – relief.

Johanan's mother was amazed to see Bukki trailing behind the others as they filed wearily through the gate in the late evening.

"My dears – who on earth is your friend?" she cried curiously, lighting the lamps for herself and jangling all her bracelets in her haste. "Of course he is welcome … but – oh! Your brother-in-law, Ammiel? Well, well! He's not a bit like I imagined. Somehow I thought he'd be – much younger – oh! I mean – older – well, different." She dropped a taper with an anxious cry and trod on it impatiently to put out the smouldering rug. "You know, perhaps different colour hair …" she added lamely. It didn't sound very convincing, but the fact was that for one awful moment she had nearly blurted out 'not so ugly'. She sank into a chair and fanned herself in confusion. "Is it warm in here, or is it just me?"

Anna's eyes twinkled at her. "Yes, Auntie, it is a bit warm in here."

"You must all have baths before we talk things over – no, I insist! That road up from the river is so horribly dusty at this time of year …"

Anna kissed the top of her elegant head. "Dear Aunt Mari – would you be surprised to know that Ammiel and I have already had one today?"

And so the story came out – first briefly – then pounced on and teased apart, and all the bits put back together again – a process repeated as each told their version, until it was threaded firmly through all the experiences of that evening, and formed a never-to-be-forgotten tapestry of events.

River-bathing, baptisms or no – Johanan's mother still shooed the menfolk off to the tiled bath in the basement. The Galileans revelled in the extraordinary experience of sitting in *really warm* water – all over! – while Loukanos and Johanan soaped themselves in a businesslike manner clearly devoid of novelty. Two servants stood by with hot water jugs, big towels, small soft brushes, rough cloths, and odd little scrapers at which Dan merely blinked in astonishment. Uncle Bukki sat blissfully with his hairy pale stomach bobbing in front of him like a child's ball and guffawed to himself over the luxury. Dan and Ammiel splashed like porpoises and marvelled at the fine scented soap which actually frothed. Meanwhile, Mari had the ancient Egyptian servant woman deal with Anna's needs in a more private setting.

"I feel like a bride already," Anna laughed at the excess of feminine attentions as her nails were trimmed and buffed to a shine with soft suede, and delicate undergarments laid out for her. "If a rather elderly one! You're too kind, Aunt Mari."

Mari shook her head at her. "Well, dear, you're not quite so much of the *elderly*, really, and deserve it all the more for waiting. When you're fanning yourself as often as I am you can talk about elderly and not before … And my fussing – yes, I know you call it fussing – is good practice for the real thing so soon to come in a week or so, when all the women will be fussing over you, including myself I hope – trotting up eagerly to funny little old Cana in a horrid wagon, just think of it! But anything's better than a nasty swaying camel – they make me feel so sick! Ugh, how I hate travelling – I think I must love you very much – and my dear old Shefi must too or she'd be finding every reason for us both to stay home. As for tonight, it's a pleasure, I assure you. A little pampering is good for a woman – just occasionally – and you leave me tomorrow so early! I'm determined to make you stay up half the night, just out of sheer greediness for an intelligent woman to talk to. Now, I mustn't sit here any longer – I have people to boss about … Shefi will make you as pretty as you like. Don't be shy of asking for anything you need."

She kissed her niece warmly and left.


Shefi was surprisingly deft and gentle despite her arthritic fingers. She massaged soft sweet ointment into Anna's skin, which was very soothing. Anna closed her eyes with a grateful sigh. The skillful hands first detangled with scented oil, and then combed the freshly washed hair, now smelling delightfully of rosewater rather than Jordan water, and braided it up carefully.

"Better for the travelling, mistress," she advised knowingly. "It will stay cleaner – less trouble."

"Very well," said Anna, amused by the thick shining plait now carefully pinned around her head like a bridal coronet. But she waved away the kohl with hasty protests.

"No, no, no, Shefi! This is not part of my tradition, at all! For you, I understand. But it is not for me."

Shefi paused with the tiny palate in her palm, her black rimmed eyes suddenly fixed on Anna's. She snapped the silver kohl case shut with a click and shut her eyes, muttering Egyptian phrases under her breath and anxiously tapping the amulet at her wrinkled throat.

"Aiee, mistress!" she whispered in awe, " Eyes which are not twins … it is not right … it is bad luck …"

Anna sighed, though she was used to this reaction. "Shefi, they are just ordinary eyes. My grandmother had them too, and lived a long and happy life …"

Shefi's almond eyes widened in horror. "You have your grandmother's eyes? Aiee!" and she turned and ran from the room, leaving Anna laughing regretfully over the misunderstanding. She picked up the soft embroidered under-shift. Mari was a sweet, generous aunt, but it would be a relief to dress herself with her own hands and not be fidgeted over.

It was an elegant meal, and the company looked elegant enough to match it. Mari surveyed her extended family proudly as they lounged at the table. Anna looked lovely, a far cry from the dusty and rather dishevelled woman in an exceedingly crumpled gown who had appeared earlier. Yes, they all looked quite as smart as city folk! Even Bukki – whose relationship to herself she was not exactly confident of – looked surprisingly tidy, clean, and well combed. Hardly recognisable as the disreputable scruffy man who plodded in through her gate only hours before. He had evidently suffered a drought of wine lately, though, she thought wryly, and was fast making up for it, so who knew how long his image would last …

Loukanos, sleek, neat and fastidious, was looking more his usual self, though she had to admit she rather liked his hair more unruly. It made him look, well, more *human*. Dan and Johanan had unusually clean clothes and shining faces, though, wait a moment … she paused mentally for a critical look at her son's upper lip, which looked a bit dirty. With a maternal heart thump she realised it wasn't dirt after all. *Oh, and he was so sweet when he was little, too!* Johanan caught the dismayed stare and winked at her, exaggeratedly twirling huge imaginary moustaches. She tutted at him crossly, and turned her attention to Ammiel.

Now there was a figure of a man – and thankful she was for him indeed, for Anna's sake. *Quite like my own departed darling, really, may he rest in peace, though he was dark, and Ammiel's fair as the sun and clear as the day. And "Terrible as an Army with Banners?"* her busy

377

mind insisted on adding, making her smile at her own thoughts and their very appropriate source from the Song of Solomon … *H'm … maybe he could be, if his blood was up!* Yes, there was no doubt Ammiel was a pleasure to look at, with his fine strong nose, his kind mouth, twinkling eyes and warm expression. Not to speak of those shoulders! Carrying all those lambs, no doubt. And fighting wolves and wildcats and lions and … and what-names … lepers? no, leopards … Thankfully her Johanan would never know such a dangerous life. She sighed happily and sentimentally and gestured to Shefi for more wine. Shefi obliged, edging around Anna cautiously.

It was a wonderful meal, and even Dan could not remember how many different and delicious dishes he sampled. Ammiel ate heartily, having recovered his normal temper completely with the comfort of overseeing Bukki's struggles with his pen, and having himself composed a brief but exultant missive to acquaint Etta with all the main events of the last few days. He knew in his heart that Anna was right about Etta managing well enough, though he was hurt that Bukki could treat her so shabbily as to make no attempt to send word of his whereabouts. But he could relax now that the letters had gone to his sister, and to Asa as well, by the entrepreneurial hand of Shalal's posts which took messages to five different collection points in the country, and Cana was one of them.

Mari told the story to gales of laughter. It was a complicated one, beginning with the unlucky timing of the fellow's birth – which took place by the Spring of Gihon due to the upheaval of the great Census. His father being a pious man had elected to name the unfortunate mite Mahershalalhashbaz, and the child had put up with far too many jokes by the time he became a man.

One day, hearing for the hundredth time, "It's quicker to write and send a letter than say your name …" the young man had had enough. He demanded thenceforth to be known merely as Shalal, and determined to shorten the vagueness of letter delivery to a predictable time. Five years later he had a thriving business, "which is growing as we speak!" Mari assured them. "Of course I still use friends when I can, it's cheaper!"

As Anna laughed her rippling, gurgling laugh for the dozenth time that night, Ammiel thought of the sound of the Jordan among the shallows, the background to their happy decision. Truly tonight she looked like a queen, with her hair for a crown, framed in a drifting veil and fittingly draped with silver coins, her fascinating eyes dancing, her family around her, her face flushed with joy like a girl's. No, he did not regret the years that had passed. And the future was all theirs.

The fun subsided as they began again to go over the last two days of their experiences with the Baptist and his followers. The conversation grew more sober and intense, but Mari intently listened to the retelling of details, and was full of new questions. Bukki excused himself and did not return. The night deepened. Shefi retired. Mari lit more lamps until the room looked like a synagogue at Chanukah. Dan's eyes began to roll, and Johanan shamelessly flopped onto cushions and appeared to doze. Loukanos, his head sunk on his chest, was clearly asleep, though rather comically sitting bolt upright, one hand still holding his cup. It was a queer knack of his. Mari rose, fanning herself, smiling.

"It is warm in here – I keep saying so. A warm spell to finish summer before the rains! And all these lamps make it stuffy. See – the children are asleep – "

"Not asleep!" mumbled Johanan, opening his eyes blearily and sitting up with a yawn. Children? He was nearly a man under the law! Dan jerked himself up bravely and blinked like an owl.

"Come!" said Mari, who was still eager for more discussion about Johannes and the prophets Isaiah, Jeremiah and Micah – and determined to make the most of an unsatisfactorily short visit. "The boys can go to bed if they like, and we will go to the roof for fresh air. And later, Ammiel, my dear, you will pray for a blessing on us all before we retire."

"With pleasure. And thank you."

Johanan and Dan knew they would wake up properly once they were outside, and insisted they were not tired at all, they were just resting their eyes and would not go to bed. So with Mari shepherding them all to the outside stairs, and each holding high a lamp, like a bridal procession, they began the steep climb to the top of the roof, where, Dan knew, a shelter waited with soft cushions and rugs against any nip in the night air.

Ammiel ran up first, his light guttering gaily above him – running lightly as a boy, leather soles slapping the whitewashed stairs – with Anna five steps behind, and the boys on her heels. Just as he reached the top there was a startled exclamation, and a stumpy figure blundered out from behind the parapet and lurched out onto the top step.

There was a grunt from Ammiel as the wind was knocked out of him. A lighted lamp wheeled high into the night and vanished. A horribly flailing body cried out. A ghastly sound smacked the pavement two storeys below. Lights wavering. Shouting. Feet scrambling down stairs. Somewhere, far away, a woman was screaming as if she would never stop. Dimly Anna wished someone would shut her up. She felt sudden pain in her throat and realised the noise was her own … Loukanos – suddenly, sharp, alert – flung himself out of the lit doorway and at the broken body twisted in the shadows. Carefully he turned it over. He bent his head. He looked up.

"Don't hurt him!" shrieked Dan, rigid with fear.

Mari cast her veil over the boy's head and pulled him inside the house without a word. Johanan was on his knees, vomiting, in gut wrenching agony. Sharp oily shards broke under her hands and knees as Anna crawled towards her brother like an animal even while he shouted at her to keep away . He shouted at her in Aramaic, in Greek, in Latin. But she didn't seem to understand, and drew her fingers numbly, wonderingly, over the sticky pavement.

Running feet, flaring lamps. Noise. Cries. Blackness. Nothing was real. Nothing was real.

Only one man was unmoved. Above the nightmare, tumbled halfway down the stairs, half singing, half mumbling, very confused, very drunk – Uncle Bukki.

## Chapter Thirty

THE world had shrunk, dwindled, vanished. Anna and Loukanos were kneeling at the bottom of a dreadful well, outside of which nothing existed but silence and blackness. Inside was only a flickering pool of sickly light which threw mocking glints from those red gold curls which were not clotted so horribly as the rest. A twisted garment exposed the broad chest – an expanse of wiry auburn hair which trembled only under the ragged breath of the watchers, and not from within. Anna bent her head – surely she was inside someone else's body – it did not feel like her own – and laid her icy face against the still chest. Warmth lingered there, and the pounding which shook her body could be an illusion for both of them. So had she dreamed of feeling his heartbeat under her cheek! She moved her bloodied, manicured fingertips tenderly over his supple skin, tracing a smeared crimson path, feeling each hair as clearly as touching a tree in a forest. A forest in which she had lost her way, a blind forest where she must feel her way out, and yet where she wanted to lie down forever. She could smell it – warm, herbal ... feel the dancing sunlight against her eyelids and grasses stroking her face ... though far beneath was blood ... and fear ...

She opened her eyes a little – just a crack – just enough to let in the gold olive light and see it play on the soft white place under his chin as her free hand gently lifted the rippling beard which felt yet alive. Yes, there it was. How beautiful. She raised her head and kissed it gently. Yes, that was how she had thought it would feel, and smell. Soft, babyish, vulnerable, still warm … She would not forget, though it should have throbbed with a vital pulse.

Her eyes moved to his lips, perfect, white and bloodless. Strange when everything else was so bloody. Her gaze must go no further. She drew the veil slowly from her head and the person beside her read her thoughts, taking it gently and covering the rest of the ruined face as tenderly as a benediction.

"Say goodbye now, sister."

The murmured words came from a long way off, but she whispered, "Yes," … gave the unresponsive, once-lovely mouth the kiss it had never presumed to ask in life … and obediently allowed someone to lift her out of the well, and into the nothingness beyond.

## Chapter Thirty-one

ETTA lifted the lid and sniffed.

"Smells right, looks right ..."

She dipped in her wooden spoon, blew cautiously, and sipped. "Ugh! Marah, are you sure about this brew?"

Marah, her capacious sleeves turned back neatly and tied behind her neck, moved her bare scarred arms briskly over the table, wiping the last fragments of greenery into her cupped hand. Tossing the scraps in the fire, she bent over to taste Etta's spoonful, and screwed up her face. "*Ptha!* This tastes like soap! Far too much caraway."

"But you *said* caraway."

"Yes, one beqa – not much more than a large pinch. What did you use – a ladle?"

"Oh dear!" Etta pulled a face. "Let me see ..."

She peered at the list Marah had charcoaled rapidly on the open door earlier in the day. "Eleven *beqa*, you wrote! Look there!" She pointed to the spot which said *XI*.

Marah looked and her eyes twinkled repentantly. "It's all your brother's fault! No, no, it's clearly my own for not washing the boards first! I'm sorry, Etta! Did he leave a message recently with a ten in it?"

"Bother the man, that he did!" Etta chuckled. "The night you came he began one for Ittai saying we'd be away at least ten days. That'll serve us right for using fancy Roman numerals!"

Marah sat down and positively roared with laughter. It had startled Etta at first to hear such a huge husky laugh from a woman, but she was used to it now. Marah did nothing by halves, and an affected laugh was an abomination anyway, thought Etta defiantly. No mincing "hee-hee" titters from Marah All-Alone. Why, she sounded more like Bukki at times!

They had their laugh out and then began to discuss the best way to rescue their herbal brew. They could water it down, but who could swallow such an amount before it went off? They argued for a while, exchanging more laughter and outrageous suggestions – finally agreeing to strain out the seeds and dry them for another use. The liquid surely was worth trying as a hair rinse, if nothing else. It was just as well they hadn't already added the precious honey! A ludicrous image of hair which attracted ants, bees, flies, beetles, wasps and no doubt spiders as well, had them going again, and they completely missed hearing Marta's call until she appeared in the doorway, blocking the light.

She waved a package at them tantalisingly.

"I thought I'd bring something to cheer you up, but it sounds like you don't need it," she teased. "Shall I go away again?"

Marah sprang up and pounced on her. "No, you don't. We promise to be miserable right away to make it worth your while!"

Marta laughed. She too was more used to Etta's house-guest now. The tragic spells came and went unpredictably, and in between

386

Marah did not seem to be deeply unhappy any more. In fact, she was often good, if mercurial, company, though there was a watchful wariness about her which never quite left her eyes. In the time she had been with Etta, since waking from her last death-like trance, the strange second sight which had her hunting newborn babes had not reappeared. Even so, Marta was glad enough of the excuse of too-heavy twins, to leave them behind with her mother-in-law when she visited here.

"What is it, Marta?" Etta demanded. "Come! Sit – sit! On your feet all day and walking here as well. You must take something to drink. But not our herbal water, which is disgusting and will probably give your babes the colic! Marah assured me it was a good cleansing tonic, at least it may have been before I misread the recipe … but there are limits … I'm not soaping my insides no matter how much good it does me." She handed her friend a cup of cold water from the jug on the table. "Have you news of that disgraceful Bukki?"

"I don't know any more," Marta replied, sitting down and gulping the water thankfully. *Those greedy babies just drink me dry! One day I'll just shrivel up like a husk and blow away in the wind!* She suppressed a giggle at her silly thoughts. "He seems to have vanished after his exploits in Tiberius. Quite vanished, like Elijah."

"Could he have taken shipping somewhere?" Marah suggested, and Etta's eyes flickered with momentary alarm. Marta patted her hand quickly and shook her head.

"You know how much he hates boats and water, Etta, so don't you go imagining drownings and other horrors. He will have crawled away to sleep it off somewhere and got lost. Or maybe he's working his way around the taverns in Decapolis. Bukki will always land on his feet – or his, you know …" She patted her behind, making the others laugh.

Etta added drily, "Or someone's feet will land on his behind, more like it!"

When they had got over their next outburst of laughter, Marta said cheerfully, "No news is good news. And speaking of news – don't you want to look at this?"

Etta tilted the black untidy writing on the package towards the light.

"How did you get this, Marta? It bears my name, but also Philip the Younger's."

Marta drained her cup and put it down with a tap. "Ittai got it from Philip, who picked it up in Cana – from that new collection point set up by some enterprising young man in Jerusalem. He calls it the Jerusalem Post, because it goes out in relays, you know. Such a wonderful idea – but expensive."

Etta had snapped the brown wax already and was pulling apart the string on the packet, fingers all thumbs in her excitement.

"It's not likely to be from Bukki, then!" she said with a twinkle. "But how exciting, to have any sort of letter at all, and so good of you to bring it, Marta. Though there can't be much news in here – it's so light! If this came all the way from Jerusalem it won't be from Asa or Samuel … it can only be from my brother!"

"Here, Etta!" Marta urged impatiently, snatching up the cooking knife. "Forget your economy for a moment and just cut it!"

"No, no, no!" Etta protested, still picking at the string laboriously.

Marta scolded, "You're as bad as Extra Pressings!" but Marah All-Alone intervened and had the knots undone in a moment.

"There."

The linen cover slipped off and three pieces of thin crackling stuff dropped out, each neatly triple-folded.

"Real papyrus!"

"Isn't it light!"

"Lovely!" they chorused.

Which to open first? Etta recognised Ammiel's hand on two pieces, but whose was the other?

"Open the mystery one first!" the women urged. Etta picked up the messiest of the three and unfolded it, twitching her nose, and reading aloud with a smile lurking.

*"From Bukki I am safe,"* she read and looked triumphantly at the others.

"I told you so," they chorused happily. "Go on!"

*"I drunk my winnings and got in some carpets. In Jericho I woke up sick and got beat hard. Begging is better if you are blind. Ammiel makes me say I am very sorry. Yes I am. See you in Cana. Bukki."*

Etta finished reading Bukki's struggling letter, sat down with a plump and rolled her eyes at her friends, who were trying not to laugh .

"Short but sweet!" she said expressively and began to chuckle. "Stupid man!" she added crossly and contradictorily, wiping her eyes. "Worrying the life out of me like that! Whoever beat him hard did me a favour!"

Marah could hold herself in no longer and out it came – a huge, man-like bellow which made the others jump and had them laughing all the more. They laughed for the funny images which Bukki's awkward prose had raised in their minds, but also because they were so relieved, Etta for Bukki, the others for her sake.

At last, Etta dabbed her eyes with the corner of her veil and said with a sigh, "He must still be fuddled. I don't know what he meant about blind begging and by seeing me in Cana, if he knew himself. But it's clear he's all right, and he's met up with Ammiel in Jerusalem somehow, so that's a relief too. "

"Do hurry and open the others, Etta," Marta pleaded, tucking her unruly strand of white hair back under her veil where it belonged. She hugged herself and groaned. "Ow – feeding time! I must get home right away."

Etta obliged by opening the dirtiest first as quickly as she could. "Why, it's from Dan, bless him!" she cried with delight and read the sprawling, smudged letters at once. *"Aunty donkeys are fun but cross we had a good trip Jerusalem is big as the sea I wish you were with us and send you love from us all Dan. Father helped me write this Dan. I will bring you a present Dan."*

"My little Dan!" said Etta, folding the letter tenderly and kissing it in a rare moment of sentimentality – Marah and Marta smiling at her – "who is growing up by the hour!" she added hastily, laughing at herself, before quickly opening the third letter.

"Ah, God is good! It is from Ammiel himself! *My dear sister, blessings and peace from all ours at Cana and Jerusalem. I write late afternoon on the sixth day, we having arrived safely, praise God. Anna's aunt Mari rejoices to have Johanan safely home and is full of kindness to us. After the Sabbath we go to find the prophet. If he is the Messiah we will know soon. I will write you again at once. Make Bukki be good to you. God be with you till we meet again. From your loving brother Ammiel."*

She looked up, full of happiness and folded the letter carefully.

"Bukki must have found them soon after this was written! How thankful I am they are all safe, and together again. I wonder if Ammiel will keep Bukki with him, or send him home? But it makes no difference now. My brother will do whatever he deems best, so I will expect Bukki when I see him, and not before."

She stowed the precious letters neatly on her beloved wooden shelves, setting a smooth striped stone on top to keep them safe. It was one Dan had brought her more than a year ago. He had tried to stick fish scales to it, but they had long since dropped off.

She turned to her friends with a smile mingled with a relieved sigh.

"I will sleep soundly tonight, and praise the Eternal for His merciful protection!"

Marta stood up, satisfied. "So will we! How wonderful to have such good news, Etta, dear! Now I must run. Here, I'll take the water jar and Ittai will bring it back in the morning."

"There is no need, Marta," said Marah impulsively. "He is a man, and busy – I will get the water."

Marta hesitated. Marah All-Alone met her eyes, though her body drooped in resignation.

"It's all right, Marta," she answered quietly. "I know they shun me, and hide their children. And the bravest of the small boys throw stones and feel like warriors! I will go very early and be gone before anyone is afraid."

"Oh, Marah!" said Marta, dropping her eyes helplessly, and ashamed of her own fears.

"It is because of these strange spirits which possess me," the woman continued drearily. "I feel them, I hear them, they drive me – and yet I feel I am dreaming and cannot wake. Sometimes I feel I am watching another person altogether and not myself. Then there is the blackness. I can't explain it any better than that. But if anyone should be afraid, surely it is I?"

"I don't understand," said Marta frankly, laying a gentle hand on her shoulder. "And yes, I am afraid when you are wild and storming. But I will try to remember that it is more fearful for you, and that you mean no harm."

"Thank you." Marah bit her lips and passed a hand over her eyes, her face draining. "I am painfully aware that *meaning* no harm does not mean ... I ... will do none ..." Her voice trailed away.

There was a moment of shocked silence. Marah's eyes fluttered.

"Marah!" Etta said sharply. "Marah! Talk to me! We are your friends!" She leant across the table and snatched up the jug, flinging its contents in Marah's face.

Marta cried out in alarm, "Etta, are you mad?" and Marah gasped, the colour rushing back into her face. Her eyes flew open and she shook her head, looking in surprise at her wet bosom and dripping hair. She pushed the dark strands back from her face automatically and blinked.

"What was I saying?"

"You were saying goodbye to Marta, who is just going," said Etta boldly, smiling firmly at Marta. She embraced her concerned young friend murmuring, "Don't worry, my dear!" in her ear, and then raising her voice to say casually, "Do you know, I believe my carry jar has a fine crack in it – perhaps Ittai could sell me another. Maybe a smaller one?"

"I'll tell him," Marta promised, with an understanding nod, and left, a little rattled, hurrying back to the babies who would be surely wailing for that feed by now – and to throw all these fresh worries upon her husband's sensible, reliable shoulders. It was a relief to talk to him and know it would go no further. She dared not say much to her mother-in-law, kind as she was. That terrible Rachel would have it out of her before three buckets were drawn.

"Let's sit in the sunshine for a little while, Marah." Etta made no attempt to explain the water splashed everywhere, and chattered on lightly. "These beans need sorting and the light's not good enough here. I saw a crafty look in young Joram's eye when we bought them, and shouldn't be surprised if they are full of gravel. My teeth won't stand for it, I can tell you, and I can't spare any at my age."

The sun would dry her quickly, and Etta was learning to manage the strange turns of mood. Sun, warmth and light, were calming after what Etta now called a 'near miss', but if Marah slipped all the way into her private place of horror, she then quickly needed somewhere cramped and dark in which to curl up and feel safe, if she was not to start raving or wandering like a sleepwalker.

Marah followed her bent older friend obediently, and together they sat on the rough bench in the sunny courtyard, sorting the beans into shallow bowls. To do young Joram justice, they had no more gravel in them than was usual, but Etta was glad to see Marah's brow clearing even as her dress and hair dried.

"Was I sinking again, Etta?" she asked unhappily, plucking at her damp bodice.

"Yes, dear."

Etta sorted busily. Marah sighed and her fingers grew still.

"Is my whole life to be driven thus?" she asked in a low, passionate voice. "Will I never be able to trust myself? You are good to me, Etta, but I can't remain here. It's time I found somewhere of my own. But I never know when it will happen! It came upon me so suddenly – after that fever … Must I never dare to step outside the house? Will I forever drive people away from me?"

Etta said nothing. She had no answers. Marah picked up a piece of gravel and dropped it back into the dish with a clack.

"Among all the people in the world … I'm like this stone among these beans, you see, Etta. I may look the same. I may fool people for a while. But sooner or later someone will get a tooth broken."

She picked it out again, and flicked it away into the bushes. She picked out another stone and tossed it idly into the water pot beside them. It sank with a plinking sound. She watched it with something curiously like envy.

"The sea is deep."

She leaned her head back against the warm whitewashed wall, and closed her eyes wearily. "That's the only answer, isn't it."

It was a statement, not a question.

Protestingly Etta shook her head, uncomprehending of such deep despair.

"How can it be? The Eternal gives us life that we may give Him glory and praise. To fling away the stone of life is to deny Him His due."

"What glory can I give Him?" Marah cried. "I have no peace! I am denied the synagogue! I can't even worship! I am chased and feared and spat on! My own race shuns me, and yet despises my association with Gentiles. Am I to live like the poor wretch over the Lake? Among the dead? How can I obey the law when I can't even do good to my neighbour!"

"Stop," Etta said firmly. "Marah, dear, stop. You can make that list as long as eternity if you wish. What we *can't* do will always be more than what we *can*. Believe me, at my age and condition, I know what I'm talking about. But why not think of the 'can' for a change?"

"Oh!" Marah tossed her head impatiently, and said rather sarcastically, "I can sort beans!"

"No you can't," Etta said with authority, peering over her shoulder and pointedly picking out three pieces of gravel from her bowl.

Marah glared at her, then as Etta winked, she snorted, and grudgingly relaxed.

"Very well, then," she conceded at last. "What *can* I do?"

Etta repeated calmly, "You can give the Eternal glory."

Marah shrugged. "What *is* giving the Eternal glory, Etta? We *say* it, but what does it *mean*? Singing praises? Praying? I told you, I'm out of the synagogue."

Thoughtfully Etta tapped her teeth with a broken fingernail. "I wonder, how many voices need to speak before God can hear? He who knows our thoughts?"

"I suppose, if you put it like that, not even one voice needs to speak aloud ..." Marah answered slowly, "... if the thoughts are directed towards Him."

"Ah!" replied Etta, frowning at a particularly large pebble which even young Joram should know could never pass for a bean. "Then if thoughts are indeed directed towards Him and He hears them – surely the sound of even one voice 'All-Alone' speaking in prayer, or singing in praise, would be an extra pleasure to His ears?"

"M'm." Marah was noncommittal, swinging her feet rebelliously, tossing the wormiest beans fretfully at the darting sparrows under the eaves.

Etta poured water into her pan and began to rub the husks from the beans with her fingertips. "Let's see. Giving God glory. First, in Godly thoughts. Then, voice of praise – in song or speech. What next?"

"I suppose actions," Marah said reluctantly. "But –"

Etta held up her plump hand. "Ssh! I'm working this out myself. When do actions give glory to the Eternal?" She snapped her fingers. "When we show how we admire or worship Him … yes … now how do we do that? Obeying the law?"

"Yes, but there's got to be more," Marah said with sudden interest, straightening herself and leaving the poor sparrows alone at last. "Or we must all be doomed! Keeping the law *exactly* as it was given has been impossible since the Exile – we all know that!"

"Ouf! Who could *ever* keep the whole law, *honestly*, the whole time!" Etta laughed, distracted momentarily from her original train of thought. "We'd have to stay in the river half the time washing, and the other half we'd be either outside the camp, or inside the tabernacle with endless sacrifices! Who – really and truly – would have time to actually *live*? I think Abraham had it much simpler, don't you?"

396

Marah shot out a hand and snatched Etta's arm so quickly that water slopped on both of them.

"Abraham didn't keep the law!" she said intently, her deepset eyes widening.

"Well, of course not," Etta lifted her bowl calmly and pulled the wet cloth on her knees to one side. "Moses wasn't born yet. Oh!" And she began to see the point.

"The promises! The blessings! The seed! First Eve ... later Abraham ... Therefore – salvation must be from *before* Moses – yes?" Marah said eagerly. "So what of the law?!"

Etta felt her world shift slightly beneath her.

"It is of God," she said abruptly, and firmly. "Necessary!" she added deliberately. Of course, a six year old could have lisped as much, and Etta uneasily realised it didn't really address the question.

Marah shook her head impatiently. "There's something more, isn't there! But I don't know what. I don't know enough. Get back to the matter of giving God the glory. What you said about actions – showing we admire Him ... let's leave the commandments and traditions out of it for a moment ..."

Etta retraced her thoughts. "H'm ... that's not easy ... showing we admire him ... Well, we always copy those we admire and try to be like them ourselves. So it would have to be by copying Him, don't you think? That must be it."

*"Of course, the Eternal Himself does not have to 'keep the commandments', does He ..."* Etta's private thoughts ran on. *"So, in copying Him exactly would we not need to keep them either?"* It was a daring thought almost amusing in its peculiarity. But probably impious. She dismissed it quickly.

Marah snatched up her bowl and began rubbing the beans quickly.

"Yes, yes, yes! Because – *What does the Lord ask of thee, but to act justly, to love mercy and to walk in humility with thy God ... !*" she recited rapidly.

Etta put her hand over the beans and drained the husk-filled water between her deeply creased fingers. She nodded, knowing they had reached a good point to stop.

"M'm! Act with justice, be humble, and *show mercy, as the Eternal shows mercy!* Now, we were talking of how Marah All-Alone can give God glory, were we not? Thinking, singing, praying – yes, this you need nobody else for, you can do it anywhere, any time and none can prevent you. Now let's add this action – showing mercy! Such as giving help and comfort to a deserted, bent old woman of no importance! Perhaps Marah gives Him glory, after all, eh?"

She stood up, stretching with a wince. Marah looked up with thoughtful eyes.

"You think so? Have I really, Etta? You make it sound possible! But how to show mercy elsewhere, when I receive none from others?"

"Hold out your hand," said Etta in an exasperated tone, with a look Dan would have recognised. Marah held it out obediently. Etta smacked it lightly.

"Not *none*, Marah dear," she said with a hint of reproach, thinking of young Marta's valiant overtures of friendship.

Marah blushed, snatched Etta's hand and kissed it impulsively. "It was you who showed mercy to me first – and I'm an ungrateful wretch."

"No, that's not what I meant, and no you're not. And as for giving something you don't receive, why – doesn't the Eternal do that every day? Maybe you're copying Him more exactly, giving Him more glory, than the rest of us! Won't that be a shock for us all on Judgement Day! Now enough of playing at Scribes – let's go inside and do something with these beans – and hope they're more successful than your tonic!"

As Marah whisked the table clear, something yellow fluttered to the ground.

"Etta! There was another letter in this parcel! Caught in a fold!"

Etta snatched it up eagerly.

"Marah, you must be good luck! However did I miss it!"

She unfolded the sheet with hasty fingers, ran her eyes over the page, and uncharacteristically burst into tears.

"Etta! Oh, what is it! Bad news? What has happened?!"

Etta sat down slowly, her fat shoulders shaking, holding her veil to her face with both hands and hugging the letter to her bosom with her arms. Marah rushed to ladle a warm draught from the pot, and Etta obediently swallowed it in one gulp. So agitated were they both that neither of them noticed it was the despised herbal water. Etta's shining eyes met Marah's gratefully, shaking her head reassuringly and sniffing.

"Oh dear – this took me so much by surprise! Serves me right for reading the last part of it first!"

She smoothed the letter out before her and found the lines.

"See – it was written only a few days after the last! Ammiel has found the prophet Johannes. *He is a Nazirite of the tribe of*

*Levi. He is not the Messiah himself after all, but has been sent from God to announce his appearing.'* So Messiah is here, somewhere, waiting! Oh, Marah! Imagine! And – Ammiel and Anna have been baptized by the prophet in the Jordan! He says *'all our old sins have been forgiven, and we start afresh by God's authority – cleansed,'* he says, *'ready to accept the Messiah!'* And they are *'coming straight back to Cana to be married right away!'*"

"How wonderful!" breathed Marah, but she was not thinking of the wedding.

Etta beamed at her.

"He says I must bring Ittai and Marta and the children – Samuel and Ada – Caleb, Extra Pressings and her husband – and hire donkeys! He says *'all our animals will survive in folds with Samuel's boys for at least a day or two.'* Just think! I am to set out for Asa's as soon as I can manage! We will all be reunited there, Dan, Bukki, friends, family and all. He sounds so happy! And look, Marah, dear – he invites you too!"

Her friend's eyes softened. "He is a kind man, and I wish him and his bride – all of you – every happiness. But Etta, though I thank him sincerely – I can't come. You have been a true friend to me in a time of great trouble, and I'm grateful ... I'll help you get ready and see you on your way, but then I must be leaving you."

Etta was stunned.

"Leaving?" she gasped. "When did you decide this?" A rare glint came into Marah's eyes.

"Just now," she said steadily. "Praise God I can still support myself, you know – and I'll get by, as long as I don't have too many more bad times at once ..."

"But where are you going?" Etta did not like the thought of the woman wandering off aimlessly, but very deep down inside, though she hated herself for it, was relief that there was no risk of any unexpected dramas at the wedding.

Marah All-Alone rose with an uplifted, determined look.

"I'm going to Bethabara, to find the prophet and hear him for myself. I think he offers me what the synagogue can't – something I need more than anything. God grant that I may be spared a visitation of misery long enough to find out. But first I must hurry back to Magdala to find my father."

## Chapter Thirty-two

"YOUR father?" Etta felt a curious sinking sensation. She rose and shut the door.

"What are you doing, Etta? Now it's dark in here!"

Etta raked out the fire, and began to busy herself straining the greenish liquid from the pot through a cloth draped over a bowl.

"Etta?"

Etta put the pot down and wrung the cloth over the bowl.

"Fetch me another plate, please, Marah."

Marah obeyed but held it at arm's length.

"Etta, will you tell me what's wrong?"

The older woman's dark wrinkled eyes looked sorrowfully at the puzzled face at the table.

"Tell me, or I drop this plate right now!" Marah said, half laughing, half threatening.

Etta sighed and motioned for the dish.

"Marah, dear. Your father is long dead."

Confused, Marah fumbled the plate onto the table.

"No, I – that was a mistake – I saw him – recently – somewhere … yes, in Magdala!"

"You have not been in Magdala recently, Marah. You have been at Banayim, in Tiberius, or here with me."

"Before then!" Marah resisted, moving her hands restlessly around the table, picking up the spoon, the pot, the knife, playing with the sodden fringes of the straining cloth. Etta watched her, feeling helpless.

*Great God, Thou the merciful Healer, help me with this poor daughter of thine!*

"What did your father die of, Marah?" she asked conversationally, though her heart began to hasten. "Was it not fever?"

"No!" Marah whispered, hurriedly covering her eyes. "Everyone thinks so, but it was not! I know what killed him, but I shan't tell! I shan't! I – can't ..."

"So he died, then?"

"Yes, of course! – No! No! I saw him! I told you – I've seen him! You are trying to trick me! And I thought I could trust you!" Marah sprang to her feet, panting.

"Peace, Marah! Peace! All is well! You are safe!" Etta cried hastily, but Marah was trembling, her voice hoarse, her eyes seeing something far away.

"He was alive! He was alive! He *is* alive ... he must be alive ... he can't be dead ... I want him alive! I loved him so much! Abba! Abba!" she moaned, pressing her face to the wall, clutching imploringly with her hands. She dropped them suddenly and turned with a swiftly changed face, now set and expressionless. She snatched up the cooking knife – Etta gasped in disbelief, her knees sinking beneath her – slash! Marah changed hands – slash! Dark blood sprang from long red stripes and dotted the scrubbed wood – the dripping knife clattered to the dirt floor, hitting the table as it fell.

Marah was silent for a frozen moment. She looked at the gashes on her forearms and gave a convulsive sob of relief.

"I'm alive! I'm alive!" she whispered feverishly. "I'm all right. I'm alive!"

Methodically she tore a strip from her veil and began to bind her wounds, not noticing the tears which spilled down her pale, sweating face, not seeing the aghast woman before her.

Etta, her body quivering, stealthily picked up the knife from whence it had fallen beside her stool, and with a swift movement flung it out of the small window into the scrub. She looked warily at Marah, who now seemed to be quite satisfied and calm, and having tied the knots with her teeth, smoothed her bandages almost complacently.

"This is all too much for me to understand, Marah," she said, very quietly and carefully.

Marah nodded matter-of-factly. "Yes. But it will be well now. I am better."

She looked up and smiled brightly. "Much better. The sword devours one as well as another, you know."

Very tightly, Etta gripped the smoothly worn edge of the table. It seemed to her that Marah was still somewhere else. *The knife is gone – she will not hurt me.* Quickly, boldly, she asked, "What sword?"

"Ssh!" anxiously Marah put a finger to her lips. "Let no one hear it! The sword that killed my father!"

"Did he not die of fever in Magdala ten years ago, Marah?" Etta whispered.

"No!" the younger woman looked furtively over her shoulder. "That was not my father. I was a pretty child, you know, and he a lonely, pious man."

"Oh," said Etta sadly. The old, old story.

Marah lifted her head in proud denial.

"I said he was pious! I was a daughter to him, nothing more. But who would believe it? Nobody knew us, but still they whispered behind their hands. Always such awkward questions about my mother. I would not say she was dead. I still saw her. Leprosy, we said! It stopped the questions."

Etta was crouched over the table, eager for answers, but more confused than ever.

"What happened to your parents?"

Marah looked up with haunted eyes. "The sword! The sword! Sometimes I hear their screams still and I am killing them all over again!"

Shaken, Etta whispered with difficulty, "You killed your parents?"

Marah clutched at Etta's nerveless fingers. "Yes!" she whispered tragically, and tears burned in her hot eyes. "And my baby brother! I killed them all!"

Suddenly Etta remembered something, and her heart turned over.

"Marah," she said gently. "When you were a little girl – did you live down south?"

Marah All-Alone looked at her warily. Etta softly persisted.

406

"Anywhere – near Bethlehem?"

Marah nodded mutely.

Etta grew still. *I am all mothers, all grandmothers! I am all sisters, all daughters! I am Rachel!* There had never been a Rachel who pulled poor Dan's hair after the feast. There had only ever been a tormented Marah All-Alone of Magdala.

"Tell me what happened," Etta's eyes filled.

Marah covered her face, red brown stains seeping through her bound arms.

"Night!" she gasped. "Hammering! Torchlight! Shouting! Smashing! Mother dragged me out of bed so roughly I shrieked in terror. Father crushed his hand over my mouth till my lips bled, – pleading with me to be silent and brave! They thrust the tiny little one into my arms and told me to run like the wind – run and hide! Keep him silent or we would both die! The door was breaking as I darted to the next room. Soldiers with torches, shouting in the name of Herod – a child had cried in that house, they swore it – and there was the cradle with bedding still warm! "Not ours!" my parents wept, "a visitor's – since gone!"

"There was no time – I sprang into the tall basket which held the winter blankets – it fell over and stunned me, but I lay still, pressing the baby's face into my neck, tumbling the blankets over us. I heard tearing cloth and my mother's screams. 'A nursing mother!' the men yelled triumphantly while my father swore his infant son was dead and buried only that very day – but they did not believe him – then came crashing and swearing and terrible choking cries – harsh shouts – a sudden silence and scuffling as they searched. Someone kicked my basket and laughed. The infant struggled and kicked, but I gripped him tighter and forced his little face against me so he could not scream. I would not let him be found! They ran a blade through the woven work and it cut my arms as I held him to me so firmly. But I would not cry out and betray us, so they never knew I was there. Then they were gone – a horrible quiet, and faint screams and commotion growing further away … it was a long time before I dared to crawl out. My father … and my mother … lay in their blood."

Marah stopped speaking. She had spoken more and more calmly as her tale grew more horrific.

Etta was weeping.

"Marah, my child! My poor, poor child! But you had saved your baby brother!"

Marah stirred the drying caraway seeds in the cloth, stirring them round with her finger and making careful, intricate patterns.

"I had saved him from the sword. But his little life was quite gone. You see, I had smothered him."

Etta shook her head, appalled. She could not speak.

Marah picked the seeds up in her fingers, destroying the pattern, and sprinkled them onto the plate. They pattered almost noiselessly on the thin wood.

"Yes. It was my scream that Herod's mercenaries heard – and broke in. So I killed my parents. And then I had crushed my infant brother in my arms and choked off his baby breath. I had nothing left – except the wounds."

She touched her arms and said pensively, "So much I had forgotten, except the cutting."

"Did you not remember at all, Marah?" Etta asked at last, incredulously.

Marah shrugged. "There was a kind of blankness, that's all. I could not – still do not – remember my own name. It was the old man who named me Marah, when he found me starving somewhere – I don't know where, but I had run for days. There were times when black feelings of guilty oppression nearly smothered me, but I could never understand why. The cutting always freed me for a while. It still does. My dear old greybeard arranged a betrothal for me when I grew to womanhood. But I was caught with my sleeves up one day – and so that was the end of it."

"Yet you can remember it all now."

"The fever I had was very bad, I think. It loosed demons in my head which had been bound for many years. Some I had kept safely chained till today. You must be a demon yourself, Etta, to charm such horrors back to the light." She shuddered.

Etta's head was reeling. Was Marah in her right mind now, or not? Reluctantly, Etta had to admit she probably was – but for how long? She took a deep breath and tried one last time.

"But, you said you had seen your mother – and your father, recently!"

Marah nodded regretfully.

"Oh yes, I see them all the time. Sometimes they forgive me, sometimes they threaten me, sometimes they plead with me to save the little ones … to atone …" She looked up with misery in her dilated eyes. "Etta, my baby brother has grown up in my mind as well. I see him too, as a young man now, a dead man walking. He is thin and dark, like my father, with burning eyes. He appears, he talks to me, tells me not to cry, that he is alive – and then melts away again – but he is real to me all the same.

"Sometimes I remember them, but forget they are dead. Mostly I forget them, or that they have gone – or why – because I have forgotten so much. What is real, what is nightmare, what is supernatural? I am often confused. All I know is, I am a murderess, and now I am a madwoman as well."

"You were a brave child," Etta protested, wiping her eyes unhappily with her fingers. "A tiny brave child who did all she could to save her little brother."

Marah shrugged again. "I was six. Not so tiny. The fact is, they all died because of me, and I lived. You see why I need to hear this Baptizer. Do you think God can forgive a murderess?"

"King David …" Etta began but Marah tossed her head impatiently.

"Don't talk to me about King David," she said scornfully. "Men are always forgiven everything! What about forgiveness for a madwoman, eh?"

Etta stood resolutely and made up the fire. She banged her pots on the hearth and stooped over to put the beans on, where they could simmer at the back.

"Is it a sin to be mad?" she asked fretfully. "Is it a sin to have a crooked back? Is it a sin to have eyes of different colours? Why ask the unanswerable of me?"

"Etta?" There was a hesitant touch on her shoulder. "Are you angry with me?"

The grey haired woman embraced Marah gingerly, careful of her arms.

"Yes," she replied. "Because you call yourself a murderess. You know full well murder is done with deliberation and evil intent. If you will insist on judging a child as an adult, you will at least grant

410

yourself the plea of manslaughter! They were dark evil days in Herod's rule – and there may be many such terrible tales as yours – but would the Eternal expect a six-year-old child to flee to a city of refuge?"

"I – don't know – I hadn't thought – you see, Etta, most of the time the thing is hidden from me. Only the anguish, the guilt, and the terror remains …" She yawned unexpectedly and her restless eyes drooped wearily. "Oh, I am so horribly tired!"

Etta unhooked the wineskin from the rafters. It was safe to leave it out now Bukki was not home. She handed a cup to Marah.

"Drink this now, and sleep. Never mind the hour. I will go to see Marta and we will begin preparations for our journey. Tomorrow we can leave – me to Cana, you to see the Baptist at Bethabara. He is a holy man of God – I am convinced he will have answers for you. There now – that's a good girl. Come, lie down – you are exhausted. You will sleep, and I will be back before you know it."

Clucking gently in this manner, Etta put the strained, pale woman to bed. Marah was suddenly limp, drained, and compliant. Turning up her veil, Etta went outside, shutting the door carefully, and hunted urgently for her sharp knife, which had caught in a saltbush near the herb patch and glinted helpfully in the sun. She tucked it safely into a leather pouch, and walked determinedly to see Marta and Ittai. She would say nothing yet of this dramatic afternoon with Marah All-Alone. There was much to think about in what she had revealed … there would be plenty of time on the journey, and little to spare today.

By sunset, Etta was home again, preparations complete, thanks to a very willing Marta and Ittai, who had agreed with delight to

411

accompany her to Cana the very next day and be part of the joyful celebration of Ammiel and Anna's wedding. Marta was itching for an occasion to wear her little ornaments and best gown, and Ittai for a chance to show off his disgracefully fat babies. He looked out one of his finest creations for a wedding gift, and sent eagerly to Magdala for three donkeys, complete with panniers to take the children. The third donkey would carry their celebration clothes, food and gifts from friends, but there would be room on it yet for Caleb, whom they meant to waylay nearer to Cana. The other guests would have to make their own way. Ittai strode around busily organising their expedition, while Marta sorrowfully tugged at her treasured festive garment – which had become very tight around the top – waxed her needle, and snipped and sewed for dear life.

Etta set the door open wide as quietly as she could, but Marah was already up and looking greatly refreshed, stirring the pot of beans, which now smelled deliciously of onion, garlic, and fennel. On the table the dried caraway seeds were tidily sitting in a small bowl, and the green liquor in a jug, the straining cloth draped over to keep out the flies. A plate of half mixed dough was beside it, and on the hearth the little clay oven stood ready. Marah smiled apologetically in welcome.

"I'm sorry, Etta. I meant to finish the bread, but I've done something to my arms and it hurts to knead. They're very sore. By the way, I can't find the knife. I've had to put the onions in whole. Don't they look funny – like jellyfish!"

Etta shivered to recall the cold-blooded way Marah had sliced her scarred flesh, and how she had seemed not to feel it at all. Now she felt it, but didn't remember.

She sighed. What would this prophet Johannes have to say to the questions strange Marah burned to ask him? That is, if she remembered to ask. How much of their last conversations would Marah remember at all? What could be done with her? What would happen to her when she ran out of friends, or her friends were tired of her unpredictable, terrifying fits of madness? Would she indeed end up like the lunatic across the Lake? This woman who struggled so bravely, who ached for peace, and who longed to serve her God even in her increasingly unreliable fragments of calm? Etta felt more than a pang of guilt herself. Marah had remembered too much that day, prompted by Etta's own questions, no matter how careful.

"Etta, you are not an exorcist!" she chided herself. "The poor woman may become worse because of your probings!"

But the following day, despite the tenderness of her arms, Marah seemed bright and responsive. Defying received wisdom both women had washed their hair after supper the previous night – rinsing with the herbal water – combing and drying it as best they could by lamplight before carefully wrapping their heads in towels and going to bed. Very early in the morning, they combed their locks anxiously – and jubilantly pronounced their failed tonic a great success. The strengthening sun found the two fresh and prinked and in holiday mood. The house was clean, swept and locked, the food and water packed, the friends arrived with happy faces and a mood to laugh over every little thing. The panniers were loaded with food, clothing, water, and the two babies, whose chins were cheerfully tickled by Marah All-Alone without a qualm.

Marah's own satchel was hastily stuffed with last minute treats – sesame cakes from Marta, a minute travel-sized pitcher with a good stopper from Ittai, and a small pot of the leftover beans and bread from Etta, who had also pressed upon her the last of the wine for emergencies. Etta was anxious for her, but Marah All-Alone was back to her energetic self. She kissed her friend warmly, loaded her with good wishes for Ammiel, Dan and Anna, and waved her off with happy smiles. The little group staggered off with squeaks of alarm from Etta, who had not been on a donkey for years, and roars of laughter from Marah, who was enjoying the spectacle as much as Ittai and Marta.

Still laughing, she shouldered her satchel and set off for Tiberius. She knew all the regular trips which were made from there to Jerusalem and it would be an easy matter to coax a ride from some of her Roman acquaintances. They were less touchy about dealing with her than the Jews, Marah thought wryly. There was a haze hanging over the previous day before, but this was often the case when her arms were stinging, and she accepted it with the stoical conviction that one day she would have the answers. One day she would be a whole person again, no longer made up of cobbled-together patches – even if she must wait till the Resurrection Day. Meanwhile, a man of God was in the Land. A man who offered forgiveness, redemption of sins! And that was a first step – to somewhere – Marah wasn't yet sure exactly where. But she would head that way, and keep walking until she got there.

And so it was that Marah All-Alone of Magdala set her face determinedly to seek for her own redemption, and passed from the life at Banayim for many months.


Meanwhile, Etta and her merry companions enjoyed a very pleasant trip to Cana over the rustling grassy ridges – collecting a joyous Caleb along the way. Etta extracted solemn promises from Samuel to make arrangements about the care of the combined flocks, and he promised to meet them in Cana within two days with his wife and Caleb's daughter and husband. Marah's unhappy story was discussed at length on the journey, Ittai clearing his throat loudly, Caleb nodding in comprehension, and Marta impulsively smothering her babies with kisses at every opportunity.

"Nobody knew this history," she said, her eyes misted as Etta finished the tale. "It is no wonder the woman is tormented!"

"She was happy enough this morning," Etta said peacefully. "Oddly enough she does not brood over the matter. In between times she is up and down, but more settled than you would imagine, once you know the whole matter."

"A brave woman!" said Caleb suddenly. "A very brave woman. It is hardest of all to fight the demons within." He knew.

Etta nodded. She suddenly felt very proud of all her friends. No doubt they were an odd bunch of no account to others, *but just look at them!* she said to herself. Caleb had overcome the death of wife and sons, the horrible compulsions of drunkenness and the loss of his own flock, to become a solidly reliable hired man, a good worker for Ammiel, and a kind of elderly uncle to Dan, who had little enough family to spread around. Ittai had grown from a besotted young dreamer to a responsible, proud father – who recognised the need to be thankful for his blessings, and adored his wife – and yet found time to treat a decrepit, insignificant old maid of no relation, like a mother. Cheerful Marta, rejoicing in her youth and strength and new motherhood, was a fitting mate to her husband, and her love for Etta was real and warm. And yes, she was proud of tragic Marah All-Alone – struggling to serve her God, helpless before terrors nobody could understand, and yet determined to seek out truth and forgiveness.

Etta beamed over them all and praised the Eternal in her heart. Such happiness was hers, and so much more to come! With Samuel's small group following – and Ammiel and Anna even now on their way to meet them at Cana! And there would be little Dan, prankish Johanan, dear, dithery Mari Jerusalem – and silly old Bukki – all together with generous Asa, whose heart expanded even in his grief to include the joy of others, instead of selfishly contracting, as was the common – though excusable – way … Even in thought one must attempt justice …

Oh – and she must not forget that extraordinary Loukanos! What an interesting person he sounded! She could not wait to meet him. Not to talk to him so much – he would quite terrify her – but he must be fascinating to listen to – and pretty handsome too, if she had understood Ammiel's casual comments correctly. H'mm! Etta had not met many Greeks in her sheltered lifetime, except for Helen herself, and Ammiel had painted quite an intriguing picture! Why, Loukanos sounded as unpredictable as Marah All-Alone. *Maybe we could marry them off,* Etta thought naughtily, and chuckled. After the recent intensity of life with Marah, it was a relief to be feeling so free and excited and clear of responsibility. She sent up a prayer that the woman would be protected and unmolested, and find the answers she sought.

The novelty of the journey dulled the pain in Etta's back sufficiently for her to daydream daringly of a later visit to the Baptizer herself. She would be afraid of nothing with strong Ammiel, capable Anna, and willing Dan as companions on the long journey! She would even take another jolting on a donkey …

*A long life is a sinful one,* she told herself, shaking her head regretfully. *And back or no back, I need forgiveness as much as poor* *deluded Marah – perhaps more – for all my impatience, and quick judgements, and snappiness at Bukki's miseries. Who knows what sins – real or imagined – weigh **him** down either?*

Etta's generous thoughts towards Bukki did her credit though, had he known them, she thought, laughing at herself, would he have been grateful – or outraged?

Blind Mordecai noted the bustling, chattering, laughing little crowd who pressed in through Asa's gate that afternoon, weary but in good spirits. He smiled to himself at the thought of all the busy preparations which had begun the day before, and how noisy Dinah had managed to organise helpful neighbours trotting to and fro down the street on errands all day. He was glad for his companion of the pavement – the large-hearted man who could have knocked him senseless for a pickpocket, and yet who sat in the street, shared his sleep and laughed with him. Yes, a pleasant thing when a surprise was a joyful one. Old Asa's house had not been in such a happy ferment for a long while. It was good to have an unexpected wedding celebration after an unexpected funeral. Too much preparation spoiled either event.

Mordecai remembered Anna's fresh honey cakes with pleasure. She'd surely send a little remembrance of titbits to him, for old times' sake. Lucky shepherd to be marrying such a wife! He wondered what had changed their minds so quickly. Well, the news would get to him sooner or later. He could always waylay that giggly Rhoda and ask outright. She was polite for a servant girl. Helen had taught her well. Not many would call a mangled beggar 'sir'.

It was late at night, and the laughter and lights had finally faded from Asa's house. Blind Mordecai sat up straighter.

"Shalom to you, tanner. You are late home tonight from your journey!"

The tanner grunted. It had been a mistake to set out so late from Ginnae without companions. He had fought off lone bandits at three different points of the road and his whipping arm was tired.

"Post for Asa, from Jerusalem. No sense in me coming right back clear across town tomorrow to give it to him. I get tired of the turned backs and turned noses, too. I declare I think sometimes Samaritans have more manners. Here, give it to him in the morning, won't you?"

Blind Mordecai held out his hand for the letter – and exclaimed with rare surprise.

"Thank you, friend! A leather cloak? Why such generosity for a simple act of no worth?"

The tanner cleared his throat. "Poor quality, Mordecai. A rejected order. It'll stink when it gets wet. But it'll keep the rain off you."

"Not stolen, Parosh, is it?" Mordecai asked drily, fingering the soapy leather and sniffing it pleasurably.

"Not stolen – given. The Baptizer at Bethabara, Mordecai. He washed away my sins. He urges a new life to prepare for the Messiah. He says – share your clothes, share your food."

"Gracious words indeed!" Mordecai said incredulously. "They must have sunk deep for you to retain them all the way from Bethabara and still act upon them."

Parosh shifted nervously. "It's not easy, so don't mock me, beggar!" he said gruffly.

418

"Not mocking!" the beggar responded hastily. "Admiring! Thankful! Praising the Eternal, I assure you. I will say a prayer for you tonight and bless God for His goodness – and for the Baptist. See the cloak fits as if made for me … and I thank you sincerely, friend. This is truly a valuable gift now the rains are coming. On your way, then, and your letter will find Asa in the morning. Blessings and peace!"

"Blessings and peace," growled Parosh, thankful to move on.

Blind Mordecai did indeed say a prayer as he promised. Underneath his gratitude was a feeling of uneasiness, as if the matter was a huge joke, and he would be the only one not laughing, while maybe under arrest for theft in the morning. But for tonight, he would enjoy the comfort and warmth – while it lasted.

Inside Asa's hospitable house, his guests were doing the same.


In the morning, Blind Mordecai delivered the letter from Jerusalem, and Rhoda cheerfully tripped with it to her master.

Blind Mordecai was warm in his cloak, which nobody took from him after all. But from inside the walls so close by him, came a sudden, terrible, loud wailing, as the warmth was stripped from the sheltered folk within.

## Chapter Thirty-three

THE glittering eagle seemed to be pasted high on the grey cloud, like the fish scales Dan had once pasted on a small rock. How pretty they had been then – and suddenly they had dropped. There – now! The watchful, shivering shepherd boy swung his sling and let the stone fly – it went wide and there was no time for reloading with cold numbed fingers. Shouting, waving his arms and flinging rough rocks scooped up in his desperate run he charged at the bird which loomed larger in the plunge, his eyes fixed on the outstretched talons as they clutched for the foolish lamb. A trip, a stumble – a lucky stone flew from the flailing chapped hands and struck the cruel beak – the eagle's balance was thrown and it was but rapidly thrashing wings which hit the soft body while the talons clawed the boulders in an unplanned scramble. Dan threw himself forward – shielding the little creature which was frozen in fear – beating ferociously with a snatched stick and screaming in rage. The eagle spiralled almost lazily into the heights, leaving Dan hugging the tottering lamb and clenching his teeth against the sobs which shook him.

"Good, my boy!" Old Caleb panted encouragingly from the protective crescent of limestone where he and the heavily labouring Queen of Sheba struggled to deliver a tangle of hoofs and heads. "You are a fine watchman!" Yes, it was good, very good, that the

421

lad screamed in anger and fought predators and cried with relief for saving the little ones.

Dan calmed down quickly – every day more quickly – and ran to the dithering mother with the lamb bundled in his arms. He saw it firmly attached to the teat, and daubed the lacerations on its quivering cheese-soft skin with a special potion of Caleb's from his scrip, before running back to the rocks, jamming the stopper into the little clay jar as he ran.

"How is she doing?" Dan wriggled the jar back into the leather pouch.

Caleb winced and shook his head. "A nose and two feet forward, but the wrong feet, and everything drying too fast. My big rough hand can do no more, and she's exhausted."

The ewe's harsh breath was quick and shallow, her eyes distressed, her chest heaving.

"Oh, Caleb! Not the Queen of Sheba! Don't let her die!"

Caleb withdrew his hand gently. "Time you learned your trade, boy. Oil and water, quickly."

Dan's eyes widened. "No! I can't!"

"You've got the hands, I've got the skill. Come on, lad, we can do this together. Bunch your fingers – long, and thin, that's it. Now, carefully – that's it – tell me what you feel …"

"I think – yes – there's a tongue – a little jaw …"

"It's the wrong one. Get your fingers around it, up to the bigger bones, and push it back – firmly but gently – as far as you can."

Dan's eyes were screwed shut in concentration. "It's gone!" he yelped.

422

"Good boy – now the feet – you feel the feet in front there? Yes? Trace them back to the body … then feel for the neck and head."

"Only one foot! The right, I think …"

"I thought as much – the cart won't run with a chocked wheel …"

"What?" gasped Dan impatiently.

"The other leg's bent back under its body, Dan – one forward, one back – and so it's jammed in the passageway, see. Trace over the chest – you need to find the left leg – now picture the little one, Dan – find the shoulder if you can …"

"Yes, here it is – now I've got a finger hooked under the armpit – is it an armpit?"

"Near enough!" Even in the tense moment Caleb's mouth flickered in a grin. "Doing well, Dan – just what I would have asked you to do – can you hook the leg forward? Slide your finger down and back as you pull …" His own eyes narrowed and his fingers twitched as he mentally guided the boy's neat fingers. Dan grimaced with the effort, his forefinger aching. It was so tight, so squashed, so hard! How did Caleb ever do this, with his big hands!

"Yes! Here it is!" Dan's eyes lit up with relief, though sweat stood on his cold forehead. "It's unfolding – knee – ankle – yes! The foot's forward!"

"Good! Good! Now quickly follow – up the chest for the neck and head position."

Dan gulped. "I think I've got it – but …" the boy looked sick. "There's no head!"

"Ah!" Caleb muttered and patted Dan reassuringly. "It's there all right, it will be twisted to the side."

"Ouch!" gasped Dan as Sheba strained. "Yes! I've got it – I can feel the gums!"

"Get a grip if you can – not the lower jaw, you might break it – and see if you can pull the nose round to the feet"

"Yes, yes – oh! this is hard!" Dan's face twisted fiercely, and then cleared. "Done it!"

"Well done, boy! Now make sure those little hooves are lying nice and prayerful – and – coax them forward … yes! I see them now. Good lad – make way, now …"

Caleb pulled gently and firmly up and forward – a blunt nose appeared, submissively on the forefeet – then a relieved grunt from both Caleb and the Queen of Sheba announced the swift arrival of the lamb.

"Alive!" Caleb crowed. "Now that's a surprise! Quickly now!"

Dan whisked it to one side and rubbed it firmly with sacking. The next bedraggled little creature followed soon after, and Caleb was jubilant, though his eyes had never stopped flickering to the sky every few moments.

"Twins again – good old Queen of Sheba!" laughed Dan, putting them under her nose to be cleaned. Caleb straightened up from his crouch and cackled heartily, pointing. Dan gasped.

"More feet?"

Caleb nodded, unable to stop chuckling. "Triplets, Dan boy! Triplets – all untangled nicely thanks to your dainty little hand – and here comes the last of them."

Dan sobered in an instant, memories tugging at his sleeve. *Triplets – that would be special, wouldn't it?* Had he really said that? *Maybe – if nothing went wrong!* had been the reply. It seemed prophetic, now. It must have been years ago – long years ago – he and Caleb, and a big, warm, laughing man, sitting by a dawn fire, and talking about an unknown woman called Anna. Dan stared at his messy hand, rubbing it clean with the sacking. A tall dark Greek had studied this hand with the scar near the thumb, and had drawn it onto papyrus. Strange that a small moment in life, the scrape of a rock, had left such an indelible mark for all to see. And that another moment – a sudden knock which threw a man off balance – which at any other time or place would likewise be unimportant … should instead be so hugely significant … so heavily weighted with tragedy … and yet leave no visible mark whatsoever …

"Bukki!" someone was roaring. "Get off your lazy backside and watch those kids! They'll have the hedge down in a moment!"

A shambling figure stumbled sulkily to the neat fold which had been built in the shelter of overhanging rocks. Within, five gawky kids and two lambs were plunging up and down in an awkward game, their mottled hairy coats nudging a tight hedge of thorn bushes which formed the wall on an uneven slope. Their mothers eyed them with sleepy indifference, chewing the cud industriously, staggering slightly when butted in the udder by their offspring, who paused for a quick refreshment from time to time. Overhead, the eagle hung in the heights as if on a silversmith's wire.

Bukki winced and sucked his fingers as they were pricked by the sharp thorns – Samuel's.

425

Eli strode over. "Peg them down properly. You'll get nowhere poking at them like that."

Bukki looked helpless, holding a sharpened stick in one hand and looking vaguely around for something to strike it with. Eli snapped, "Use a rock!" and snatched one for himself, pounding the stakes with hard blows. He had done four before Bukki had fixed one. It was his own fault the stakes were loose, Eli thought crossly. Fancy giving the job to that fool in the first place!

"Look sharp, Bukki! Post yourself in front of the hedge and keep them off it. We don't want their skin scratched!" Eli threw his rock away and stamped off, warning Bukki for the fourth time about looking out for the eagle.

Bukki huddled miserably in the nursery fold. Samuel and Caleb had put the best young ones here, determined to produce a good number of unblemished animals for the Passover market. They weren't interested in whether Bukki's skin got scratched, or his feet stamped on by sharp hooves. Bukki didn't like the look of the goats' horns, and the queer window-slit pupils. He'd never thought much of sheep, but they at least looked semi-human, not like these devilish goats with their mad eyes and their scornful beards. He shivered. They looked for all the world like the worst kind of Pharisee.

It was cold, but firelighting time was hours off yet. The overcast day was ideal birthing weather, and the shepherds had been moving quickly and quietly around the flocks for hours. Bukki watched as Dan charged suddenly towards a clump of bushes, swinging his sling. It wasn't fair that the boy was allowed such a weapon. Just because Bukki had knocked a sheep senseless one day with an unlucky shot …

There was a whisk of bushy tail and Dan raised his arms with a triumphant grin as the fox scampered over the hill. Carefully the boy coaxed Hephzibah from her dangerous hiding place and led her back to the others.

"Come to Abba, Hephzibah," he called gently, raising his voice in the remembered cadences, and swallowing the stone in his throat. There was no buzz in the light voice, such as Hephzibah had been used to, but she knew the loving words and melody and was learning to accept the change. Obediently she came, thin legs waddling around her tight belly, nibbling at the boy's scrip, scenting the dried figs within, pausing every now and then while her flanks tightened. Dan lifted her fat tail and called to Caleb.

"I think she'll be next, Caleb! I'll put her with Holah and Geba."

With Hephzibah safely folded, Dan ran off to answer a call from Samuel. Soon he was back fetching water, running with sacks, or darting to ward off slinking shapes on the fringes, drawn by the scent of birth and the sound of newborn bleats. The grey sky darkened suddenly and rain dropped with a sudden hiss on the damp ground. Samuel scowled at the heavens as he knelt in the mud wiping bubbles of mucus from the mouth of a kid which seemed disinterested in breathing. Rain poured from a fold of his greasy headcloth like a spout, directly onto the half-conscious creature and into its crumpled nostrils and slack mouth. Samuel swore, but even in the heat of the moment, looking up guiltily lest Dan be near. He was.

"Here, Samuel!" The boy leant over him with a heavy goat-hair cloak, felted and waterproof, extending his arms in a makeshift tent. Beneath it, the rain stopped, and Samuel snatched up a cloth gratefully, working hurriedly over his charge. He had been initially dubious about the suggestion of combining their flocks, but old Etta and the boy must not starve, and selling the animals would have been only a temporary solution. Dan would be a man in a few years and what a waste if his inheritance were squandered before then. Caleb's idea had worked surprisingly well all winter, and the arrangement looked fair to become permanent.

Samuel's younger sons liked the sociability of the larger operation, and were not displeased to have their big brother out of their hair most of the time. As for Eli – he had no time to be bored these days. It had been a shock to him to find how different sheep were, despite their similar appearance, and a few hard lessons had been learnt there. At least the young man had all the variety he needed, with old Caleb as a patient and valuable teacher – yes, Samuel was grateful that his son had the chance to add an extra string to his lute. And Dan – now there was a willing lad – quick and useful in a thousand ways, and hungry to learn, with a sad kind of desperation in his eagerness. Unlike his uncle.

An anxious motherly nose nudged the supine kid. Samuel shook his head in frustration and snatched up the slack little body, holding it head downwards between his leathery palms. Dan sprang back, knowing what was coming. Samuel jumped from his crouch and swung the half-alive creature at full arms' length in a rapid arc – once, twice, thrice – there was a watery gurgle – out came the cloth again – thick fingers rubbed the chest – a cough, a splutter – a tiny bleat. Samuel and Dan exchanged huge grins. It was not long before the scraggy black kid was sheltering beside the thick hairy coat of its mother, submitting to a thorough licking, and looking as blissfully smug as if it had saved itself. Samuel clapped Dan heavily on the back as the doe finally turned her attention to the afterbirth.

428

"They'll be fine now."

"Bukki!" screamed Eli and Caleb together.

Bukki looked up as the eagle dropped. He uttered a yell of terror and scrambled for the rocks, his arm over his eyes.

"The kids!" roared Samuel, running and uttering a shrill whistle to his dogs. Eli tore towards the fold, swinging his club around his head and shouting as the barking dogs flew past. Dan could not outrun them. He tugged out his sling, hastily loaded, and began whirling up all the force he could. The eagle lifted a writhing brown body in his claws – powerful wings beating them steadily out of reach – Bukki was scrabbling up and over the walls of the fold, his frantic feet kicking a wide breach in the stones as he fled. Holding his breath, Dan let fly just as Eli hurled his club.

The tiny kid plummeted as the eagle made an ungainly escape with a broken wingtip. Caleb threw himself towards the falling body like a diving cormorant, but there never had been a chance he might catch it. The perfect kid had been sacrificed too early. Eli's club and Dan's rock thudded to earth. Caleb struck the slushy ground and rolled, a huge graze wiped rawly onto his forearm in an instant. Sharply Samuel whistled off the eager dogs and caught their rope collars, ordering them away now the damage was done. With blazing eyes Eli picked up the screaming, broken little body. At a glum nod from Samuel he broke its neck.

Dan turned away, retching, hating himself for it, but unable to help it. There was too much about that incident which seemed horribly familiar. Caleb clambered wretchedly to his feet rubbing his wrist. Torn muddy tunic clinging to his bony legs, he hurried back to Hephzibah, squeezing Dan's shoulder kindly on the way. *Ach!* It *would* be his right arm! That would sting nicely inside a ewe later! Just as well for Dan's fine bones … when all else failed and the others were busy, Dan had already proved his worth in an emergency. And bad luck to Bukki, he thought grimly.

Dan spat and wiped his mouth impatiently. He turned urgently to the broken fold which Eli was mending as rapidly as he could. The goats had sprung to a crevice in the rock-face previously occupied by Uncle Bukki, but the two sheep were running about in panic and bleating wildly.

"I'll fix this – you quieten your sheep," Eli panted even as Dan began to murmur to them, climbing in without haste or fuss.

"Hush! Gomer, hush Ruah, you are safe! Quiet, my darlings!" Ruah's lamb! It was gone.

Black Gomer steadied herself a little at Dan's reassuring voice, and butted her lamb behind her, but mottled Ruah threw up her head and bolted for the thorn hedge – and the section which Bukki had even yet not pinned firmly. It gave way at once and the heavy sheep, wool caught in its brambles, tore half of it with her in her mad flight to find the lamb. Dan dived at her and somehow clutched a hoof , but she kicked it free of his boy-weak hand as easily as pulling it from a mud hole, leaving Dan winded on the slimy stubble, the pelting rain erasing her fleeing tracks.

It had been a long, cold, wet, windy afternoon. And it became a long night. Sheep and goats, newborns, and labouring mothers, all were now safe. Samuel and Caleb had risked moving the animals and now had them securely folded together in a half-cave, fires lighted around, hedges and walls hurriedly built by Samuel's willing sons while Dan and Caleb searched in vain. Now they took a torch and set out again, the pitch-impregnated cloth spitting flames into the wind. Dan looked grimly at Caleb's shadowy face. The uncertain light spilling around them was swallowed up by great gulps of blackness. The rain hampered them and spat stinging hail, the night grew colder than ever, the stars were hidden, the moon hiding behind huge mountains of angry cloud. How could they hope to find Ruah in this awful night, let alone her lamb? It seemed hopeless. But surely someone, long ago, had said, "If a lamb cries, it may be heard, and may be saved."

"Ruah! Come to me! Come to Abba!" *Oh that I might cry "Abba, come to me!"*

How often had he impressed upon Dan that a lost lamb might cry to its dam or a lost sheep to its shepherd – and though the night be dark as the grave he would still hear. How could they give up? What if she were to cry, and the shepherd not be there to listen? So they went on.

"Take great care, Dan lad," Caleb cautioned. "Test each step with your rod. A rock may be but a lump of sand with a nasty drop below it."

"Ruah!" Dan called again, and again.

"Come to Abba!" Caleb chirruped in his own way. There was more hope of the creature responding to him, but Ruah knew Dan's voice as a friendly one at least so let the boy call. They were a long way from the camp now, and soon the decision would have to be made – to give up, or go on regardless. Every sheep lost meant loss of income. Every one was valuable for her milk and her wool, and eventually, her meat and hide. Not to speak of the lambs she would produce. Caleb resolved to go on. It was his old friend's legacy in every animal – and Dan's future.

An inhuman groan floated through the night. Dan clutched Caleb's arm. The old man pricked up his ears.

"This way!"

Picking their way carefully they came to a black cleft in a shadowy rock. The sound came again. Caleb held the torch high and the flames flapped in the wind.

"There!"

An eerie glint of frightened eyes way below – jammed into the cleft was Ruah, with scarce room for breath.

"Hold the torch, Dan."

Caleb lay flat and reached down with his crook, shaking his head at last.

"She's too far down – I can't even get a rope around her."

Dan was already unwinding his own rope from his middle.

"You can't, but I can!" he said eagerly.

Caleb saw what he meant at once. The lad was light and nimble, it was worth a try. And at least the hail had stopped.

Down he clambered, feeling his way cautiously in the raggedly unsteady splash of light, the rope around his waist firmly tied to a sturdy branch pinned behind two boulders, and paid out by the old man. The torch hung over the crevice, jammed in place, wafting occasional embers of burning cloth down into the depths to spit in Dan's wet hair. Soon the boy was astride the unfortunate Ruah, murmuring reassurances, and searching for a gap behind her front legs.

"That's it, Dan!" Caleb called encouragingly, and dropped the second rope. the knotted end struck his head but Dan hardly felt it. Splayed over the wide quivering body like a nervous jockey in a Roman circus, he gritted his teeth, face buried in Ruah's pungent wet wool, arms reaching wildly around her bulk.

432

With a huge struggle, he passed Caleb's doubled rope around the animal's body, and threaded the ends through the loop before scrambling up again to help him pull. Dan's muscles strained to cracking point under the weight. He was astonished at the strength in Caleb's stringy old arms, and glad of the stunted tree as a windlass which held the slippery wet rope tightly between each pull. Slowly the helpless animal was drawn free and dragged to safety, her faint, distressed grunts soon, ominously, ceasing. Caleb examined her anxiously, but the fall had broken her ribs and a leg, and the rope which saved her from the rocks had hastened her death.

Caleb shook his head sadly and pulled out his flaying knife. "Bring the torch closer, quickly, Dan. There'll be nothing much left of the poor old girl by morning, but we can save her skin at least."

Dan was leaning to free the torch when he glanced down again at the crevice, so black and threatening. A flicker of something pale caught his eye – and then a thin sound.

"Caleb!" he cried, dashing the pouring rain from his face and rubbing his eyes. "I think the lamb is here too!"

In an instant Caleb was peering intently into the blackness, and the decision was made. Down went Dan again, with Caleb at full stretch above and holding the torch.

"Quickly, Dan, this light won't last another hour, and the rain is too heavy already."

"I can't quite reach him!" Dan was frustrated.

"Watch out – here comes my crook! And remember your life is worth more than a lamb!" Caleb added hastily, though the line was tied securely enough above.

Below, Dan put up a hand as Caleb's crook rattled down to him, jerking on its rope, and knocking scabs off his knuckles. Gently he hooked the pale body of the bewildered lamb, and tugged it towards him till he could just get his fingers in its wool.

"Got it!" he gritted.

Oh, but it was a heavy thing for one hand to hold. Another effort – and the little creature was dragged, swung over the gap with desperate fingers, clutched with eager arms, and hugged to his chest. Dan leant back on the wet rock, suddenly forgetting the cold, panting and flashing his teeth in a grin which was half grimace. Stuffed inside Dan's tunic the exhausted lamb radiated heat against his wet skin like a little furnace, its tiny heart thudding like a shower of figs shaken down at harvest. It felt like nothing in the world or out of it – a crystal moment for Dan which ever would sparkle in his memory. Gladness and elation, victory over death! Nearby he heard the sly cough of a jackal – *"Cheated!"* Dan thought with ferocious satisfaction.

Up he came, slowly, carefully – and triumphantly. Caleb wrapped him in his cloak, lamb and all.

"You're a true shepherd, Dan boy. Your father would be proud."

The weariness of the long day, the tense search, the stumbling tramp back to camp, resolved into a feeling of deep contentment as Dan sat around the welcome fire with the men and older boys, avidly chewing his bread and figs, drinking hot soup, listening to Caleb's praises as he told the tale, and anointing all his scrapes and bruises with soothing wool fat. Dan instantly named his little orphan Moses, "because I drew him out of the rock" he laughed. Moses had been tied up in the skin of the dead kid and put to the teats of its bereaved mother. The unlucky Ruah's skin had been rolled with salt and would soon be on its way to the tanner.

Bukki had not reappeared since his ignominious flight before the eagle, and somehow everyone was carefully avoiding his name.

In the morning Dan and Eli ran to the nursery pen to check on Moses. He was doing well with his foster mother, who was nibbling curiously on something flat and muddy. Eli tugged it from her teeth.

"All we need now is for her to choke!" he said drily, and was about to throw the object away when he stopped. He gaped at Dan.

"It's a letter! Now, how in the world did that come to be here?" He snapped his fingers. "Bukki! It must have dropped from his clothes when he took off, the waster!" He glanced apologetically at Dan. "Sorry, Dan. It's easy to forget he's your uncle."

He turned it over. The seal was broken, crumbling, and the damp, smeared papyrus had been refolded several times. Clearly, the letter had already been read.

Dan grabbed it eagerly and gasped. "Eli! It's – it's got my name on it!"

"Oh really?" Eli's mouth twisted. "It'll be for you, then."

He looked down at Dan's trembling fingers as they fumbled with the cover.

"Odd your uncle never mentioned it, hey?"

## Chapter Thirty-four

BUKKI rolled out of his blankets in a corner of the small new room which had somehow become his alone. His nearset bleary eyes glowered at his sister-in-law, who bent over him angrily, waving a dirty letter in his face.

"Can't a man get some sleep?" he demanded defensively, scratching his tangled beard.

"Get to your feet, Bukki ben Bezaleel, and answer me like a man!"

Bukki got up slowly and stretched, looking down at her. With every week he felt himself growing taller by comparison.

"The fishmonger gave it me," he said at last, sulkily. "Just after I left for the pasture."

"That was days ago," Dan said in amazement. "And you said nothing of it!"

Bukki rubbed his untidy head crossly. "Must have done."

"You said nothing," Dan repeated bleakly. "And it was still in your clothes!"

He had been puzzling over it the whole time he and Samuel had been walking to Magdala with the older lambs and kids for the market, taking Ruah's skin for the tanner. The young animals were scatty and fearful, but the dogs had adapted to sheep quickly and their skill freed the other boys to stay with the main flock. Samuel had told Dan to make a detour to Etta's while he transacted his business. He would collect him on the way back – a visit to Etta's was something which Samuel was itching to make for his own reasons. Meanwhile, he was as angry as Dan about the letter, which should have been given to the boy at once, in his opinion, not carted about for days on Bukki's person and dropped carelessly in the mud! Letters were precious – especially to a lonely boy.

"And you've read it yourself a few times, by the looks," said Etta grimly, interrupting Dan's train of thought.

"My letter." Dan could hardly believe it yet. "I've been waiting weeks and weeks for one! *My* letter from Anna and Johanan!"

Bukki pulled on his coat.

"What do they want with the boy? He's nothing to them now."

He yawned carefully, combing his unruly hair with dirty fingernails. He settled a new turban on his head, shuffling out to the kitchen, and jingling the purse at his belt. Samuel paid him to watch the sheep, and in real money too, not cheese or milk which would mean the further effort of trading. He loathed the life in the fields, but it was neither heavy labouring nor begging in dirt, so it would do, and explained his recent spending. There was enough in the pouch to warrant a stroll to Tiberius, and plenty in reserve in the money belt under his tunic. He smiled smugly to himself. Yes, plenty in reserve, though to all appearances, he could make a little go a very long way. Etta liked that, and it saved the housekeeping. So she was grateful. Her gratitude made a pleasant change from nagging.

Bukki chuckled to himself over his growing prosperity. You never knew – a tasty young wife might be next! Someone to wash

438

his clothes – admire his cleverness – keep him warm on cold nights? He shook his head regretfully. No, a young wife, even with a tidy dowry, meant children and an everlasting outlay of funds – and to a man who liked to enjoy his money in peace and quiet – a bad idea! An older woman would be less trouble – and grateful to be saved from the disgrace of being unwanted. It wouldn't matter much if she was ugly, as long as she knew her place, held her tongue and was a decent worker. As for Etta – she wasn't good for much any more and would have to take a humbler seat. Bukki and his new wife would rule the roost! Meanwhile, he would tread softly enough.

He tied his new coat cheerfully. No doubt they wouldn't want him back for a little while after that embarrassing business with the savage eagle. Mad, all of these shepherds. It was a wonder they had any eyes left if they went through this performance every lambing. Now, if he could keep Etta and the boy off his back a little longer, they would drop this inconvenient questioning and he could get away to his favourite tavern.

Aunt Etta took Dan aside into the still-empty long room, their footsteps echoing faintly in the cold air. She tapped the papyrus with a stained fingernail and looked sad.

"Of course, it was very wrong of Uncle Bukki to treat your letter so lightly. But there may be something in what he says, Dan," she said quietly. "Have we not written to Anna and even Johanan several times? Yet so long before a reply! And such an unsatisfactory reply at that. We must face the fact that perhaps we are painful reminders to Anna. She may not be strong enough to bear her double loss – mother *and* husband, poor girl! – while we are so much under her notice."

Angry tears sprang to Dan's eyes.

"And what of *our* loss, Aunt Etta? I can't believe it of Anna!"

Aunt Etta shook her head regretfully.

"Neither can I, not really. But see here, she says nothing in answer to anything you wrote. She sounds uncertain of you. And this post script from Johanan seems very cool and stilted, not like him at all."

From the kitchen, Bukki's jaunty whistling struck a jarring note. Etta's lips compressed.

"I'm not happy about this, Dan. Something's all wrong somewhere. Do you suppose Loukanos has had a hand in this?"

Dan felt an odd pang. It was a painful thought. Perhaps it was possible, but he had believed, strangely enough, that Loukanos actually liked him, a little …

Suddenly the whistling stopped and there was a flurry of movement in the warm kitchen. Uncle Bukki bolted past into his room, just as there was a tremendous thumping on the door.

"Bukki ben Bezaleel!" shouted Samuel, scarcely nodding to Etta as she swung the lock. "I saw you through the window! Come out – no use hiding!"

Bukki crept out of his room and bowed his head ingratiatingly to his employer.

Samuel stopped shouting and looked at him as if he was something which had crawled out from under a rock, instead of a fine man in new clothes. Bukki stopped bowing and bridled a little.

"I've treated you kindly for the sake of my dear friend, your brother-in-law, may he rest in peace," Samuel said more quietly, a note of disgust in his voice. "In the short time you have been working for me you have done little good. You have startled the flock many times, worked haphazardly, accidentally killed one animal, and blinded another, and allowed a bird of prey to attack the helpless – and because of your carelessness and your miserable cowardice another ewe has lately met her death … Without Caleb's persistence and Dan's pluck, we would have lost her lamb as well. And lucky it is for you, that no harm came to them in the rescue of it. To crown it all, you basely deserted the flock at a moment of danger."

Carefully Samuel laid a denarius on the well scrubbed table. "That's the last money you'll have from me – or anyone else in this district worth his salt. Not only do I want no more of your dubious services – if you come anywhere near our flocks again I'll set the dogs on you. That's a promise."

"That's an insult!" Bukki puffed himself up. With a calculating eye, he snatched up the coin. "I did my best for you," he cried, uncertain of whether to strike a whining or a blustering tone.

Samuel looked at him coldly. "I know. That's what makes it so pitiful."

He turned on his heel, and rashly added, "You're better off here carrying water and going to market for Etta."

Etta's hand flew up in warning, but it was too late. Bukki flushed angrily.

"Women's work, eh! That finishes it!"

He stalked into his room and snatched up a few belongings – his old cloak, stout stick, and blanket, and from the kitchen coolly unhooked the wineskin from the beams, lifted a rattling clay flask from a dark corner- and stuffed them into Etta's best market basket. Positively swelling with rage he marched to the door,

441

shoving rudely past Etta, Dan and Samuel, who stood transfixed with astonishment.

"Goodbye, Etta," he said stiffly, looking down his oily nose at her. "I'll send for my things when I'm settled."

Dan recovered first. "Where are you going?" he cried, following him outside. "What will you do?"

Bukki stamped grandly through the scrub with the basket on his shoulder, his ears defiant. "Many places!" he shouted impressively. "Many things!"

And he was gone.

"I'll fetch him back!" Samuel offered guiltily, but Etta shook her head with a sudden blur in her eyes.

"Sit down, Samuel. Sit. Sit." She waved her hand agitatedly. "It was only a matter of time. Poor Bukki – he knows he is useless, you see. A man can't stand that forever."

She sniffed determinedly. "Perhaps you did him a favour, Samuel. He must work in good earnest now, or starve."

"Or beg!" Dan put in, remembering Blind Bukki by the riverbank. His mind swung quickly away from the other huge memories of that sparkling day which held out their arms to him in painful clarity, and he tried to focus on the comical spectacle of the fraudulent beggar peering out from under his bandage. Suddenly he was weeping, and painfully aware of every sting and smart, bruise and cut, scratch and graze and ache in his body. Aunt Etta pulled him to her lap and hugged him as if he still had his milk teeth, instead of sturdy milestones grown fully down, if a little crooked.

"He drives himself from dawn to dusk – and beyond," Samuel said briefly, at a look from Etta.

Instantly Dan wriggled free determinedly, dragging his sleeve over his eyes.

"Will he starve, really, Samuel?" he gulped, though his tears were not exactly for Bukki.

Samuel punched him playfully in the chest. "Starve? Not your Uncle Bukki! He'll have a trick or two up his sleeve yet, you'll see."

"A weighted dice or two up his sleeve, more like it," said Etta, cheering up on Bukki's account, but her mind was working quickly and anxiously. How could she stay here alone for weeks without a soul? It was still early spring and cold, and there were days now when her back simply froze and she could not move at all for an hour, even with the precious stick which was her brother's last legacy of thoughtfulness. Marta and Ittai couldn't possibly play nurse to her forever. And with Dan now a prentice shepherd – what would she do?

Samuel rose to go.

"I've done your house no favours this day, Etta," he said soberly. "I will send Ada to you soon – and you must let her help you if she can. She will have ideas, no doubt … Dan – it's a hard blue sky and no softness in the air. There'll be few births today, though maybe a couple overnight if it should turn foggy. We'll be in the lambing field for several days yet, but I can spare you for today, and tomorrow is the Sabbath, so let's pray the sheep respect it and do no labouring! Take your aunty to the synagogue, and spare a prayer for a blundering fool. Come back to the field on the First day."

Whistling to his two yellow dogs, which, being unclean, had been trained to sit obediently at a respectful distance from the house, Samuel was gone, leaving Dan and Aunt Etta staring at each other, shocked anew to find out how quickly life could spin around on a pinhead. A sudden rattle and splashing on the hearth was followed by a sputtering hiss. Dan darted to the pots and rescued the soup for which Aunt Etta had been savagely chopping vegetables as if chopping heads while he had told her about the letter. Wearily, his aunt smiled a little to herself as she watched the boy sniffing the pot eagerly.

*Marah All-Alone would make a joke about not forgetting eleven beqa of caraway! And then she'd laugh fit to blow out the fire.* She sighed. *I wonder what she would make of all this?* Right gladly would Etta have had Marah live with her now, demons or no demons. It was tempting now to wish she had never gone, but the woman had set her face in a brave quest. She wondered how her unusual friend had fared in her search for forgiveness and truth. Not a word had she heard. Was she at peace? Was she in chains? Alive, abused or dead? Anything could be true.

Dan looked through the doorway to Uncle Bukki's untidy room. The room which ought to have been for a man and wife finding late happiness. Aunt Etta touched his shoulder gently and he came back to the present with an effort.

"It must be yours now, Dan. Bukki will not be back for a long time. If ever."

Dan set his lips. "He should not have left you."

"His pride was touched," she answered simply. "And he had so little to be proud of, he could not spare any loss of it."

"Uncle Bukki often behaved without pride!" Dan protested. "What of pretending to be a blind man?"

"Ah, that's different," she mused. "That was his own idea. But having another man shame you openly before your family is a wound not easily healed. Now busy yourself, my Dan, and make the room sweet again. All his private things can go in that box, and the blankets will air nicely over the sage bushes today. Then you can set out your own little treasures and put your own mat and blankets there. I declare, while you're away in the fields, I will feel like the Shunamite with a room for Elisha! And it's time we made use of the long room, you know … such a foolish waste otherwise, hey, Dan? I'll talk to Ada about finding a boarder who'll work for his keep, or maybe a nice young couple with no corner to call their own would be glad of such a chance – see I'm full of ideas already …"

As she chattered on brightly, Dan recovered himself, though he was still pained by the odd stiffness in Anna and Johanan's letter which made him worry that Aunt Etta was right about their estrangement. After all they had shared – could it be possible? And what of Loukanos, and Asa – and Mari – and – and – yes, all right, what of Rhoda? No answers had come to these questions. It seemed to Dan that he had lost more than a father – he had lost a whole family – which in his eyes was almost a tribe.

He didn't care for Aunt Etta's sudden idea of total strangers living in the long room, even though it may be a solution to Uncle Bukki's desertion. He thought that someone like Rhoda would have been an ideal companion to help Aunt Etta, but – he sighed – well, perhaps Samuel's Ada would have a better suggestion.

Frowning over these thoughts Dan rolled up the tattered sleeping mat. Aunt Etta now found it struggle enough to air her own bedding, and so the able-bodied Bukki was meant to do his own. Clearly he had not bothered to fling his mat over a bush for a long time. It was damp, spotted with mould, and must be burnt. Such a waste. There was a definite hollow where his body had lain night after night, and the mat had taken on his shape to fit. Dan

445

amused himself by stamping his foot into the place where Uncle Bukki's generous rear must have been, half-guiltily, half-pleasurably giving him a well deserved kick by proxy. Something crackled under his toes and he drew up his foot hastily, thinking of scorpions. Suddenly he bent down and peered, then poked, then scrabbled.

"Aunt Etta!" Dan's voice sounded queer, even to himself. He drifted into the kitchen, holding something in his hands.

"What is it? Sit down, child, you're pale as parchment!"

Dan looked at her miserably, and upended a small brown cloth bag onto the table. Out of it cascaded a small stream of folded papyrus with broken seals.

Open-mouthed, Etta snatched at them breathlessly. "*Etta bath Amos, near Banayim. Etta bath Amos, near Banayim. Dan ben Ammiel, near Banayim. Dan ben Ammiel ... Dan, shepherd's house, near Banayim ... Etta ...*"

With shaking hands she rattled open the pages, one after the other, answers to letters they had never written.

"*My darling Dan, you distress me with your last note. Of course you must go to school, as your father intended. The enclosed will buy your tablets and stylus, and the new sandals you need ... My dear Etta, it grieves me to hear you are in want. It is hard to be at the mercy of the merciless, and Samuel's dealings are deplorable. Please accept the help I would have given you as your sister-in-law. I would send goods but money is more practical while I am still in Jerusalem ... To Dan – Anna has been very ill. Loukanos will not let her travel. He is always in a bad mood ...*

*To Dan – Anna worries about you always needing money. Please ask me, not her, it makes her worse. Loukanos said he will tear up your*

446

*letters if you don't stop … Dear Etta, it is too dreadful that the foundations of the new room have collapsed and you must pay workmen to make it safe. Let me help you …"*

Etta looked sick. She clutched at her hair in anguish – hair which had turned so rapidly from grey to frost that a white tide stood at the roots for a full three fingers' breadth. Dan stared at it steadily, as if keeping his eyes there would stop time, while he struggled to understand the enormity of it all. Aunt Etta's eyes met his at last. Then she put her old head down and wailed – tears of anger, of humiliation, of loss and pride, and bitter distress.

Dan felt a cold queasy feeling sink down through his frame. He set his jaw, though his limbs were trembling.

"It's just as well for Uncle Bukki that he's gone," he said through stiff lips.

He shut his eyes, but stark, clamouring images of *"Justice"* rose coldly and grimly, unasked, behind them. *My own mother's brother!* He opened his eyes determinedly, and the images faded and grew mute.

Aunt Etta cried noisily, unheedingly. Dan laid his cheek against her quivering shoulder and put a darkly tanned arm around her broad, bowed back which heaved with sobs. *Horrible. It was horrible.* Was this really the same Uncle Bukki who had once stomped easily with him to Cana – and taught him to whistle? Who, for that little while, had actually behaved like a real uncle … Dan felt sourly that he would never care to whistle again.

His breath came hard and fast. Was it not enough for the man that nobody rejected him or even blamed him openly for – for – even accidentally – though his drunkenness was no accident – *killing* someone? There! He had said it! But the thought was too dark and frightening, and Dan shied away from it like a nervous lamb, his mind not daring to go further with the words even while his body seemed to cry out the accusation from an icy prison. He quickly returned to the shock of their discovery almost in relief.

*Praise God for Samuel's bluntness!* Dan thought defiantly, though his body felt frozen yet. How long would Bukki have kept this up, had Dan not been turning out his room, had Eli's sharp eyes not noticed the letter in the mud? And was it too late to repair the damage? With a feeling akin to panic Dan thought of the joyous times he had shared with Johanan, and the promise of loving warmth, of admiration and understanding, which had wafted his way from Anna like a subtle perfume. Even the arguments and discussions with Loukanos, the robust kindness of Asa, and the fun of the tantalising Rhoda ... these could have remained his in some form, but now they were snatched away and besmirched – and with them, some of his most precious memories of his father.

Feeling flooded back into his face, and into his heart. The chill of despair gave way to a hot surge of wrath. Dan sprang to his feet, his cheeks crimson, and clenched his teeth angrily. *Beware, Bukki!* – he would never call him 'uncle' again – what he wouldn't do to him right now if he were here! Dan stormed around the room, his fists itching to destroy something – *hah!* There was Bukki's pet flask which had been filled with many a sly drop – pushed behind the door where it seemed Aunt Etta had hidden it – and serve him right too! It was nothing special in itself, in fact just like any other, but the fact it was Bukki's filled Dan with wrath.

A very nasty thought curled into his mind like a wisp of dirty smoke. Smashing was too good for it! Dan snatched up the flask – which Aunt Etta seemed to have filled with sand and pebbles in her own defiance of Bukki, and put for a doorstop – and tore out

448

to the little privy in the scrub. He kicked the cover off the deep hole in the ground and flung the flask down into the sharp-smelling depths with a savage sense of satisfaction. He dumped a bail of earth into the hole as custom dictated and dropped the wooden cover back in place with a thud. Even if Bukki ever found it – which he certainly wouldn't – he would not be wanting to use *that* particular flask ever again! Had Bukki not been so fond of furtive guzzling in the first place, *maybe he never would have got so drunk on that terrible night when* – but Dan ran back to the house, pounding the thoughts away with his feet, splashing them away in the water barrel before striding determinedly back into the house – his agitated mind seizing on another idea at once.

"I won't!" he blurted out to his weeping aunt. *"I won't!"* Aunt Etta struggled for control. She raised her head and mopped her eyes and took a shuddering breath. Tears smeared her sagging brown face, and her untidy grey eyebrows were smudged a weird green from the mint she had been chopping earlier and which had rubbed off her fingertips. A large drop hung from her curved nose. She was not a beautiful sight, but Dan looked at her protectively in his surge of masculine rage.

"I *won't* lose *everything*!" he repeated savagely. "And neither will you!"

Aunt Etta blew her nose fiercely. "But what can we do about it?" she asked helplessly, hunting for a dry patch on her handkerchief and blowing again. "More letters? They will probably be too disgusted with us to open them. And what happened to those we entrusted to Bukki?"

"They need proof!" Dan raced back and began flinging Bukki's belongings about in a frantic search. "Remember when I left Jerusalem, Mari gave me a block of ink, a new pen and a leather cover with twenty sheets of papyrus inside, and told me we must write them often."

Etta wiped her eyes again. "Yes, she was so thoughtful and kind to you in those dreadful first days. Such a generous gift."

Dan was shaking clothes, beating cushions and poking the floor.

"Expensive," he agreed. "And very useful. Especially to Bukki. I don't think he would have thrown them away, auntie. He had to keep track of what we wrote to Jerusalem, and copy our writing too. I think he would have kept our letters somewhere and maybe used the backs to practice on.."

He came out eventually, shaking his head. "There's nothing more in here."

"Maybe they're somewhere obvious," his aunt suggested. "Maybe we can't see for looking."

*The trouble with the obvious is that it's never obvious.* Surely Dan had heard that somewhere before ... He looked up.

"How many sheets did we use of the twenty?" he asked. "Four or five?"

"Yes, about that, I suppose." Etta put her handkerchief away resolutely and struggled to her feet. "We wrote small – so as not to waste the lovely papers, and – oh!"

Dan nodded vigorously. "Uncle Bukki had to use it too when he wrote in our names – or they'd wonder why. But then the sheets would disappear from the case too fast and we would notice. So ..."

450

Etta was already waddling determinedly to her wooden shelves. She plucked the flat leather folder down and unlaced it quickly. Licking his finger Dan flicked through the top edges of the pages.

"About fifteen here – so it looks right …" He tugged the thin wad of pages free from the tight case and spread them on the table. There were ten blank sheets, underneath which were five more, carefully written in two different hands and bearing creases where they had once been folded. The backs – scrawled all over with variations on Dan and Etta's signatures and fragments of copied sentences – made it plain that Bukki had practised his forgeries. Aunt Etta pursed her lips.

"I think I must have misjudged your Uncle Bukki all these years. This was clever – or perhaps cunning would be a better word. But he took a terrible risk of discovery, keeping the sheets all together."

Dan sat down suddenly.. "We always pulled out the top one without looking." He felt oddly let down … "But maybe he knew he would be found out sooner or later – and didn't care – maybe he always meant to leave us when he had money, anyway."

It seemed so wrong that Bukki would leave them by choice, as if they weren't worth staying for, even for the sake of appearance. Dan had once almost thought that – maybe he did care about them – just a little – just a crumb. *Out of habit, you know,* he excused his lame belief crossly. Etta shook her head and her eyes filled again. "I never did know what went on inside that man's head!" she mourned.

Dan pushed their unsent letters and the blank sheets back into the satchel, and bundled them together with all those found under Bukki's bed. He ran to the door and glanced at the sun.

"Aunt Etta," he said quickly, "have you any money?"

Etta blinked. "A little, Dan, dear. For what?"

"Enough to hire a donkey for a day?" Dan asked eagerly.

"Why, yes, I believe so – it was a good shearing last year, the best for some time, and you know, Samuel and old Caleb have managed the flock so well over winter – but what do you want with a donkey?"

Dan looked at her imploringly. "Sabbath at nightfall – but we can be there by then if we hurry."

"Be where?" Etta was bewildered.

"Oh, Aunt Etta – don't you see? We can't explain properly to Johanan and Mari or Anna – Jerusalem is too far away. So we have to go to Asa, and show him all that has happened. He will believe us! I could go alone – though you would never let me. But I know the way, and you can come on the donkey. You've done it before ..." he added, his voice faltering a little.

"Cana! On a donkey!" Etta pressed her lined hand to her deep bosom and drew a startled breath. Yes, indeed she had done it before – in laughing joy and promise of happiness so cruelly dashed. She stood up, tugging her money pouch from the depths of her neckline, pulled the cord up over her head – and tossed it lightly into Dan's outstretched hand.

"What I have done before, I can do again! Run to the pottery and take instructions from Ittai. He knows all about hiring donkeys in a hurry. Dan, you are right! This thing must be put right at once, for all our sakes, and you have two days grace from Samuel. Truly the Eternal is still with us!"

Dan nodded and a spark of light crept back into his darkly shadowed eyes.

"Truly He is still with us," he replied firmly. Then raced out of the door, fleet of foot, to find Ittai.

As he ran, a persistent itch niggled at the back of his mind, something which he had not noticed at the time, and which now insisted on being addressed.

*What in the world did Bukki want with Aunt Etta's shell collection?*

## Chapter Thirty-five

MARTA, having bundled her babies into the eager arms of her mother-in-law, came rushing through the scrub, hot with indignation, the rebellious silver streak blowing wild in the breeze, calling to Etta almost before the house was in sight. She flew inside, flung her arms around her old friend and burst into tears of sympathy, babbling furiously her long-suppressed opinions of Bukki. While Etta calmed her down, Ittai was doing much the same sort of babbling to Dan, hardly pausing to wash the miry streaks from his arms and chest before bounding along on the track towards Magdala, towing Dan as relentlessly as if he had been Bukki himself being dragged off to the galleys, which Ittai expostulated were far too good for him.

"Whoa there! Watch your step, brother!" and the fishmonger's shout of warning jerked the angry young potter to attention. He and Dan sprang from the track as the laden donkeys skittered before them. The turn in the path had been sudden, and neither of them had noticed the nodding noses rounding the rocks. Apologising, Ittai grabbed Philip's arm and poured out the story of Bukki's perfidy. Philip's thick eyebrows lifted then scowled.

"A tool of Bukki's!" he complained bitterly. "Me! Carrying letters to and from the post at Cana – thinking I do Etta and the boy good and earning merit for myself – pah!"

"We have to go there right away," Dan explained earnestly, jiggling with impatience. "We have to show Asa it was all lies."

"We?"

"Aunt Etta won't let me go alone. So we're hiring a donkey from Magdala for her."

"No, you're not!" Philip growled. "Sabbath tonight and little enough time as it is. And I had my part to play in this disgrace, unwitting though it was. I'll take you myself, boy, right now, since I'm on my way already – and you'll spare your aunt the shaking of her poor old bones."

Ittai's dirty face beamed. "That's the spirit, hey, Dan?" and he turned on his heel and loped joyfully back towards Banayim, unable to resist spreading his arms wide, clicking his fingers and dancing a few hopping steps of glee.

"You hold hard there," Philip warned with a grin. "Upset my donkeys and we'll have the fish to catch all over again!"

But Aunt Etta would have none of it.

"Oh, no, no!" she said grimly. "For ten years or more I have been in this house and rarely journeyed more than a few miles – and yet in the last months I have been offered donkeys and Jerusalem and Cana and the moon itself with one hand and had them snatched away again with another. Then the only chance I had was ruined with misery. I'll have no more of it, and no more of sitting here worrying on my own. I thank you kindly for your offer, Philip, but if you take Dan, you take me too!"

Philip the Younger and Dan looked at her stout, stooped, grey, determined figure, as she dabbed the crook of her precious stick at the satchel she had already packed. They exchanged grins as she fished it up from the floor and stared at them defiantly. Philip shrugged resignedly and Etta nodded, satisfied Determinedly she chalked a message for Marta on the door. *'Gone with Dan – Etta'*.

"Douse the fire, Dan, and pin the shutters!" she ordered, whisking her thick cloak into her arms and fussing Dan into his own. "And Philip – pick me a soft spot on your fattest donkey. I'll carry your fish baskets strapped to my hips if need be … !"

Dan laughed at the idea and Philip looked at her admiringly. Aunt Etta picked up the wool pillow so happily stitched long months ago, remembering that nasty bony ridge in the centre of a donkey's back which not even her cushioning fat could make comfortable. *This pillow is a friend which is going to stick closer than a brother!* – she smiled at her thoughts, but the sigh came too. While Philip and Dan bustled obediently, Etta was unable to stop herself wondering nervously what could go wrong this time, either before or after they reached Cana.

"Let's away then! Time waits for no man, and fish wait for neither," Philip said briskly. "Etta, you'll take my beast, while Dan and I walk."

Etta looked guilty. "Only one donkey spare? What about you?"

Philip rumbled and patted his stomach regretfully. "My disrespectful wife tells me I grow stouter by the day, and nags me constantly to work myself more and my donkeys less! She'll be grateful to you, no doubt. I declare she would have been quite at home in her own country cracking the whip and bawling at me to find straw to make bricks …"

Which was quite disgraceful of Philip the Younger, whose soft-spoken, black-skinned Aida pampered and clucked over him like an old hen and daily insulted him with tender solicitations about wrapping up warmly and taking care on the road. But it had the desired effect of clearing Etta's brow with a laugh, and so they were off at last.

Scarcely had they cleared the low scrub and disappeared around the curve of the hillside to the spring-flowering orchard slopes when a thickset figure rose cautiously from the top of the hill behind the house and hurried down into the courtyard. The fresh scrawl on the door told him he would be undisturbed. He lifted the bar on the door and slid inside, rubbing his hands, unable to believe his good fortune. Yes, he fancied he'd made a most impressive exit earlier in the day, and had not relished a sheepish return which would be hard to explain. It had been a very nasty shock – like cold water trickling down his spine – when he had realised that the rattling flask he'd scooped up was the one full of Dan's rubbishy collection of stones and shells, and not the one full of the silver and gold extracted from Anna over the months. True, he had topped his own jar with pebbles and things himself in case of prying eyes, but that pesky Etta was forever tidying things up and the two had somehow changed places.

What a piece of luck that they'd gone off with the fishmonger! That meant Cana, and Asa's family, no doubt, or Etta would never have been on a donkey again. Odd she hadn't mentioned it before. Or maybe she had … a man couldn't listen to half what a woman prattled about or he'd scramble his thoughts like eggs. But meanwhile there was no hurry at all and none would even know he had crept back! Bukki put his greasy hooked nose into various pots and jars in the storeroom. He'd have time now to make the best of things, well and truly. He agonised delightfully over the advantage of buying a beast to carry provisions, as opposed to the disadvantage of having to lug things around and feed a donkey, finally deciding that to travel light was preferable after all. Now, where was that jar?!

Hurrying into his room, Bukki stopped short when he saw that his hiding place under the sleeping mat had been discovered – and realised with a momentary queasy feeling that Etta's trip to Cana must be to expose him. How or why they'd even thought to look for the evidence he couldn't think, but no doubt Dan's inquisitiveness would be to blame. Well, they'd all know the worst now, but it would make no difference. They would have found out sooner or later anyway, and meanwhile Bukki had realised his long cherished dream at last. How he had hugged the knowledge to himself! All that long day in the dreary weather of Yom Kippur, while all around were dutifully fasting and "afflicting their souls" – how hard it had been to look sad and solemn! For once he had not found the day boring. It was pleasant to hide behind his mournful face while romping with joy within, and making many plans for his freedom and future. The idea of marrying and taking over Etta's house had only just occurred to him, but with or without that variation, he was a made man! To have a good sum of money to live on, without working for it, and which could set him up in some nice little business somewhere … maybe even money-lending! Yes, wife or no, he'd be better appreciated in a more sophisticated community after all. That Anna was a generous woman. He almost regretted the ease with which he'd deceived her. Impatiently Bukki flung the shutters wide for light, itching to find his cache of coins.

He had no doubts that Etta and Dan would be all right, they had many friends. It wasn't as if he was making their lives any worse. After all, neither Etta nor the boy would ever have had the sense to ask anything for themselves from Anna's family, so things would just be as they were meant to be. *Except that I'm better off at*

459

*last. And as for them, why, they'll think life's even better too without me around!* So he justified himself, though faintly aware of an uneasy warp in his own reasoning at that point.

His original half-formed plans of gaining control of Ammiel's flock had been dismissed earlier – *where was that flask?* – in the bitter teeth of winter. And he had no taste for it, no patience, no liking. He did not say to himself, no strength – though that stringy old Caleb seemed to be made of iron yet and more like to die of rust than human weakness – all very galling. But – a horrible feeling of panic was beginning to wind its treacherous tentacles about Bukki's chest.

"Where is that flask!" he shouted desperately, now pushing, kicking, knocking and throwing. Bukki's room – Dan's bed – Etta's bed – pulled apart! The long room – empty! The lower storage level – broom-scraped, cushion-kicked, basket-jumbled. The kitchen-pots smashed, meal spilled from sacks, mending tipped in a flurry of yarn and cloth to snarl on the floor – the crowded wooden shelves struck clear with an angry hand. Alone and frantic, Bukki roared and stirred up his private cyclone of anger, tearing his hair, desperate, ridiculous – despairing.

For hours he combed through the mud and stone house near Banayim – up and down – in and around – the water jar was plumbed, the water barrel dragged, the roof and the reproachful half-finished booth searched, the rafters fumbled – even the woven twig and reed ceiling overhead poked savagely enough to snap Etta's tangled distaff, bringing down dust, knots of shrivelled mud, insects, a nest of indignant mice, and tumbling impertinently down on Bukki's startled head, a dusty toy whistle whittled years ago by a proud father during long lonely watches, and jammed impatiently out of sight by a young mother with a headache …

With a howl Bukki stamped on the beaten earth – recklessly stabbing the floor all over with the precious kitchen knife in case – somehow – he had buried his treasure while half drunk and forgotten it … the bushes outside were combed, the trees climbed, the privy shelter shaken … and finally in fruitless misery, Bukki wailed his way back into the house, overthrew the table, kicked the dead fire to pieces and pulled up the very hearth.

Gone. It was gone. No doubt Dan's sharp eyes had spied it, and the money which should have been Bukki's was now on its way to Cana! Cheated by fate! Dan's small-souled uncle could not help seeing the frustrating irony of the fact that the money had been sent for Dan and Etta. It was too much that it should have reached that destination after all!

Bukki was beside himself. He did not mind exposure while he had his escape route wide open – but here he was, exposed as an utter scoundrel – for to himself Bukki did not deign to use the term 'thief' – and all for nothing. Oh yes, he had enough money in his belt to get by for a little while, but what then? Etta would not take him back, Samuel would not give him more of the tedious work in the field, and nor would anyone else by the sound of it. Samuel did not make idle threats. Bukki knew by humiliating experience that he could do well enough by begging, especially if blindfolded, but it did not appeal. There was no scope in begging for an expansive man to attract an approving circle of friends – and Bukki felt he had unappreciated talents to share yet. He wasn't sure quite what they were but no doubt they would emerge in a less cramped atmosphere than the house at Banayim.

The death of his brother-in-law had been a great blow to Bukki. There was no real link to a supportive family any more, except the blood tie to Dan, who, being dependent, didn't count. Yet.

Bukki cast his mind frantically back over the past year, and realised he should have made more effort to wriggle his way into Asa's good graces. Now, he had nobody to fall back on. He looked up sourly at the baggy wineskin which dangled from the beams. Scarcely a cup or two left.

For some time Bukki tried to keep hope alive – sifting through everything over and over, totally losing hope of his treasure, and disgusted with Etta's lack of vanity which provided him with no more than a few poor copper and silver trinkets – family gifts – with which to barter. Her daily ornaments were mostly clumsy things – clay beads, threaded shells, wood and leather pendants and other such clutter, laboriously made with earnest, childish fingers and worn with no awareness of their ugliness. The only gold was in the thin old earrings she never removed! Etta boasted no heavy bracelets such as Anna wore or even the jewelled nose rings which Dan's mother had left her. Etta may have overheard Bukki's ungracious mutterings about the foolishness of jewels of gold in a swine's snout or she may not. But she had handed them straight to Bukki, and they had long since gone.

"What kind of woman doesn't want decent jewellery?!" he shouted in frustration.

*Far away, in a noisy temple courtyard the din seemed to fade into the ever present haze as a woman enveloped by a great sense of stillness and purpose, removed all her ornaments, even to the few coins on her forehead ...*

Brooding savagely, Bukki unhooked the wineskin and squeezed the final stream of wine into his greedily open mouth, shaking the last drops out, and tossing the skin away.

*Standing by, a father heard his daughter forswear all that came from the vine ...*

Still thirsty, Bukki plunged his whole head rudely into the drinking-water pot, sucked at the clean water, and flicked his head out, spraying water from his oiled hair in a wide arc. Gasping, and blowing, with malicious satisfaction at having fouled Etta's meticulous housekeeping for once and all, Bukki raked the wet hair out of his eyes with his dirty-nailed fingers. He had planned a luxurious time at the hot-baths in Tiberius with his gold – even a Roman barber to wash and cut his hair, which was growing over-long. And now that pleasure was denied him, along with all the other little comforts he had promised himself.

*The priest folded back the veil from the woman's head, revealing the truth beneath.. Hair patchily streaked with queer colours, shockingly short – which kinked oddly and with bald patches yet – which told of acute sickness and struggle. Unruly, mannish hair which robbed her thin face of what little beauty it possessed.*

Bukki toweled his head and fashioned a neat turban from a length of embroidered cloth Etta had been saving to make Dan a special coat for his first Jerusalem Passover.

*Her ugliness exposed, the woman turned to her father, exchanging the feminine, embroidered veil she would wear no more, for one of stark simplicity, and spoke the final words of her vow with steadiness and clarity. His mouth opened involuntarily. Her calm eyes sparked fleetingly with a warning plea. Obediently he closed his mouth, biting his lips to keep them still.*

463

"They'll be sorry!" Bukki gritted his teeth, churning his sorrow afresh and bringing forth more anger. "I'm not going to crawl back to an old woman and a puppy! I've got a friend or two at the garrison, and a good set of dice – one day I'll be back just to show them what I'm really good for, and then let's see who has the last laugh … Me! I swear it!"

*The priest looked over at the father, who dropped his eyes in acceptance, with tears sliding down his rugged cheeks and his fingers laid to his lips. So it was acknowledged. He had heard her vow and shut his mouth. The priest gave his blessing, and walked away.*

For the rest of that day Bukki camped in the chaos and litter he had created, stuffing himself with the choicest of Etta's carefully stored supplies, warming himself by a lavish fire of Dan's diligently collected dried cow dung and even wood, filling his basket at leisure with clothes, food, and useful bits and pieces. Sunset approached, and the Sabbath, but the Tiberius gaming pavement awaited, and few would be abroad to comment. As families all over the land gathered to sing their prayers and kindle the Sabbath lights, Bukki walked contemptuously out of the home a shepherd had built lovingly for his family – leaving the door swinging, shutters yawning and the bedraggled fire to burn itself out – feeling as strong-minded as he was, in reality, weak spirited.

*Unseeing, unhearing of the nudges and whispers from others in the Court, the father lovingly stroked the ravaged, uncovered head beside him. He kissed it tenderly, with tears.*

*"My child! My darling! My little Nazirite!" he murmured, and she submitted gratefully to his embrace. Then veiling herself once*

*more, she took his arm, and walked courageously out of the Temple towards her new life.*

Aunt Etta and Dan sat in the synagogue in Cana. Dan was down with the men; Aunt Etta, Rhoda, and Old Dinah up in the women's gallery. Blind Mordecai was sitting outside leaning his head against the wall, yearning over the activities within, singing the responses under his breath and straining to hear the voice of the nervous young man who was reading for the first time. Philip the Younger was not there. Aida had detected a sniffle when he arrived in the late afternoon and had poured so much spiced wine down his throat as a remedy against cold that by the Sabbath morning he would have been incapable of movement even had he not been swaddled with foul-smelling chest plasters. His wife pinched his cheek lovingly, gathered her children, and trotted off to Synagogue with a pleasant consciousness that afterwards they might linger as long as they pleased.

Etta found the larger congregation uplifting to her spirit. The thrum of the massed voices gave her a thrill such as rarely came in the cramped synagogue in the humbler part of Magdala. The sense of sisterhood, however, which insinuated itself as she stood beside old Dinah and young Rhoda and dozens of other women she knew not, was a feeling she was used to; the gossamer touch of invisible threads of faith which bound them together. With the stabilising centre of the family gone, and even Bukki out of their lives, Etta realised with a queer lurch of the heart that she was now the centre, the head of this tiny family. There was only herself and Dan! Just an ageing woman and a young lad, though if he grew fast enough and she lived long enough, she would see a family grow again, if God willed. But even if there was never to be more than the two of them – *did* it matter, after all?

Almost a sense of adventure possessed her, a sense of freedom, as she recalled the haste in which she had left all that was solid and concrete in her life – the house at Banayim – and set off to right a most grievous wrong. *Why truly, living is all that matters! Living and praising the Eternal! Not a house, not a dynasty, just breathing in and out, in faith, in hope and in love!*

Etta was amazed at her own thoughts. This was what she and Marah had been discussing, yet Marah All-Alone had been living it seriously, while until this moment, for herself (oh, for shame! she could see it now) it had just been words. Correct words, and very sincere, but here she was, the earthly ties loosed, finally living it. *Yes, it is freedom! We have enough to eat, clothes to wear, and praise God!, a flock to sustain us and friends as well!* Etta felt her heart swelling with a revelation which brought her close to tears. *Why, we are rich, Dan and I! And I thought we had been stripped of everything!* Truly God was good, though His ways indeed hard to bear at times, and certainly past finding out.

What did it matter that they had not found Asa at home after all? The matter could wait. Dinah and Rhoda had been emphatic in their assurance that they expected his return from Jerusalem very soon – indeed, on the Third day. *Surely the Master would be angry if we did not keep you here to bring him joy!* So Rhoda had pleaded. Dan and Etta had been astonished to hear this, and relieved as well. Anna must have said nothing to Asa about their "begging letters" if he felt this way, and probably had silenced Loukanos and Johanan too, to avoid further distressing her still-grieving father. Praise God for such a rare woman! Etta had readily agreed to wait, and determined to use the time as well as Old Dinah would allow her. She had already noticed that neither of the servants were good needlewomen, however good they were with cooking and cleaning, and there would be some mending and patching to see to, she'd be bound. And it would do Dan good to have a break from the damp spring fields.

She sought her boy from the gallery, eyeing him narrowly as his thin face below, lit by a stray shaft of sunlight, lifted towards the reader. The lad was looking peaky. He was growing fast, and the bone-ache kept him awake some nights, she knew. As for this latest shock over Bukki, in Dan it had turned to anger and determination. Pray God, healing for this was possible, and soon. For the boy's other, deeper sorrow, it was not a matter of healing. Grief had settled into him and become part of his growing. His father would live on within him.

The reader traced the words with the long pointer, careful to avoid touching the holy words on the sacred page, as he intoned from the book of Numbers.

*"The words of Balaam the son of Beor,*
*and the prophecy of one whose eye is open,*
*knowing the knowledge of the Most High.*
*Who has a vision of the Almighty, swooning, yet seeing."*

Dan thought he knew what that felt like. He had felt like it himself, some months before, his eyes seeing something too shocking to believe it was real.

*"I see him, but not here. I behold him, but not near.*
*A Star shall come forth from Jacob, a Sceptre rise from Israel!"*

The Star and the Sceptre! The Bethlehem Star and the Sceptre of the King, the Messiah! Dan hung on the words. *In our very own days – my days – they have already come true! Oh, where is he and when will we see him! Can he really wipe away our tears, as the scribes*

467

*say? Will he really care about me, Dan? Or only about Israel – all of us in a lump?*

Dan's mind made a rapid, sparkling leap. He remembered the night he realised that the whole of Israel made a unified glow created of many smaller lights. *The Star out of Jacob? – yes!* If only he could cry out or clap! He could see it now – *So shall thy seed be!* All of them blessing and being blessed. Why, the Messiah was one of the stars too – if the biggest. So of course he would care! Just like Johannes the prophet – whose words were blunt, but actions kind – who asked people's names, and talked to them, and touched them and baptized them one by one with his own lean, hairy hands. Johannes, the Baptizer, the great man – prophesied in scripture like Messiah so Anna had told him – had actually smiled and touched and baptized Dan's very own father … So why wouldn't the Messiah be just as caring!

> *"He will crush Moab's head, pull down all the offspring of Sheth.*
> *And Edom will be a possession! And Seir also!*
> *While Israel does valiantly."*

Dan watched the sparse curling side-whiskers of the young reader bristling up and down as his lips moved earnestly, mouth tasting the syllables of the Holy Writ. Terrible words for Moab and Edom … Suddenly Dan's imagination transported him to the Palace of Herod the Great, and saw a scribe of nearly thirty years ago nervously reading to the King, the Idumean – the Edomite. The Star which heralded the King – would crush Edom! No wonder Herod flew into a panic and jealous rage! No wonder he wanted to kill the Messiah, the Star and Sceptre of Jacob.

> *"The descendant of Jacob shall be dominant*
> *And destroy the remnant from its cities."*

Yes, that was the Messiah part people usually liked to consider. Victory and crushing! Dominance for Israel at last, and destruction of the remnant of oppressors. It was strange, then, that the Baptizer had said nothing about it. He spoke of the victory of good living, destroying bad habits – the victory of Godliness, destroying sin. Dan was not sure what it all meant, but it was clear to him that Messiah would not want wasters in his newly restored Kingdom of Israel.

The reader tremblingly stepped down from the stand and the service continued, but Dan and Etta, each wrapped in their own private revelations, felt rather than heard it washing over them in comforting waves. Finally the closing benedictions were recited, the congregation dismissed.

As they stepped out into the cold sunlight and found each other in the crowd again, Dan and Aunt Etta smiled at each other. Miles from home, their muscles still recalling the journey of yesterday, an absent host, and the original purpose of their visit frustrated for the present – somehow none of it seemed to be as important as it was last night. The Eternal was in control. His purpose was being outworked under their very noses. Whatever came, they were blessed already.

The blessing of Abraham – the possession of the earth and the Kingdom restored and the promises and everything – would be real one day. And soon! Was not Messiah already here? But in the meantime, there *was* indeed a *present* blessing – as Dan had thought about so long ago. The *something new and good* – Dan could feel the idea of it creeping slowly into his bones – why! it was not something you were given, or something you could possess, or even something which happened to you. It was something new and good about the way you *thought* – the way you *looked* at what happened to you.

And so they found each other in the bustling crowd, and smiling with contentment, Dan, at a nod and touch from Aunt Etta, dropped several small coins into lap of the blind man who was resting soberly against the building. Blind Mordecai was careful to say nothing and do nothing except raise a hand in thanks when he heard the coins chink and felt their delicate pressure depress the tunic which was tightly stretched over his crossed legs. He whisked the alms into his belt. It would not do to appear to be working on the Sabbath.

A sudden spat of rain rattled on the hood of his leather cloak, the sop to the conscience of the freshly baptized tanner. The thought still made Mordecai smile a little. He pulled it around his body, tucked his knees underneath, and sent a thankful, if slightly puzzled, blessing in the direction of Johannes the baptizing prophet.

The flurry of rain fell only on Cana and its district. It did not spread as far east as Banayim, where it might have done good … but in any case, the sly red flickers which had crept out of Etta's destroyed hearth to lick exploratively at the fallen straw and twigs and rubbish on the floor, though fanned into a steady blaze from the draught through the open door and window, had not yet burned through the roof.

## *Chapter Thirty-six*

RHODA sat half guiltily watching Dan's attempts to mend her broom. She had been sweeping mud from the entry when Antioch Hassim's camel train came by laden with bales of far-eastern silks and luxury goods on the way to Jerusalem. The markets there would do a roaring trade at the coming Passover when the city was jammed with pilgrims. Rhoda didn't mind cattle or donkeys or horses, but she had a shrinking fear of camels, and had dropped her broom and whisked back into the courtyard with a squeal which drew the supercilious attention of the leading beast. It seemed to find scornful delight in treading all over the abandoned broom, and its example was followed by the five haughty creatures behind it. When Rhoda crept out, abashed, to reclaim her broom, the ends were crushed past repair.

Dan looked at it glumly, regretting his initial impulse to impress the servant girl. He struggled for a while with frayed twine and splintering twigs, then looked up and caught her watching. There was, mixed with gratitude and admiration, amusement behind those eyes. He threw the broom down, laughing ruefully.

"It's no good, Rhoda. I thought I'd be clever, but this broom is past mending. Could you still use it if I rebound the top, cut all the broken ends off and just made it shorter?"

Rhoda giggled appreciatively.

"I could use it for beating off that wild rooster when I feed the chickens. He went straight for me this morning, horrible thing. I'll be glad when he's in the pot! But for sweeping, I will need a new broom. Never mind – this one was well worn, and it was my own fault."

Blind Mordecai listened to their laughter as they ran out of the gate, pursued by Old Dinah's stream of advice on haggling for the best price. Nothing exciting there – just a visit to Hushed Lamech's for a broom, and a message to be sent to Shepherd Samuel about the boy being delayed. But it was good to hear some life in that house. The place had been almost as silent as the Lamechs themselves of late – discounting Old Dinah, whose endless cluckings merely blended in with the chickens – and little Rhoda needed another youngster to bring out her giggles. He hoped they would keep up their cheerful chattering at the broom-makers. A quiet place that was indeed, with mother, daughter and son afflicted with a dumb spirit. Silently, busily, sorting, twisting, tying, binding, and good brooms they made too. Speaking to each other in signs as complex and swift as the movements they made in fashioning their work. But folk forgot they had ears, just as folk forgot Mordecai had a mind.

How strange it was that before the dumb, so many were struck dumb, trying to make themselves understood by signs, or mouthing exaggeratedly, assuming that the speechless could not hear – whereas before Mordecai they became blind – blind to the fact that he was not a witless simpleton simply because he could not see their faces. How strange indeed that faced with someone with an obvious defect, people preferred to bestow another of their own choice! It was a puzzle that curled Mordecai's lip sardonically.

Yet, he reminded himself, before he was cursed, was he not the same? *How different it is on the other side of the gate!* he sneered at himself. He wondered how the strange Baptizer would communicate with the blind, the dumb, the lame.

Interesting it was that this prophet went beyond the law which required that one must not hinder the afflicted, in that he commanded actively helping them. A nice change from those who regarded one's affliction as punishment for a past unworthy life. Mordecai sighed. Of late he had heard so much about the Baptizer. The whole countryside seemed to be talking of nothing else. And there were even those like Parosh, who not only began to reform their lives, but actually kept on with it. Though the gruff tanner had always borne a soft heart under his sharp dealings. Oh yes, Mordecai knew all about that unspoken alliance with the enigmatic Loukanos! But the prophet had forced Parosh to make a clearcut decision about his way of life which could not be hidden, and though his very vocal struggles for holiness amused Mordecai, it was clear the man was in earnest. The Baptizer said Messiah was coming and Parosh had decided he must be ready, and that was that. People went in droves to the dark Nazirite Johannes, to be tantalised, frightened or thrilled – according to their secret hearts – and hundreds were convinced and baptized. All were in a fever of impatience for the Messiah whom Johannes said would come soon. But when?

Ah – what wouldn't he give to hear a man of God for himself! For surely, if only in the heart-changes he accomplished, the fellow was of God and not of man? But what hope of that, with so many miles between them, and neither family, friends nor money to take him? The beggar scrubbed his head savagely, his habitual coolness deserting him for a moment. He *existed* well enough here in Cana, where folk knew him – but did he *live*? The gatherer of information, weaver of gossip and assumptions, hoarder of the titbits of other people's lives – yes – he had made his own private world as rich as possible for a long time and fought bitterness successfully for the most part. But now he was no longer satisfied with living on the fringe of life, sipping the dregs of other people's affairs. A long-suppressed longing rose and gripped him with sudden misery – a longing to *live* again, as a whole man – a longing which had nothing to do with regaining his sight. He would gladly remain a blind man, if he could only live with a purpose, with something more to work towards than surviving another day. But who cared whether he lived or died?

He dropped his bandaged face into his hands and groaned.

Aunt Etta had not said much to Rhoda or Old Dinah about the purpose of their visit, unsure that it would be appropriate to discuss their affairs with Asa's servants. But Dan was constrained by none such reticence, and by the time they had returned home with a new broom and had Dinah's approval for the style and the price, Rhoda knew the whole story. Her dark eyes first grew round in disbelief, then narrowed with disgust.

"Loukanos will be wild as a bear when he hears this!" she said in an awed voice. "My dear mistress Anna has been terribly sick with a slow burning fever, and for so long her brother has worn himself out making her well. He would have been very angry about any letters which upset or worried her! The master has been fretted to distraction about both of them. He has been in Jerusalem with them for weeks, you know, and wouldn't leave till Anna was safe – and how lucky you came now, when he is about to return."

Dan bit his lip. His heart had fluttered anxiously at the thought of Anna being seriously ill. The brief scraps from Johanan's long-lost letters had not been enough to reassure him. Thankfully she had recovered – Praise the Eternal! – though she must have suffered a great deal. How dreadful it would have been if she had died – and died thinking so badly of them! At least, if Asa was returning to Cana, she must be finally out of danger. It was a great relief. He thought again about Rhoda's words which had puzzled him.

"I don't understand. What do you mean about Loukanos wearing himself out to make Anna well? Was her aunt Mari not caring for her? Or was Loukanos trying to sell those horrible paintings to pay for medicines? But they have money. It makes no sense."

Rhoda clapped a hand over her mouth in dismay.

"Oh dear! I am not supposed to say anything."

Dan looked at her indignantly. "It's a bit late for secrets now – and there's been too many of them already. Tell me."

Rhoda hesitated, but there was something in what Dan said, and it *was* delicious to be able to tell a secret. She flushed, giggled, then hurried into speech.

"Loukanos paints for pleasure only."

Dan snorted. "His pleasure, maybe. Probably not anyone else's."

Rhoda giggled again and waved a slim brown finger.

"You mustn't interrupt. And you mustn't be unkind." She lowered her voice and whispered into Dan's ear with a wriggle of delightful importance, *"Loukanos is a physician."*

Dan goggled. "What?" He rubbed his ear hard to take away the tickle.

She nodded vigorously. "Yes – and a very fine one too."

"But – why? Why hide it?"

Rhoda looked more sober. "In Greece he did not. He was held in great honour in Philippi, so my mistress told me. But you know, in Galilee, and particularly in Judea, a physician is not respected as he is there! Sickness is from the Eternal, or visitations of demons, or of course, a punishment for misdeeds in another life!"

"That's just silly," Dan said stoutly, nevertheless realising uneasily how ignorant he was of many things ... of how much his life until so recently, had been so limited, so sheltered, so unaware of many ideas outside his own four walls, so bounded by the simple yet sensible convictions of his father and aunt – and Caleb. "Since when does God agree with demons? And how many lives can one person have? Have some sense!"

Rhoda shrugged off Dan's abrupt answer loftily.

"*I* do not presume to know more than the learned ones! There are many who despise a physician for meddling with the bodies of men, which the great God requires should be cured with prayer and devotion. And Loukanos learned his doctoring from Greeks and Egyptians! Just imagine that! How would you feel if you were a holy Pharisee and your prayers were no use? What would you think about asking help from such a man!"

Dan looked at Rhoda with new respect, remembering his own confusion about the unanswered prayers for his mother. Would his father have seen fit to go to a Gentile physician either? If only he could ask him! Meanwhile, it was clear that the giggles and fun were only the surface of the hard working Rhoda. He held his peace and let her proceed.

She glanced at him with a little grin, sitting on her hands, and swinging her slender, neatly crossed ankles, as they sat on the bench in the cold sunlight.

"People around here are not quite so holy, perhaps? Loukanos has been treating the poor in Cana ever since he came here. Every night he would go out to the tanner's house and doctor any who came to him in need. Of course most law-abiding people wouldn't go anywhere near a smelly old tanner's and make themselves unclean, so it meant the desperate did so undisturbed. But Loukanos forbade any of us to speak of it." She giggled at the memory. "You should have heard him stamping around and shouting about refusing to have idle rich matrons pestering him to attend their hysterias and their overfed spoiled brats with the stomach ache and making eyes at him behind their husband's backs! So of course, he had his own way, and my late mistress Helen, may she rest in peace, was so proud of him!

"At first, Loukanos went to the poorer quarters and sought out those in need – particularly among the beggars – and Blind Mordecai could lead him to others he'd heard of. Later on, tanner Parosh gave him a room where needy people could come to him. The word got around about the doctor who came by night, and asked no fee but discretion. Only those who were not ill, and the rich with their own cures and prayers, knew nothing. They had no need of him, after all."

Dan's eyes sparkled as he heard this surprising tale. *To think of Big, Bad, Bold, Black Loukanos being such a Greek hero!* He had been so secretive about it, surely his left hand had not known what his right was doing! Dan rejoiced to see Loukanos in this unexpected light. But – "If he likes to do good, why is he always so bad tempered?" Dan couldn't help asking.

Rhoda picked at the frayed threads on her sacking apron.

"Anna said he didn't get enough sleep, and was always distressed for those he couldn't help. And she told me more one day – when he spoke sharply to me and I wept over it. She said he is angry because Helen's God did not save her. And he is angrier with himself because he could not save her either."

Dan thought of Helen's last happy morning, rejoicing in the knowledge of the Messiah. Was not that help from God?

"Everyone has to die," he said flatly, "but there is the Resurrection afterwards. Better to die and live again, than to just go on being sick and cured by doctors over and over." A sudden thought struck him.

"Rhoda? Did you find out anything about the *forbidden* drawings?"

Rhoda dropped her eyes and shuddered.

"Yes. Oh, they gave me nightmares! Anna came to me one night when I woke up screaming, and I had to tell her what I had seen. She told me that in Egypt – Loukanos learned to –"

She looked up dubiously, but Dan gestured impatiently. The girl gulped and went on.

"He learned to cut up dead bodies to see how they are made," she confessed in an awed whisper. "He draws what he saw, and it helps him to set bones, and stitch up broken skin and muscles so they still work properly. He can even restore sight to some who have the cataracts – if they are brave enough to face his blade! Imagine!"

Dan didn't like to imagine such operations much more than Rhoda did. Of course, it was forbidden – not just the drawings, but the cutting up of the dead! Why, Jews were not allowed to cut themselves – let alone anyone else, dead or not! Cutting up animals to eat them was one thing – but bodies of men? It was just as well Loukanos didn't follow the law or he'd be unclean all the time and nobody would get near him to be made well. An irritating thought crossed his mind, that it was a shame a person was made unclean for trying to learn how to help people. But the thought also came to him that now he knew what the drawings were, it would be rather fascinating to look at them. He stared at his hands, wriggling the fingers and seeing the tendons move under supple brown skin. Yes – a fascinating thing!

He jumped off the bench as Aunt Etta came looking for them.

"Dan – Rhoda – sitting around when there is much to do? That new broom ought to be sweeping the courtyard this very minute, with Asa expected by sunset! Cold and stiff he'll be too, after lurching and swaying on the back of a camel for more than a day, Dinah tells me – ugh! sheer madness! – though admittedly there's not much to chose between a swift camel which makes you sick, or a slow donkey which makes you sore. Dan fetch some wood from the pile for Dinah, won't you? Thick stuff for decent coals, not twigs. And Rhoda, you're needed in the kitchen!"

So scolding, Aunt Etta bustled about as if she had not been doing so from the instant Sabbath was over. Dinah and Rhoda had turned out the clothes and household linen for Etta's inspection as obediently as if she had a perfect right to ask, and Etta had rejoiced over the mending of every tiny hole and tear. Praise the Eternal her eyes were still good, and her fingers nimble, and she was still useful for something. Asa must see that she and Dan were not beggars – but more than this, it was a pleasure to do a good deed for a good man.

There were some articles once belonging to Helen which gladdened her feminine heart in their daintiness and delicacy. Rhoda explained sadly that Loukanos believed they would make useful bandages and fine dressings for wounds. Etta was scandalised.

"Such a waste, child! So like a man! Why should a poor woman not appreciate a pretty garment as much – nay, more! – than a rich lady? And such a nice addition to a girl's dowry some of these things would be! New clothing is a luxury few can afford, and one of these lovely shawls would buy three changes of dress for a child and sandals besides. Perhaps I can suggest something about this to Asa later myself. As for Master Loukanos – I'd rather give him my own shift to rip up than see these lovely things wasted on festering wounds when they could be doing more good elsewhere."

There was a bustle outside the gate, the jingling of bits, barked instructions, slap of leather, the unmistakable peevish groaning of camels as they knelt – and the wicket was rattled impatiently. Dan on the hearth feeding the fire, Rhoda with her new broom, Aunt Etta with her sewing, and Old Dinah, stuffing a chicken which a rather squeamish Dan had plucked and drawn under her loquacious instructions – all looked up in astonishment.

"Can this be he? So early, too!" Aunt Etta, startled, folded her work hurriedly.

"Rhoda!" barked a voice loudly. "Wake up, girl, and open the gate!"

Rhoda, as flustered as Aunt Etta, threw down her new broom and rushed to the gate, squeaked, and rushed back into the kitchen with a pale face.

"It's Loukanos!" she panted wildly. *"Loukanos!"*

"Loukanos? Not Asa?!"

"Rhoda! What are you playing at! Come back and open this gate!" cried the impatient voice from outside.

480

"Go on, then, girl!" Old Dinah urged, rolling her eyes and jerking gate-wards with a rough chapped elbow. "Let the man in!"

Flapping her hands in confusion, poor Rhoda scurried outside again to the gate and fumbled with the latch and bar.

Loukanos strode through, brushing aside her stammered apologies.

"Is there a good fire?"

"Yes, sir. Dan has just made it up in the long room in preparation for your father. And there is hot soup ready, and a chicken being prepared this moment."

"Good girl. Put some bricks by the fire, won't you? I want the bed well warmed."

He stopped. "Did you say *Dan*? That grasping little – "

"Yes, sir," faltered Rhoda. "He and his aunt have been here since Sabbath."

She plucked nervously at his sleeve and gabbled hastily, all a-tremble at her own audacity, but determined to make him hear.

"They have come to right a terrible wrong, sir. Things are not as they appeared. Please hear them before you speak hastily!"

There – that was as much as she dared! She darted into the house and shut herself safely in the kitchen with Dinah and the chicken.

Loukanos stared after her in surprise. Unwonted courage from timid Rhoda! There must be something in what she said after all. Well, that matter could wait – he had other things to attend to. And wonder of wonders, here was the old woman herself coming nervously to greet him. By the stars, the poor creature was more bent than ever he had expected.

"Blessings and peace, Loukanos of Philippi," Etta said meekly, bending her head even lower in a polite bow, then meeting his eyes bravely nonetheless. "I am Etta bath Amos, for whom I know you will have little respect, and yet from a cause not of my making, as you will hear later. Our presence here is a shock for you, I am sure. And a surprise for Dan and myself too, for we awaited your father. Is he well?"

"He is well," Loukanos answered shortly, though intrigued by her words. "Do you occupy Anna's room?"

"Why no!" Etta was shocked. "Dan and I are in the guest chamber. I have not seen Anna's room, but Asa's is ready for him. I aired the bedding myself this day and Dan has warmed it with a brazier. These spring evenings are yet unkind to old bones."

Loukanos looked at her keenly, and appeared satisfied.

"It is an unusual introduction for us both, Etta bath Amos," he said, less abruptly. "But in truth, I am half glad to find you here, regardless. Will you have Rhoda put the bricks in Asa's bed? I must see to the unloading."

He disappeared. Dan emerging from the guest chamber whence he had bolted at the sound of Loukanos' voice, was abashed at his own cowardice. It was easier to have courage when you had no time to think! This slow waiting, and then finding the fiery Loukanos instead of Asa at the gate, had unnerved him momentarily. He squared his shoulders and said to Aunt Etta,

"I'll go and help him. Rhoda won't go near camels for anything."

Dan ran out to the gate to make himself useful and the camel driver obligingly began to load him with packages till he could scarcely see over them. Loukanos was very gently helping someone out of the litter. Someone who clung to his neck for support, veiled and swaddled in blankets to keep out the cold spring air. What had happened to Asa that he should grow so thin?! Dan dropped a parcel and as he bent to collect it from the dust, Loukanos and his charge passed slowly into the house. Dan hurried after them as best he could and deposited his bundles in the vestibule. At a sharp command from their driver, the camels in the street rocked reluctantly from their calloused knees to their feet, and padded on their protesting way.

Rhoda and Dinah kept to the kitchen, but beside the fire Loukanos was unwinding blankets and wraps. As Dan entered, the gaunt figure emerged, and held out thin hands to his aunt.

"Etta!"

There was a gasp – shakily Etta took several steps forward, grasping the hands and kissing them, touching them to her forehead. Dan stared, and his lips trembled. The face was turned towards him – thin and strained, but still with those extraordinary eyes and the crooked smile.

"Dan!"

"Anna!"

She held out her arms, and Dan flew into them, squeezing his eyes shut and holding her tightly. How bony she was! She seemed to have shrunk – or was it just that he had grown? She was still tall, but how had he ever imagined her as a giantess? How good it was to be together again – as if nothing had happened. Was it possible for her still to care about him? Despite everything?

She bent her head and kissed him.

"Ah, my Dan – I have missed you!"

Yes, it was possible, and he *would* think it!

A tear splashed on Dan's nose and he looked up, surprised. The Anna he knew rarely wept.

"Forgive me, I am still a little weak," she confessed with a self-deprecating laugh, dashing away the drops and recovering quickly.

Loukanos muttered something about Rhoda and hot bricks and dived into the kitchen.

Anna smiled her lopsided smile. "Louki would roast me alive, if I let him. I am quite warm – almost too warm, already."

She sat down beside Dan, and held Etta's hands in her own, pretending not to see the tears which rolled down the old woman's face. Etta's heart yearned for the younger woman. *Such a shock to see the poor dear looking so dreadful! She must have suffered so much, and we in total ignorance – as if we didn't care – and apparently sending begging letters the while!*

Anna patted Etta's work-hard hands playfully.

"I am so happy to see you both again! There was a time when I wondered if I ever should ..." Her voice trailed off. Dan wanted desperately to rush in and tell her everything about evil Bukki and the letters, but he must wait till Loukanos was there.

"Dan, dear – are you doing well at school?"

Loukanos came back with a bowl of soup and held it out to her.

"Drink." He looked at Dan. "Well – are you?"

"Am I? ..."

"Doing well at school?"

Dan glanced miserably at Aunt Etta and jumped up restlessly. He caught his foot in the end of Anna's veil which jerked from her head, hot soup splashing out of the bowl and down over her dress. Anna gasped and snatched the steaming cloth away from her body. Incongruously, she began to laugh.

"It's not hot enough to burn me, don't look so startled! It's been my year for having things spilled over me, I'm afraid. At least the soup hadn't been drunk yet!" Deliberately she thought of the harmless things – Dan's breakfast, Rhoda's lunch, and now this soup. The splattered dress, with the dark smears where her knees had crawled through blood and brains was wrapped and stored like a forbidden, sacred thing back in Jerusalem, and she would not think of it now.

She smiled again at Dan and Etta's still-shocked faces, puzzled.

"I'm not hurt!" she repeated brightly. Then she remembered. "Oh." Her hand went to her head.

"It was the fever," Loukanos said matter-of-factly, picking up her veil with a shake and covering her again. Anna tugged Dan's curls lightly.

"Will you lend me some of these for a while, Dan-boy?" she teased. "Louki tells me my hair will be very peculiar like this for a few months before it starts to grow back properly."

"Oh, my dear!" Etta mopped her eyes.

"Now, now, Etta!" Anna said gently. "It's only *hair* which fell out! If it had been my teeth I would have had something to complain about, I can tell you!"

She shivered a little, despite the fire, and her earlier protestations about being warm. Loukanos replaced one of the blankets around her shoulders.

"Let's try again with that soup," he said, and beckoned Etta to the kitchen.

"Rhoda tells me you have important things to tell us, Etta," he said in a low tone. "She thinks I have gravely misjudged you. But my sister needs rest more than anything tonight, so for her sake you will wait to discuss these problems, till tomorrow?"

"Of course, sir," Etta replied with feeling. "We would do anything for her, and in any case, she seems to bear no grudge against us, for which I thank the Eternal. And I thank you too, for not turning us out without a hearing. Indeed I would be happiest if we could tell our tale to you first, if you please."

Loukanos grunted in agreement, and glanced back at his sister, who was sitting by the fire with an arm around Dan. Neither of them spoke, as they gazed contentedly into the flames. Rhoda was already bustling around with warm water for her face and feet, crying with joy for seeing her mistress again after so long, while shedding tears of sorrow at her appearance.

Anna drank the fresh bowl of soup without incident and insisted on opening letters which had come in their absence. Most were condolences from afar, and these she put aside quickly for a private time. Only one she read aloud with bitter-sweet pleasure.

"Uncle Joseph has given us – *me* – the shore house as a wedding present! He wants me to keep it in the family, use it for charitable purposes, or sell it – as I see fit." She looked up with a sad, lopsided smile. "Of course, his letter has crossed with Aunt Mari's. He will know the whole story by now."

Dan didn't know whether to be happy or not. *What use was a house if you didn't live in it?* But maybe Anna or Johanan and his mother would come and stay in it from time to time, or perhaps even Loukanos would visit there. Anna seemed to be puzzling out the matter herself. Her straight black eyebrows were frowning a little, and she was rubbing her temples.

"Enough, Anna." She must go to bed at once, Loukanos decreed. The bed was warmed, the room cheerful, and if she was still awake and hungry later he would have food sent in to her.

"You still look a bit pale for my liking," he said critically, as he pulled her to her feet. "If I had my way you'd take some strong, sweet wine before bed, to nourish your blood."

Anna gave him one of her old looks, and he shrugged.

"I'll fetch it!" Dan cried, though Rhoda had already darted out to the kitchen before Loukanos had even finished his sentence – but Anna smiled at him and shook her head.

"No wine for me, Dan."

"Nor grapes, nor raisins, nor spirits of wine, nor wine vinegar, nor dolmades, nor toothpicks made of vine wood," said Loukanos rather irritably.

Etta's mouth dropped open. "No!" she said.

"Yes," Anna answered simply. "I have taken a Nazirite vow."

Dan looked at her in amazement. She was a Separated One! He had never known one before. Except for the prophet Johannes, and of course, it was what you might expect from a prophet. But an ordinary person! Dedicated to the Eternal!

"As if this baptism thing wasn't enough," Loukanos said to nobody in particular, but he said it with resignation. Anna would never do things by halves, and if she did, she wouldn't be his sister.

Aunt Etta closed her mouth and swallowed hard. Tears were too readily at hand these days. *Do you want to turn into a maudlin old sponge like great aunt Lilith?* she scolded herself, *shedding water whenever you're the slightest bit touched?*

487

She could understand without being told, why Anna had done this thing. But she asked, gently, "For how long have you undertaken to hold this vow?"

Thirty days was the minimum period, indeed, almost the usual time, though there were vain Absaloms who undertook it that they might, as men, avoid cutting their hair, if it was beautiful. Apart from such spurious reasons, for those who were genuine it was not as easy as it sounded.

"To bed, Anna!" Loukanos repeated firmly as she opened her mouth to reply.

"For how long?" Dan repeated anxiously.

She slipped from Loukanos's shepherding arms and put her hands lightly on Dan's shoulders. With an apologetic glance at Etta she replied steadily,

"Dan, I loved your father, and lost him – twice. So much love, and so much despair, must be redirected wholesomely if it is not to turn selfish and poisonous. I tell you this so you may understand why I have vowed to remain a Nazirite until I see him face to face."

There was a silence. Dan looked back into her weary brown and hazel eyes.

"Face to face! But – that means – until the resurrection ..."

She kissed his forehead lightly and touched his cheek lingeringly.

"Yes, Dan. Until the resurrection! Goodnight."


Dan and Etta watched Rhoda lead her to Asa's room, fussing over her mistress like a tiny hen with an enormous chick.

Etta took a shaking breath and made a helpless movement. Dan stood by her shoulder and rubbed her back thoughtfully. With a gesture of impatience Loukanos picked up the jug Rhoda had fetched so quickly, and poured recklessly.

"Here, Etta bath Amos! The rest of us need not abstain! I'll answer your questions about Asa staying in Jerusalem before you ask them, then you can try and explain away those abominable letters. Then I'll decide whether you're friend, foe or family – and tonight we can eat Dinah's chicken on a settled stomach."

Dan listened with grim satisfaction. At least Loukanos always cut straight to the point. Dan picked up his cup and saluted the lean handsome Greek and the stout old woman opposite him.

"To the truth!" he said firmly.

They saluted him in return, Etta gratefully, Loukanos ironically.

"To the truth!" they answered.

## Chapter Thirty-seven

BLIND Mordecai munched on the flat bread, scooping up the last luxurious dollops of spiced lentils from the wooden bowl around which Anna had pressed his fingers.

"You are one of the few who give me fresh food," he told her, wiping his mouth gratefully. "I grow tired of bread like stones, and addled eggs with a bite like a scorpion! Some would give me a sea-serpent for a fish if they thought I wouldn't notice, and still expect merit for alms-giving."

Anna did not answer. Last year she would have laughed with that delightful gurgle which was a treat to his ears. She was still there though – standing silently, no longer smelling of the fragrant oil she once used on her hair. He tried again, dropping his bantering tone.

"I am glad you are back, Anna bath Asa," he said quietly. "I know you have suffered much, and they say you are now a Nazirite. Is this true?"

"Yes."

Still she stood there – praying? Weeping? Watching? Why did she not walk away?

Carefully Mordecai stretched out his hand and touched the hem of her robe. Yes, the usual fringe was there, the fabric was

491

the light wool she favoured, and not harsh sack-cloth as he had feared. His fingers brushed her feet so lightly they might have been a passing fly. Her feet were not bare. Good. He tugged her dress gently.

"Lady? Will you deign to sit with me a moment? It is very early, the streets are bare, none will comment."

A gentle sigh above his head, and she did so. Mordecai could feel her breath just above his hair. Her silence disturbed him, and he probed carefully.

"The bitter waves have advanced and retreated and advanced again! – and near drowned you, have they not? First your mother – then your betrothed – and now as they retreat again you fear another blow and hold your breath?"

There was a pause.

"You too have been to the Great Sea," she murmured. "It is exactly as you say. The waves boom there like thunder … As they retreat the water rushes back past your feet, dragging away the sand on which you stand – and while you watch, they make you dizzy. You turn to run, your feet are sinking – and while you stagger, the next wave breaks over your head to choke you with its bitter water."

Mordecai put down the bowl. "You have been reading too much Job, I suspect, and must reread the final chapter. Tell me – what does a Nazirite do for her safety on the shore of sorrow?" He wished he could see her face.

She folded her hands carefully, deliberately, studying the blue network of veins under the sallow skin, and replied in a low voice.

"Shall I lift my eyes to the hills? From whence comes my safety? The Lord Adonai is my salvation in time of trouble, and in prayer He is my strength."

"Aye, so a Nazirite prays," the beggar replied, deliberately offhand. "Good. So should we all – and …?"

She bit her lip, but the revelations which had crept upon her in the sleepless nights would not be denied, and tumbled forth.

"And sometimes is too busy praying about her own fear and misery to see it in others! In my selfishness I let Dan and his aunt return home after the first seven days of mourning, and did not go to them later when they wrote for help. I – I gave money instead of myself. Detestable! Had I gone to share their troubles in person, I would have discovered from the very first that their begging letters were forgeries, written by that perfidious Bukki! They were badly written, but Dan and Etta have had scant schooling … I did not expect more … but I was too weak even to question this extraordinary change in their characters – it was easier simply to forgive their importunity – and imagine I was being compassionate, even generous. In so doing, I wronged them terribly … and allowed Bukki to go on and become hardened in his crime. I did him no favours either in this."

"You had become very ill," Mordecai reminded her gently.

She shrugged. Unseen, yet he sensed it.

"I was selfish there too – selfish to whet the sharpness of my pain by spurning food and warmth and rest, refusing to let anyone help me or give me comfort. I fancied this was pious courage – such nonsense! I did not stop to consider what distress I caused my poor father, who may have lost me as well."

"Yes, perhaps selfish," the blind man softly replied, a shadowy tower of his own selfish deeds rising to reproach him. "But where is it written how a woman must grieve?"

Anna folded her arms around her knees like a child and rested her chin on them. It was a relief to talk to someone whose gaze you did not have to meet. Confession was easier, and the burden of being seen as better than she was, must be laid down before it crushed her.

"I am a coward, Mordecai, am I not?" she said drearily. "I have been hiding, wrapped in my sorrow and a stream of prayers which at times have been mere shrieks of desperation – almost afraid to move lest something hurts or breaks. And yet at other times I have felt such rebellion! Wild, frantic impulses to do dreadful, destructive things – extraordinary, desperate thoughts such as I have never thought before and never wish to again – bizarre thoughts which are so contrary to Godliness of any kind they astound me. I don't know where they come from and they frighten me."

Mordecai breathed, "Ah yes! Ah, yes!"

"You know?"

He nodded. "So I was when I lost my sight. I mourned as tenderly and bitterly for myself as if I had died. And I was angry – oh yes! Angry and rebellious with it. I, Mordecai the Good!" He gave a sardonic snort. "I too had no idea of what slept beneath my untested goodness!"

Anna picked up the wooden bowl and toyed with it, spinning it around with her finger like a child's top.

"I have become a Nazirite out of fear, Mordecai," she said slowly, letting the bowl spin down to a wobbling stop. "I am afraid

494

of my thoughts, afraid of myself. I cannot confess this to my father, who thinks I am strong enough for both of us. My brother would only scoff." Her voice faded.

Patiently Mordecai waited – she would not stop here – and after a time she continued quietly,

"I have taken on this discipline of my body in order to make me discipline my mind towards the only place where any lasting happiness lies. I *know* that I must go further, I just don't know *how* yet. But there is one thing which I have struggled with, and have now come to understand … a thing I knew before in my head, but now feel in my very bones – and it is this. That devotion to the Eternal – as a Nazirite or not – is expressed more than anything in living devoutly. Not knowledge, or deeds, or obedience to jots and tittles … *Living*, not existing in a sanctified cave where none go in or out."

"Aye – and more than living!" Mordecai said abruptly, reluctantly, out of his own wrestlings the day before. "Living *joyously!*"

"Oh – but how can that be possible," Anna whispered, a heavy tear swelling over the rim of her hazel eye. "I am so weary of hearing *'life goes on!'* yet I bow to its truth – but now you say living *joyously?*"

The brown eye brimmed unnoticed, two drops clinging to the lower lashes like dew on frost-blackened grass.

Mordecai tugged his crinkled greying beard, trampling ferociously through his mind, beating its bushes for the quarry which eluded him. The knowledge which had escaped – half-forgotten words which would help them both! It had been so long … so long … Of what help now was his once-precious Mishnah and its half a dozen Sedarim – its sixty three webs, five hundred and twenty five chapters and four thousand one hundred and eighty seven verses! *Pah!* What he needed was an arrow flying cleanly out of scripture to pierce the heart. Translation – translation! – of principle into action! *Eternal Creator of the Universe, speak to me through Thy word! Help me to help this charitable daughter of Israel and give me peace of mind for myself!*

With a surge of something surprisingly like excitement he found what he sought. He grasped one of the sky blue tassels on Anna's hem and jerked it suddenly.

"Walking in the circle of blue!" He spoke roughly, startling her. "What is that about?"

"Walking – in holiness – as if in heaven – in the presence of God ..." Anna stammered.

"Aye! What is in the presence of God, Anna bath Asa? Tell me that? Misery? Darkness? Pain? Resentment? Anger? What is in the presence of God?"

"Light ... beauty ..." Anna faltered,

" ... glory ... purity ... peace ... joy ... *Oh!*"

She covered her face with her hands and took a deep breath.

"Is the Eternal distressed and pained by sin and death, ugliness and misery?" Mordecai continued relentlessly. "Yes! But in His presence is eternal joy, eh? How so? Because the immortality of His Goodness overrides the mere mortality of our evil day! Let us walk in that knowledge! You will embrace your Ammiel again – and your mother – and I will have my eyes, eh? Do we believe this or not? *Do* we? Then let's live as if we do and praise God for it!"

Anna buried her face in her arms, her heart swelling – the morbid wave of bitterness, which she had been trying so long to control, rising up, spilling out and breaking in a healing gush of tears. Mordecai sat listening to her sobs, his grimy hands gripped together. It was not for such as he to as much as touch her shoulder in comfort. He settled his face ready for when she should lift her head. It was long enough for the street to be heard waking to morning life. Slowly the shaking body beside him calmed, and the final gasps became long trembling breaths. Mordecai's expression became resolutely neutral.

"Praise God for *you*, Mordecai," Anna said brokenly at last. She pulled a handkerchief from her belt and blew her nose resolutely. "I have been a self-absorbed creature ... thinking I was battling bravely ... and all the while locked in a fortress, fighting through a keyhole. I need to break out – get up into the tower – and see the whole war in perspective."

Mordecai nodded slowly. "Selah. Take it to a high place, and consider."

Up, out of the depths! Fly to the high place – to the tower! Why, passivity was not enough. He saw it now. How could he ever have thought that meekly accepting his fate earned him merit! The Eternal demanded more of a man! Despite all his cleverness, he had never realized it before. Until a woman sat in the dust beside him and confessed her wretchedness.

Anna looked at the sun – she took a deep breath, steady this time, wiping her eyes. She must get back – wash her face – Dan must not see that she had been weeping. There was a ripping sound as she tore the tassel from her band of blue –and tucked it firmly into Mordecai's fingers.

"A talisman for a good friend. Pray for me whenever you laugh at finding it in your purse – and I will pray for you whenever I see the gap in my hem."

She got to her feet in one lithe movement.

"Wait." Blind Mordecai lifted a hand. "Do you have any books of the law?"

"Yes, we are fortunate – we have all five, the Psalms, Job and most of the prophets as well."

Mordecai whistled enviously. "For me, the letters fade, since sight cannot refresh my memory. But when you are able, take the fifth book ..."

"Yes?"

He handed back the wooden bowl. "Halfway through the Cursings you will find the reason – the only reason – why such terrors would be brought upon us. It's a milestone for direction if ever I knew one. I'm grateful to you for reminding me."

And Mordecai waited until he heard the wicket gate creak closed, before he took the heavy blue tassel in his hand, and – lightly as a woman's fingertips – stroked it softly across his mutilated cheeks. She would pray for him! He touched it to his lips and winced. *Now – hypocrite! – look what you must live up to!*

An hour later, her eyes still unhappy from the onions she had hastened to peel when cold water had not disguised the traces of her tears, Anna unrolled the heavy scroll of Deuteronomy before Dan and Etta's respectful faces. A whole scroll of the law! Dan had never seen one outside a synagogue. Aunt Etta smiled at him. *How like dear Anna to give the boy such a special thing to do just before we leave!* While Aunt Etta listened proudly, Anna sat Dan beside her and helped him stumble slowly through the lines. *Oh, but the boy must return to school soon! The sheep will always be there, but the time to learn easily will be lost!* Yes, there it was, Mordecai's milestone. She made Dan read it again and he read more surely this time.

*"All these curses shall descend on thee, and heap up and overrun thee to destruction, because thou hearkened not to the voice of Adonai thy God to keep his commandments and statutes – these curses which shall be an everlasting sign and wonder upon thy seed – because thou served not Adonai thy God with joyfulness, and with gladness of heart, for the abundance of all things."*

Dan looked up with glowing eyes. "Look at that, Aunt Etta! I always thought the curses were a punishment for wickedness. But they are for not having joy and gladness of heart!"

Aunt Etta was trying to puzzle that out, when Loukanos butted in, looking up from the sketch he was openly making of Aunt Etta's gnarled hands.

"So He's not so savage after all," he commented, blowing charcoal dust off his papyrus. "You can sin as long as you're happy about it."

Dan gave him an indignant look. "Of course not! He doesn't say to be joyful about sinning – He wants gladness in *serving* Him."

Loukanos winked at Anna and Dan caught him at it.

"You already know what it means!" he accused, exasperated.

"Well, good," Aunt Etta said drily. "Perhaps he can explain it to me."

"Perhaps he can," invited Anna cautiously, looking sidelong at her brother.

He shrugged good-humouredly and rubbed the charcoal critically with his thumb. "It's about gratitude. If you are joyful for *His* gifts, you want to make Him joyful with *yours*, as it were.

499

A person with that attitude may sin out of weakness, but won't hold their God in contempt."

Aunt Etta sniffed. "Thank you, Loukanos. You have just explained why Bukki has sunk so low."

Dan raised his eyes, and Aunt Etta softened her contemptuous expression to look at him regretfully. "I'm afraid he never was grateful for his blessings, Dan – and ended up with no respect for those who gave them."

"Yes," Anna said softly. "It is a terrible trap to be ungrateful. No wonder the Eternal commands that we praise Him for His goodness continually."

"Can you do that even now, Anna?" Loukanos asked with frank and faintly challenging curiosity.

Anna put her chin in her hands and leant her elbows on the table, staring down at the scroll before them.

"I thought I had been doing it," she said slowly, "until I talked to Blind Mordecai, and realised I was only thanking Him with my head and not my heart. Now I will lift my head – and praise the Eternal for the happiness I had, and not despair for what I lost."

On a rare impulse, Loukanos put an arm around her shoulders and pulled her close, resting his shaven cheek briefly against her patchy hair. Her left arm went around him even as she reached out for Dan, who rubbed his face on her sleeve like a yearling lamb, and had his right hand imprisoned in Aunt Etta's.

"And I will praise Him for the long years of comfort and love my brother gave me." Etta was determined to back her up.

Dan felt it and racked his brains

"I praise Him for making my father in the first place!" he offered. For a fleeting moment the four were linked in mutual sympathy, but then Loukanos laughed.

"Is it my turn? Well then, perhaps I should praise Him for a blind man who has made my sister see good in evil. Roll up your scroll now, and have Dinah find me an inkhorn, or Asa will get an unreadable letter in charcoal smudges. I must write at once and tell him how that preposterous Bukki deceived us all."

"May I please add a few lines to Johanan?" Dan asked eagerly and Loukanos nodded. Dan ran to the kitchen for Old Dinah, who was outside, scrubbing with sand the clay pot in which the chicken had been baked the night before. In her absence the ink was found by Rhoda, who had been as much agog as Dan when Loukanos told them about his stepfather refusing to leave Jerusalem.

"You will stay with your sister in Cana," Asa had said to Loukanos. "And I will remain with mine here in Jerusalem. I don't want to tie Anna to me now any more than before, and besides this, I need to be needed, not coddled. Mari does need me, and so does Johanan – especially now he's growing to manhood with no father and too many servants. The lad needs a man with authority in the house or he will be quite spoiled. As for Anna – you will see to it that she uses her vow for good in her life, and not evil. Do not allow her to slip into melancholy – keep her busy – make her laugh. And remember the goal of finding the Messiah!"

Loukanos nodded. "Sometimes I think your experience is worth all my medicines. I agree with you about Anna. The time of shock and disbelief is over – and it is time she began to look about her lest she stay dazed for ever. Do you think this vow will help her?"

Asa pulled at his lower lip meditatively. "I do – it was at least a decision for beginning a new life, and she had her reasons. It is a good thing for her, but she will still need encouragement."

This last part of the conversation, Loukanos had not relayed to the others, but he thought it over now. While Dan was busy labouring over his letter to Johanan – whom Dan sensed would be a little dismayed to inherit his quick-witted Uncle Asa as a permanent fixture – Loukanos slipped outside to the beggar's corner.

"I don't know what you said to my sister," he said soberly, "but you have put a light back into her eyes and made me less anxious over her. Is there any way I can thank you?"

Mordecai heard the ready chink of coins and shook his head vehemently.

"Not money."

Loukanos paused, surprised. Mordecai was not usually slow in accepting alms.

"Do you mean what you ask me?" the blind man asked abruptly.

Loukanos jerked his glossy black waves proudly. "Of course."

"Then help me get to hear Johannes the prophet."

The physician raked his sensitive fingers through his thick hair and groaned inwardly. This country – these people – had a common fixation! And he had just *returned* from the south a week ago! But the man had done a service that day, more valuable than he could suspect, and Loukanos had given his word. Besides, perhaps it would do Anna good to hear fresh news of the prophet, and maybe old Etta and Dan might stay on to fuss over her nicely while he went. Yes, that would be a good plan. No need for Anna to retrace her steps – anyway, it would not be wise until she was stronger.

"Very well. I will take you myself."

Mordecai clutched Loukanos by the knees in a convulsive movement of joy.

"Thank you, brother! A man of honour! Praise the Eternal!"

Loukanos detached himself carefully.

"Not so much of the *'brother'*, Mordecai. I'm a Greek."

Mordecai found the bandage on his eyes had damp edges. It had been a long time since he had been surprised into such emotion.

"Ah!" he retorted. "Not so much of the *Greek*, Loukanos! You're a brother in my adversity."

Loukanos snorted fiercely to cover an inconvenient stab of gratification.

"I will come for you in two days." He strode back to the house.

It was only when he saw Rhoda packing cold drumsticks and pickles into a satchel for Dan and Etta's journey home that Loukanos realised his mistake. The fishmonger Philip was calling for them in an hour and they would be on their way. Taking Mordecai to the Baptist was just not practical! He had forgotten that Dan was not a carefree child these days. He had to go back to work, and Etta would not want to stay behind for another week without him.

What to do? Loukanos would not leave Anna alone, nor could he take her all the way back to Jerusalem! But he had given his word. Not only that, he remembered with a jolt, he had promised Helen not to leave Anna's side. He was not fool enough to take this completely literally – a day or two away would sometimes be unavoidable, and be neither here nor there – but he must not leave her for a whole week or more. Especially as she was not yet strong. *Zeus take it! – a man can't be in two places at once!*

"If I had a beard I'd pull it!" he muttered crossly, and stamped back into the now-busy street to confess his difficulty to Mordecai. His shoulder was jolted rudely by a passer by.

"Mind your step, sir!" cried Samson, the tiny weaver (whose diminutive parents had named him with touching optimism) staggering past with a brightly patterned roll of carpet balanced on his bald little head. Loukanos looked down at him with a grin, despite his exasperation.

"Well met, Samson," he said ironically, rubbing his shoulder. "What news?"

Samson paused and wheeled round, puffing. Two dumpy young women squawked as the rolled carpet clipped them unexpectedly on the head, and they scuttled away, tongues clattering angrily. Samson swung around in alarm at their cries and thumped Loukanos on the other shoulder.

"By the stars! Hold still, man!" Loukanos snatched the heavy roll hastily and forced the little man to stop his dangerous manouevres. "We'd all be knocked senseless if you grew another span."

The carpet slid to the ground.

"News," Samson panted, unconcerned. This sort of thing happened all the time. People should just look out, that's all. Did a man have eyes on stalks like a snail? He mopped his itching scalp with a cloth … clay-coloured skin impressed like a signet seal, with a pattern of knots from his handiwork.

504

"Nothing much new in Cana. But the Baptizer has been driving the Pharisees down south frantic. Heh, heh! They even sent priests – and brother Levites – to him, and demanded some answers!"

"What answers?" Loukanos was briefly curious.

"Answers to some direct questions … for a change! Such as *Are you the Messiah – yes or no?*" Samson rubbed his sunburnt neck which was aching. *Hi-yi!*, a man grew old too soon!

"He said No, not the Messiah. And he's not Elijah. Nor the prophet promised by Moses. Oh, they were frustrated all right! If he wasn't any of them – *what did he think he was doing?* Heh, heh! A lone Levite stirring up the countryside and never a word about the knots in their carpet!"

"Speak plainly, tadpole!" grumbled Loukanos. "Knots in their carpet?"

Samson pulled his own carpet from the tall man and hoisted it back to its original position.

"They make a pretty pattern for themselves out of the law," he puffed. "Oh, very pretty tufts on top – yes, it all looks very fine … but how's the picture made? Underneath, that's how – by millions of hard little knots of tradition, tightly tied! Terrified of loose ends, they are. Heh, heh! And where's the real law and commandments from the Eternal, hey?"

"You tell me!" Loukanos rolled his eyes impatiently.

Samson chuckled again.

"Hidden, that's what! Why, it's the canvas in the middle! Pray the Eternal it will still be there when the pretty bits which stab it through are rubbed bare! Heh, heh! Well, the Baptist's moved up river from Perea to Decapolis now to get out of their hair. He's preaching at Bethabara now, they say."

Loukanos started.

"Bethabara?" he cried.

Samson stared at him. *What a strange fellow he is, to be sure. His nerves must be stretched as long as his legs.*

"Yes – the place of passage – house of the ferryboat – you know it?"

Loukanos gave a shout of laughter.

"I do – and it's less than thirty miles away!" he gloated. "On your way, Samson! I apologise sincerely for calling you a tadpole!"

Samson nodded cheerfully, causing the carpet to dip and rise, and clout an unlucky dog which was scavenging scraps. As it yelped indignantly down the street, Loukanos loped back to the house in time to put his new plan to the others. Anna's eyes glinted. She would eat, she would rest, swallow potions, anything the doctor ordered, anything – but she would not be left behind! Loukanos felt her pulse, rejoiced at her heightened colour – and gave in. If she came, and stayed with Etta, he and Mordecai could continue on to Bethabara without haste.

An hour later, Philip the Younger found to his astonishment that he had not two but *five* people to accompany his journey to Banayim. He was even more astonished that one of them was the man who gave Blind Corner its name.

"I'm turning into a caravan!" he complained loudly at the sight of the extra donkeys, but inwardly was delighted. Perhaps he should bring Aida next time and make a thorough holiday of it, he joked to himself. Loukanos explained that Dan would rejoin the shepherds along the way. The rest would go on to Etta's where there was plenty of room for them all to stay overnight. In the morning, Loukanos and Blind Mordecai could set out early straight down the Jordan valley to the crossing of Bethabara and be back in a couple of days. Simple – it was all going to be quite simple, he reassured them.

Nobody argued with this logic, and Anna again declared herself quite fit to sit on a beast for a few hours. Blind Mordecai was enraptured with every step, laughing loudly at every mishap with his donkey, to which he clung like a limpet, unable to believe his good fortune, and treasuring every new scent and sound for the blank years ahead. Dan ran off happily as they met up with the shepherds, (Moses gambolling to meet him like a long lost brother), proud that Anna could see he was learning his trade like a man. The adults were glad to see him so cheerfully rejoining his rough life without a murmur.

A few hours later, they were even gladder that Dan had left them. The little chain of donkeys was creaking around the last curve of the limestone hill near Banayim, when Mordecai lifted his head and sniffed exploratively.

"There's been a fire here," he announced, but by then the others knew.

Before them was once Etta's house of mudbrick and stone – crumbled, blackened, a breeze breathing fine ash into the air from the ruins, giving the illusion that they were still smoking. There was a little low moan, and Etta's heavy body slumped from her animal. Loukanos sprang to her side but could not hold her weight. Stocky Philip leapt forward to help, and the two men lowered her gently to the ground.

Mordecai cried out for information as Loukanos examined Etta's eyes, pulse, and bones and Philip hurried to survey the ruins.

Anna obliged, her voice calm as she knelt over the crumpled old woman and straightened her disarranged clothes.

"Poor Etta has swooned with shock. She's not hurt and will soon recover. But her house is burned to the ground."

"Another blow!" Mordecai was stunned. "Yet another wave beats upon you!"

Anna drew herself up with decision.

"No, Mordecai," she said slowly. "Not this time. Praise the Eternal – nobody has died."

"Where will you go now?" Philip called as he ran back to them. "Nothing is salvageable here. And the walls will be dangerous."

Anna was loosening the veil around Etta's plump neck. Loukanos had raised Etta's knees on her wool cushion. She stirred and Loukanos nodded, pleased.

"We will all go to my house!" said Anna suddenly. She looked up at Philip. "My house by the shore."

## Chapter Thirty-eight

RETURNING to Cana with his fish, Philip the Younger spied the sheep and goats in the hillside pasture sooner than he wanted. Glumly he wished somebody else had the task of telling such bad news to a mere lad.

"Burnt?" Dan gasped. "How? I put out the fire so carefully! Is it *all* gone?"

As Philip nodded miserably, Dan turned to Caleb, who stood dismayed and unbelieving, and wept tears of shock on his scrawny chest.

Caleb's faded eyes were full of distress. *Alas for Dan! Alas for Etta! Alas for the house where I ate so well – which was built with joy by my friend and master! May he rest in peace!*

"Don't cry, Dan, don't cry," urged the old man painfully – tears pouring down his own cheeks as the boy's forlorn body shook against him. He sniffed desperately, stroking Dan's head awkwardly with his big hands. "We must not despair for a house – which can be rebuilt, eh? The Eternal gives, the Eternal takes away, you know. Blessed be the name of the Eternal."

So murmuring, he drew the lad aside.

Samuel stopped shaking his head at last. He looked at Philip blankly.

"What now, fishmonger?"

"What now indeed, shepherd!" Philip said uncomfortably. "The boy has had a hard time of it in the last year. Next he will be imagining he caused the fire himself."

Samuel shook his head. "Brought up by an old woman? I never saw a boy so careful with fires! If he said it was out, it was."

Philip lurched sideways as the Queen of Sheba shoved him heavily, trying to reach the figs in his scrip. "You know, Anna believes he ought to be a schoolboy, not a man before his time, but what can be done? He is not her son, and the flock is his inheritance."

Samuel sighed. "There's no easy answer to that. And now there is the problem of where old Etta will live. Some of the flock must be sold to pay for a new house, however small. And not even that miserable Bukki to help in the building." He caught Eli's eye, and beckoned him over. "We are Etta's friends, are we not?" he continued. "Her brother was as my brother – his son as my nephew. We must think this over together. Can you spare an hour?"

Philip cocked a bushy eyebrow at the sky as Eli obediently jumped to his feet and ran up to them, eager to find out what was wrong with young Dan. "A cold crisp day for Spring – so, yes I can – but only an hour. I have lost time already. The days are longer, the market earlier, my sleep shorter and my temper with it. Aida declares I am unbearable come high summer and will take to me with a carpet beater if I don't get home by the sixth hour after noon."

510

Samuel grunted understandingly. Wives were obsessed with time – until *they* had to be governed by it, when miraculously they could stretch it out as they pleased.

He put a hand on Eli's shoulder. "Son – stand with us for a moment. We may need a young fellow's ideas, and Dan is in no state to make suggestions. We'll leave him to Old Caleb and they can comfort each other while we decide how to help his family."

Eli felt a glow of pride as he nodded. At last his father was seeing him as more than a hired hand. He straightened his shoulders, listened hard, and resolved to astound them with his astuteness.

Dan and Caleb crouched together against the rocks of the fold which held the perfect lambs and their mothers, their first stormy outburst of grief finally subsiding.

"That's right, lad," Caleb encouraged them both, wiping his rough sleeve across his eyes and creating clean smears on his craggy face. "A time to weep, and a time to refrain from weeping, eh? A time for everything, the wise king said – so a time to build up will be next, you'll see."

He mopped quickly at two more tears which sprang from his eyes at the sight of Dan's wretchedness. *Alas, my dear master! A poor comforter I must be to your boy, but who could stand in for you, my friend?*

Dan cradled Moses in his arms and buried his face in the shaggy little coat. The lamb lay unprotesting as Dan squeezed him hard at every fresh remembrance of the house which had been his only home. As for Old Caleb, he contented himself by grinding his remaining teeth at every recollection, not of the home, but of Bukki. Dan had told the whole story of the letters, and

Caleb was soon darkly convinced that Bukki was at the bottom of the mysterious fire.

"But he left the house before we did," Dan said unhappily. "It couldn't have been he. What do you think happened? I know I was careful. I know I was!"

"Hush, boy!" Caleb patted his back. "Of course you were. But who knows what happened once you left? Perhaps one of your auntie's friends called to see her – and opened the door – a draught? A little dry grass whirled in by the breeze and – pouf! – up in smoke?"

Dan shook his head firmly. "I doused it, Caleb. The ashes were wet! What about lightning?"

Caleb sighed. "Well, Dan, not likely – there's been no rain, no storm since you left. Perhaps if we looked at the ruins we would find a clue somewhere, but I doubt it."

Dan gave Moses another fierce hug and rubbed his cheek on the alert, bony little head. Moses nibbled hopefully at his ear and nuzzled his wet nose in Dan's neck.

"Philip says Anna has taken Aunt Etta and the men to her house on the shore. I wish I could go to Aunt Etta, Caleb," he said, swallowing hard. "She will be crying over all her burnt things. Especially her lovely shelves."

Inwardly he was still crying himself – for the memories which would never again be evoked by familiar shapes and textures. For the rough plastered wall upon which he used to watch the shadow play of his aunt … and his beloved father … (Dan expunging from the scenes his now detested uncle) in the lamplight. The rough twig and reed ceiling hung with herbs and ladles, spoons, a broom, an old crook, the mat beater. The empty place in the

512

corner where Ammiel had slept, and towards which Dan had for months sent a silent good night every time Aunt Etta blew out the lamp, every time the shepherds on the hills banked the night fires and rolled into their thick mantles. The lower level where precious or sickly animals shared hard winters. The stillness of the empty long room which was to have hosted the wedding banquet – which was to have been furnished and made homely by Anna's own hands. The glistening whitewash on the newly plastered walls which made the house look like giant cubes of cheese ... But he would not miss the sagging, drunken, half finished booth which spoke too plainly of Bukki's broken promises.

Dan bit his lip and rubbed his cold face on Moses' hot little body. "Caleb?"

"Yes, lad?"

"I feel as if I have – lost ... even more ... pieces ... of my father ... with the house," he whispered.

Caleb's arm tightened around Dan's hunched shoulders and he sighed again, deeply.

"Aye, Dan – I know what you mean. It's hard to separate them, eh? Well, thanks to him – and Etta – it was a rare place for hospitality of the soul as well as body. I will miss your house too and no mistake. But Ammiel will never be lost, lad. Not a jot. Out with the sheep like this you'll have plenty to remind you, eh? You'll have him always in your mind as long as you live, and one day he'll put his arms around us both – come the glad day when mourning turns to dancing. The Eternal has promised, boy."

His throat tight, Dan welcomed the pressure of the stringy arm about him and nestled closer to the old man who shared his sorrow so sincerely. The man, the boy and the lamb were so huddled when the sturdy Eli ran up. In the distance, Philip was moving away, raising an arm in farewell and glad to go before having to see the boy's stricken face again.

"Get your things, Dan," ordered Samuel's eldest with a friendly grin. "Father's sending you home."

"But – I just got here today!" Dan scrambled to his feet in consternation. "Have I done something wrong?"

Eli laughed and shook his head. "He thinks your Aunt Etta needs you more than we do at the moment. You're to take her this cheese, too."

Dan's sad eyes lit up, but not because of the cheese.

Caleb gave a snaggle-toothed smile. "Run along, Dan boy."

"You'd better run along yourself," Eli nodded to him. "He's not going alone."

Old Caleb gave a cry of joy and hurried to Samuel.

"Can you spare us, Samuel? " he asked anxiously. "What of lambing?"

Samuel picked his teeth with a thumbnail, carelessly. "Get along, old man. The sheep are all done but for a handful, and the goats are my affair. We're not moving for a week anyway. Come back then without fail or I'll see to it you're back in the market – crook in hand and wool pinned to your coat, awaiting hire by a master who'll beat you."

So threatening with a twinkle in his eye and a thump on the back, Samuel dismissed two of his most willing workers. When they were out of earshot he said quietly to Eli,

"Send Shaul to Ephraim in the next valley, will you, son? A perfect passover lamb for his collection if he'll lend me a good man for a week, and I'll pay the wages myself."

514

Aunt Etta buried Dan in a mutually damp embrace, then proceeded to work at making him smile by comically describing how she had fainted and fallen off her donkey. Loukanos caught the boy's sharp look of inquiry over Etta's head, and gave him a *thumbs up* signal, forgetting it was all as good as Greek to the boy. Dan's puzzlement had Aunt Etta demanding explanations, so Loukanos explained about the Roman circuses, and gladiators, and how the Emperor would signal with his thumb that a man should live or die, and the roaring crowds would demand their say with their own thumbs up or down.

"Hmph!" was Aunt Etta's opinion of this disagreeable matter. "So I'll live then? Well, thank you kindly, and isn't that a relief!"

Caleb cackled, and the others smiled, even Dan. The little house was full of bodies – Blind Mordecai, Caleb, Loukanos, Aunt Etta, Anna and Dan – and full of bustle. Anna gave a thankful prayer for Johanan, who had thoughtfully swept and made up the fireplace before they had left the shore so long ago. Everything – though dusty – was ready for instant occupation, right down to the box of fuel in the corner. So had they arranged it to be ready for any charitable need. *And tonight we ourselves are the needy!* she thought with wry amusement. *Whoever would have thought it?*

Loukanos installed Mordecai safely in an angle of the stairs and set Caleb to talk to him, then made Aunt Etta rest in the upper room, where he squatted, questioning her in detail about her back, and making notes on a wax tablet. Dan was sent running off to borrow food from Marta and Ittai's at the end of the village.

Marta kissed him and cried over him a little, but she was a sensible young woman and put her tears away with the handkerchief very smartly when she recalled how fast the lad was growing. Recovering herself, she stuffed a heavy babe into Dan's

515

arms and set him to rubbing its gums with some foul-smelling tincture while she did the same with its twin.

"Dan, how can we tell you how sorry we are?" she said, as sadly as was possible while struggling with her fractious infant. "We all got such a fright when we saw the smoke, not realising at first that Etta had insisted on going to Cana with you after all. Half the village ran with buckets – even the Dabab herself – terrified until we read the chalk on the door, which was not yet burnt. There was nothing we could do to save the things inside – and afterwards it was almost worse. There was your house burnt to the ground, and a message to Cana was pointless! You would be almost ready to return anyway – and what good would it do? We decided to leave you to accomplish your visit with peace of mind. Did we do right, do you think?"

Dan ducked to avoid a blow from an enthusiastic little fist which was waving perilously close to his nose. He wiped his slimy fingers on the baby's gown and jiggled the child on his knee. It smelt most unpleasant – like the bucks in Samuel's herd.

"Yes," he said, after a moment's thought. "I think Aunt Etta would say the same. We couldn't have done anything – it would only have spoiled our visit – Oh, *no!*" He scowled at the babe, which was now grinning toothlessly, and gave Marta a pained look. "Your baby has just wet me. I think Moses has better manners."

Marta went off into a peal of laughter which stopped her asking who Moses was, but before long Dan was in a threadbare old tunic of Ittai's – well knotted up at the waist – and his own soaking in a glazed bowl of vinegar water.

"I'm sorry, Dan, but if I don't, it'll stink by morning," Marta confessed. "They've been eating a lot of goat curd lately and Hairy

Job *will* pen that disgusting old buck of his too close to the milking does. It makes the milk reek, and of course, the curd, and so the children, and so on ..."

"You should get it from Samuel," Dan advised in a superior fashion. "He's much more watchful of his bucks than Hairy Job, and Ada makes better curd anyway."

Marta smiled in her heart to hear Dan's display of knowledge, but she nodded seriously and promised to take his advice. Having heard all about Moses while finding dry clothes for both Dan and her chortling child, she insisted on having all the news from Cana while filling a basket with food.

"Dear Anna!" she said wonderingly. "A Nazirite! It's a long time since I heard of anyone taking this upon themselves. An unusual Nazirite she'll make too, with almost no hair, poor woman. Is her brother really sure it will come right one day? And he a *physician* – well, well! And fancy old Asa staying in Jerusalem to help his sister bring up Johanan, while Loukanos looks after *his* sister in Cana! What a turnaround for everyone." She piled flat bread into the basket and ladled a pot of barley soup. "It sounds like you have quite a houseful – a doctor and a blind beggar are unusual guests, hey, Dan?"

Dan scrambled up from the lower floor where in this house babies played safely instead of orphan lambs, and took the basket carefully, mindful of the soup.

"Thank you, Marta. Aunt Etta will be very glad of it. It was lucky she took her money with us, anyway. I suppose it would have melted in the fire. She'll repay you after market day, she said."

"Ouf! Nonsense!" Marta loaded him up with blankets and waved him off hastily. "Send her all my love. I would come at once, but the babes are a handful and your house must be busy enough. I will bring your clothes in the morning and find some spare for Etta if I can." She hopped down the step and pulled the babies into her lap. "Be warned, little ones," she told them seriously. "Your darling Amma will be delayed a long time at the well tomorrow with so much news to tell, so you be good for your Abba, do you hear me?" She lifted the little boy's shift and blew noisily on his wriggling body. "And that'll be one in the eye for the Dabab!" she chuckled suddenly.

Dan arrived back at Anna's house, lumbered with his basket, and clutching the slipping blankets draped around his neck. As he pushed the door open with his foot he heard Anna's low voice.

"What think you – Caleb? Loukanos? Mordecai? – of this note of Samuel's? I would know before I discuss matters with Etta."

"What note?" Dan cried. The mention of notes or letters made him nervous.

"Thank you, Dan!" Anna lifted the heavy blankets from his shoulders and took the basket. "There was a note for me from Samuel – tied in with the cheese." What a friend in need young Marta was! Bread, pickles, garlic, onions, even a cucumber! And soup! She put the pot by the fire.

"Nothing to fear, Dan boy," comforted Caleb. "You have good friends here. Good friends. A little patience."

Anna nodded and patted the bench next to her. Dan sat anxiously looking from one to the other. "Of course he must!" was Loukanos' decided opinion.

"I will be sad to lose him," Caleb said resignedly. "But it is best."

518

"Why do you ask a blind beggar?" Blind Mordecai was almost shocked. "A mere trespasser on your charity!"

"I have my reasons," was Anna's quiet reply. "Speak, if you please."

Mordecai leaned forward, turned his ruined face towards her and spread his hands deprecatingly. "Since you ask me … well, I agree with your friends. Already there is much ground to be made up, but if you can give some extra time to the basics, he will be glad of it later."

Dan was fizzing with impatience.

"Oh, what is it? Who are you talking about? Me? Eli? Moses?"

"Ssh!" Anna put her finger to her still pale lips and smiled at him reassuringly. "Aunt Etta must be consulted first. And even before then, we must eat."

She took the soup from the hearth to the table and looked around. It was her house now. And a man must ask the blessing. Not Loukanos of course … and Mordecai was overwhelmed enough …

"Caleb?" she asked gently. "Will you grace my new house by asking the first blessing?"

Caleb's eyes widened in amazement and his mouth fell open.

"Please," she said.

With a pounding heart, the old man closed his eyes. *Me! – an ignorant hireling, praying before a sophisticated Greek – and an educated Jewess?* Never had he imagined such an honour! But before the Eternal, was it not all the same? He lifted up his hands in a simple gesture to pray for the damaged folk whose individual suffering had brought them together in this unlikely group. A simple gesture –

519

and a simple, common prayer with an extra touch from lips which were now clay.

*"Blessed art Thou, Adonai our God, King of the world, who causes to come forth bread from the earth ..."* he quavered. *"Thou our Shepherd, lead us beside still waters, and show us thy Messiah. Amen."*

"Amen!" they responded. Anna's heart was full. She caught Dan's expression as he looked proudly at the old shepherd, and the tenderness she had always felt for the boy became love at that very moment. Was it for him alone? Was it for Ammiel? Who could tell? And did it matter? In her heart, Dan was as much hers as he was Etta's from then on.

"You remembered father's prayer!" Dan said gratefully, his face brightening.

Caleb nodded, a little abashed, and hid his face in his soup.

"Show Mordecai where the privy is, Dan," Loukanos instructed after the meal, "we have a little matter to discuss with your aunt over her dinner." He loaded a tray and whisked it upstairs, followed more sedately by Anna. She sent him back down almost at once, saying, "A little women's business first, please Louki. But when I call you, please bring Caleb up here as well."

Outside, wandering slowly about, Dan and Blind Mordecai breathed in the fresh night air. The discussion in the upper room was still going on. The moon was bright, and on a whim, Dan led the blind man to the water's edge, less than a stone's throw from the house. The water bit hard, but Blind Mordecai revelled in it and stripped to the skin. Up to his knees, Dan stood obediently as a marker while Mordecai knelt beside him to wash vigorously,

gasping happily with the cold. Oh! How wonderful! To be clean
– all over! He unwound the bandage from his eyes and plunged his
darkened face into the lake with relish, scrubbing the dust from his
hair and beard, squeezing out the drops, combing with his eager
fingers, rejoicing in the glorious abundance of fresh water. He
found Dan's elbow and they splashed back to the pebble strewn
beach.

Mordecai pulled on his clothes. Together they sat in the dark
listening to the murmur of the night wind and the gentle crisping
of wavelets, the lonely cry of a stray gull, the clucking of water
against worn rocks. The blind man took a lingering breath of the
fresh, moist air.

"Are there stars tonight, Dan? Will you describe them to me?
It is a long time since I have seen the stars."

Dan huddled his arms around his knees and gazed at the dark
shimmering sky which was brocaded with tiny gems – the
mysterious, far-off stars. How could he describe them so Mordecai
could see without eyes?

"They are high, high up, sharp and bright – like salt crystals
flashing in noon-day sun. The sky is very dark, and soft-looking,
but not really black. It's deep blue if you look very hard, with
purplish edges touching the hills. The stars are scattered over it
thickly – like, um, like sesame seed spilled on a blanket."

"*So shall thy seed be,*" murmured the blind man.

"Yes!" Oh, how it all came back to him, and how long ago it
seemed that he had struggled for understanding! Dan dug his
hardened heels and toes through the shingle into the sand, feeling
the large grains gritting against his sensitive instep.

*"As the sand which is on the sea shore for multitude,"* he added, and it was Mordecai's turn to nod.

"Aye, the promises!" he agreed wistfully. "If Messiah is really coming they will come to pass soon!"

"But he is!" Dan said eagerly. "He is here already. He will show himself soon, the prophet says so! Then we will know everything at last!"

Mordecai sighed. "I will hear Johannes the Baptizer soon and judge for myself. Go on about the stars."

Dan's heart missed a beat. *"Go on about the stars."* A phrase last heard in thick golden sunlight from a warm, rich voice filled with love and laughter, on a day of happy, careless anticipation. How different it sounded in a night of sadness, in this thin, cool starlight, in the cautious voice of a beggar he barely knew!

But why grudge anyone who asked so humbly? Dan would answer the blind man as carefully as if his father was listening. "They sparkle – like hoar frost at sunrise," the boy continued obediently, squinting hard and hunting for words. "Some are white and pointy. Some are more smudged and faintly coloured … blue, or pale red … a few just glow without twinkling. Some look like bright dust, and others are big sparks. Each is tiny – but altogether, they fill the sky. They're beautiful. Oh! And there's one falling! – it's gone!"

Dan felt a lump rising in his throat. The falling star had recalled a high, falling lamp … and his father. One of the seed, and therefore one of the stars. A bright light in his life which fell and vanished. "Gone," he whispered to himself painfully.

Mordecai heard. "Your house?"

"My father." Dan hadn't believed there would still be any tears left to cry.

Mordecai was slowly refolding his eye bandage. One day he would tell Dan about the night Ammiel shared his mat, and his trust. But not tonight.

"Not gone for long, young man. *Precious in the eyes of the Eternal is the death of his chosen ones,* you know. So says the Psalmist. Everything about your father is treasured in the mind of his Creator, all ready to be recreated the moment the resurrection command trumpets forth, do you see? *Precious.* The Eternal doesn't lose His treasure. *They shall be mine, in the day when I claim my special treasure,* Dan. That's Malachi for you."

Dan was silent for a long time, the brief spurt of tears already dry. His father – precious in the eyes of the Eternal! Oh, what a wonderful thought that was. How did the blind beggar know so much! But the man wasn't born a beggar. Who knew what other knowledge he had? Just then, the disfigured man turned his face longingly up to the moon, and by a trick of the light, Dan suddenly saw among its shadows the face Mordecai once possessed. It was gone just as suddenly, leaving Dan with a new understanding which was hard to put into words. This was not a blind beggar – this was a man. There was a long pause. Mordecai grunted and carefully, reluctantly, replaced his bandage.

"Mordecai?" Dan said quietly at last, with an odd new note of respect, "Do you know why stars fall? And what happens when they do? Or what they are?"

"No-one really knows."

"I asked my father, once. That's what he said, too."

"Then he was right."

"I said they might be bits of sun, because they're like the bits of the sun you see through a screen of leaves ..." Dan offered shyly. Mordecai smiled slowly.

"Good. I like that." The boy thought for himself. He hoped they wouldn't spoil him.

"Thanks, Dan, for being my eyes tonight." They got to their feet. "Just for a moment, as you spoke, I almost believed I was seeing the night for myself. That was a gift worth more than alms."


Back inside, Dan was called upstairs to the dim chamber where the others waited. Aunt Etta, propped up with cushions in the very spot where once Dan had lain unconscious, was looking well and almost happy. Her eyes suspiciously bright, she held out her hands.

"Dan – you are a lucky boy to have such kind friends. And I am a lucky woman. Praise God for His blessings, Dan! For He is truly good to us in our adversity!"

Confused, Dan looked at his aunt, Anna, Loukanos, Caleb. Anna had said Aunt Etta was to be consulted about something before he was told. The men had been giving their opinions about it. What was it? He waited for the explanation. But first there was something which the men had not known of.

"Dan, " Anna asked carefully, "you were glad once – were you not? – for me to become your new mother?"

"Yes," he answered, wondering.

"Would you still accept me as such, even though your father is gone?" she asked, trembling.

"Yes," he answered simply. There was no need to think about it. Thoughts, dreams, wishes and impossibilities – they had all been in his mind for a long time … why hesitate when they suddenly took shape!

Her voice shook as she took his hand, and Etta's.

"Then you are my son from now on. And Etta is my sister." Now she raised her voice so that Mordecai downstairs could hear her, and spoke firmly. "You men here are my witnesses before God, that I take Dan ben Ammiel, and Etta bath Amos as my own family from this day forth."

"We are witnesses."

"Amen," added Loukanos unexpectedly.

Etta put out her sagging arms to embrace Anna and Dan both. The moment was too deep even for tears. She looked over Anna's ugly hair to Loukanos, with an unfathomable expression.

"I know," he responded flatly. "But I'm in this too – and who are we to deny Anna?" He leaned over and dropped a smacking kiss on her grey head. "So, like it or not – welcome to the family." He turned Dan's glowing face up towards him roughly.

"Yes, Loukanos?" Dan said timidly, and Loukanos plucked him from Etta's arms, growling, "That's *Uncle* Loukanos to you!" while Caleb cackled delightedly and the tension was broken in a gale of laughter.

Downstairs they tumbled in a turmoil of irrepressible feeling, where a refreshed Mordecai – who had heard every astounding word and joined in the affirmation loudly – suddenly pulled a reed pipe from his belt – Caleb grabbed two brass plates for cymbals – Anna snatched up the lamps to set them safely on the stairs – and already Loukanos was throwing up his head, calling a beat, lifting his arms with easy grace to snap his fingers in invitation – beginning to dance elegantly around the crowded table, crossing his ankles back and forth in a lilting shuffle – pulling Anna after him, followed by a laughing Dan. As they stepped and turned and beat the time with their feet, Mordecai took his lips from the pipe and sang – the clear carrying voice of a man who had once led synagogues in sacred song –

*"God has turned my mourning into dancing for me*
*He has taken off my sackcloth!*
*He has turned my mourning into dancing!"*

*Clap-clap-clap!* went three pairs of hands, *clock-clock-clock!* went the wooden pipe against a stool, *tang-tang-tang!* went Caleb's brass – then Aunt Etta's voice came warbling determinedly down the stairs to join in the refrain, and Dan laughed harder than ever to hear the rhythmic slapping together of sandals – worn on her hands – as if she was dancing herself.

*"God has turned my mourning into dancing for me*
*He has clothed me with gladness!*
*He has turned my mourning into dancing!"*

Dizzily Dan remembered Caleb's words, earlier in that day which had been so dreadful, and was now so strangely happy. The day when mourning turns to dancing had sounded so far off and impossible – but the night was not yet over and here they were doing it already! Oh yes, it was true that something new and good just kept on happening, and today, just when you need it! How could you not praise God?

*"God has turned my mourning into dancing for me!*
*Now I sing His praises unsilenced.*
*He has clothed me with gladness!*
*Adonai my God – forever I will thank thee!"*

Anna wished she could catch Blind Mordecai's eye at these words, but had to content herself with laughing at Loukanos as he whirled around and snatched Caleb to his feet. "Dance, shepherd," he cried. "Move your old bones!"

Anna sank breathlessly down beside Mordecai as Caleb took her place, laughing all the more as Loukanos shouted to her, "For pity's sake, don't sing, Anna!"

*"God has turned my mourning into dancing for me*
*He has clothed me with gladness!"*

She hummed, but obediently did not sing, rapidly clapping her hands in complicated counterpoint as her new son and his new uncle stamped rowdily around the table, upon which Caleb was now hopping dangerously, triumphantly clicking his fingers and dancing with his elbows while uttering long whoops of joy. Mordecai was piping again at a terrific rate, his fingers flying over the stops, and it was a wonder nobody had thrown rocks on the roof by now for the noise.

When they had calmed down, she would tell Dan the rest of it. Etta and Dan would live with her in this house – the place where they had first met. And the men's decision? The boy – her son! – *Oh, Ammiel! Ammiel!* – would return to school for three years and learn all he could of the law and prophets, reading, writing, and figuring. Meanwhile Caleb would be the master of the flock until such time as Dan was ready to take up his inheritance.

A new life had begun from the ashes of the old. *I feel it! Praise God! I feel it!* Yes, she felt it. And Dan felt it.

Two days later, submitting to the terror of being deliberately sunk in rushing water he could not see, Blind Mordecai felt it too.

## Chapter Thirty-nine

"SAD," Johanan remarked, kicking experimentally at a charred lump of wood, which broke apart with a chinking sound. "Nothing saved?"

Dan shook his head.

"Nothing," he said flatly. "Only the privy hut over there. I suppose that's quite funny when you think about it." Except that Dan wasn't laughing much. "The villagers saved it spreading, though. It would have been awful if the whole hill had gone up. Aunt Etta couldn't face sifting through the ashes. She said what was done was done. This is only the second time I've come back to see it."

"H'mm!" said Johanan.

"It's been months – you should clear and rebuild," Johanan had urged two days before, almost as soon as he and Dan had finished a joyous wrestle at meeting again. "Or someone else will, and when you marry there'll be no house for your family."

Dan shrugged. "But there's no money to rebuild, you know. And Aunt Etta won't hear of Uncle Asa or even Amma giving any. She says I am already well provided for with a good trade waiting, and must make my own way just as father had to."

"Do you agree with her? Does Anna?"

"Yes both times."

"Very honourable!" Johanan laughed, but he meant it. He was impressed too by the easy way Dan said *Amma*, mother, and said so, but Dan said that it was so like *Anna* it was not much of a change. There was no need for him to remind Johanan how thankful he was to belong to the family. They were all glad of it, and it did not have to be said.

Dan himself was lost in admiration of Johanan's new deep voice – which finally had lost its gargling quality – and the short, wispy moustache which no longer could be mistaken for a smudge of dirt, though the same could not yet be said of the down on his cheeks. But it was the same Johanan underneath, and besides, Dan himself had begun to sprout like a mustard seed, and was catching up in height. Letters had flown to and from Jerusalem over the months – Dan's writing more confident by the day – and though both boys had been kept hard at their studies, Uncle Asa had just released Johanan for a long-awaited holiday. To his jubilation, when the Day of Atonement had passed, and the harvest time was almost upon them, Johanan was packed off to spend the Festival of Booths with Dan at Banayim.

Loukanos was not there – he was on one of his regular trips to Cana, where Old Dinah reigned supreme in the family house, tantalising Blind Mordecai with glorious smells from the kitchen, and prattling undisturbed to those who crowded into the courtyard to see the physician on market day. The tanner's house had become less convenient when Parosh and his wife had been agreeably startled by the unexpected advent of a very noisy miniature Parosh whom they called Manna as a joke, and who was in fact about the same age as some of their grandchildren.

Mordecai? A busy man, these days. In the mornings he taught *Mishnah* and *Halakhah* – the Oral Law and Traditions – in Asa's courtyard, and woe betide any man or boy who thought the blind man could not see with his ears. *Haggadah* – that heavy burden of humanly embellished ordinances which would crush any willing heart or mind, and which could not be substantiated from any scripture – he refused to discuss. Any pupil of any age, who cared to sit under the tree with him, he would accept without question. Fathers brought their sons to learn the law, and stayed to argue about the Baptist and Messiah. From time to time Anna sent Dan to Mordecai to widen his thinking, and test the competence of the new Magdala rabbi, the previous, sharp-tempered teacher having moved on to terrorise young boys in Tiberius. In the afternoons the blind scribe compounded ingredients for Loukanos' remedies with mortar and pestle, classifying by taste, touch and smell; his sharp stylus inscribing wax tablets which his fingertips could read. In the evenings he sat in his old corner to gather the daily news and direct alms givers to the drooling palsied young woman who crouched behind the market booths frightening children with her harsh cries and moans as she struggled to make herself understood.

"Repent!" Nazirite Johannes had cried but he had shown what must follow. "Honesty! Charity! Humility! Prepare ye – for surely Messiah and his Kingdom comes!"

*Aye – only by giving, will one truly receive!* As one who had tasted both pride and poverty, Mordecai the beggar understood this now.

Little Rhoda, in floods of bitter tears at leaving beautiful Galilee, had been sent to Jerusalem where she cheered up rapidly under

Mari's fluttery kindness, and strained her pretty ears for every mention of Dan. Johanan took pity on her and began covertly to teach her letters so she might read Dan's scrawls from time to time, and bore with him to the lakeside a dirty fragment scratched with a single row of wobbly characters which being interpreted meant "Greetings to Dan from Rhoda".

Johanan's long journey had not tired him in the slightest, and along with the rest of the hamlet, he and Dan threw themselves enthusiastically into preparing the booth in which the family would spend the festive week. Dan was greatly amused when Johanan pointed out conveniently that as they were both fatherless, they had full gleaning rights which ought to be exercised so their womenfolk would not be over-burdened with feeding them. Simply out of a sense of duty, as Johanan said with a grin, they raided the luxuriant hillside groves for fruit which had survived the recent harvesting, while gathering leafy armfuls of mulberry, apple, fig and quince trees. The boys cut and lashed young saplings of poplar and myrtle under Aunt Etta's experienced eye, shaping the framework, driving it into the soft shingle at the back of the house.

Anna pinned back her sleeves, tied her unreliable veil like a turban – a rare concession – and worked steadily alongside them, weaving tidily all the smaller willowy branches and tying down sharp-edged palm leaves while the boys foraged widely for more greenery, or scampered off to help Marta and Ittai by way of a change. Ittai gave them a spare bundle of mixed green stuff for their own booth, and Dan sorted through it before bringing it home, meticulously separating out any vine, which now that the grapes were gathered in, was a popular choice of many. Should even a fragment of leaf or bark fall in Anna's cup, her vow would be broken.

Women were not obliged to sleep in the booths, so after the first rather cramped night of the Festival, Anna and Etta returned thankfully to their own beds, declaring they would have quite enough to do with cooking and camping out during the daytime, as the law required. While the women slept peacefully upstairs, the boys sprawled in the booth and evolved their plan for the ruined house. They talked happily in hoarse, daring whispers, in an airy, rustling space where nothing was fixed and everything seemed possible, staring at the starry skies through the fragrant boughs, and seeing things which were not, as clearly as those which were.

They would dismantle the ruins and sort them through, to see what could be salvaged. Then, at every opportunity they could seize, they would do a little more – even if it was merely to set a few more stones in their courses. Maybe, before the rains, they could try their hand at some mud bricks, which required less skill and which seemed like fun. Perhaps Ittai could be in on the plot and give them advice. But they would do as much as they could on their own.

"We must have learned *something* from building the new room last year!" they reasoned.

While Johanan visited, the work would be faster, but Dan would not stop when he left. It would cost nothing, it didn't matter how long it took, they would have a lot of satisfaction trying – and maybe keep future squatters away from the family plot. So now, here they were, up with the sun, excited by the secrecy and stifling any qualms at the size of the task. The ruins were rendered even more forlorn by the cries of geckos, and the presence of a heavy, melancholy pelican standing in what had once been Bukki's corner. The bird stood mournfully digesting his last catch, beak pressed against his chest, eyes closed, and looking eerily like Bukki himself after a long night at Tiberius.

"Right!" Johanan was ready for work. He shooed the large bird away unmercifully, took a deep breath and girded up his tunic firmly. His thin legs were sprinkled lavishly with long dark hairs and looked about as attractive as a spider's, but Dan felt only envy. Why, even his toes were hairy, lucky Johanan! Dan looked mournfully at his own smooth brown legs and innocent toes, as he likewise pulled the back hem of his tunic up through his legs and tucked it into the front of his belt to form breeches. Well, at least he looked like a worker now, and there'd be no looks from Aunt Etta which spoke volumes about dirty hems, rips, and careless boys! Johanan read Dan's long-suffering expression and laughed.

"Keep the women happy, I say," he agreed feelingly. "Now let's clear the burnt stuff first. Then see what's underneath. No mud walls left … but the new stone is only half down. Might be better than it looks."

For over an hour they dragged charred beams and cleared rubble. The cracked remains of the ash-covered water jar was the only recognisable object. The acrid smell of burnt wood was still faintly detectable in the damp morning air, and their hands and clothes, legs and feet were soon scratched and covered in soot.

"Plenty of charcoal for Uncle Louki, hey?" panted Dan, wiping his sweaty forehead and creating an artistic grey smear. A Palm Dove in a distant terebinth tree promptly answered, "Hoo-hoo-hoo!" Was it laughing or crying? The ambiguity seemed appropriate. Johanan grinned at his friend. Good old Dan, making a joke of what couldn't be changed. He shoved a blackened rock from the tumbled pile where the hearth used to stand.

"Look here!" he said with interest. Lying over a fallen section of the old mud wall was a wide, warped slab of wood, pinned by a fallen beam. Burnt to charcoal, yet intact, with fissures that crawled all over its surface, it looked like ebony snakeskin.

"Why – it's our table!"

Johanan was shaking his head in amazement as he pushed away the remains of the beam. "Jericho!"

"What?"

"*And the walls fell flat!* Straight on their backs. Bang."

"Oh." Dan pulled sadly at the peculiar remains of the little table around which so many meals had been shared. It sheared in half, and shattered into large chunks as Dan attempted to haul it upright.

"Well, will you look at that!" cried Johanan, astonished out of his usual matter-of-factness. Beneath the protection of the table, the rough plaster on the flattened wall was intact, and even clean. But the surprise was not the wall itself.

"Oh, Johanan! I don't believe it!" Dan gasped. "Aunt Etta's shelves! Her shelves!"

Defying the fire, shielded by the hospitality of the sacrificed table, they were still firmly held in their plastered niche, no longer shiny – dull and smoke-stained – but unhurt by flame. Dan fell on his knees beside them and tugged frantically. They did not move.

"I must get them out! Break the wall around them – but carefully!"

Wild with excitement, the boys snatched up small rocks and chipped away at the fired clay and plaster around the smooth wood.

"It's coming!"

Suddenly a mud corner crumbled, hardened lime sheared off – and the triple-shelved frame slid out cleanly, backing boards and all. Superbly crafted – not a single neatly-pegged joint was split. Dan, with a wobbly feeling in his knees, hugged the precious item to himself as if it was a living thing, and swallowed the inconvenient stone in his throat.

"A resurrection!" Johanan was impressed. He wiped his hands before stroking the smooth wood respectfully with his short fingers. He glanced back at the flattened wall, then blinked.

"Dan," he said slowly, bending down and poking sharply at the plaster – he broke off a thin chalky slice – "did you know *this* was here?"

Dan stared through his tears of joy- and they dried up in sheer surprise. A patchy section at the back of the niche had cracked as the shelves came out, revealing a small cavity behind. Within it sat an old leather pouch. A very heavy, full, but yielding, leather pouch.

Dan fumbled eagerly with the stiff thongs which drew it shut. He dragged the bunched leather open , and his mouth went dry.

"Silver?" His voice was hushed. He looked up at his friend, wide eyes staring. "And an ostraca addressed to Aunt Etta … !"

He jerked the neck of the pouch together smartly and crammed it into Johanan's hands. "She must read this first, not me! Come on!" He picked up the shelves, wrapped them in his coat and ran like an Asahel.


It was still early in the morning. The women had not yet stepped outdoors and had no idea that the boys were even awake. At first alarmed by the tangle of filthy arms, legs, and blackened faces which hurled themselves shouting through the door, they were almost past speech when Dan opened his coat and showed what he was clutching to his chest. Aunt Etta was like one that dreamed, her stooped body bent over the precious shelves, running her creased fingers wonderingly over them, caressing them, even kissing them with half-guilty tears, and a hasty prayer that this may not be counted as idolatry. Finally she lifted her head, though her back remained bent – as it always did now, despite Loukanos's best ministrations of powdered bone, hot barley compresses and gentle manipulation.

"A miracle! A miracle of miracles!" she whispered, still incredulous. "Praise God for His kindness! To give me back a precious thing I thought was lost!"

"Praise God, indeed, Etta!" rejoined Anna delightedly, hugging her son proudly and beaming at her sooty cousin, whose teeth flashed in his black face like an Ethiopian's.

Dan was overflowing with gladness. The kind of light, spreading gladness which had first come to him when he first began to understand about the Promises. *Imagine the Master of the Universe caring so much about Aunt Etta's little shelves!* Or rather – he corrected himself – *caring so much about her!* For in the whole world surely only Etta bath Asa could have found such happiness in the salvation of this particular item.

Struck by this thought, Dan cautiously felt a little further and then it came to him … a dizzying, glowing truth which was to uphold his faith his whole life long. *How wonderful!* **Each star, each grain of sand – matters!** Not just as one of millions needed to group together to form the whole heaven, or the whole beach – but as special – yes, *precious* – on its own as well. Again Dan held his breath, feeling that surge of 'rightness' as this new realisation clicked into its place. He exhaled slowly, the uneven tips of his strong ivory teeth showing in a private smile of pure satisfaction. But not so private that Johanan wouldn't hear all about it the moment he got a chance!

"Come on! Wake up!" that young man hissed into his ear. "Tell them what else!"

He grinned hugely at Johanan – who was hopping up and down with impatience, the pouch being stuffed inside his tunic – and nodded. With a flourish, his friend dumped their find on the table with a heavy metallic sound. Aunt Etta went pale and sat down with a thud.

"What is this, boys?"

Dan sprang to her side, put an arm about her wide shoulders and squeezed reassuringly.

"Auntie, did you ever know about a hiding place behind your shelves?"

"What, Dan?" she gasped breathlessly. "No, no indeed!"

"I think father must have made it," he said quietly. "There is a message in this pouch for you. And money."

The old woman seemed unable to move. Wordlessly, Anna sank down beside her and with chilled fingertips loosened the dusty leather cords – pulled apart the dry leather folds – lifted the sagging pouch – poured the contents onto the smooth scrubbed table. There was a moment's silence, broken only by the tapping of several tarnished silver coins which slid down the heap, rolled off the table, hit the bench, and then bounced along the stone floor to be brought up short by the hearth. There was a faint tink as they turned over and lay still.

Anna picked out the palm sized pottery shard from the heap and handed it to Etta. The ink was still black, but it was written very small, and on both sides. Etta held it at arm's length, squinted, brought it closer, shook her head – and handed it back, her hand shaking.

"It needs younger eyes – Anna – please," she quavered.

The room was still. A voice was about to speak from the grave.

*"My dear Etta," read Anna quietly, her breath coming quickly. "My pretty Michal is gone, alas! so now I direct this to you. This my Legacy – safe from Bukki – I will tell you of should I ever be sore injured, or mortally sick. A yearly tithing begun on Dan's birth, for such injury, illness, old age or my death. May the bag be full and the years long before you read this. All I have is yours and Dan's. To Bukki the wastrel give no money, but daily bread and shelter, that God be not dishonoured. Guard well my little Dan – my son, my heart, my pride. Until the resurrection! I kiss you both tenderly. Ammiel ben Amos."*

Anna put down the *ostraca* carefully and cupped her thin face in her hands, her misted gaze fixed on something which was not in the room. The boys were equally silent. But Aunt Etta was shaking her head, sobbing and laughing and talking all at the same time.

"Ah, my brother! My beloved brother! The times I scolded you for shutting us outside while you whitewashed that wall like a sepulchre! *A waste of money!* I said each time. *It will only discolour again with the cooking,* I said. And why shut us out the while? 'Oh, just to enjoy your happy face when I reveal it all suddenly fresh and finished,' he would say. Such feeble excuses and I never once imagined what he was up to!"

"Nor did Bukki," Dan pointed out proudly, while his heart beat joyfully the rhythm – *I was his heart – I was his pride!*

539

He looked at his mother, who came out of her reverie as he spoke. "Now we can rebuild properly, can't we?"

Her arm around Etta, who had thrown her veil over her face and gone on crying happily, Anna nodded, her face gentle.

"We must consider the matter carefully first. But yes, my son, the Shepherd's house will stand again."

She stood up, and calmly smoothed down the rebellious tufts of short hair – finally growing back in its normal rich brown – tufts which, amongst the ragged pale longer strands, stuck out fluffily like dark down through a striped pillow. No comb could touch it, for the Rabbis declared that combing drew hairs from the head and nullified the Nazirite vow. She pulled the veil up from her shoulders, where it had slipped – again – and kissed the overwrought Etta, stroking the painful back, and coaxing her gently outside to stand in the lush airy booth which overlooked the sparkling sea. With a glad smile she waved her hand around them.

"Look about you, Etta!"

The narrow seaside street was gay with greenery, and smelled like a forest. Fronds, sprays and reeds tossed in the mellow air beside each dwelling. Each booth told something of the family it sheltered. Marta and Ittai's shelter had half chewed leaves poking out below knee height, and odd sticks poked through it where the babies had decided to help. Two little woven slings swung from the framework and rocked the meddlesome pair to sleep. The straggly booth beside them belonged to wily old Zaccheus, who had hung it with strings of his hard dried figs in the hope of a sly sale or two. Little Huldah and her mother had brightened their booth with red anemones, purple cyclamens and yellow camomile, replenishing them determinedly as fast as they wilted or were pulled out by small, equally determined Tirzah. Rachel the Dabab had made her husband build a loose-woven affair with plenty of gaps so she could keep an eye on things. As Etta calmed down and obediently surveyed the scene with Anna, they spied the irrepressible ben Zebedees skimming over the waves with a perfectly ridiculous little booth of salt-bush sitting cheekily in the bow of their fishing boat. By the roars of laughter rolling over the water, it was clear they thought it was a huge joke.

Anna gave Etta's shoulders an affectionate squeeze.

"My sister, praise God for our boys!" she encouraged cheerfully. "In discovering the loving provision of our dear Ammiel, surely the Eternal blesses us most fittingly for this Week of all weeks, and does all things well!"

Etta looked blank, and inclined her cheek to wipe it with a corner of her veil. Dan hunted mentally for the connection which he knew was there.

"Yes!" cried Johanan, laughing, who saw the point and relished it. "See, Dan? The festival of temporary shelter, the time of fruit harvest, looking forward to God's promise of an everlasting home …"

Dan gave a shout of recognition and jumped around to snatch and swing Aunt Etta's hands exuberantly. "That's us, isn't it! Here we are – Praise the Eternal, auntie! – gathering the fruit sown by my father over the years – looking forward to the promise of rebuilding our house!"

As Etta's olive complexion lit up and she began to laugh also, Johanan and Dan capered about the women, crowing like mad things until they were all giddy, and Anna begged for mercy.

"You'll have the whole thing over in a moment!" She shooed them out to fetch and carry, calling, "Loukanos returns tonight – we will call our friends – and celebrate the finding of that which was lost!"

There was a happy bustle as they each hurried to their individual tasks, with the refrain of *lost and found!* running through their minds, but in fact only Johanan – diligently stacking sticks and dried dung by the pot-bellied clay oven – was thinking literally of lost and found shelves, or a burnt house which could now be replaced. To tell the truth, he was almost disappointed that their private project was no longer necessary. But perhaps they would still have a hand in the matter, for money ought not be wasted on unskilled labour while there were strong young men in the family! Johanan settled his shoulders like an ox taking the yoke. He resolved that clearing the site, at least – would still be undertaken as they had planned.

Dan, ladling water from the main jar with a wooden dipper, realised with glad surprise, *I lost a father, but found a mother! God is good!*

*Praise the Eternal!* agreed Etta's thoughts as she kneaded her dough energetically. *I lost a brother but found a family. I lost my house and found loving shelter.*

Anna gazed out at the fishing boats which skipped over the waves so carelessly.

*I lost my mother, and my husband, and nearly lost my mind. But I have found a son, a sister, and peace.*

542

She remained wrapped in her reverie for a moment longer. Cool wafts of wind off the rustling sea fingered her scalp through the short hair, and she laughed at herself.

"You lost your hair, too, Anna bath Asa, – now there's freedom for you! It's almost a pity you're regaining that!"

It was true she disliked the ugliness of her patchily cropped appearance, but how cool and simple it was – no combing, no pulling when she turned over in bed and put her elbows on it, no braiding, no laborious washing, drying or oiling, no hair flying everywhere in the wind …

"Enjoy it while it lasts," she reminded herself with her lopsided smile, coiling up her veil again neatly. She hoisted the water jar to the resulting pad on her head and made for the crowded, chattering well.

"What a commotion at your house this morning," commented the Dabab by way of baiting her hook. Anna smiled sweetly at her, put down her jar, and waited for more.

"Of course, one can *expect* boys of that age to give trouble and grief," Rachel began angling, hopefully. "Answering back, teasing about one's appearance …" (here she looked significantly at Anna's head) " … refusing to do their tasks! Ah, yes, *well* I know it, and you needn't be ashamed my dear, for you are very inexperienced, everyone knows. So difficult to take on instant motherhood at *your* age! Though very noble of you, to be sure. At least, some people say so, which is encouraging, don't you think? I declare my heart nearly stopped when those gangling lads came racing up to your house this morning covered in soot and hooting like savages – goodness *knows* what they'd been up to. But as I say – youths are so hard for a woman to handle!"

Still wordlessly, Anna caught Marta's eye and bit her lips to hold back a laugh. Huldah's plump mother watched them shrewdly, enjoying Rachel's discomfort. The other women giggled behind their hands. The poor Dabab always had uphill work with that Anna! Marta was wont to say that while Rachel was able to exaggerate like any fisherman about her catches of information, Anna always remained the one that got away.

"Yes, it's a trial to control boys! Especially with no man in the house!" Rachel was almost desperate. Was the woman a *sphinx?* She deliberately allowed the rope to slip through her hands and the leather bucket hit the water far below with a distant splash, and had to be hauled up afresh. But delay as she would, probe as she might, nothing more was forthcoming from this infuriating woman who was as tall and cropped as a man, and who walked – even Rachel had to admit it, however reluctantly – who walked like a queen.

Anna put out a hand to steady the bucket for the widowed Thaddeus' nervous servant girl, Judith – an unhappy victim of the Dabab's most recent insinuations. The poor maid was forever sousing herself as she tried to fill her pot, trembling under Rachel's calculating eyes. But Anna relented at last.

"Rachel – how kind of you to take such an interest! Our lovely boys brought us glad news indeed this morning."

She looked around at the eager faces at the well mouth. *Even Rachel has her own private torments, no doubt, which poison her tongue. And why be selfish in our happiness?* Her hazel and brown eyes softened with affection.

"Rejoice with us, my friends, for that which was lost has been found! Dan and Johanan have discovered something very precious in the ruins of Etta's house and my dear sister is beside herself with happiness. Please come and celebrate our unexpected 'harvest' with us tonight, on this the second day of the Ingathering."

There was an excited clamour of questions, but Anna didn't even hear them. She had just caught sight of two men further down the path.

"Louki?" she cried, putting down her still-empty jar with a hollow clunk. "Louki!"

She picked up her skirts and ran like a girl.

"Now, now!" Loukanos fanned her flushed face. "Remember your age and inches."

"But I didn't expect you till this evening!" she panted gladly. "Have you walked half the night?"

"Nonsense," he said robustly. "No women or children needing endless bush stops and rests and food and water ... or awkward donkeys to slow us down? A matter of a few hours!"

He grinned at his companion, who was nodding and chuckling happily.

Anna recovered herself. "Caleb! Dear old man, what a treat to see you! Blessings and peace to you, my friend! How happy our Dan will be! You must tell him all about his beloved flock – especially the Queen of Sheba and Moses! And as for Johanan – why, he has missed meeting you so many times he declares you must be Dan's imaginary friend."

"Run along to your task, you chattering woman," said Loukanos teasingly. "How I will stamp and swear if there's no water for our weary feet!"

"There's still plenty at home," she laughed, kissing him impulsively. "I will not be far behind you, and I must hear all the news, so save it till I'm there."

She turned to go, but hearing an amused aside, stopped in her tracks.

Loukanos had muttered to Caleb, "And they say *men* never notice anything!"

"Why, Louki!" she said slowly, astonished at herself for not seeing, and at him for his appearance. "What a blind, stupid sister you have!"

She reached up and caressed his lean face wonderingly. "It's curly, too! How lovely."

Loukanos pulled her hands away.

"Stop that. It's still ticklish." In retaliation he ruffled her own hair playfully. "You're turning curly yourself! Well, it's often the way with regrowth after fever. You'll be a beauty yet, eh? But we can't have this ridiculous business with your veil sliding off all the time, you hussy."

Anna pulled it up, laughing apologetically. "I can't pin it you know, with hair this short – pins would drop out. Even if it was longer, the weight would drag them and pull hair from my head, which must not be. And I don't like to tie it on like a man."

Loukanos reached into his satchel and handed her an intricately knotted open-work cap with a soft silken fringe around the edge.

"There. Found it in Nain on my usual circuit. It stretches to fit, see? Pretty, eh? And not a fussy bead in sight. This over your hair, veil over the top. Pin it to the cap if you like."

546

He looked at her critically. The pale blue fringing lent softness to her strong face, and the veil stayed put. Old Caleb clapped his hands approvingly and Anna thanked them with a twinkling eye before walking sedately back to the well to complete her task.

"The latest fashion, no doubt!" sniffed the Dabab disapprovingly, eyeing the delicate cap jealously. Even without natural beauty, or a coin head-dress, bangles, earrings, beads, or the necklaces which stored a family's wealth, Anna looked more queen-like than ever. What was this Greek doctor fellow doing, meddling with female finery? Did he not have enough to do? That reminded her, she'd had these awful palpitations lately … maybe she could bring the matter up in conversation tonight, and find out a cure without having to pay … Rachel changed her tune abruptly and managed a sickly smile.

"Very becoming, dear. Makes you look quite feminine."

It was too much for Huldah's mother, who had to turn away sharply in a hastily assumed fit of coughing. She marched off home with her jar shuddering suspiciously. The complacent Rachel had no idea that it was not *Anna* who was being laughed at, so she remained content. Meanwhile the hapless young Judith went home quite cheerful. As for Marta, and Anna herself, they laughed all the way home.

Anna breathed deeply in the crisp autumn air and wondered at her own lightness of heart. The universe was making sense again, that's what it was. The Messiah *was* here in the land – somewhere! – and in God's grace she had been given time to prepare for him. A blotting out of past mistakes, and selfishness and sins … a time to look deeply inward … and then a time to turn around and see outside of herself with courage. She was ready for him now, and saw at last, that she had not been ready before. *Oh, may I recognise him! May he come soon!*

As she heard the jumble of voices old and young in the myrtle-scented booth behind the house, unexpectedly she paused – and her heart smote her reproachfully. In truth there was a selfishness, even yet, in her thoughts! Why had she not seen it before? There was a lonely old man … to whom she had given nothing but common hospitality … who had given her Dan so much of his heart, his knowledge, his respect for the Faith. What had she done for his striving, starving spirit? She knew it was there, and it had scant nourishment from his own family. And, oh Anna! Anna! *How could you overlook the brave old woman who never asked a favour of you yet! God forgive you!*

She swung the heavy, double handled jar gracefully from her head, and deposited it carefully inside the door. She would mend matters at once! And then – to work! Though all would bring a share, she was the hostess, and there was a feast to prepare. *Look out, boys!* she sang within herself. *It will be a busy day!*

## Chapter Forty

THE second night of the Festival of Booths that year was long remembered by the inhabitants of Banayim. At sunset the crowded tabernacles emptied their families into the street – a happy jumble of folk in celebration mood, who clustered around a tipsy shelter on the shore, a first attempt, creditably done, built by two lads and a woman. The amazing story of the discoveries in the ruins was told and gasped over. Johanan and Dan – and the Eternal's great goodness! – were praised fulsomely. Not one grudged Etta's turn of fortune, and even Rachel the Dabab herself thought the poor old creature probably deserved it, while edging closer to the useful Loukanos – who was skilfully avoiding her, noticing the glint in her beady eye and groaning within himself at what it had in store for him.

There were blessings, there were benedictions, there was eating and drinking, and the usual frantic flapping away of thirsty yellow wasps and hungry black flies. There was singing, and laughing, and dancing in the street. Old Zack pranced solemnly arm in arm with Old Caleb, the pair wailing an ancient melody nobody else knew. Rachel, having given up on the slippery physician for a time, lifted up a surprisingly attractive voice in a strident solo of harvest time, with the men stamping out a vigorous reaping dance to the tune – everyone chanting the compelling chorus, with a subtle accompaniment muttered behind various hands about *"sweet voices and sour singers"*. Huldah's buxom mother ignored toddler Tirzah clamouring at her skirts, to sing a tragic tale of a fisherman drowned on the treacherous lake before them, and as the women keened a haunting, breathy chorus of woe, Dan could almost see the hefty singer transformed into a slim, weeping, lonely girl yearning on the rocks, desperately searching the horizon for her lover. His hand stole into his mother's, and they pressed each other's fingers in silent sympathy.

As the sun slid behind the encircling hills, draining them of colour, torches were lit. Their extravagant flames, leaping doubly above and below the dark waves, seemed to dance with the village mood. The ben Zebedees, who had been out late, slid into the cove and beached unbidden on the shore which was splashed with welcoming light and music. Soon the fishermen were frying fish on the shingle for everyone, telling noisy stories, pretending to shut naughty children in their tiny booth, demanding their favourite songs, and making even the Dabab cry with laughter over their best jokes.

Mingled with the heroic tales, nonsense and tragedy of folk songs and dances were the evocative, lilting psalms of praise and joy. *Let Everything that Has Breath Praise Him!* rang out as cheerfully as once it had in the little house in the hollow of the hills, though Etta wondered regretfully where Bukki's harsh voice was being heard tonight. But could he have rejoiced with them now? He was one who had taken all, lost all – and found nothing. Would they ever see him again? Was there hope he would ever change? Even the very ladle he had dented in his enthusiasm on that happy night, was now a mere puddle of brass amongst ashes.

550

But there was no time for moodiness, and no need for self-reproach. Etta's black eyes gleamed softly as a joyful memory was re-enacted before her – because finally, came The Victory – the swaggering dance of mixed couples in which there was nothing to choose between the thrill of taking part, or being the pleasure of being a spectator. There was a catch in Dan's throat, and a sting in his eyes as he watched again two people he loved dancing it together – a bitter-sweet echo of a Shearing Feast held – was it really? – so long ago. The skirts swirled, the women minced, the men roared, the elbows strutted, the music rang to the stars above and pounded the sand beneath. Caleb's battered old pipe twittered, Johanan's drum banged, Etta's finger-cymbals tinkled, Dan's gourd of beans shook delightfully – shaka-shaka-shaka! – while around them folk clapped, tapped, shook, plucked, blew, clashed and stamped or sang with all their might.

"You should have been dancing this with Ammiel, sister," murmured Loukanos at Anna's flushed cheek, his arm caught around her waist. She flung him a look over her shoulder as she whirled around him to begin the link with outstretched hand.

"I know it," she answered breathlessly, with a brief flash of pain in her eyes, "yet glad I am to dance in this Festival with you, brother!"

The chain of dancers wove its way around the circle and back to their partners and as Loukanos swung his sister wildly with both hands, her face glowed, while the dark veil, kept neatly in place by the silken cap beneath, streamed out behind her like flowing hair – and her face suddenly kindled with a rare visitation of beauty. Loukanos felt his heart contract, and without invitation his eyes welled. This woman who had suffered so much under the hand of her God was glad, and at peace amidst the clamour. And he, who had so much, who served no god – not even Zeus, in his heart – was restless and unfulfilled. What good did he really do in the world, anyway? Had he saved his mother from a slow death? Or Ammiel from a sudden end? He could not even effectively fight the disease in poor old Etta's back, nor cure Mordecai's curdled blind eyes, Caleb's stiffening hands or keep dry the slack, stammering lips of the twisted girl in the Cana market. The very best he could do for anyone was temporary, undone in a moment by accident or misfortune. *Thank God Anna's fever responded at last! Thank God he had saved her at least!*

Something inside him leapt painfully. What had he said? *Thank whom?* Unsettled, he led Anna back to the blanket – where the others sat shouting enthusiastic applause – rubbing the crisp new beard which curled around his sensitive lips and chin. *A reflex*, he told himself crossly. *Louki, my son, you've been around these Jews too long, and the beard proves it.* He thought of Anna's plans for the next day, and a small tendril of fear snaked around his heart. He bounded to his feet.

"Another Victory, friends! Who has not yet danced? Come – this is your last chance!"

He pounced on little Huldah, who blushed furiously and cast an agonised look at her mother, who laughed till she had a stitch in her side.

"Time you learned this one!" she encouraged, and settled down to watch proudly as her plump daughter puffed through the women's part in terrible confusion, and all those who had thought to escape the exercise protested loudly and insincerely as they were likewise dragged in for the fun. Only the normally shrinking maid Judith did not protest. It was a long while since she'd had such a good time. She took Old Caleb's gnarled hands as gladly as if he had been a handsome youth and beamed at him till he was dazzled.

Meanwhile sad, brooding Thaddeus found himself tugged to his feet by Loukanos and planted in front of the stately widow Shana, whose painful propriety was constantly besieged by her boisterous nature. He took her fat hands reluctantly, looking at her aloof expression with a sigh of relief which soon changed to alarm as she lost the struggle to be ladylike, and hauled him about, ululating hilariously. But at last even this torture ended with the dance, and the celebrations broke up in happy exhaustion and buoyant good wishes. A final benediction was pronounced by Zaccheus, who sounded impressively pious, and the Amen rejoined fervently by all.

Before long the village had settled down, and was quiet. Even Marta's smothered giggles stopped, and Ittai's monotonous lullabies as he sleepily swung the babies to sleep, ceased lumbering down the street from their booth to annoy Johanan. He thought scornfully that the poor children must have gone to sleep in self-defence, but soon found himself floating off too. Caleb in the shelter and Aunt Etta upstairs, lay awake for a long time, scarcely daring to dream of the promise of the next day. Next to the old shepherd, Johanan snored like a man.

Too elated to sleep, Dan and Anna – and a less elated Loukanos – splashed their hot hands and faces and walked the brooding shore, cooling their feet in the inky, starlit lake. They leaned lazily on the fishermen's gently creaking boat while Loukanos pointed out the constellations far above. There was so much in the world to see, to hear about, to learn about! thought Dan. Would he ever find a time to hear it all? His days were so full already. And yet, perhaps the time to *hear it all* was in fact a whole lifetime … a slow, certain gathering of knowledge and wisdom …

"Louki," Anna interrupted cautiously, knowing he had something on his mind. "We can go alone tomorrow, you know, if you prefer."

"No," he said carelessly. "No need."

Though the fear was still there, deep down.

Dan tugged at her arm indignantly and she ruffled his curls, laughing.

"I was going to surprise you, my Dan. But that was a foolish idea anyway, with your sharp ears, hey? What do you think! Tomorrow we take Aunt Etta and Caleb to Bethabara to hear Johannes the prophet! I am disgusted with myself that I never thought before how badly they want to go. Louki will take us, since he knows the way so well."

Loukanos looked at the eager young face at his elbow and said offhandedly, "Well, your auntie could never go on her own, and Caleb rarely has enough time to scratch himself. But he's got leave for the whole Festival, so off we go."

"Oh, Anna! Uncle Louki!" Dan launched himself at them and hugged them both fiercely.

"Here! Stop rocking the boat!" barked a rough Galilean accent. Anna yelped with surprise and one of the fishermen stuck his tousled head over the edge. "Isn't it enough that you keep us awake with your prattle?"

Dan and Anna stifled their laughter while Loukanos apologised handsomely. They had not known anyone was actually sleeping on board, he said. The bushy-haired fishermen waved away his explanation good-humouredly enough.

"Going to see the Baptist, are you now?" they said, yawning mightily. "Why – we've been meaning to do it for weeks and kept putting it off while the catches were so good. We planned to take the boat as far down as possible, too."

The brothers looked at each other, and seemed to wake up properly.

"We didn't do so well today ..."

"Yes! Why wait?" the shorter man agreed eagerly. "Father won't mind if the hired boys do the fishing for a few days – he knows we're unpredictable."

They guffawed happily. "Save your legs – come with us! A return for your hospitality."

"And an adventure!" begged Dan, forgetting how sick he had been on his memorable tenth birthday.

Anna looked at her brother, her straight black brows raised in query.

"Why not?" he shrugged. "The boys will enjoy it, the old ones will find it easier, and you have been hankering to hear the man again for months." He looked at the boat warily. "But can you fit in an extra six?"

The taller brother slapped the sturdy planks affectionately. "Room for a dozen plus one!" he boasted. "See you all in the morning!"

They took the hint and padded back along the beach to the house.

Anna slipped upstairs, but Loukanos stretched himself beside Caleb and the boys, wondering at himself afresh, and remembering almost against his will, the Festival of Booths in his childhood.

When his mother and stepfather, himself and little Anna, curled up together in their tabernacle of olive and laurel, smelling the golden autumn days through a spicy screen of dusty blue-green leaves. Watching the lazy bees blundering amongst the white blossoms Helen would tuck into the branches, woman-like; listening to Asa as he taught them the constellations; tying Anna's lustrous hair surreptitiously to a pole and hearing her shriek as it was nearly torn out by the roots when she moved. *Why, oh why did I ever think that was funny!* Trying to make her laugh during Sabbath prayers ... his mother singing as she lit the lamps ... The pride he felt as a small child asking each Passover ... 'Father, what mean ye by this ritual?' and the thrill of the perpetual reply, 'It is the sacrifice of Adonai's passover ... when we were slaves in Egypt ...'

Except of course he came to realise that no part of Loukanos of Philippi had ever been 'slaves in Egypt'. Not *his* ancestors – never! And one day he found the gumption to say so to his shocked parents. So why did he feel like a slave in bondage now? In bondage to what? Oh, it was perfectly ridiculous! Loukanos turned over impatiently and scratched his beard. What had possessed him to grow it? Did he want to look like a Jew? Maybe it was time he married. *But what could I teach my sons? I would have no answers for them, only questions I dare not ask.* He rolled over on his elbow and studied Dan's sleep-slack face, mottled with leafy moonlight. The boy was a thinker – a Galilean if you please – but undoubtedly a thinker. It was one of the reasons Anna loved him ... for certainly he looked nothing like his father ... but how did he get that way, living beyond the influence of sophistry and cant – even that of his own impossible religion? How did he weigh and test his thoughts without a wider experience of men's thinking? *Compare scripture with scripture!* he heard a younger Asa say pleadingly to a rebellious

556

stepson. *Never hide from the truth – it's a waste of time!* he heard the aged Helen say firmly to a grown man.

Loukanos sighed heavily, dragged a pillow over his face in defiance of his own advice, and plodded gloomily off towards a sleep full of nightmares. The dreamily drifting thought came that the sooner Anna found her Messiah, the happier he'd be. She'd be all right now, whatever happened, and Praise the Eternal for *that*, anyway. He twitched sharply and pulled the pillow off his face. *"I didn't mean that!"* he complained to the sky, and buried himself again.

The clouds scudded across a sky which was piling up darkness. The boat dipped and pulled at the grey water, and the fishermen busily hauled ropes, eyed the flapping canvas and shouted to each other happily. There was a lowering rumble from the sky. Aunt Etta's hard fingers bit into Loukanos's thigh and he jumped.

"Hey, now – what's wrong, Etta!"

Rigid faced, she was unable to answer, huddling miserably in her shawl.

"Are you afraid, Etta?" Anna put her arm around the old woman, and Etta shook her head firmly and untruthfully. *Hi-yi! but I must be out of my senses! That I would ever see myself riding the sea like a porpoise!*

"You're sick, aren't you?" cried Dan (who wasn't, this time) – deeply sympathetic.

This at least was true and no disgrace. Teeth clenched, she nodded grimly and Loukanos grinned. He pulled a small phial from his belt and held it to her lips.

"Be brave, Etta – swallow this!"

Her pale face screwed tightly, Etta reluctantly obeyed. Her eyes bulged, streaming indignant tears, and a deep shudder shook her. She gulped. and gasped.

"What – are you a demon from Tophet, man?" she gasped. "What poison was in that fire water?"

Loukanos threw back his head and laughed, lurching from side to side with the waves, and patting her back cheerfully. "It's a rare root from the orient – and fiery is right! But tell me, how do you feel now?"

Etta looked surprised. "I am perfectly well!" she said proudly. "Already! Thank you!"

Caleb turned and groaned. "Better pass it this way ..." he begged, the spray from the bouncing, smacking waves sprinkling his beard like heavy dew.

How they all laughed – but only once the swaying boat was safely beached at the southern end of the Sea, and their feet splashed down to solid shingle beneath the knee-high water. The fishermen procured a pair of small coracles from a ferryman, whom they knew, and with four in each boat they steered easily down river, oars skilfully working with the current, avoiding calamity against Etta's most dire predictions, their boisterous spirits not at all dampened by the light drizzle.

By noon the rain had dried, and the crumbling water of the Bethabara ford was first visible ... next, a ferryboat dancing over the eddies to link the banks like a weaver's shuttle. Then the crowds, heaving and massing on the lush banks, crowding out the wild creatures, all except the indifferent storks resting in the rustling reeds.

558

Still they came from Jerusalem and Judea, still they had followed the windburnt Johannes as he moved up-river – and still the people from Cana – Nazareth – Nain – Bethshean – Pella – came to see and hear. They flocked to the prophet from regions of Galilee – the fringes of Samaria – from Decapolis, Trachonitis and Perea. They trickled through the rift valley from as far away as Nabataea – Idumea! Jostled and half-hidden, Dan was bewildered by the crowds – thicker far than those near Jericho – and as to what became of the benign fishermen or their borrowed boats, he could not have said to save himself.

Here and there folk had built leafy shelters, but whether thrown up in token for the Festival which they were missing, or for a practicality which spoke even more poignantly of the Festival's meaning, was a matter of conjecture.

Loukanos told the boys to keep close and make their own way, while he put a strong arm around the wide-eyed Etta, and Anna linked her arm firmly in Caleb's. Edging, creeping, ducking, pushing – *Your pardon, friend ... I'm sorry, old mother ... , Excuse me, young man ... , Please may I just ... ? Sorry, boy ... Mind your head, little one ... Thank you ... Thank you ... Blessings and peace to you too ... No, friend, it doesn't hurt a bit – my fault ... Thank you ... Thank you ...*

The ford was swarming with people – curious people, anxious people; people who were earnest, cynical, unhappy, suspicious; those who were hopeful, glad, rejoicing – and those who trembled with anticipation and longing for the fulfilment of the dearest prophecy in The Book – *Messiah – Restoration – Deliverance!* All left their goods, their farms, their trades, their homes and neighbours – and came eagerly to see the man who refused to be anything to them but a Voice which cried –

"Prepare!"

They found no effete ascetic, nor crazed bellower, neither a mere reed whistling in the wind, but a clarion call which transcended the man who was its medium. Baptist, Baptizer, Dipper of Men, Washer, Watchman of Jordan, Prophet in the Water ... any of these names were his, and more. His name was his mission. *Johannes – who?* The people did not care, and could not remember. He was simply the one who was born when the time for birth was past, who tumbled into his aged parents' world as if narrowly to beat death in a race against time – the one whose own name had been submerged in his work to become simply *The Baptizer*. The prophet who wore the effacing, desert-rough garb of Elijah, in which he seemed to blend and become part of the rocks – as if it were the very stones which cried out!

The pools of water surged more strongly here than down in Bethany-over-Jordan, but the man's sinewy strength never flagged. In and out of the shaded, palm-fringed shallows he plunged – down and under and up he raised the suppliants. *"Comes the Kingdom! Comes the King!"* was the message which never wearied, though the man himself somehow seemed to fade as the Voice grew bolder. Fewer approached him now with private questions as they had in Bethany. More had come to watch, to listen, or to be baptized by the Prophet – but the man Johannes they were content to leave beyond their own reach. Johanan observed this, and wondered at it. Was this, then, the lot of one who came only to serve? To lose touch with one's fellow? To find the service acknowledged with gratitude, no doubt, but perhaps to be less valued as a flesh and blood man with his own needs? *Service like this – self-effacing, sacrificing – must bring conflict. I couldn't do it. Not like him.* Humbled, Johanan listened the more carefully.

560

"I am but the herald – unworthy even to stoop and unlace the sandals of the one who follows me. I am baptising you now with water, but he will baptize you with the Holy Spirit. The time is close! Repent ye, for the Kingdom of Heaven is at hand."

Dan and Johanan were struck dumb. There was so much they still did not understand about this prophecy – what did it mean, to baptize with the Holy Spirit? And what, *the Kingdom of Heaven*, exactly? Yes, the Kingdom would be restored … yes, it was God's Kingdom … but on earth! So why 'of Heaven' … and no mention of 'The Kingdom of Israel'? Would the Baptizer tell them? Would the Messiah?

They thought guiltily of the whole matter of Johannes' preaching – the preparing for Messiah – which had been going in *and* out of their busy thoughts for so long … meanwhile, all the time they had been carelessly playing, learning, growing, planning – absorbed in their own schemes, tragedies and challenges – all this time had a homeless, comfortless man been tirelessly, faithfully at work.

"He has been doing *this* – all this time!" breathed Dan, his eyes and Johanan's meeting in mutual wonder.

"All this time!" repeated Aunt Etta, chins quivering, her voice full. "All this time to hear his message – and I have delayed so long! *Thanks be to the Eternal for preserving my life to this day.*" She handed Dan her precious stick, bundled her coat and veil into Anna's willing arms and looked appealingly at Loukanos as she sat heavily to unlace her sandals.

"All this time to hear what I *said* I craved to know," shame filling him, Old Caleb's withered lips stuck to his teeth and he licked them nervously, "but I never before sought him out. Praise the Eternal for Loukanos and Anna that they brought me here

561

before it was too late! Surely *I have heard of him by the hearing of my ears – but now mine eye seeth him …*"

And the shepherd stripped off his shabby cloak, gripping the muscular young arm beside him in anticipation of what must come.

Resisting, Loukanos folded his arms in a gesture of protest. *And all this time I have been hanging about this disorganised country waiting for a Messiah who never comes.* He looked down at the old woman, the old man, who clutched at his support, and then to his sister. But who else could do it? The water was swift, they needed a man, not a boy or a woman. He met Dan's hopeful glance, Johanan's appraising look.

"Wait," he said coolly.

Off came his coat, his scrip, his robe, his jaunty half turban, the neatly tooled sandals. There Loukanos of Philippi stood in his breeches, creamy gold skin puckering impatiently with cold. Gripping Caleb firmly with one arm, and supporting Etta's bulk with the other, he waded into the choppy water. Caleb clung to him heavily like a stiff stick insect, Etta soon bobbed like a pomegranate on the waves, her gown bulging with air and puffing up under her chin. All were nearly breathless with the cold, the heavy water hugging their chests.

The sun-blackened Baptist slid from a worn boulder which was barely warmer than the chest-deep water. His fingernails were blue, the fingertips pulpy. Long matted cords of hair and beard streamed over his shoulders and tossed in the current. He reached out to the shivering trio before him, grasping Etta and Caleb's nervous hands to steady them, and looking a query at Loukanos with his clear, dark eyes.

562

"Ah! The man on the bank at Bethany, who could see that a seed of Abraham is not always a son of God! Welcome! Perhaps you now see that a son of God is not always a son of Abraham. It is good to see you in these waters."

For a moment, as the four were joined in a circle as if ready for a dance of praise, Loukanos met his gaze boldly. But his heart was hammering foolishly, his nervous mind snapping at him – *Mass emotion, Loukanos! That's all! Mere mass emotion!* He shook his head firmly.

"Not me, Baptist. These two."

"Not you?" Johannes answered with an odd inflection. "Or not yet?"

Loukanos stared at him, appalled.

"I am a Greek! An unbeliever!" he said roughly. "These are your penitents. Make haste, for they are aged and their bones protest the cold."

Johannes took fat Etta into his long arms as her legs were swept up alarmingly by the current. She was almost speechless with anxiety, but her determination never wavered. She would be baptized if she drowned in the attempt!

"Why do you come to me, daughter? ... What is your name? ... Etta bath Amos, by the commandment of God I baptize you for the remission of your sins ..."

Spluttering and gasping, Etta came up, streaming grey hair and water – almost delirious with relief. Loukanos held her tightly as Johannes gently transferred Caleb's iron grip to his own body.

Caleb's eyes were nearly starting out of his head, and his teeth chattering like crickets, but he clutched at the Baptist's scanty camel-hair tunic, thin old legs kicking wildly to keep him upright, his heart burning with a gift he urgently wanted to give to the ambassador of God's Anointed, who would rebuild the Kingdom on earth. Oh, Caleb had no trouble understanding *'of Heaven'*! Had he not seen Heaven itself opening to rejoice over the child who would be King?

"I was *there*, prophet!" he blurted out feverishly, his fingers working anxiously. In the midst of the rushing current, a calm look of encouragement – and Caleb gabbled on desperately. He must tell him! He must!

"I was there in the fields – a shepherd – at Ramah – the tower of the flock, you know! *'Unto thee shall it come'* and it did, *'even the first dominion'* and I was there! And me a sinner, God forgive me."

Johannes stared at him in wonder. "You were there, old man?"

"Yes, master!" stammered Caleb. "When Messiah was born! I heard the angels! Khabod! they sang – and oh! such glory! And then I saw the child! I know your words are true!" A sudden sob heaved his chest. "You see, Master –" he gasped, weeping, "in a very feeble way ... I, too, have been his herald ... have I not?"

"Ah!" The Baptizer snatched Caleb's chilled and scrawny body to a broad chest warm under coldly sodden cloth – an impulsive embrace which dashed water high and astonished the onlookers. "I am not your master, but a servant." His rich voice was low, his eyes swimming bright with deep gratitude. "The Anointed is my master, and yours. But, friend, what a blessing to hear your words! Surely my voice has never been entirely alone, while others have shared this work. Praise God, shepherd! I would that more in Israel were such as you!" He released the old man gently, and the wet ringlets of his Nazirite beard split into a full and frank smile which almost rendered Caleb incapable of further speech. "And now – ?"

"My name is Caleb ben Shimei," Caleb choked quickly, before he was asked, before his voice failed him altogether. "I come repenting the sins of a lifetime – baptize me now I pray – so that the babe I saw thirty years ago may not be ashamed of me, now he is a man!"

"Gladly!"

As Caleb came bubbling to the surface with wild eyes, Johannes delivered him back to Loukanos and the shivering Etta, who was clutching him round his bare neck shamelessly, in fear of being whirled downstream. The young physician gripped the old shepherd's belt.

"I've got you, Caleb. Now let's get you both dry!" He nodded briefly to the Baptizer.

"Thank you, Grecian." The hunger-shadowed eyes were still aglow with rare pleasure. "Do not forget this day."

Anna and Dan were waiting with dry clothes and towels warmed against their own bodies. Johanan, ever the worker, was already blowing a small fire in a space he had managed to claim from a family which was departing the riverbank, disgruntled that the scene was so tame, the prophet so plain, the message so demanding. Loukanos almost burned the skin off Caleb's back with vigorous rubbing, in his insistence that nobody would take cold if he could help it and that they had been in the water far too long. Anna, radiant with shared joy, toweled Etta briskly and wrung out her hair, deftly stripping off the wet clothes under a voluminous blanket. Etta was still shivering and overcome, and could only flap her hands helplessly and sniff apologetically when spoken to. Dan wrapped a warmed cloak around Loukanos' naked back.

"Take your own medicine, Uncle Louki!" he cried gaily and jumped back to avoid a friendly cuff.

"That reminds me, Dan, pass them my flask, will you?"

Aunt Etta sniffed it suspiciously and swallowed bravely. She pulled a face, and spluttered a little, but found her voice at last.

"Isn't this the same horrible stuff you gave me on the boat?" she croaked.

Loukanos grinned up at her as he collected his sandals. "But this is a much weaker version – with honey in it, Etta! And it will warm you up."

Caleb's teeth were still clenched, his lips blue. He rattled the clay neck against his teeth and gulped regardless of the burning, bitter, aromatic taste – and hung out his tongue to cool it afterwards.

"Warms you up, all right," he chuckled, clearing his throat noisily. They'd all need it, too, if those clouds overhead grew thicker and dumped rain.

Loukanos took a pull at the flask himself and made for the warmth of Johanan's rather smoky fire. Brr! – the mixture was horrible. He coughed hastily, and to cover his disgusted expression hustled on his clothes, while Johanan, a grin unsuccessfully compressed, poked the fire about, quite unnecessarily.

Dan looked up from retying his aunt's sandals, to exchange a laughing look with Anna, who was busily braiding up Etta's damp grey hair to keep her bowed back dry. Dan's fingers slowed. Anna followed his fixed gaze. Etta, with difficulty, looked over her shoulder, leaning on her curved, glossy stick.

"Don't we know that young man? He looks familiar."

He came down the bank with a sense of purpose, removing his coat as he came, dropping it carelessly from one hand as he passed, not seeming to notice that it covered the bared feet of a tall thin Greek man and his youthful Jewish cousin who with their backs to him, were kneeling over their little fire. But they felt it with surprise, and turned to pick it up, placing it on a rock, and observing him curiously.

His eyes sought the Baptizer's even as he slid the sandals from his feet, tossed them behind him, and waded far into the busy water. The prophet's hands reached out – and froze. He flushed, then paled. There was a quiet, intense exchange, which Loukanos and Johanan strained to hear, and Anna, Dan and Etta heard not at all.

The most extraordinary look had come over the Baptist's dark face – he was shutting his eyes – biting his lip in concentration – plunging the young man beneath the grey water – and as the dark head rose from the ripples before him – the prophet sank back into a depth where he must surely tread water. The young man emerged with his eyes still closed, his head bowed, and covered his face with his strong hands … how different from all others who jerked their heads high up out of the water, hurriedly wiping it from their faces, gasping, spluttering, eyes and mouths wide, as they sucked in gratefully the air they had relinquished for such a short time! He lifted his head and hands to the dark sky, his face tense.

"He's praying!" Dan murmured to his mother. "And he seems to be in pain! Do you think he's all right?"

Her lips parted, but what Anna had been about to reply nobody ever knew, including herself, for at that moment a dazzling shaft of light shot down from the glowering clouds above the leaden water and flashed off the glistening wet head – where a dove beat its wings – and the rocks trembled with a deep, rolling thunder which petrified all who heard it.

Oh! Oh! An earthquake? What was that? Did you hear words? Thunder? No – someone spoke! Impossible! What? Something about David – the beloved? You're hearing things! A voice from heaven? What – are you a pagan? Thunder gods, next, eh? Words. There *were* words. I heard them. I could *not* have heard them.

Loukanos was stamping on the tiny fire, ash flying up to smudge his garments.

"Put it out!" he said to Johanan, trembling. "We're leaving."

Johanan was trembling too. "You heard it. You know you heard it."

Dan – white faced – "Mother!" – flung himself into Anna's arms.

"Hush, my Dan." Anna's lips scarcely moved as she folded her cloak about him.

Caleb and Etta were gripping each other's hands and praying fervently.

The young man walked out of the water, his short, blue-trimmed robe clinging heavily to reveal a thin, muscular body – the wiry build of a labourer. The light faded, the dove fluttered a moment longer, its soft voice still and small – then it was gone – was there a dove? Nobody saw where it went.

He passed close by the two at the fire, scooping up his coat as he came, close enough for them to hear the creaking of his sodden sandals, close enough for drops of water to flick upon them from his body as he moved. He turned to look across the water at the tall, rope-haired man in the rough wet girdle, who had waded to the opposite bank. Each raised a hand in silent farewell.

Suddenly – the Baptist's hand flung out – "BEHOLD YE!" he thundered, – yea, now at last he truly thundered! – his mighty voice booming across the water – shattering the fragile silence with startling power.

"BEHOLD THE LAMB OF GOD, WHICH TAKETH AWAY THE SIN OF THE WORLD! THE ONE OF WHOM I SPOKE! THIS IS HE!"

Dan's heart pounded until he thought he would faint. Pressed to his ear, Anna's heart was thudding like the feet of a hundred dancers stamping the sand. Johanan was on his knees, as were Etta and Caleb. Loukanos stood frozen. The young man had disappeared.

Anna tried to move, but her legs failed and she and Dan slid to the ground. On her knees she crawled to her brother over the rough stones, and reached up to clasp his loose-hanging hands, her face distorted with emotion, her eyes shining. She kissed his nerveless fingers, as Dan scrambled to join her.

"Dearest brother! Dear Louki! You have been faithful to your vow," she panted, tears blotting out the difference of her eyes. "I love you for it and I thank you! But – now – now you can go home at last, Louki. Praise God! You are free."

Dan got shakily to his feet and wondered if a heart could burst with dread fear and delirious joy.

"Yes, Uncle Louki!" he gasped.

He took a huge, trembling breath and with glowing eyes looked at the stricken face above him.

"You are free!" he repeated breathlessly. "Our Messiah has come!"